PRAGUE FATALE

Philip Kerr is the author of eight previous Bernie Gunther novels, most recently *Prague Fatale* and *Field Gray*, both *New York Times* bestsellers. Kerr has been a finalist for the Mystery Writers of America's Best Novel Award and the Shamus Award for Best Hardcover Fiction, and he received the British Crime Writers' Association's 2009 Ellis Peters Award for Historical Crime Fiction for *If the Dead Rise Not*. As P. B. Kerr, he is the author of the young adult series Children of the Lamp. He lives in London.

BY PHILIP KERR

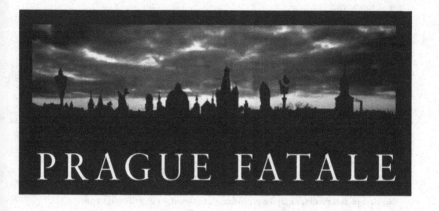

PRAGUE FATALE

A BERNIE GUNTHER NOVEL

Philip Kerr

PENGUIN BOOKS

PENGUIN BOOKS
Published by the Penguin Group
Penguin Group (USA) Inc., 375 Hudson Street, New York, New York 10014, USA

USA | Canada | UK | Ireland | Australia | New Zealand | India | South Africa | China
Penguin Books Ltd, Registered Offices: 80 Strand, London WC2R 0RL, England
For more information about the Penguin Group visit penguin.com

First published in Great Britain by Quercus in 2011
First published in the United States of America by Marian Wood Books,
a member of Penguin Group (USA) Inc. 2012
Published in Penguin Books 2013

THE LIBRARY OF CONGRESS HAS CATALOGED THE HARDCOVER EDITION AS FOLLOWS:
Kerr, Philip.
Prague fatale / Philip Kerr.—1st U.S. ed.
p.   cm.
ISBN 978-0-399-15902-2 (hc.)
ISBN 978-0-14-312284-5 (pbk.)
1. Gunther, Bernhard (Fictitious character)—Fiction.
2. Private investigators—Fiction.   3. Prague (Czech Republic)—History—
20th century—Fiction.   4. Mystery fiction.   I. Title.
PR6061.E784P73   2012   2011051632
823'.914—dc23

Printed in the United States of America
10 9 8 7 6 5 4 3 2 1

BOOK DESIGN BY AMANDA DEWEY

PUBLISHER'S NOTE
This is a work of fiction. Names, characters, places, and incidents either are
the product of the author's imagination or are used fictitiously, and any
resemblance to actual persons, living or dead, businesses, companies, events,
or locales is entirely coincidental.

Once again, to Jane

Acclaim for the eighth Bernie Gunther novel, *Prague Fatale*

"Inside this mesmerizing novel, set mainly in a country house outside Prague, is a tantalizing locked-door murder mystery that will thrill fans of Philip Kerr's Bernie Gunther novels."
—Carol Memmott, *USA Today*

"In *Prague Fatale*, [Bernie Gunther] is back in the early days of the Second World War, dealing with a case that combines espionage, terrorism, and a locked-room mystery. . . . Philip Kerr does his usual fine job of setting the scenes and portraying the personalities of the era. His Nazis are note-perfect creations, as are the other characters, fictional and historical, of Second World War–era Europe, all of it flavored by the wisecracking, tough-talking Gunther, who has been called the Sam Spade of Germany. Kerr knows his modern German history, and is gifted at storytelling, and Gunther is a dark antihero for the ages."
—H. J. Kirchhoff, *The Globe and Mail* (Toronto)

"*Prague Fatale* is classic Philip Kerr, a first-person noir detective story worthy of Dashiell Hammett or Raymond Chandler in every regard, seamlessly transplanted to war-era Europe. Every time I finish another Gunther novel, I think, 'This is as good as it gets.' Then inevitably, the next one comes along and is even better!"
—Bruce Tierney, BookPage.com

Praise for Philip Kerr

Just as youth is wasted on the young, history is wasted on historians. It ought to be the exclusive property of novelists—but only if they are as clever and knowledgeable as Philip Kerr."
—Julia Keller, *Chicago Tribune*

"Thanks to the series' settings, it has a moral gravity rarely seen in the detective genre. The mean streets Gunther walks down don't come any meaner."
—Mark Feeney, *The Boston Globe*

PRAGUE FATALE

PROLOGUE

It was a fine, warm day when, together with SS-Obergruppen-führer Reinhard Tristan Eugen Heydrich, the Reichsprotector of Bohemia and Moravia, I arrived back from Prague at Berlin's Anhalter Station. We were both wearing SD uniforms but, unlike the general, I was a man with a spring in my step, a tune in my head, and a smile in my heart. I was glad to be home in the city of my birth. I was looking forward to a quiet evening with a good bottle of Mackenstedter and some Kemals I had liberated from Heydrich's personal supply at his office in Hradschin Castle. But I wasn't in the least worried he might discover this petty theft. I wasn't worried about anything very much. I was everything that Heydrich was not. I was alive.

The Berlin newspapers gave out that the unfortunate Reichs-protector had been assassinated by a team of terrorists who had parachuted into Bohemia from England. It was a little more complicated than this, only I wasn't about to say as much. Not yet. Not for a long time. Maybe not ever.

It's difficult to say what happened to Heydrich's soul, assuming he ever had one. I expect Dante Alighieri could have pointed me in the approximate direction if ever I felt inclined to go and search for it, somewhere in the Underworld. On the other hand, I've a pretty good idea of what happened to his body.

Everyone enjoys a good funeral, and the Nazis were certainly no exception, giving Heydrich the best send-off that any psychopathically murderous criminal could have hoped for. The whole event was mounted on such a grand scale, you would have thought some satrap in the Persian Empire had died after winning a great battle; and it seemed that everything had been laid on, except the ritual sacrifice of a few hundred slaves—although, as things turned out for a small Czech mining village called Lidice, I was wrong about that.

From Anhalter Station Heydrich was carried to the Conference Hall of Gestapo headquarters, where six honor guards wearing black dress uniforms watched over his lying-in-state. For a lot of Berliners it was a chance to sing "Ding-Dong! The Witch Is Dead!" while sneaking a wary tiptoe look inside the Prinz-Albrecht Palace. On a par with other semi-hazardous activities, such as climbing to the top of the old radio tower in Charlottenburg or driving on the bank at the AVUS speedway, it was nice to be able to say that you'd done it.

On the radio that night the Leader eulogized the dead Heydrich, describing him as "the man with the iron heart," which I assume he meant to be a compliment. Then again, it's possible that our own wicked wizard of Oz might simply have confused the Tin Man with the Cowardly Lion.

The next day, wearing civilian clothes and feeling altogether more human, I joined thousands of other Berliners outside the New Reich Chancellery and tried to look suitably gloomy as the whole ants' nest of Hitler's myrmidons came bursting out of the Mosaic Hall to follow the gleaming gun carriage as it bore Heydrich's flag-draped coffin east along Voss Strasse and then north up Wilhelmstrasse toward the general's final resting place in the Invaliden

Cemetery, alongside some real German heroes, such as von Scharnhorst, Ernst Udet, and Manfred von Richthofen.

There was no doubting Heydrich's bravery: his impetuous part-time active service with the Luftwaffe while most of the top brass stayed safe in their wolves' redoubts and their fur-lined bunkers was the most obvious example of this courage. I suppose Hegel might just have recognized Heydrich's heroism as the incarnation of the spirit of our despotic times. But for my money, heroes need to have a working relationship with the gods, not the titan forces of darkness and disorder. Especially in Germany. So I wasn't the least bit sorry to see him dead. Because of Heydrich, I was an officer in the SD. And pressed into the tarnished silver cap-badge that was the loathsome symbol of my long acquaintance with Heydrich were the hallmarks of hatred, fear, and, after my return from Belorussia, guilt.

That was nine months ago. Mostly I try not to think about it, but as another famous German lunatic once observed, it's hard to look over the edge of the abyss without the abyss looking back into you.

1

The thought of suicide is a real comfort to me: sometimes it's the only way I can get through a sleepless night.

On such a night—and there were plenty of them—I used to dismantle my Walther automatic pistol and meticulously oil the metal jigsaw of pieces. I'd seen too many misfires for the want of a well-oiled gun, and too many suicides gone badly wrong because a bullet entered a man's skull at an acute angle. I would even unload the tiny staircase that was the single-stack magazine and polish each bullet, lining them up in a rank like neat little brass soldiers before selecting the cleanest and the brightest and the keenest to please to sit on top of the rest. I wanted only the best of them to blast a hole in the wall of the prison cell that was my thick skull, and then bore a tunnel through the gray coils of despond that were my brain.

All of this may explain why so many suicides go wrongly reported to the cops. "He was just cleaning his gun and it went off," said the dead man's wife.

Of course guns go off all the time, and sometimes they even kill the person holding them; but first you have to put the cold barrel against your head—the back of the head is best—and pull the damned trigger.

Once or twice I even laid a couple of folded bath towels under the pillow on my bed and lay down with the firm intent of actually going through with it. A lot of blood leaks out of a head with even a small hole in it. I would lie there and stare at the suicide note written on my best paper—bought in Paris—and placed carefully on the mantelpiece, addressed to no one in particular.

No one in particular and I had a pretty close relationship in the late summer of 1941.

After a while, sometimes I would go to sleep. But the dreams I had were unsuitable for anyone under the age of twenty-one. Probably they were unsuitable for Conrad Veidt or Max Schreck. Once I awoke from such a terrible, vivid, heart-stopping dream that I actually fired my pistol as I sat bolt upright on the bed. The clock in my bedroom—my mother's walnut Vienna wall clock—was never the same.

On other nights I just lay there and waited for the gray light to strengthen at the edge of the dusty curtains and the total emptiness of another day.

Courage was no good anymore. Nor was being brave. The endless interrogation of my wretched self produced not regret but only more self-loathing. To all outside eyes I was the same man I had always been: Bernie Gunther, Kriminal Commissar, from the Alex; yet I was merely a blur of who I had been. An imposter. A knot of emotions felt with gritted teeth and a lump in the throat and an awful echoing lonely cavern in the pit of my stomach.

But after my return from Belorussia, it wasn't just I who felt different, it was Berlin, too. We were almost two thousand kilometers from the front, but the war was very much in the air. This wasn't anything to do with the British Royal Air Force, which, despite Fat Hermann's empty promises that no English bomb would ever fall on the German capital, had managed to put in irregular but nonetheless destructive appearances in our night skies. But by the summer of 1941 they hardly visited us at all. No, it was Russia that now affected each and every aspect of our lives, from what was in the shops to how you occupied your spare time—for a while dancing had been forbidden—to how you got around the city.

"The Jews are our misfortune" proclaimed the Nazi newspapers, but by the autumn of 1941 nobody really believed von Treitschke's slogan; and certainly not when there was the more obvious and self-inflicted disaster that was Russia with which to compare it. Already the campaign in the East was running out of momentum; and because of Russia and the overriding needs of our Army, Berlin felt more like the capital of a banana republic that had run out of bananas, as well as almost everything else you could think of.

There was very little beer and often none at all. Taverns and bars closed for one day a week, then two, sometimes altogether, and after a while there were only four bars in the city where you could regularly obtain a pot of beer. Not that it tasted like beer when you did manage to track some down. The sour, brown, brackish water that we nursed bitterly in our glasses reminded me most of the liquid-filled shell holes and still pools of no-man's-land in which, sometimes, we had been obliged to take cover. For a Berliner, that really was a misfortune. Spirits were impossible to come by, and all of this meant that it was almost impossible to get drunk and escape from oneself, which, late at night, often left me cleaning my pistol.

The meat ration was no less disappointing to a population for whom the sausage in all its forms was a way of life. Allegedly we were each of us entitled to five hundred grams a week, but even when meat was available, you were just as likely to receive only fifty grams for a hundred-gram coupon.

Following a poor harvest, potatoes disappeared altogether. So did the horses that pulled the milk wagons; not that this mattered very much, as there was no milk in the churns. There was only powdered milk and powdered eggs, both of which tasted like the masonry dust shaken from our ceilings by RAF bombs. Bread tasted like sawdust and many swore that that's exactly what it was. Clothing coupons paid for an emperor's new clothes and not much else. You couldn't buy a new pair of shoes and it was almost impossible to find a cobbler to repair your old ones. Like everyone else with a trade, most of Berlin's cobblers were in the Army.

Ersatz or second-rate goods were everywhere. String snapped when you tried to pull it tight. New buttons broke in your fingers even while you were trying to sew them on. Toothpaste was just chalk and water with a bit of peppermint flavoring, and there was more lather to be had in queuing for soap than in the crumbling, biscuit-sized shard you were allocated to keep yourself clean. For a whole month. Even those of us who weren't Party members were starting to smell a bit.

With all of the tradesmen in the Army, there was no one to maintain the trams and buses, and as a result whole routes—like the number 1, which went down Unter den Linden—were simply done away with, while half of Berlin's trains were physically removed to help supply the Russian campaign with all the meat and potatoes and beer and soap and toothpaste you couldn't find at home.

And it wasn't just machinery that went neglected. Everywhere you looked, the paint was peeling off walls and woodwork. Doorknobs came away in your hand. Plumbing and heating systems broke down. Scaffolding on bomb-damaged buildings became more or less permanent, as no roofers were left to carry out repairs. Bullets worked perfectly of course, just like always. German munitions were always good; I could testify to the continuing excellence of ammunition and the weapons that fired it. But everything else was broken or second-rate or substitute or closed or unavailable or in short supply. And tempers, like rations, were in the shortest supply of all. The cross-looking black bear on our proud city's coat of arms began to look like a typical Berliner, growling at a fellow passenger on the S-Bahn, roaring at an indifferent butcher as he gave you only half of the bacon your card said you were entitled to, or threatening a neighbor in your building with some Party big shot who would come and fix him good.

Perhaps the quickest tempers were to be found in the lengthening queues for tobacco. The ration was just three johnnies a day, but when you were extravagant enough actually to smoke one it was easier to understand why Hitler didn't smoke himself: they tasted like burned toast. Sometimes people smoked tea, that is when you could get any tea, but if you could, it was always better to pour boiling water on the stuff and drink it.

Around police headquarters at Alexanderplatz—this area also happened to be the center of Berlin's black market, which, despite the very serious penalties inflicted on those who got caught, was about the only thing in the city that could have been described as thriving—the scarcity of petrol hit us almost as hard as the tobacco and alcohol shortages. We took trains and buses to our crime scenes, and when these weren't running, we walked, often through the blackout, which was not without hazard. Almost one third of all accidental deaths in Berlin were a result of the blackout. Not that any of my colleagues in Kripo were interested in attending crime scenes or in solving anything other than the enduring problem of where to find a new source of sausage, beer, and cigarettes. Sometimes we joked that crime was decreasing: no one was stealing money for the simple reason that there wasn't anything in the shops to spend it on. Like most jokes in Berlin in the autumn of 1941, that one was funnier because it was also true.

Of course, there was still plenty of theft about: coupons, laundry, petrol, furniture—thieves used it for firewood—curtains (people used them to make clothes), the rabbits and guinea pigs that people kept on their balconies for fresh meat; you name it, Berliners stole it. And with the blackout there was real crime, violent crime, if you were interested in looking for it. The blackout was great if you were a rapist.

For a while I was back in Homicide. Berliners were still killing each other, although not a moment passed when I didn't think it risible that I should continue to believe that this mattered very much, knowing what I now knew about what was happening in the East. There wasn't a day when I didn't remember the sight of old Jewish men and women being herded toward execution pits, where they were dispatched by drunken, laughing SS firing squads. Still I went through the motions of being a proper detective, although it often felt as if I were trying to put out a fire in an ashtray when, down the road, a whole city was the scene of a major conflagration.

It was while I was investigating the several homicides that came my way in early September 1941 that I discovered some new motives for murder that weren't in the jurisprudence books. Motives that stemmed from the quaint new realities of Berlin life. The small holder in Weissensee who drove himself mad with coarse, home-made vodka and then killed the postwoman with an ax. A butcher in Wilmersdorf who was stabbed with his own knife by the local air-raid warden in a dispute about a short ration of bacon. The young nurse from the Rudolf Virchow Hospital who, because of the city's acute accommodation crisis, poisoned a sixty-five-year-old spinster in Plotzensee so that she might have the victim's better-appointed room. An SS sergeant back on leave from Riga who, habituated to the mass killings that were going on in Latvia, shot his parents because he could see no reason not to shoot them. But most of the soldiers who came home from the eastern front and were in a mood to kill someone killed themselves.

I might have done it myself but for the certainty that I wouldn't be missed at all; and the sure knowledge that there were many others—Jews, mostly—who seemed to soldier on with so much less in life than I had. Yes. In the late summer of 1941 it was the Jews and what was happening to the Jews that helped persuade me against killing myself.

Of course, the old-fashioned sort of Berlin murders—the ones that used to sell newspapers—were still committed. Husbands continued to murder their wives, just like before. And on occasion wives murdered their husbands. From where I sat, most of the husbands who got murdered—bullies too free with their fists and their criticism—had it coming. I've never hit a woman unless we'd talked about it first. Prostitutes got their throats cut or were battered to death, as before. And not just prostitutes. In the summer preceding my return from Belorussia a lust killer named Paul Ogorzow pleaded guilty to the rapes and murders of eight women and the attempted murders of at least eight more. The popular press dubbed him the S-Bahn murderer because most of his attacks were carried out on trains or near S-Bahn stations.

That is why Paul Ogorzow came to mind when, late one night in the second week of September 1941, I was called to take a look at a body found close to the line between the S-Bahn stations at Jannowitzbrücke and Schlesischer. In the blackout nobody was quite sure if the body was a man's or a woman's, which was more understandable when you took into account that it had been hit by a train and was missing its head. Sudden death is rarely ever tidy. If it was, they wouldn't need detectives. But this one was as untidy as anything I'd seen since the Great War, when a mine or a howitzer shell could reduce a man to a mangled heap of bloody clothes and jagged bone in the blink of an eye. Perhaps that was why I was able to look at it with such detachment. I hope so. The alternative— that my recent experience in the murder ghettoes of Belorussia had left me indifferent to the sight of human suffering—was too awful to contemplate.

The other investigating detectives were Wilhelm Wurth, a sergeant who was a big noise in the police sports movement, and Gottfried Lehnhoff, an inspector who had returned to the Alex after having retired.

Wurth was on the fencing team, and the previous winter he

had taken part in Heydrich's skiing competition for the German police and won a medal. Wurth would have been in the Army but for the fact that he was a year or two too old. But he was a useful man to have along on a murder investigation in the event that the victim had skied onto the point of a sword. He was a thin, quiet man with ears like bell pulls and an upper lip that was as full as a walrus's mustache. It was a good face for a detective in the modern Berlin police force, but he wasn't quite as stupid as he looked. He wore a plain gray double-breasted suit, carried a thick walking stick, and chewed on the stem of a cherrywood pipe that was almost always empty but somehow he managed to smell of tobacco.

Lehnhoff had a neck and head like a pear, but he wasn't green. Like a lot of other cops, he'd been drawing his pension, but with so many younger officers now serving in police battalions on the eastern front, he had come back into the force to make a nice cozy corner for himself at the Alex. The little Party pin he wore in the lapel of his cheap suit would only have made it easier for him to do as little real policing as possible.

We walked south down Dircksenstrasse to Jannowitzbrücke, and then along the S-Bahn line with the river under our feet. There was an almost full moon, and most of the time we didn't need the flashlights we'd brought, but we felt safer with them when the line veered back over the gasworks on Holtmarkt Strasse and the old Julius Pintsch lighting factory; there wasn't much of a fence and it would have been easy to step off the line and fall badly.

Over the gasworks, we came across a group of uniformed policemen and railway workers. Farther down the track I could just make out the shape of a train in Schlesischer Station.

"I'm Commissar Gunther, from the Alex," I said. There seemed no point in showing him my beer-token. "This is Inspector Lehnhoff and Sergeant Wurth. Who called it in?"

"Me, sir." One of the cops moved toward me and saluted. "Sergeant Stumm."

"No relation, I hope," said Lehnhoff.

There had been a Johannes Stumm who had been forced to leave the political police by Fat Hermann because he wasn't a Nazi.

"No, sir." Sergeant Stumm smiled patiently.

"Tell me, Sergeant," I said, "why did you think that this might be a murder, and not a suicide or an accident?"

"Well, it's true, stepping in front of a train is a most popular way to kill yourself these days," said Sergeant Stumm. "Especially if you're a woman. Me, I'd use a firearm if I wanted to kill myself. But women aren't as comfortable with guns as men are. Now, with this victim, all of the pockets have been turned inside out, sir. It's not something you'd do if you were planning to kill yourself. And it's not something that a train would normally take the trouble to do, either. So that rules out its being an accident, see?"

"Maybe someone else found him before you did," I suggested. "And just robbed him."

"A copper, maybe," offered Wurth.

Wisely, Sergeant Stumm ignored the suggestion.

"Unlikely, sir. I'm pretty sure I was the first on the scene. The train driver saw someone on the track as he started to gain speed out of Jannowitz. He hit the brakes, but by the time the train stopped, it was too late."

"All right. Let's have a look at him."

"Not a pretty sight, sir. Even in the dark."

"Believe me, I've seen worse."

"I'll take your word for that, sir."

The uniformed sergeant led the way along the track and paused for a moment to switch on his flashlight and illuminate a severed hand that lay on the ground. I looked at it for a minute or so before we walked on to where another police officer was waiting patiently beside a collection of ragged clothes and mangled remains that had once been a human being. For a moment I might have been looking at myself.

"Hold the flash on him while we take a look."

The body looked as if it had been chewed up and spat out by a prehistoric monster. The corrugated legs were barely attached to an impossibly flat pelvis. The man was wearing a workman's blue overalls with mitten-sized pockets that were indeed inside out as the sergeant had described; so were the pockets in the oily rag that was his twisted flannel jacket. Where the head had been was now a glistening, jagged harpoon of bloody bone and sinew. There was a strong smell of shit from bowels that had been crushed and emptied under the enormous pressure of a locomotive's wheels.

"I can't imagine what you've seen that could look worse than this poor Fritz," said Sergeant Stumm.

"Me neither," Wurth observed, and turned away in disgust.

"I daresay we'll all see some interesting sights before this war is over," I said. "Has anyone looked for the head?"

"I've got a couple of lads searching the area for it now," said the sergeant. "One on the track and the other down below, in case it fell into the gasworks or the factory yard."

"I think you're probably correct," I said. "It looks like a murder, all right. Quite apart from the pockets, which have been turned out, there's that hand we saw."

"The hand?" This was Lehnhoff talking. "What about it?"

I led them back along the track to take another look at the severed hand, which I picked up and turned in my hands as if it were a historic artifact, or perhaps a souvenir once owned by the prophet Daniel.

"These cuts on the fingers look defensive to me," I said. "As if he might have caught the knife of someone trying to stab him."

"I don't know how you can tell that after a train just ran over him," said Lehnhoff.

"Because these cuts are much too thin to have been inflicted by the train. And just look where they are. Along the flesh of the inside of the fingers and on the hand between the thumb and the forefinger. That's a textbook defensive injury if I ever saw one, Gottfried."

"All right," Lehnhoff said, almost grudgingly. "I suppose you are the expert. On murder."

"Perhaps. Only of late I've had a lot of competition. There are plenty of cops out east, young cops, who know a lot more about murder than I do."

"I wouldn't know," said Lehnhoff.

"Take my word for it. There's a whole new generation of police experts out there." I let this remark settle for a moment before adding, very carefully, for appearance's sake, "I find that very reassuring sometimes. That there are so many good men to take my place. Eh, Sergeant Stumm?"

"Yes, sir." But I could hear the doubt in the uniformed sergeant's voice.

"Walk with us," I said, warming to him. In a country where ill temper and petulance were the order of the day—Hitler and Goebbels were forever ranting angrily about something—the sergeant's imperturbability was heartening. "Come back to the bridge. Another pair of eyes might be useful."

"Yes, sir."

"What are we looking for now?" There was a weary sigh in Lehnhoff's voice, as if he could hardly see the point of investigating this case any further.

"An elephant."

"What?"

"Something. Evidence. You'll certainly know it when you see it," I said.

Back up the track we found some blood spots on a railway sleeper and then some more on the edge of the platform outside the echoing glasshouse that was the station at Jannowitz Bridge.

Below, someone aboard a river barge that was quietly chugging through one of the many red-brick arches in the bridge shouted at us to extinguish our lights. This was Lehnhoff's cue to start throwing his weight around. It was almost as if he'd been waiting to get tough with someone, and it didn't matter who.

"We're the police," he yelled down at the barge. Lehnhoff was yet another angry German. "And we're investigating a murder up here. So mind your own business or I'll come aboard and search you just because I can."

"It's everyone's business if the Tommy bombers see your lights," said the voice, not unreasonably.

Wurth's nose wrinkled with disbelief. "I shouldn't think that's very likely at all. Do you, sir? It's been a while since the RAF came this far east."

"They probably can't get the petrol, either," I said.

I pointed my flashlight on the ground and followed a trail of blood along the platform to a place where it seemed to start.

"From the amount of blood on the ground, he was probably stabbed here. Then he staggered along the platform a ways before falling onto the track. Picked himself up. Walked a bit more and then got hit by the train to Friedrichshagen."

"It was the last one," said Sergeant Stumm. "The one o'clock."

"Lucky he didn't miss it," said Lehnhoff.

Ignoring him, I glanced at my watch. It was three a.m. "Well, that gives us an approximate time of death."

I started to walk along the track in front of the platform and after a while I found a grayish green passport-sized book lying on the ground. It was an employment identification document, much like my own, except that this one was for foreigners. Inside was all of the information about the dead man I needed: his name, nationality, address, photograph, and employer.

"Foreign worker's book, is it?" said Lehnhoff, glancing over my shoulder as I studied the victim's details under my flashlight.

I nodded. The dead man was Geert Vranken, age thirty-nine, born in Dordrecht, in the Netherlands, a volunteer railway worker;

living at a hostel in Wuhlheide. The face in the photograph was wary-looking, with a cleft chin that was slightly unshaven. The eyebrows were short and the hair thinning to one side. He appeared to be wearing the same thick flannel jacket as the one on the body, and a collarless shirt buttoned up to the neck. Even as we were reading the bare details of Geert Vranken's shortish life, another policeman was coming up the stairs of Jannowitz Station with what, in the darkness, looked like a small, round bag.

"I found the head, sir," reported the policeman. "It was on the roof of the Pintsch factory." He was holding the head by the ear, which, in the absence of much hair, looked as good a way to carry around a severed head as anyone could have thought of. "I didn't like to leave it up there, sir."

"No, you were right to bring it along, lad," Sergeant Stumm said, and, taking hold of the other ear, carefully laid the dead man's head on the railway platform so that it was staring up at us.

"Not a sight you see every day," Wurth said, and looked away.

"You want to get yourself up to Plotzensee," I remarked. "I hear the falling ax is very busy these days."

"That's him, all right," said Lehnhoff. "The man in the worker's book. Wouldn't you say?"

"I agree," I said. "And I suppose someone might have tried to rob him. Or else why go through his pockets?"

"You're sticking to the theory that this is a murder, and not an accident, then?" inquired Lehnhoff.

"Yes. I am. For that reason."

Sergeant Stumm tutted loudly and then rubbed his stubbly jaw, which sounded almost as loud. "Bad luck for him. But bad luck for the murderer, too."

"What do you mean?" I asked.

"Well, if he was a foreign worker, I can't imagine there was much more than fluff in his pockets. It's a hell of a disappointing thing to kill a man with the intent of robbing him and then find that he had nothing worth stealing. I mean, these poor fellows aren't exactly well paid, are they?"

"It's a job," objected Lehnhoff. "Better a job in Germany than no job back in Holland."

"And whose fault is that?" said Sergeant Stumm.

"I don't think I like your insinuation, Sergeant," said Lehnhoff.

"Leave it, Lehnhoff," I said. "This isn't the time or the place for a political argument. A man is dead, after all."

Lehnhoff grunted and tapped the head with the toe of his shoe, which was enough to make me want to kick him off the platform.

"Well, if someone did kill him, like you say, Herr Commissar, it'll be another of them foreign workers that probably did it. You see if I'm wrong. It's dog-eat-dog in these foreign-worker hostels."

"Don't knock it," I said. "Dogs know the importance of getting a square meal now and again. And, speaking for myself, if it's a choice between fifty grams of dog and a hundred grams of nothing, then I'll eat the dog anytime."

"Not me," said Lehnhoff. "I draw the line at guinea pigs. So there's no way I'd ever eat a dog."

"It's one thing saying that, sir," said Sergeant Stumm. "But it's another thing altogether trying to tell the difference. Maybe you haven't heard, but the cops over at Zoo Station are having to put on night patrols in the zoo. On account of how poachers have been breaking in and stealing the animals. Apparently they just had their tapir taken."

"What's a tapir?" asked Wurth.

"It looks a bit like pork," I said. "So I expect that's what some unscrupulous butcher is calling it now."

"Good luck to him," said Sergeant Stumm.

"You don't mean that," said Lehnhoff.

"A man needs more than a stirring speech by the Mahatma Propaganddhi to fill his stomach," I said.

"Amen," said Sergeant Stumm.

"So you'd look the other way if you knew what it was?"

"I don't know about that," I said, getting careful again. I might have been suicidal but I wasn't stupid: Lehnhoff was just the type to report a fellow to the Gestapo for wearing English shoes, and I hardly wanted to spend a week in the cells, removed from the comfort of my warm, nighttime pistol. "But this is Berlin, Gottfried. Looking the other way is what we're good at."

I pointed at the severed head that lay at our feet.

"You just see if I'm wrong."

2

About a lot of things I'm not always right. But about the Nazis I wasn't often wrong.

Geert Vranken was a voluntary worker and had come to Berlin in search of a better job than the one that was available to him in Holland. Berlin's railway, which was experiencing a self-inflicted crisis in recruiting maintenance staff, had been glad to have an experienced track engineer; Berlin's police was less keen to investigate his murder. In fact, it didn't want to investigate the case at all. But there was no doubting that the Dutchman had been murdered. When eventually his body was given its grudging, cursory examination by the ancient doctor brought back from retirement to handle forensic pathology for the Berlin police, six stab wounds were found on what remained of his torso.

Commissioner Friedrich-Wilhelm Lüdtke, who was now in

charge of the Berlin Criminal Police, wasn't a bad detective. It was Lüdtke who had successfully headed the S-Bahn murder investigation that led to the arrest and execution of Paul Ogorzow. But as he himself explained to me in his newly carpeted office on the top floor of the Alex, there was an important new law coming down the pipe from the Wilhelmstrasse, and Lüdtke's boss, Wilhelm Frick, minister of the interior, had ordered him to prioritize its enforcement at the expense of all other investigative matters. Lüdtke, a doctor of law, was almost embarrassed to tell me what this important new law amounted to.

"From September nineteenth," he said, "all Jews in Germany and the Protectorate of Bohemia and Moravia will be obliged to wear a yellow star inscribed with the word 'Jew' on their outer garments."

"You mean like in the Middle Ages?"

"Yes, like in the Middle Ages."

"Well, that should make them easier to spot. Great idea. Until recently I've found it rather hard to recognize who is a Jew and who isn't. Of late they do look thinner and hungrier than the rest of us. But that's about it. Frankly, I've yet to see just one who looks anything like those stupid cartoons in *Der Stürmer*." I nodded with fake enthusiasm. "Yes, this will certainly prevent them from looking exactly like the rest of us."

Lüdtke, looking uncomfortable, adjusted his well-starched cuffs and collar. He was a big man with thick, dark hair neatly combed off a broad, tanned forehead. He wore a navy-blue suit and a dark tie with a knot that was as small as the Party badge in his lapel; probably it felt just as tight on his neck when it came to speaking the truth. A matching navy-blue bowler hat was positioned on the corner of his double partner's desk, as if to hide something. Perhaps it was his lunch. Or just his conscience. I wondered how the hat would look with a yellow star on the crown. Like a Keystone Kop's helmet, I thought. Something idiotic, anyway.

"I don't like this any more than you," he said, scratching the backs of his hands nervously. I could tell he was dying for a smoke. We both were. Without cigarettes, the Alex felt like an ashtray in a no-smoking lounge.

"I'd like it a whole lot less, I think, if I were Jewish," I said.

"Yes, but you know what makes it almost unforgivable?" He opened a box of matches and bit one. "Right now there's an acute shortage of material."

"Yellow material."

Lüdtke nodded.

"I might have guessed. Mind if I have one of those?"

"Help yourself." He tossed the matches across the desk and watched as I fished one out and put it in the corner of my mouth. "I'm told they're good for your throat."

"Are you worried about your health, Wilhelm?"

"Isn't everyone? That's why we do what we're told. In case we come down with a dose of the Gestapo."

"You mean like making sure Jews wear their yellow stars?"

"That's right."

"Oh sure, sure. And while I can see the obvious importance of a law like that, there's still the matter of the dead Dutchman. In case you'd forgotten, he was stabbed six times."

Lüdtke shrugged. "If he was German it would be different, Bernie. But the Ogorzow case was a very expensive investigation for this department. We went way over budget. You've no idea how much it cost to catch that bastard. Undercover police officers, half the city's rail workers interviewed, increased police presence at stations—the overtime we had to pay out was enormous. It really was a very difficult time for Kripo. To say nothing of the pressure we came under from the Propaganda Ministry. It's hard catching anyone when the newspapers aren't even allowed to write about a case."

"Geert Vranken was a rail worker," I said.

"And you think the ministry is going to be happy to learn that there's another killer at work on the S-Bahn?"

"This killer is different. As far as I can tell, nobody raped him. And unless you count the train that drove over him, nobody tried to mutilate him, either."

"But murder is murder, and frankly I know exactly what they'll say. That there's enough bad news around right now. In case you hadn't noticed, Bernie, this city's morale is already lower than a badger's arse. Besides, we need those foreign workers. That's what they're going to tell me. The last thing we want is Germans thinking that there's a problem with our guest workers. We had enough of that during the Ogorzow case. Everyone in Berlin was convinced that a German couldn't possibly have murdered all those women. A lot of foreign workers were harassed and beaten up by irate Berliners who thought that one of them must have done it. You don't want to see any more of that, do you? Christ, there are problems enough on the trains and the underground as it is. It took me almost an hour to come to work this morning."

"I wonder why we bother to come in at all, given that the Ministry of Propaganda is now deciding what we can and what we can't investigate. Are we really supposed to find people who look Jewish and check to see if they're wearing the right embroidery? It's laughable."

"I'm afraid that's just how it is. Perhaps if there are any more stabbings like this one, then we can devote some resources to an investigation, but for now I'd rather you left this Dutchie alone."

"All right, Wilhelm, if that's the way you want it." I bit hard on my match. "But I'm beginning to understand your twenty-a-day match habit. I guess it's easier not to scream when you're chewing down on one of these."

As I stood up to leave, I glanced up at the picture on the wall. The Leader stared me down in triumph, but for a change he wasn't saying very much. If anyone needed a yellow star it was him; and sewn just over his heart, assuming he had one—an aiming spot for a firing squad.

The Berlin city map on Lüdtke's wall told me nothing, either. When Bernhard Weiss, one of Lüdtke's predecessors, had been in charge of Berlin Kripo, the map had been covered with little flags marking the incidents of crime in the city. Now it was empty. There was, it seemed, no crime to speak of. Another great victory for National Socialism.

"Oh, by the way, shouldn't someone tell the Vranken family back in Holland that their major breadwinner stopped a train with his face?"

"I will speak to the State Labor Service," said Lüdtke. "You can safely leave it to them."

I sighed, and rolled my head wearily on my shoulders; it felt thick and heavy, like an old medicine ball.

"I feel reassured already."

"You don't look it," he said. "What's the matter with you, these days, Bernie? You're a real bat in the balls, do you know that? Whenever you walk in here it's like rain coming in at the eaves. It's like you've given up."

"Maybe I have."

"Well, don't. I'm ordering you to pull yourself together."

I shrugged. "Wilhelm? If I knew how to swim I'd first untie the anvil that's tied around my legs."

3

Prussia has always been an interesting place to live in, especially if you were Jewish. Even before the Nazis, Jews were singled out for special treatment by their neighbors. Back in 1881 and 1900, the synagogues in Neustettin and Könitz—and probably in several other Prussian towns, too—were burned down. Then, in 1923, when there were food riots and I was a young cop in uniform, the many Jewish shops of Scheuenviertel—which is one of Berlin's toughest neighborhoods—were singled out for special treatment because Jews were suspected of price gouging or hoarding, or both, it didn't matter: Jews were Jews and not to be trusted.

Most of the city's synagogues were destroyed of course in November 1938. At the top of Fasanenstrasse, where I owned a small apartment, a vast but ruined synagogue remained standing and looking to all the world as if the future Roman emperor Titus had just finished teaching the city of Jerusalem a lesson. It seems that not much has changed since AD 70; certainly not in Berlin, and it could be only a matter of time before we started crucifying Jews on the streets.

I never walked past this ruin without a small sense of shame. But it was quite a while before I realized there were Jews living in my own building. For a long time I was quite unaware of their presence so close to me. Lately, however, these Jews had become easily recognizable to anyone that had eyes to see. Despite what I'd said to Commissioner Lüdtke, you didn't need a yellow star or a set of calipers to measure the length of someone's nose to know who was Jewish. Denied every amenity; subject to a nine o'clock curfew; forbidden "luxuries" such as fruit, tobacco, or alcohol; and allowed to do their shopping only for one hour at the end of the day, when the shops were usually empty; Jews had the most miserable of lives; and you could see that in their faces. Every time I saw one, I thought of a rat, only the rat had a Kripo beer-token in his coat pocket with my name and number inscribed on it. I admired their resilience. So did many other Berliners, even some Nazis.

I thought less about hating or even killing myself whenever I considered what the Jews had to put up with. To survive as a Jew in Berlin in the autumn of 1941 was to be a person of courage and strength. Even so, it was hard to see the two Fridmann sisters, who occupied the flat underneath my own, surviving for much longer. One of them, Raisa, was married, with a son, Efim, but both he and Raisa's husband, Mikhail, arrested in 1938, were still in prison. The daughter, Sarra, escaped to France in 1934 and had not been heard from since. These two sisters—the older one was Tsilia— knew I was a policeman and were rightly wary of me. We rarely ever exchanged much more than a nod or a "good morning." Besides, contact between Jews and Aryans was strictly forbidden, and since the block leader would have reported this to the Gestapo, I judged it better, for their sake, to keep my distance.

After Belorussia I ought not to have been so horrified at the yellow star, but I was. Maybe this new law seemed worse to me because of what I knew awaited those Jews who were deported east, but after my conversation with Commissioner Lüdtke I resolved to do something, although it was a day or two before I figured out what this might be.

My wife had been dead for twenty years, but I still had some of her dresses and sometimes, when I'd managed to overcome the shortages and have a drink or two and I was feeling sorry for myself and, more particularly, for her, I'd get one of her old garments out of the closet and press the material to my nose and mouth and inhale her memory. For a long time after she was gone that was what I called a home life. When she'd been alive we had soap, so my memories were all pleasant ones; these days things were rather less fragrant, and if you were wise you boarded the S-Bahn holding an orange stuffed with cloves, like a medieval pope going out among the common people. Especially in summer. In the dog days of 1941, even the prettiest girl smelled like a stevedore.

At first I figured on giving the two Fridmann sisters the yellow dress so that they could use it for making yellow stars, only there was something about this I didn't like. I suppose it made me feel complicit in the whole horrible police order. Especially since I was a policeman. So, halfway downstairs with the yellow dress draped over my arm, I went back to my flat and fetched all of the dresses that were in my closet. But even this felt inadequate and, as I handed over my wife's remaining wardrobe to these harmless women, I quietly decided to do something more.

It isn't exactly a page from some heroic tale as described by Winckelmann or Hölderlin, but that's how this whole story got started: if it hadn't been for the decision to help the Fridmann sisters I'd never have met Arianne Tauber and what happened wouldn't have happened.

Back inside my apartment, I smoked the last of my cigarettes and contemplated putting my nose in some records at the Alex, just to see if Mikhail and Efim Fridmann were still alive. Well, that was one thing I could do, but for those with a purple J on their ration cards, it wasn't going to help feed them. Two women who looked as thin as the Fridmann sisters were going to need something more substantial than just some information about their loved ones.

After a while I had what I thought was a good idea and fetched a German Army bread bag from my closet. In the bread bag was a kilo of Algerian coffee beans I'd purloined in Paris and that I'd been planning to trade for some cigarettes. I left my flat and took a tram east as far as Potsdamer Platz Station.

It was a warm evening, not yet dark. Couples were strolling arm in arm through the Tiergarten, and it seemed almost impossible that two thousand kilometers to the east, the German Army was surrounding Kiev and slowly tightening its stranglehold on Leningrad. I walked up to Pariser Platz. I was on my way to the Hotel Adlon to see the maître d' with the aim of trading the coffee for some food that I could give to the two sisters.

The maître d' at the Adlon that year was Willy Thümmel, a fat Sudeten German who was always busy and so light on his toes that it made me wonder how he ever got fat in the first place. With his rosy cheeks, his easy smile, and his impeccable clothes he always reminded me of Hermann Göring. Without a doubt both men enjoyed their food, although the Reichsmarshal had always given me the impression that he might just have eaten me, too, if he'd been hungry enough. Willy liked his food; but he liked people more.

There were no customers in the restaurant—not yet—and Willy was checking the blackout curtains when I poked my nose around the door. Like any good maître d' he spotted me immediately and quickly came my way on invisible casters.

"Bernie. You look troubled. Are you all right?"

"What's the point of complaining, Willy?"

"I don't know; the wheel that squeaks the loudest in Germany these days usually gets the most grease. What brings you here?"

"A word in private, Willy."

We went down a small flight of stairs to an office. Willy closed the door and poured two small glasses of sherry. I knew he was seldom away from the restaurant for longer than it took to inspect the china in the men's room, so I came straight to the point.

"When I was in Paris I liberated some coffee," I said. "Real coffee, not the muck we get in Germany. Beans. Algerian beans. A whole kilo." I put the bread bag on Willy's desk and let him inspect the contents.

For a moment he just closed his eyes and inhaled the aroma; then he groaned a groan that I'd seldom heard outside a bedroom.

"You've certainly earned that drink. I'd forgotten what real coffee smells like."

I hit my tonsils with the sherry.

"A kilo, you say? That's a hundred marks on the black market, last time I tried to get any. And since there isn't any coffee to be had anywhere, it's probably more. No wonder we invaded France. For coffee like this I'd crawl into Leningrad."

"They haven't got any there, either." I let him refill my glass. The sherry was hardly the best, but then nothing was, not even in the Adlon. Not anymore. "I was thinking that you might like to treat some of your special guests."

"Yes, I might." He frowned. "But you can't want money. Not for something as precious as this, Bernie. Even the devil has to drink mud with powdered milk in it these days."

He took another noseful of the aroma and shook his head. "So what do you want? The Adlon is at your disposal."

"I don't want that much. I just want some food."

"You disappoint me. There's nothing we have in our kitchens that's worthy of coffee like this. And don't be fooled by what's on the menu." He collected a menu off the desk and handed it to me. "There are two meat dishes on the menu when the kitchen can actually serve only one. But we put two on for the sake of appearances. What can you do? We have a reputation to uphold."

"Suppose someone asks for the dish you don't have?" I said.

"Impossible." Willy shook his head. "As the first customer comes through the door we cross off the second dish. It's Hitler's choice. Which is to say it's no choice at all."

He paused.

"You want food for this coffee? What kind of food?"

"I want food in cans."

"Ah."

"The quality isn't important as long as it's edible. Canned meat, canned fruit, canned milk, canned vegetables. Whatever you can find. Enough to last for a while."

"You know canned goods are strictly forbidden, don't you? That's the law. All canned goods are for the war front. If you're stopped on the street with canned food, you'd be in serious trouble. All that precious metal. They'll think you're going to sell it to the RAF."

"I know it. But I need food that can last, and this is the best place to get it."

"You don't look like a man who can't get to the shops, Bernie."

"It isn't for me, Willy."

"I thought not. In which case it's none of my business what you want it for. But I tell you what, Commissar, for coffee like this I am ready to commit a crime against the state. Just as long as you don't tell anyone. Now come with me. I think we have some canned goods from before the war."

We went along to the hotel storeroom. It was as big as the lockup underneath the Alex but easier on the ear and the nose. The door was secured with more padlocks than the German National Bank. In there he filled my bread bag with as many cans as it could carry.

"When these cans are gone come and get some more, if you're still at liberty. And if you're not, then please forget you ever met me."

"Thanks, Willy."

"Now I have a small favor to ask you, Bernie. Which might even be to your advantage. There's an American journalist staying here in the hotel. One of several, as it happens. His name is Paul Dickson, and he works for the Mutual Broadcasting System. He would dearly like to visit the war front, but apparently such things are forbidden. Everything is forbidden now. The only way we know what's permitted is if we do something and manage to stay out of prison.

"Now, I know you are recently returned from the front. And you notice I don't ask what it's like out there. In the East. Just seeing a compass these days makes me feel sick. I don't ask because I don't want to know. You might even say this is why I went into the hotel business: because the outside world is of no concern to me. The guests in this hotel are my world, and that's all the world I need to know. Their happiness and satisfaction are all that I care about.

"So, for Mr. Dickson's happiness and satisfaction, I ask that you meet with him. But not here in the hotel. No, not here. It's hardly safe to talk in the Adlon. There are several suites of rooms on the top floor that have been taken over by people from the Foreign Office. And these people are guarded by German soldiers wearing steel helmets. Can you imagine it. Soldiers, here in the Adlon. Intolerable. It's just like 1919 all over again, but without the barricades."

"What are workers from the Foreign Office doing here that they can't do in the ministry?"

"Some of them are destined for the new Foreign Travel Office, when it's finished. But the rest are typing. Morning, noon, and night, they're typing. Like it's for a speech by the Mahatma."

"What are they typing?"

"They're typing up releases for the American press, most of whom are also staying here. Which means that there are Gestapo in the bar. Possibly there are even secret microphones. I don't know for sure, but this is what I heard. Which is another source of grief for us."

"This Dickson fellow. Is he in the hotel right now?"

Willy thought for a moment. "I think so."

"Don't mention my name. Just tell him that if he's interested in a bit of 'Life Poetry and Truth,' I'll be beside the Goethe statue in the Tiergarten."

"I know it. Just off Hermann-Göring-Strasse."

"I'll wait fifteen minutes for him. And if he comes, he should come alone. No friends. Just him and me and Goethe. I don't want any witnesses when I speak to him. These days there are plenty of Amis who work for the Gestapo. And I'm not sure about Goethe."

I hoisted the bread bag onto my back and walked out of the Adlon onto Pariser Platz, where it was already getting dark. One of the only good things about the blackout was that you couldn't see the Nazi flags, but the brutal outlines of Speer's partly constructed Foreign Travel Office were still visible in the distance against the purpling night sky, dominating the landscape west of the Brandenburg Gate. Rumor had it that Hitler's favorite architect, Albert Speer, was using Russian POWs to help complete a building that no one other than Hitler seemed to want. Rumor also had it that there was a new network of tunnels under construction connecting government buildings on Wilhelmstrasse with secret bunkers that extended under Hermann-Göring-Strasse as far as the Tiergarten. It was never good to pay too much attention to rumors in Berlin for the simple reason that they were usually true.

I stood by the statue of Goethe and waited. After a while I heard a 109 quite low in the sky as it headed southeast toward the airfield at Tempelhof, and then another. For anyone who'd been in Russia, it was an instantly recognizable and reassuring sound, like an enormous but friendly lion yawning in an empty cave, and quite different from the noise of the much slower RAF Whitleys, which occasionally plowed through Berlin skies like tractors of death and destruction.

"Good evening," said the man walking toward me. "I'm Paul Dickson. The American from the Adlon."

He hardly needed the introduction. His Old Spice and Virginia tobacco came ahead of him like a motorcycle outrider with a pennant on his mudguard. Solid footsteps bespoke sturdy wingtip shoes that could have ferried him across the Delaware. The hand that pumped mine was part of a body that still consumed nutritious food. His sweet and minty breath smelled of real toothpaste and testified to his having access to a dentist with teeth in his head who was still a decade off retirement. And although it was dark, I could almost feel his tan. As we exchanged cigarettes and conversational bromides, I wondered if the real reason Berliners disliked Americans was less to do with Roosevelt and his anti-German rhetoric and more to do with their better health, their better hair, their better clothes, and their altogether better lives.

"Willy said you've just come back from the front," he said, speaking German that was also better than I had expected.

"Yes, that's right."

"Care to talk about it?"

"Talking about it is about the only means of committing suicide for which I seem to have the nerve," I confessed.

"I can assure you, sir, I am nothing to do with the Gestapo. If that's what you're implying. I daresay that's exactly what someone who was a Gestapo informer would tell you. But to be quite frank with you, there's nothing they have that I want. Except perhaps a good story. I'd kill for a good story."

"Have you killed many?"

"Frankly, I don't see how I could have done. As soon as they know I'm an American, most Berliners seem to want to hit me. They seem to hold me personally responsible for all the ships we've been giving to the British."

"Don't worry; Berliners have never been interested in having a navy," I said. "That kind of thing matters more in Hamburg and Bremen. In Berlin, you can count yourself lucky that Roosevelt never gave the Tommies any beer or sausage, or you'd be dead by now." I pointed toward Potsdamer Platz. "Come on. Let's walk."

"Sure," he said, and followed me south, out of the park. "Anywhere in particular?"

"No. But I need a few minutes to address the ball, so to speak."

"Golfing man, huh?"

"I used to play a bit. Before the Nazis. But it's never really caught on since Hitler. It's too easy to be bad at it, which is not something Nazis can deal with."

"I appreciate your talking to me like this."

"I haven't told you anything yet. Right now I'm still wondering how much I can tell you without feeling like—what was his name? The traitor. Benedict—?"

"Benedict Arnold?"

"That's right."

We crossed Potsdamer onto Leipziger Platz.

"I hope we're not headed for the Press Club," said Dickson. "I'd feel like a bit of a fool if you took me in there to tell me your story." He pointed at a door on the other side of the square, where several official-looking cars were parked. "I hear all kinds of bullshit in that place."

"You don't say."

"Dr. Froehlich, the Propaganda Ministry's liaison officer for the American media, he is always summoning us in there for special press conferences to announce yet another decisive victory for German forces against the Red Army. Him or one of those other doctors. Brauweiler or Dietrich. The doctors of deceit, that's what we call them."

"Not forgetting the biggest deceiver of them all," I said. "Dr. Goebbels."

Dickson laughed bitterly. "It's got so bad that when my own doctor says there's nothing wrong with me, I just don't believe him."

"You can believe him. You're American. Provided you don't do anything stupid, like declare war on Russia, most of you should live forever."

Dickson followed me across to Wertheim department store. In the moonlight you could see the huge map of the Soviet Union that occupied the main window, so that any patriotic German might look at it and follow the heroic progress of our brave armed forces. It wasn't like there was anything else in the store to put in the window. When the place had been owned and run by Jews, it had been the best store in Germany. Now it was little better than a warehouse, and an empty one at that. The shop assistants spent most of their time gossiping and ignoring the spectators—you could hardly call them customers—who wandered around the store in search of merchandise that simply wasn't there. Even the elevators weren't working.

There was no one on the sidewalk in front of the window, and it seemed as good a place as any to tell the American radio journalist the truth about our great patriotic war against the Russians and the Jews.

"Give me another one of your cigarettes. If I'm going to cough up the whole story I want something inside me to help it along."

He handed me an almost full pack of American cigarettes and told me to keep it. I lit one quickly and let the nicotine go and play in my brain. For a moment I felt giddy and light-headed, as if it were the first time I ever smoked. But that was how it should have been. It wouldn't have been right to have told Dickson about the police battalions and resettlement and special actions and the Belorussia ghetto and pits full of dead Jews without feeling a little sick inside.

Which is exactly what I told him.

"And you saw all of this?" Now it was Dickson who sounded sick inside.

"I'm a captain in the SD," I said. "I saw it all."

"Jesus. It's hard to believe."

"You wanted to know. I told you. That's how it is. Worse than you could possibly imagine. When they don't let you go somewhere, it's because they can't boast about what they're doing. You could have worked it out for yourself. I'd be there right now but for the fact that I'm a bit particular about who I pull the trigger on. They sent me home, in disgrace. I'm lucky they didn't send me to a punishment battalion."

"You were in the SD?" Dickson sounded just a bit nervous.

"Correct."

"That's like the Gestapo, isn't it?"

"Not exactly. It's the intelligence wing of the SS. The Abwehr's ugly little sister. Like a lot of men in the SD, I came in through a side door marked No Bloody Choice. I was a policeman at the Alex before I was in the SD. A proper policeman. The kind who started out helping old ladies across the road. Not all of us make Jews clean the street with a toothbrush, you know. I want you to know that. Me, I'm a bit like Frankenstein's monster with the little girl at the lake. There's a part of me that really wants to make friends and to be good."

Dickson was quiet for a moment. "No one back home is going to believe this," he said eventually. "Not that I'd ever get it past the local press censor. This is the trouble with radio. You have to clear your copy in advance."

"So leave the country. Go home and buy a typewriter. Write it up in the newspapers and tell the world."

"I wonder if anyone would believe me."

"There is that. I can hardly believe it myself and I was there. I saw it. Every night I go to bed in the hope that I'll wake up and find that I imagined the whole thing."

"Perhaps if you told another American besides myself. That would make the story more believable."

"No. That's your problem, not mine."

"Look," said Dickson, "the man you should really meet is Guido Enderis. He's the chief of the *New York Times* Berlin office. I think you should tell him what you just told me."

"I think I've talked enough for one evening. Odd, but it makes me feel guilty in a whole new way. Before I only felt like a murderer. Now I feel like a traitor, too."

"Please."

"You know there's a limit to how guilty I can feel before I want to throw up or jump in front of a train."

"Don't do that, Captain—whatever your name is. The whole world needs to know what's happening on the eastern front. The only way that's going to happen is if people like you are willing to talk about it."

"And then what? Do you think it's going to make a difference? If America's not prepared to come into the war for the sake of the British, I can't believe they're going to do it for the sake of Russia's Jews."

"Maybe, maybe not. But you know, sometimes one thing leads to another."

"Yeah? Look what happened back at Munich in 1938. One thing led to absolutely nothing at all. And your lot weren't even at the negotiating table. They were back home, pretending it was nothing to do with the U.S.A."

Dickson couldn't argue with that.

"How can I get in contact with you, Captain?"

"You can't. I'll speak to Willy and leave a message with him if I decide I'm ready to puke another fur ball."

"If it's a question of money—"

"It's not."

Instinctively we both glanced up as another 109 came rifling in from the northwest, and I saw the moon illuminate the anxiety on Dickson's smooth face. When the sound was just a footnote on the horizon I heard him let out a breath.

"I can't get used to that," he confessed. "The way these fighters fly so low. I keep expecting to see something blow up on the ground in front of me."

"Sometimes I wish it would. But take my word for it: a fighter tends to buzz a little louder when it decides to sting."

"Talking of things blowing up," he said, "the Three Kings. You hear anything? Only, the doctors of deceit have been giving us the runaround. Back in May they said they had picked up two of the leaders and that it was only a matter of time before they got their hands on the third. Since then we've heard nothing. We keep asking, but no one says anything, so we figure that number three must still be at liberty. Any truth in that, you think?"

"I really can't say."

"Can't or just won't?" A cloud drifted across the moon like something dark over my soul.

"C'mon, Captain. You must know something."

"I'm just back from Belorussia so I'm a little behind with what's been happening here in Berlin. But if they'd caught Melchior, I think you'd have heard all about that, don't you? Through a megaphone."

"Melchior?"

"And I thought it was just the Germans who were a godless race."

I walked away.

"Hey," said Dickson. "I saw that movie *Frankenstein*. And I remember that scene now. Doesn't the monster throw the little girl in the water?"

"Yes. Sad, isn't it?"

I STROLLED SOUTH, down to Bülowstrasse, where I turned west. I might have walked all the way home but I noticed there was a hole in my shoe, and at Nolli I decided to get on the S-Bahn. Normally I would have taken the tram, but the 33 was no longer running; and since it was after nine o'clock, the only taxis around were those that were called by the police for the service of the sick, the lame, the old, or travelers from railway stations with heavy bags. And senior Nazi Party members, of course. They never had a problem getting a cab home after nine.

Nolli was almost deserted, which was not uncommon in the blackout. All you could see were occasional cigarette ends moving through the darkness like fireflies, or sometimes the phosphorescent lapel badge of someone keen to avoid a collision with another pedestrian; all you could hear were the trains as they moved invisibly in and out of the art nouveau glass dome of the station overhead, or disembodied voices, snatches of passing conversations, as if Berlin were one big open-air séance—a ghostly effect enhanced by infrequent flashes of electric light from the rail track. It was as if some modern-day Moses—and who could have blamed him?—had stretched out his strong hand toward the sky to spread a palpable darkness over the land of Germany. Surely it was time to let the Israelites leave, or at least to release them from their bondage.

I was almost on the stairs when, from under the arches, I heard the sound of a struggle. I stopped for a moment, looked around, and as a cloud shifted lazily off the moon I got a *son et lumière* view of a man attacking a woman. She was lying on the ground, trying to fight him off as, with one hand over her mouth, he fumbled under her skirt. I heard a curse, a muffled scream, and then my own footsteps as they clattered down the stairs.

"Hey, leave her alone," I yelled.

The man appeared to punch the woman, and as he stood up to face me I heard a click and caught a glimpse of the blade that was now in his hand. If I'd been on duty I might have been carrying a firearm, but I wasn't, and as the man came toward me, I shrugged the bread bag containing the food cans off my shoulder and swung it hard like a medieval ball and chain. The bag hit him on his extended arm, knocking the blade out of his hand, and he turned and fled, with me in halfhearted pursuit. The moonlight dimmed momentarily and I lost sight of him altogether. A few moments later I heard a squeal of tires from the corner of Motzstrasse and, arriving in front of the American Church, I found a taxi with its door open and the driver staring at his front fender.

"He just ran out in front of me," said the driver.

"You hit him?"

"I didn't have a chance."

"Well, he's not here now."

"He ran off, I think."

"Where did he go?"

"Toward the cinema theater."

"Stay where you are; I'm a police officer," I told the driver and crossed the street, but I might as well have looked inside a magician's top hat. There was no sign of him. So I went back to the taxi.

"Find him?"

"No. How hard did you hit him?"

"I wasn't going fast, if that's what you mean. Ten or fifteen kilometers an hour, like you're supposed to do, see? But still, I think I gave him a good old clunk. He went right over the hood and landed on his head, like he was off some nag at the Hoppegarten."

"Pull into the side of the road and stay there," I told the driver.

"Here," he said. "How do I know you're a cop? Where's your warrant disk?"

"It's in my office at Alex. We can go straight there if you like and you can spend the next hour or two making out a report. Or you can do what I say. The fellow you knocked down attacked a woman back there. That's why he was running away. Because I chased him. I was thinking you might take the lady home."

"Yeah, all right."

I went back to the station on Nollendorfplatz.

The girl who'd been attacked was sitting up and rubbing her chin between adjusting her clothes and looking for her handbag.

"Are you all right?"

"I think so. My bag. He threw it on the ground somewhere."

I glanced around. "He got away. But if it's any consolation, a taxi knocked him down."

I kept on looking for her bag but didn't find it. Instead I found the switchblade.

"Here it is," she said. "I've found it."

"Are you all right?"

"I feel a bit sick," she said, holding her jaw uncomfortably.

I wasn't feeling very comfortable myself. I didn't have my beer-token and had a bag full of canned food that, within the limited purview of a uniformed bull, would have marked me out as a black marketer, for which the penalties were very severe. It was not uncommon for *Schmarotzers* to receive death sentences, especially if these also happened to be people who needed to be made an example of, such as policemen. So I was anxious to be away from there; no more did I want to accompany her to the local police station and report the matter. Not while I was still carrying the bread bag.

"Look, I kept the taxi waiting. Where do you live? I'll take you home."

"Just off the Kurfürstendamm. Next to the Theater Center."

"Good. That's near me."

I helped her along to the taxi, which was where I'd left it, on the corner of Motzstrasse, and told the driver where to go. Then we drove west along Kleiststrasse with the driver telling me in exhaustive detail just what had happened and how it wasn't his fault and that he couldn't believe the fellow he'd collided with hadn't been more seriously injured.

"How do you know he wasn't?"

"He ran off, didn't he? Can't run with a broken leg. Believe me, I know. I was in the last war and I tried."

When we got to Kurfürstendamm, I helped the girl out of the car, and she was promptly sick in the gutter.

"Must be my lucky night," said the taxi driver.

"You've got a funny idea of luck, friend."

"That's the only kind that's going these days." The driver leaned out of the window and slammed the door shut behind us. "What I mean is, she could have been sick in the cab. And that Fritz I hit. I could have killed him, see?"

"How much?" I asked.

"That all depends on whether you're going to report this."

"I don't know what the lady will want to do," I said. "But if I were you I'd get going before she makes up her mind."

"See?" The driver put the taxi cab in gear. "I was right. It is my lucky night."

Inside the building I helped the girl upstairs, which is when I got a better look at her.

She was wearing a navy-blue linen suit with a lace-cotton blouse underneath. The blouse was torn and a stocking was hanging down over one of her shoes. These were plum colored like her handbag and the mark under one of her eyes from when she'd been punched. There was a strong smell of perfume on her clothes and I recognized Guerlain Shalimar. By the time we reached her door I had concluded she was about thirty years old. She had shoulder-length blond hair, a wide forehead, a broad nose, high cheekbones, and a sulky mouth. Then again, she had a lot to feel sulky about. She was about 175 centimeters tall, and, against my arm felt strong and muscular: strong enough to put up a fight when she was attacked but not strong enough to walk away without help. I was glad about that. She was good-looking in a catlike way with narrow eyes and a tail that seemed to have a whole life of its own and made me want to have her on my lap for a while so that I could stroke it.

She found a door key and fumbled for the lock until I caught her hand and steered the key into the ABUS and turned it for her.

"Thanks," she said. "I'll be all right from here, I think."

And but for the fact that she started to sit down on the floor

I might have left her there. Instead I gathered her up in my arms and swung her through the door like an exhausted bride.

Advancing into the barely furnished hall, I encountered the house guard dog: a barely dressed woman of about fifty with short, bottle-blond hair and more makeup than seemed strictly necessary outside of a circus tent. Almost at once and with a voice like Baron Ochs, she started to reproach the half-conscious girl I was carrying for bringing disrespect upon her house, but from the going-over the landlady's eyebrows were giving me, I judged that much of that seemed directed my way. I didn't mind that. For a while it made me feel quite nostalgic for my Army days when some ugly sergeant would chew my ear off for nothing but the hell of it.

"What kind of house do you think I'm running here, Fräulein Tauber? You should be ashamed to even think of coming back here in such a state as this, with a strange man. I'm a respectable woman. I've told you about this before, Fräulein Tauber. I have my rules. I have my standards. This is not to be tolerated."

All of this told me two things. One was that the woman in my arms was Fräulein Tauber. And the other was that I was hardly through protecting her from attack.

"Someone tried to rape her," I said. "So you can either help or you can go and put on some more makeup. The end of your nose looks like it could use some red paint."

"Well, really," the landlady gasped. "There's no need to be rude. Raped, you say. Yes, of course I'll help. Her room is along here."

She led the way down the hall, found a key from the bunch in the pocket of her sagging dressing gown, opened a door, and, switching on the ceiling light, illuminated a neat, well-furnished room that was cozier than a cashmere-lined leather glove, and about the same size.

I laid Fräulein Tauber down on a sofa of the kind that was comfortable only if you were wearing a whalebone corset, and kneeling at her feet, I started to slap some life into her hands and face.

"When she started working at the Golden Horseshoe I told her something like this might happen," said the old woman.

This was one of the few remaining nightclubs in Berlin and probably the least offensive, so the chain of causation that was being suggested was hardly obvious to me; but, containing any argument because I'd already been too rough on the woman, I asked her, politely, if she could fetch a cold compress and a cup of strong tea or coffee. The tea or coffee was a long shot, but in an emergency there's no telling what Berlin women can come up with.

Fräulein Tauber started to come around again, and I helped her to sit up. Seeing me, she smiled a half smile.

"Are you still here?"

The smile must have been painful because she flexed her jaw and then winced.

"Just take it easy. That was quite a left hook he handed you. I'll say one thing for you, Fräulein Tauber, you can take a punch."

"Yeah? Maybe you should manage my fights. I could use a big purse. How'd you know my name, anyway, Parsifal?"

"Your landlady. She's fetching a cold compress and a hot drink for that eye of yours. It's just possible that we can stop it from going blue."

Fräulein Tauber glanced over at the door and shook her head. "If she's fetching me a hot drink, you must have told her I was dying."

The landlady returned with the cold compress and handed it to me. I laid it carefully on Fräulein Tauber's eye, took her hand, and laid it on top.

"Keep some pressure on it," I told her.

"There's tea on the way," said the landlady. "I had just enough left for a small pot." She shrugged and gathered her dressing gown closer to a chest that was bigger than the cushions on the sofa.

I stood up, stretched a smile onto my face, and offered the landlady one of my American cigarettes.

"Smoke?"

The old woman's eyes lit up as if she were looking at the Koh-i-Noor diamond.

"Please." She took one tentatively, almost as if she thought that I might snatch it away again.

"It's a fair exchange for a cup of tea," I said, lighting her cigarette. I didn't smoke one myself. I hardly wanted either of them thinking I was Gustav Krupp.

The old woman took an ecstatic puff of her cigarette, smiled, and went back into the kitchen.

"And here I was, thinking you were just Parsifal. Looks like you've got the touch. Healing lepers is easier than raising a smile on her face."

"But I get the feeling she disapproves of you, Fräulein Tauber."

"You make that sound almost benign. Like my old school mistress." Fräulein Tauber laughed bitterly. "Frau Lippert—that's her name—she hates me. If I were Jewish she couldn't hate me more."

"And what's your name? I can't keep calling you Fräulein Tauber."

"Why not? Everyone else does."

"The man who attacked you. Did you get a good look at him?"

"He was about your height. Dark clothes, dark eyes, dark hair, dark complexion. In fact everything about him was dark, on account of the fact that it was dark, see? If I drew you a picture he'd look exactly like your shadow."

"Is that all you can remember about him?"

"Come to think of it, he had nice, fruity breath. Like he'd been eating Haribos."

"It's not much to go on."

"That all depends on where you were thinking of going."

"The man was trying to rape you."

"Was he? I guess he was."

I shrugged. "Maybe you should report it. I don't know."

"To the police?"

"I certainly didn't mean the newspapers."

"Women in this city get attacked all the time, Parsifal. Why do you think the police would be interested in one more?"

"He had a knife, that's why. He might have used it on you."

"Listen, mister, thanks for helping me. Don't think I'm not grateful, because I am. But I don't much like the police."

I shrugged. "They're just people."

"Where did you get that idea? All right, Parsifal, I'll spell it out for you. I work at the Golden Horseshoe. And sometimes the New World, when they're not closed for lack of beer. I make an honest living but that won't stop the cops from thinking otherwise. I can hear their patter now. Like it was a movie. You left the Horseshoe with a man, didn't you? He'd paid you to have sex with him. Only you took his money and tried to dodge him in the dark. Isn't that what really happened, Fräulein Tauber? Get out of here. You're lucky we don't throw you in Ravensbrück for being on the sledge."

I had to admit she had a point. Berlin cops had stopped being people when they married into the Reich Main Security Office—the RSHA—and joined a Gothic-looking family that included the Gestapo, the SS, and the SD.

"Anyway," she added, "you don't want the police buzzing in your ears any more than me. Not with your American cigarettes and all those cans in that bag of yours. No, I should think they might ask you some very awkward questions, which you don't look able to answer."

"I guess you do have a point, there, at that."

"Especially not wearing a suit like that."

Her visible eye was giving me the up-and-down.

"What's wrong with it?"

"Nothing. It's a nice suit. And that's the point. It doesn't look like you've been wearing it very much lately. Which is unusual in Berlin for a man with your accent. Which makes me think you must have been wearing something else. Most likely a uniform. That would explain the cigarettes and your quaint opinions about the police. And the tin cans, for all I know. I'll bet you you're in the Army. And you've been in Paris, if that tie is what I think it is: silk. It matches your prewar manners, Parsifal. Manners are something else you can't get in Berlin anymore. But every German officer gets to behave like a real gentleman when he's stationed in Paris. That's what I've heard, anyway. So, you're not a professional blackie. Just an amateur blackie, making a little money on the side while you're home on leave. This is the only reason you're naïvely talking about the police and reporting what happened to me this evening."

"You should have been a cop yourself." I grinned.

"No. Not me. I like to sleep at night. But the way things are going, before very long we're all going to be cops, whether we like it or not, spying on each other, informing." She nodded meaningfully at the door. "If you know what I mean."

I didn't say anything as Frau Lippert came back carrying a tray with two cups of tea.

"That's what I mean," added Fräulein Tauber in case I was too dumb to understand her the first time.

"Drink your tea," I said. "It'll help keep that eye down."

"I don't see how."

"This is good tea," I told Frau Lippert.

"Thank you, Herr——?"

"That is, I don't see how it can help a blue eye."

I nodded, appreciating the interruption: it was Fräulein Tauber's turn to help me. It wasn't a good idea to tell Frau Lippert my name. I could see that now. The old woman wasn't just the house guard dog; she was also the building's Gestapo bloodhound.

"Caffeine," I said. "It causes the blood vessels to constrict. You want to reduce the amount of blood that can reach your eye. The more blood that seeps out of the damaged capillaries on that lovely face of yours, the bluer your eye will get. Here. Let me have a look."

I took away the cold compress for a moment and then nodded.

"It's not so blue," I said.

"Not when I look at you, it's not."

"Mm-hmm."

"You know, you sound just like a doctor, Parsifal."

"You can tell that from mm-hmm?"

"Sure. Doctors say it all the time. To me, anyway."

Frau Lippert had been out of this conversation since it started and must have felt that it lacked her own imprimatur. "She's right," said the old woman. "They do."

I kept on looking at the girl with the cold compress in her hand. "You're mistaken, Fräulein. It's not mm-hmm your doctor is saying. It's shorter, simpler, more direct than that. It's just 'mmm.'"

I drained my teacup and placed it back on the tray. "Mmm, thank you."

"I'm glad you liked it," said Frau Lippert.

"Very much."

I grinned at her and picked my bag of canned food off the floor. It was nice to see her smile back.

"Well, I'd better be going. I'll look in again sometime just to see you're all right."

"There's no need, Parsifal. I'm all right now."

"I like to know how all my patients are doing, Fräulein. Especially the ones wearing Guerlain Shalimar."

4

The Pathological Institute was at the Charité Hospital just across the canal from Lehrter Station. With its red-brick exterior, its Alpine-style wooden loggias, its clock and distinctive corner tower, the oldest teaching hospital in the city was much the same as it had always been. Inside, however, things were different. Within the main administrative building, the portraits of more than a few of the Charité's famous physicians and scientists had been removed. The Jews were Germany's misfortune, after all. These were the only spaces available in the hospital, and if they could have put some beds on the walls, they would have done it. The wards and corridors—even the landings outside the elevators—were full of men who had been maimed or injured on the front.

Meanwhile, the morgue in the institute was full to overflowing with dead soldiers and the still-unidentified civilian victims of RAF bombings and blackout accidents. Not that their problems were over. The Army Information Center wasn't always very efficient in notifying the families of those servicemen who had died; in many cases the Army felt that the responsibility fell on the Ministry of Health. But however the deaths were caused, the Ministry of Health believed responsibility for dealing with deaths in Berlin lay properly with the Ministry of the Interior, which, of course, was only too willing to leave such matters to the city authorities, who themselves were inclined to dump this role on the police. So you might say that the crisis at the morgue—and that's exactly what it smelled like—was all my fault. Me and others like me.

It was, however, with the hope of taking advantage of this bureaucratic incompetence that I went there in search of Geert Vranken's corpse. And I found what was left of it sharing a drawer in the cold room with a dead prostitute from Lichterfelde and a man from Wedding—most likely a suicide—who had been killed in a gas explosion. I had the mortuary attendant lay out the Dutchman's remains on a slab that looked and smelled worse than it ought to have done, but with an extreme shortage of cleaners in the hospital—not to mention carbolic soap—the dead assumed less and less of the hospital's dwindling resources.

"Pity," grumbled the attendant.

"What is?"

"That you're not from the State Labor Service, so I can get rid of him."

"I didn't know he was looking for a job."

"He was a foreign worker. So I'm waiting on the paperwork that will enable me to send his remains down to the incinerator."

"I'm from the Alex, like I said. I'm sure there are jobs there that could be done by dead men. My job, for example."

For a moment the morgue attendant smiled but then thought better of it.

"I'll only be a minute," I said, and took out the switchblade I had found on the ground under Nolli Station.

At the sight of the long blade in my hand, the attendant backed off nervously. "Here, what's your game?"

"It's all right. I'm trying to establish if this knife matches the victim's stab wounds."

Relaxing a little, he nodded at Vranken's remains. "Least of his problems, I should have thought: being stabbed."

"You'd think so, wouldn't you? But before a train ran him over—"

"That would explain a lot."

". . . someone stabbed him. Several times."

"Evidently not his lucky day."

I slid the blade into one of the more obvious wounds in the dead man's pale torso. "Before the war you used to get a proper lab report with photographs and descriptions so that you didn't have to do this kind of thing."

"Before the war you used to get beer that tasted like beer." Remembering who and more particularly what I was, he added quickly, "Not that there's anything wrong with the beer now, of course."

I didn't say anything. I was glad he'd spoken out of turn. It meant I could probably avoid filling out the morgue's paperwork— Commissioner Lüdtke had told me to drop the case, after all—as a quid pro quo for ignoring the attendant's "unpatriotic" remark about German beer. Besides I was paying nearly all of my attention to the knife in the stab wound. I couldn't say for sure that it was the murder weapon, but it could have been. It was long enough and sharp enough, with just one edge and a blunter upper side that matched the wound almost perfectly.

I pulled the blade out and looked for something to wipe it with. Being a fussy type, I'm particular about the switchblades I keep in my coat pocket. And I figured I'd already encountered enough germs and bacteria just walking through the hospital without squirreling away a private cache of my own.

"Got anything to wipe this with?"

"Here," he said, and, taking it from me, he wiped it with the corner of his lab coat.

"Thanks," I said.

I could see that he was anxious to get rid of me, and when

I suggested that there was probably no need to bother with the paperwork, he agreed with alacrity.

"I don't think he'll tell, do you?" said the attendant. "Besides, I don't have a pen that works."

I went outside. It was a nice day so I decided to walk back to the Alex and eat lunch at a counter I knew on Karl Strasse, but that one was closed because of a lack of sausage. So was the one on Oranienburger Strasse. Finally I got a sandwich and a paper at a place near the Stock Exchange, only there was even less of interest in the sandwich than there was in the paper, and probably in the Stock Exchange, too. But it's foolish to give up eating bread because you can't get the sausage to put in it. At least I was free to still think of the bread as a sandwich.

Then again, I'm a typical Berliner, so maybe I'm just hard to please.

WHEN I GOT BACK to the Alex I had the files on all of the summer's S-Bahn murders sent up to my office. I suppose I wanted to make doubly sure that Paul Ogorzow was the real killer and not someone who'd been made to measure for it. It wouldn't have been the first time that a Kripo run by the Nazis had done something like that. The only surprise was that they hadn't already tried to pin the murders of Wallenstein, Baldur, Siegfried, and Cock Robin on some hapless Jew.

It turned out that I wasn't the first to review the Ogorzow files. The record memo showed that the Abwehr—military intelligence—had also looked at the files, and recently. I wondered why. At least I did until I remembered all the foreign workers who had been interviewed during the course of the investigation. But Paul Ogorzow had been a German railway-worker; rape and a violent hatred of women had been his motives; he hadn't stabbed any of his victims, he had battered them to death. There was no telling if Fräulein Tauber's attacker would have battered her or stabbed her after he'd finished raping her, but from the blow he'd given her face, I could tell there was no doubting his dislike of women. Of course, lust murders were hardly uncommon in Berlin. Before Paul Ogorzow, there had been other violent, sometimes cannibalistic killers; doubtless there would be others after him.

Much to my surprise, I was impressed at the thoroughness and scale of Commissioner Lüdtke's investigation. Thousands of interviews had been conducted and almost one hundred suspects brought in for interrogation; at one stage male police officers had even dressed up as women and traveled the S-Bahn at night in the hope of luring the murderer into an attack. A reward of ten thousand Reichsmarks had been posted and, finally, one of Paul Ogorzow's workmates—another railway employee—had fingered him as the murderer instead of one of the many foreign workers. But among those foreign workers who had been interviewed was Geert Vranken. I shouldn't have been surprised to discover his name on the list of those who had been interviewed, yet I was. I read the transcript with interest.

A science graduate from The Hague University, Vranken had been quickly eliminated from Lüdtke's inquiry when his alibi checked out; but, hardly wanting to rely on this alone—after all, his alibi relied on other foreign workers—he had been at pains to adduce evidence of his good character, and to this end he had offered the name of a German whom he'd met before the war, in The Hague. Lüdtke's team of detectives, several of whom I knew, hardly needed to take up this reference because, a week or so after Vranken's interview, Paul Ogorzow was arrested. The certainty—on my part—that for once the right man had been sent to the guillotine at Plotzensee, in July 1941, gradually gave way to a feeling of pity for Geert Vranken and, more particularly, the wife and baby he had left behind in the Netherlands. How many other families, I wondered, would be similarly destroyed before the war was over?

Of course, this was hardly normal for me. I'd seen plenty of murder victims in my time at the Alex, many of them in circumstances even more tragic than these. After Belorussia I suppose my conscience was easily pricked. Whatever the reasons, I determined to find out if, as Commissioner Lüdtke had said it would, the State Labor Service had yet informed Vranken's family that he had met with a fatal accident. Thus it was that I spent a fruitless hour on the telephone being rerouted from one bureaucrat to another before I finally gave up and wrote a letter myself, this to an address in The Hague that was in Vranken's work book and that, prior to its issue by the State Labor Service, was where he had been previously employed. In my letter I made no mention of the fact that Geert Vranken had been murdered, only that he had been hit by a train and killed. His being stabbed six times was more than any family needed to be told.

5

I had an office in the Police Praesidium, on the third floor—a small room on the corner underneath the tower and overlooking the U-Bahn station on Alexanderplatz. The view out of the window on a late-summer evening was the best thing about it. At that kind of altitude, life didn't look quite so dismal. I couldn't smell the people or see their pale, undernourished, and sometimes just plain hopeless faces. All the streets came together in one big square just the same as they had before the war, with trams clanging and taxis honking their horns and the city growling in the distance the way it always did. Sitting on the windowsill with my face in the sun, I found it easy to pretend there was no war, no front, no Hitler, and that none of it had anything to do with me. Outside there wasn't a swastika in sight, just the many varieties of specimens in my own favorite game of girl spotting. It was a sport I was always passionate about and at which I excelled. I liked the way it helped me tune in to the natural world, and because girls in Berlin are visible in a way that other Berlin wildlife is not, I never seemed to grow tired of it. There are so many different girls out there. Mostly I was on the lookout for the rarer varieties: exotic blondes that hadn't been seen since 1938 and fabulous redheads wearing summer plumage that was very nearly transparent. I'd thought about putting a feeder on my windowsill but knew it was hopeless. The climb up to the third floor was simply too much for them.

The only creatures that ever made it up to my office were the rats. Somehow they never ran out of energy, and when I turned back to face the room, with its awful portrait of the Leader and the SD uniform that was hanging in an open closet, like a terrible reminder of the other man I'd been for much of the summer, two of them were coming through the glass door. Neither of them said anything until they were seated with their hats in their hands and had stared at me for several seconds with preternatural calm, as if I were some lesser being, which of course I was, because these rats were from the Gestapo.

One of the men wore a double-breasted navy chalk stripe, and the other, a dark gray three-piece suit with a watch chain that glittered like his eyes. The one wearing the chalk stripe had a full head of short, fair hair that was as carefully arranged as the lines on a sheet of writing paper; the other was even fairer but losing it on the front, almost as if his forehead had been plucked like one of those medieval ladies in a rather dull oil painting. On their faces were smiles that were insolent or self-satisfied or cynical but mostly all three at the same time, and they regarded me and my office and probably my very existence with some amusement. But that was okay, because I felt much the same way myself.

"You're Bernhard Gunther?"

I nodded.

The man with the chalk stripe suit checked his neatly combed hair fastidiously, as if he had just stepped out of the barber's chair at the KaDeWe. A decent haircut was about the only thing in Berlin that was not in short supply.

"With a reputation like yours, I was expecting a pair of Persian slippers and a calabash." He smiled. "Like Sherlock Holmes."

I sat down behind my desk facing the pair and smiled back. "These days I find that a three-pipe problem's just the same as a one-pipe problem. I can't find the tobacco to smoke in it. So I keep the calabash hidden in the drawer alongside my gold-plated syringe and some orange pips."

They kept on looking, saying nothing, just sizing me up.

"You fellows should have brought along a blackjack if you were expecting me to talk first."

"Is that what you think of us?"

"I'm not the only one with a colorful reputation."

"True."

"Are you here to ask questions or for a favor?"

"We don't need to ask favors," said the one with the basilica skull designed by Brunelleschi. "Usually we get all the cooperation we require without having to ask anyone a favor." He glanced at his colleague and did some more smiling. "Isn't that right?"

"Yes, that's right." The one with the neat hair was like a thicker-set version of von Ribbentrop. He had no eyebrows to speak of and big shoulders: I didn't think he was a man you wanted to see taking off his coat and rolling up his sleeves in search of answers. "Most people are only too willing to help us, and it's rare we are ever obliged to ask for something as quaint as a favor."

"Is that so?" I put a match in my mouth and started to chew it slowly. I figured that as long as I didn't try inhaling it, my lungs would stay healthy. "All right. I'm listening." I leaned forward and clasped my hands with an earnest reverence that bordered on the sarcastic. "And if it persuades you to come quickly to the point, then this is me looking all ready and willing to help the Gestapo in any way that I can. Only do stop trying to make me feel very small or I'll start to question the wisdom of letting you sit in my office with your hats in your hands."

Chalk Stripe pinched the crown of his hat and inspected the lining. For all I knew, it had his name and rank written there, just in case he forgot them.

"You know my name. So why don't you introduce yourselves?"

"I'm Commissar Sachse. And this is Inspector Wandel."

I nodded politely. "Delighted, I'm sure."

"How much do you know about the Three Kings? And please don't mention the Bible or I shall conclude that I'm not going to like you."

"You're talking about the three men who came to Berlin from Czechoslovakia in early 1938, aren't you? I'm sorry, Bohemia and Moravia, although I'm never quite sure of the difference and, anyway, who cares? The Three Kings are three Czech nationalists and officers of the defeated Czech Army who, having conducted a series of terrorist attacks in Prague—it is still called Prague, isn't it? Good. Well, then, having orchestrated a campaign of sabotage there, they decided to bring their war here, to the streets of Berlin. And as far as I know, for a while they were quite successful. They planted a bomb at the Aviation Ministry in September 1939. Not to mention one in the doorway here at the Alex. Yes, that was embarrassing for us all, wasn't it? No wonder the Press and radio didn't mention it. Then there was the attempt on Himmler's life at the

Anhalter Station in February of this year. I expect that was even more embarrassing, for the Gestapo, anyway. I believe the bomb was placed in the left-luggage office, which is an obvious place and one that should certainly have been searched in advance of the Reichsführer-SS's arrival in the station. I bet someone had a lot of explaining to do after that."

Their smiles were fading a little now and their chairs were starting to look uncomfortable; as the two Gestapo men shifted their backsides around, the wagon-wheel backs creaked like a haunted house. Chalk Stripe checked his hair again, almost as if he'd left the source of his ability to intimidate me on the barbershop floor. The other man, Wandel, bit his lip, trying to keep the death's-head moth of a smile pinned to his delinquent mug. I might have stopped my little history there and then out of fear of what their organization was capable of, but I was enjoying myself too much.

I hadn't considered the concept of suicide by Gestapo until now, but I could see its advantages. At least I might enjoy the process a little more than just blowing my own brains out. All the same, I wasn't about to throw my life away on some small-timers like these two; if ever I did decide to blow a raspberry in some senior Nazi's face, I was going to make it count. Besides, it was now plain to me that they really were after a favor.

"You know the word here in Kripo is that the Three Kings get a kick out of embarrassing the Gestapo. There's one particular story making the rounds that one of them even stole Oskar Fleischer's overcoat."

Fleischer was head of the Gestapo's Counterintelligence Section in Prague.

"And that the same brazen fellow won a bet that he could cadge a light for his cigarette off Fleischer's cigar."

"There's always a lot of gossip in a place like this," said Sachse.

"Oh sure. But that's how cops work, Herr Commissar. A nudge here. A wink there. A whisper in a bar. A fellow tells you that someone else says that his pal heard this or that. Personally, I've always put a vague rumor ahead of anything as imaginative as three pipes' worth of deductive reasoning. It's elementary, my dear Sachse. Oh yes, and didn't these Three Kings send the Gestapo a complimentary copy of their own underground newspaper? That's the gossip."

"Since you appear to be so well informed—"

I shook my head. "It's common knowledge, here on the third floor."

". . . then I daresay you will also know that two of the Three Kings—Josef Balabán and Josef Mašín—have already been arrested. As have many other of their collaborators. In Prague. And here in Berlin. It's only a matter of time before we catch Melchior."

"I don't get it," I said. "You caught Josef A in April; and Josef B in May. Or maybe it was the other way around. But here we are in September, and you still haven't managed to shake the third king out of their sleeves. You boys must be going soft."

Of course I knew this couldn't be true. The Gestapo had moved heaven and earth in search of the third man, but mostly they'd employed a more infernal sort of help. Because there was another rumor around the Alex: that the Prague Gestapo had enlisted the services of their most notorious torturer in Bohemia, a sadist called Paul Soppa, who was the commander of Pankrác Prison in Prague, to work on the two Czechs in his custody. I didn't give much for their chances but, in the light of the continued liberty of Melchior, the certainty that neither man had talked was proof positive of their enormous courage and bravery.

"There are different ways of approaching every problem," said Wandel. "And right now we should like you to help us with this problem. Colonel Schellenberg speaks very highly of you."

Walter Schellenberg was close to General Heydrich, who was chief of the whole RSHA, of which Kripo was now one part.

"I know who Schellenberg is," I said. "At least, I remember meeting him. But I don't know what he is. Not these days."

"He's the acting chief of foreign intelligence within the RSHA," said Sachse.

"Is this problem a foreign intelligence matter?"

"It might be. But right now it's a homicide. Which is where you come in."

"Well, anything to help Colonel Schellenberg, of course," I said.

"You know the Heinrich von Kleist Park?"

"Of course. It used to be Berlin's botanical garden before the Botanical Gardens were built in Steglitz."

"A body was found there this morning."

"Oh? I wonder why I haven't heard about it."

"You're hearing about it now. We'd like you to come and take a look at it, Gunther."

I shrugged. "Have you got any petrol?"

Sachse frowned.

"For your car," I added. "I wasn't proposing that we burn the body."

"Yes, of course we have petrol."

"Then I'd love to go to the park with you, Commissar Sachse."

KLEIST PARK IN SCHÖNEBERG had something to do with a famous German Romantic writer. He might have been called Kleist. There were lots of trees, a statue of the goddess Diana, and on the western border of the park, the Court of Appeal. Not that Hitler's Germany had much use for a Court of Appeal. Those who were convicted and condemned in a Nazi court of first instance usually stayed that way.

On the southern border was a building I had half an idea might once have been the Prussian Academy of Arts, but given that the

Gestapo was now headquartered in the old School for Industrial Arts and Crafts on Prinz-Albrecht-Strasse, there seemed to be little or no chance that anyone was being taught how to paint someone's portrait in the Prussian Academy of Arts; not when they could more usefully be taught how to torture people. It was a fact that the Gestapo had always taken its share of the city's best public buildings. That was to be expected. But lately they'd started confiscating the premises of shops and businesses that had been abandoned as a result of the shortages. A friend of mine had gone into the Singer sewing machine salesroom on Wittenbergplatz looking for a new treadle belt only to discover that the place was now being used as an arsenal by the SS. Meyer's Wine Shop, on Olivaer Platz, where once I'd been a regular customer, was now an SS "information bureau." Whatever that was.

In the center of the park was a curving promenade where people could walk or perhaps sit, but only on the grass, since all of the city's many wooden park benches had been taken away for the war effort; sometimes I imagined a fat Wehrmacht general conducting the siege of Leningrad while warming his hands over a brazier that was fueled with one of these. On the eastern edge of this promenade, and bordering Potsdamer Strasse, was an area of shrubs and trees that had been closed off to the public by several uniformed policemen. The dead body of a man lay under a huge rhododendron that was in late flower, but only just, since he was covered with red petals that looked like multiple stab wounds. He was wearing a dark blouson-type jacket, a lighter brown pair of flannel trousers, and a pair of severely down-at-heel brown boots. I couldn't see his face, as one of my new Gestapo friends was blocking the sun, as was their habit, so I asked him to move, and as he stepped out of the way, I squatted down on my haunches to take a closer look.

It was a typical mortuary photograph: the mouth open, as if awaiting the attentions of a dentist—although the teeth were in remarkably good condition and certainly better than mine—the wide eyes staring straight ahead so that, all things considered, he looked more surprised to see me than I was to see him. He was about twenty-five, with a small mustache, and on the front of his left forehead, below the line of his dark hair, a contusion that was the shape and color of an outsized amethyst and that more than likely was the cause of death.

"Who found the body?" I asked Sachse. "And when?"

"A uniformed cop on patrol. From the Potsdamer Platz Station. About six o'clock this morning."

"And how is it that you picked up the order?"

"The duty detective from Kripo telephoned it in. Fellow named Lehnhoff."

"That was clever of him. Lehnhoff's not usually so quick on his toes. And what did this Fritz have in his pocket that marked him out as your meat? A Czech passport?"

"No. This."

Sachse dipped into his pocket and then handed me a gun. It was a little Model 9 Walther, a palm-sized .25 caliber automatic. Smaller than the Baby Browning I had at home for when I wasn't expecting visitors, but quite accurate.

"A bit more lethal than a set of door keys, wouldn't you say so?" said Sachse.

"That will open a door for you," I agreed.

"Be careful. It's still loaded."

I nodded and handed the gun back to him.

"This makes it a Gestapo matter."

"Automatically," I said. "I can see that. But I still don't see how this connects him with the Three Kings."

"One of our officers from the Documentation Section looked over his papers and found some discrepancies."

Wandel handed me a yellow card with the dead man's photograph in the top left-hand corner. It was his employment certificate. He said, "Notice anything wrong with it?"

I shrugged. "The staples in the picture are a bit rusty. Otherwise it looks all right to me. Name of Victor Keil. Doesn't ring any bells."

"The impression of the rubber stamp on the corner of the photograph can hardly be seen," said Wandel. "No German official would have permitted that." Then he handed me the dead man's identity card. "And this? What do you make of this, Herr Commissar?"

I rubbed the document in my fingers, which drew a nod of approval from Sachse.

"You're right to check it that way first," he said. "The forgeries just don't feel right. Like they're made of linen. But that's not what gives this one away as a fake."

I opened it up and took a closer look at the contents. The photograph on the ID card had two corner stamps, one on the top right-hand corner and the other on the top left, and both of these looked clear enough. The two fingerprints were similarly clear, as was the police precinct stamp. I shook my head. "Beats me what's wrong with it. It looks completely right."

"The quality is actually quite good," admitted Sachse. "Except for one thing. Whoever made that can't spell *forefinger.*

"My God, yes, you're right."

Sachse was starting to look satisfied with himself once more.

"All of which prompted us to investigate further," he said. "It seems that the real Victor Keil was killed during a bombing raid in Hamburg last year. And we now know, or at least we strongly suspect, that this man isn't a German at all, but a Czech terrorist by the name of Franz Koci. Our sources in Prague tell us that he was one of the last Czech agents operating here in Berlin. And he certainly fits the last description we had of him. Until October 1938 he was a lieutenant in a Czech regiment of artillery that was deployed to the Sudetenland. After the capitulation of the Beneš government at Munich, he disappeared, along with many others who subsequently worked for the Three Kings."

I shrugged. "It sounds like you know everything about him," I said. "I can't imagine why you need me to look at his fingernails."

"We don't know who killed him," said Wandel. "Or why. Or even how."

I nodded. "For the how, you'll need a doctor. Preferably a doctor of medicine." I smiled at my joke, thinking of the American, Dickson, and his aversion to the doctors of deceit at the Ministry of Propaganda. But it wasn't a joke for sharing, especially with the Gestapo. "As for the who and the why, maybe I could take a closer look." I pointed at the body. "Do you mind?"

"Be my guest," said Sachse.

I took out my handkerchief and then laid it neatly beside the body. "Somewhere to lay any evidence I find. You see, I intend going through the dead man's pockets."

"Help yourself. But all of the useful evidence has already been collected."

"Oh, I don't doubt that. If there's anything of value that the uniforms and Inspector Lehnhoff have left behind, I'll be pleasantly surprised."

Sachse frowned. "You don't mean—"

"Cops in this city are just as crooked as anyone else. Sometimes they're even as crooked as the crooks. These days, most of them join only so they can steal a man's watch without getting caught."

I lifted the dead man's left arm by way of illustration. There was a tan mark on his wrist, only the watch that might have made it wasn't there.

"Yes, I see what you mean," said Sachse.

"The body's a little stiff, which means that rigor is setting in or passing off. It takes about twelve hours to get established, lasts about twelve hours, and takes another twelve hours to pass." I tugged at the dead man's cheek. "It starts in the face, however, and this fellow's face is soft to the touch, which probably means the rigor is passing off. You understand that all of this is very crude, but I'd say your man has been dead for at least a day or so. Of course, I might be wrong, but I've seen plenty of dead men who would say I'm probably right about that."

I undid the buttons on the blouson and then pulled open the shirt to inspect the torso. "This man took a hard fall. Or received a substantial impact. There is substantial bruising on the left side of his body." I pressed hard directly on the bruise and on the lowest part of the rib cage. "Feels like one of the ribs has separated from the chest wall. In other words, it's broken."

I took out my pocketknife, unfolded it carefully, and starting at the cuff, began to cut up the length of the dead man's trouser leg, but only because I didn't want to start unbuttoning his fly buttons. Generally speaking, I prefer to know a man a little better before I will do that. On the left thigh there was another heavy bruise that matched the broken rib and the contusion on the head. I was trying not to appear nervous, but on top of the bad feeling I had most of the time, I now had a bad feeling about the dead man, too. The distance between Kleist Park and Nollendorfplatz was about a kilometer, and even a man who had collided with a taxi on the corner of Motzstrasse might have staggered to the park in less than thirty minutes. This wouldn't have been the only traffic accident in Berlin that night, but it was almost certainly the only one to have gone unreported.

"You want to know what I think?"

"Of course."

"This man has been involved in a road traffic accident. Of course that's hardly uncommon, what with the blackout and Berlin drivers."

I was quite certain I was looking at the man who had attacked

Fräulein Tauber and who had collided with the taxi. A hundred different thoughts started to run through my mind. Did the Gestapo know that already? Was that what this was all about? To see how I would react when presented with the dead body, like Hagen's treachery uncovered when he stands beside Siegfried's bier? No. How could they know? None of the other parties involved—Fräulein Tauber, Frau Lippert, the taxi driver—even knew I was a cop, let alone my name. But for a moment my hand started to shake. I folded the knife and returned it to my coat pocket.

"Anything wrong, Gunther?"

"No, I like working with the dead. On most nights when I'm not contemplating cutting my own throat you can catch me down at the local cemetery with my good friend, Count Orlok." Biting my lip, I steeled myself to go through the dead man's pockets.

"We've searched his pockets," said Sachse. "There's nothing important left in them."

From the dead man's pocket I took out a packet of Haribos and showed them to the two Gestapo officers.

"I don't know what that tells us," objected Wandel.

"It tells us that the man had a sweet tooth," I said, although it told me a lot more than that. Any doubts that this was the man who had attacked Fräulein Tauber were now removed. Hadn't she mentioned the smell of Haribos on his breath?

"Apart from the false documentation," said Sachse, "and the gun, of course, all we found was a money clip, a door key, and a pocket diary."

"May I see them?"

I stood up. The money clip was silver and in its fold were about fifty Reichsmarks in twenties and singles, but it was loose on the notes and made me think that it had held more money than was now present; and it was all too easy to suppose that the policemen who had stolen Franz Koci's watch had also relieved him of at least half of his cash. That would only be typical. The door key was on a steel chain that must have been attached to his belt: it was a key for an old mortise lock made by the Ferdinand Garbe Lock Company of Berlin. The diary was the most interesting item. It was a red leather Army pocket diary for 1941 that was handed out to German officers: there was a little wallet at the front and at the back there was a useful guide to recognizing German Army ranks and insignias. As a boy I'd had a diary with a similar guide for recognizing the footprints of animals—almost invaluable in a big city like Berlin. I turned to the current week and noted the only entry for the last forty-eight hours: "N.P. 9.15 p.m." It had been nine thirty when I had interrupted Franz Koci's attack on Fräulein Tauber, which was time enough for them to meet on Nolli at nine fifteen.

But why would a Czech terrorist intent on avoiding the attention of the police risk carrying out a sexual assault on someone at an S-Bahn station? Someone he had arranged to meet there. Unless the person he had arranged to meet hadn't turned up and, in frustration, he attacked the girl. But that made no sense, either.

I handed the diary back to Sachse. "These diaries are even more useful to spies than they are for our men, don't you think? They tell the enemy who's worth killing and who's not."

"I imagine he must have stolen it," said Wandel, redundantly. "Our intelligence suggests that some of these Czechos are damn good pickpockets."

I nodded. That sounded fair enough to me, considering that we had stolen their country.

I had a lot of thinking to do, and decided to do it at the Golden Horseshoe. That was probably against the rules. Anyone with a thought in his head wouldn't ever go to the Golden Horseshoe, so I figured a man with my checkered history was worth a discount.

It was a big round room with small round tables around a big round dance floor. The floor was mostly given over to a mechanical horse on which the club hostesses and female customers were invited to take a musical ride and, in the process, flash a stocking-top or something more intimate. If you'd had a lot of beer, it was possibly a lot of fun, but in the middle of Berlin's drought, a quiet game of cribbage had it beat.

One of the hostesses was perhaps the last black woman in Berlin. Her name was Ella. She sat at a table playing solitaire, using a pack of cards featuring photographic portraits of our beloved Nazi leaders. I joined her and watched for a while, and she said that it improved her luck, so I bought her a glass of lemonade and talked out the right cards for her; when I gave her one of my precious American cigarettes she was all smiles and offered to ride the horse for me.

"For fifty pfennigs you can see my thighs. For seventy-five you can see the mouse and everything in its mouth. I'm not wearing any underwear."

"Actually I was rather hoping to see Fräulein Tauber."

"She doesn't work here anymore. Not for a long time."

"Where does she work now?"

Ella took a lazy puff of her cigarette and remained silent.

I pushed a note across the table. There were no pictures on it like the ones on the backs of the cards, but she hardly minded about that. I let her reach for it and then put my finger on the little black eagle in the corner.

"Is she at the New World?"

"That dump? I should say not. She tell you that she works there?" She laughed. "It means she doesn't want to see you again, darling. So why don't you forget her and watch me ride that pony."

The Negress was tapping Morse code on the other end of the bill. I let it go and watched it disappear into a brassiere as large as a barrage balloon.

"So where *does* she work?"

"Arianne? She runs the cloakroom at the Jockey Bar. Has for a while. For a girl like Arianne, there's plenty of money to be made at the Jockey."

"In the cloakroom?"

"You can do a lot more in a cloakroom than just hang a coat, honey."

"I guess so."

"We got a cloakroom here, Fritz. It's nice and dark in there. For five marks, I could take real care of all your valuables. In my mouth, if you wanted."

"You'd be wasting your time, Ella. The only reason they let me come back from the front was because I don't have any valuables. Not anymore."

"I'm sorry. That's too bad. Nice-looking fellow like you."

Her face fell a little, and for a moment, seeing her sympathy, I felt bad about lying to her like that. She had a kind way about her.

I changed the subject.

"The Jockey," I said. "Sure I know it. It's that place off Wittenbergplatz, on Martin-Luther-Strasse. Used to be a Russian place called Yar."

The Negress nodded.

"I've only ever seen it from the outside. What's it like?"

"Expensive. Full of Amis and big shots from the Foreign Ministry. They still play American jazz there. The real stuff. I'd go myself but for one rather obvious disadvantage. Coloreds ain't welcome."

I frowned. "The Nazis don't like anyone except Germans. You should know that by now, gorgeous."

She smiled. "Oh, I wasn't talking about them. It's the Amis who don't like coloreds in the place."

FROM THE OUTSIDE, the Jockey Bar certainly sounded like the old Berlin from before the war, with its easy morals and vulgar charms.

Others thought so, too. A small crowd of jazz fans stood on the sidewalk in the dark, enjoying the music but unwilling to pay the prohibitive cost of going inside. To save paying the entrance fee myself, I flashed the beer-token in my raincoat—a little brass oval that said I was police. Unlike most Berlin cops, I'm not fond of trying to score a free one off an honest business, but the Jockey Bar was hardly that. Five marks just to walk downstairs was little better than theft. Not that there weren't plenty of people already down there who seemed more than willing to be robbed. Most of them were smart types, with quite a few wearing evening dress and Party buttons. They say crime doesn't pay. Not as well as a job does at the Foreign Office or the Ministry of Propaganda. There were also plenty of Americans, as Ella had said there would be. You could recognize them by their loud ties and their even louder voices. The Jockey Bar was probably the one place in Berlin you could speak English without some fool in a uniform trying to remind you that Roosevelt was a gangster, a Negroid maniac, a warmonger in a wheelchair, and a depraved Jewish scoundrel; and the Germans who really disliked him had some even more unpleasant things to say.

At the bottom of the stairs was a cloakroom, where a girl was filing her nails or reading a magazine, and sometimes she managed to do both at the same time. You could tell that she was clever. She had dark hair and plenty of it, but it was tied up at the back of her head like a velvet curtain. She was thin, wearing a black dress, and I suppose she was good-looking in an obvious sort of way, which, lacking all subtlety, is the way I usually like my women; but she wasn't Arianne Tauber.

I waited for the girl to finish her nail or her picture caption and to notice me, and that seemed to take longer than it ought to have done with the lights on.

"This is a cloakroom, isn't it?"

She looked up, gave me the up-and-down, and then, with a

well-manicured hand, ushered my eyes to the coats—some of them made of fur—that were hanging on the rail behind her.

"What do those look like? Icicles?"

"From here it looks as if I'm in the wrong line of work. You, too, if I'm not mistaken. I had the strange idea that you're supposed to be the first line of welcome in this up-market shell hole."

I took off my coat and laid it on the counter, and she stared at it with distaste for a moment before dragging it away like she was planning to kill it and then handing me a ticket.

"Is Arianne here tonight?"

"Arianne?"

"Arianne Tauber. That's Tauber, as in Richard Tauber, only I wouldn't like to have him sitting on my lap."

"She's not here right now."

"Not here as in not working, or not here as in she just stepped outside for a few minutes?"

"Who wants to know?"

"Just tell her that Parsifal is here. That's Parsifal as in the Holy Grail. Talking of which, I'll be in the bar if she does show up."

"You and everyone else, I guess. There's the bar and then there's the bar, see? And if you get bored in there, you can try the bar. That's bar as in Jockey Bar."

"You were listening, after all."

I went into the bar. The place needed a coat of paint and a new carpet, but not as much as I needed a drink and a set of earplugs. I like music when I'm drinking. I even like jazz sometimes, just so long as they remember where they left the melody. The band at the Jockey Bar was a three-piece trio, and while they knew all the notes of "Avalon," these were in no particular order. I sat down at a table and picked up the drinks card. The prices felt like mustard gas on my eyeballs, and when I'd picked myself off the floor, I ordered a beer. The waitress came back almost immediately, carrying a tray on which stood a tall glass filled with gold, which was the nearest thing to the Holy Grail I'd seen since the last time I bought a forty-pfennig stamp. I tasted it and found myself smiling like an idiot. It tasted exactly like beer.

"I must be dead."

"That can be arranged," said a voice.

"Oh?"

"Take a look around, Parsifal. This louse house is jumping with important Nazis. Any one of these stuffed shirts could pick up the telephone and get you a seat on tomorrow's partisan express."

I stood up and pulled out a chair for her. "I'm impressed. That you know about the partisan express."

The partisan express was what German soldiers called the troop train that traveled between Berlin and the eastern front.

"I've got a brother in the Army," she explained.

"That's hardly an exclusive club. Not anymore."

"Nor is this place. I guess that must be why they let you in." Arianne Tauber smiled and sat down. "But you can buy me a drink, if you like."

"At these prices? It would be cheaper to buy you a Mercedes-Benz."

"What would be the point? You can't get the petrol. So a drink will do just fine."

I waved the waitress toward me and let Arianne order a beer for herself.

"Got any more of those Ami cigarettes?"

"No," I lied. Buying her a beer felt extravagant enough without throwing caution out of the window and giving her a smoke as well.

She shrugged. "That's all right. I've got some Luckies."

Arianne reached for her bag, and that gave me time to have another look at her. She was wearing a plain navy-blue dress with short sleeves. Around her waist was a purple leather belt with a series of shiny black or maybe blue lozenges that were arranged like the jewels on a crown. On her shoulder was an interesting bronze brooch of the Hindu goddess Kali. Her purple leather bag was round and on a long strap and a bit like a water carrier, and out of it she took a silver cigarette box with three bits of inlaid turquoise that were as big as thrush eggs. On the side was a little matching compartment for a lighter but that contained a roll of banknotes, and for a moment I pictured her lighting a cigarette with a five-mark note. As a way of wasting money, that was only a little less profligate than buying a girl a drink at the Jockey Bar.

When she opened the little cigarette case I took one and rolled it in my fingers for a moment and passed it under my nostrils to remind myself that it was better to have America as a friend than an enemy, before poking it between my lips and dipping my head onto a match from a book off the table that was in her scented hand.

"Guerlain Shalimar," I said, and puffed my cigarette happily for a second before adding, "You were wearing it when I last saw you."

"A gift from an admirer. Seems like every Fritz who comes back on leave from Paris brings a girl perfume. It's the one thing there's no shortage of here in Berlin. I swear I could open a shop, the amount of perfume I've been given since the war started. Men. Why don't they bring something useful, like shoelaces or toilet paper?" She shook her head. "Cooking oil. Have you tried buying cooking oil? Forget it."

"Maybe they figure you smell better wearing the perfume."

She smiled. "You must think I'm really ungrateful."

"The next time I'm in Paris I'll buy you some paper clips and put you to the test."

"No, really. The other night I didn't get a chance to thank you properly, Parsifal."

"Skip it. You were in no state to be throwing me a cocktail

party." I took hold of her chin and turned her profile toward me. "The eye looks fine. Maybe just a little bruised around the edges. Then again, I always go simple for blue eyes."

For a moment she looked bashful. Then she hardened again. "I don't want you being nice to me."

"That's all right. I didn't bring any perfume."

"Not until I've apologized to you. For not being honest."

"It's a national habit."

She took a sip of her beer and then a kiss from her cigarette. Her hand was shaking a little.

"Really. There's nothing to apologize for."

"All the same, I would like to explain something."

I shrugged. "If you want. Take your time. There's no one waiting for me at home."

She nodded and then picked out another smile to wear. This one was looking sheepish.

"First of all, I want you to know I'm not some joy girl. Sometimes, when I'm in here, I'll let a man buy me a drink. Or give me a present. Like these cigarettes. But that's as far as it goes unless— well, we're all human, aren't we?"

"I certainly used to believe that."

"That's the truth, Parsifal. Anyway, being the cloakroom girl in a place like this is a good job. The Amis—even a few of the Germans—they tip well. There's nothing much to spend it on, but I figure you still have to put something away for the bad times. And I've got an ugly feeling that there's plenty of those yet to come. Worse than now, I mean. My brother says so. He says—"

Whatever her brother had said, she seemed to think better of telling me about it. A lot of Berliners were forgetful like that. They would start talking, then remember a little thing called the Gestapo and just stop midsentence, and stare into the distance for a minute and then say something like what she said next.

"Skip it. What I was saying. It wasn't anything important."

"Sure."

"What's important is you know I'm not selling it, Parsifal."

"I understand," I said, hardly caring if she was selling it or not. But I was keen to hear her out, although I was still wondering why she felt obliged to explain herself at all.

"I hope so." She picked a piece of tobacco off her tongue and her fingers came away red from her lipstick. "Okay. Here's what happened that night. Household, building, contents, everything because I figure I have to tell someone, and I get the feeling you might be interested. Say if you're not and I'll just shut up. But you were interested enough to come down here and look for me, right?"

I nodded.

"And as a matter of fact it's in here that the story starts. It was during my break. Magda—she's the girl you met, in the cloakroom—was behind the desk and I was in the bar. When we have our break, we're supposed to come in here and have a drink with the customers. Like you and me are doing now."

She tried on another smile. This one looked wry.

"Some break. Frankly, it's not a break at all. The Fritzes here are generous with their drinks and their cigarettes, and usually I'm glad to get back to the cloakroom to have a rest and try to clear my head." She shrugged. "I was never much of a drinker, but that kind of excuse really doesn't work in here."

"I can imagine."

I glanced around and tried not to grimace. There's something obscene about a nightclub in wartime. All of those people having a good time while our boys are away fighting Popovs, or flying sorties over England. Somehow it didn't feel right to have a photograph of the English film star Leslie Howard on the Jockey Club wall. For a while, after the outbreak of war, the Nazis had been sensitive enough to ban all public dancing, but following our early victories that ban had been lifted and now things were going so wonderfully for the German Army that it was thought to be fine for men and women to let down their hair and throw themselves around on a dance floor. But I didn't care for it at all. And I liked it even less when I thought about the Fridmann sisters in the apartment beneath my own.

"Sometimes when I go home I can hardly walk I'm so heavy with the stuff."

"I can see I'm going to have to come here again. This must be the only bar in Berlin where the beer still tastes like beer."

"But at a price. And what a price. Anyway, I was going to tell you about this fellow called Gustav and how I came to be hanging around Nollendorfplatz in the dark the other night."

"Were you?"

"Come on, Parsifal, pay attention. A few nights ago when I'm in here I start talking to this Fritz. He said his name was Gustav, but I have my doubts about that. He also said that he was a civil servant on Wilhelmstrasse. And that is what he looked like, I suppose. A real smooth type. Thin prick accent. Gold bird in his lapel. Silk handkerchief and spats. Oh yes, and he had this little gold cigarette holder that he brought out of a little velvet box every time he wanted a smoke. Just watching him was kind of fascinating in an irritating way. I asked him if he did that in the morning, too—I mean, if he used the little gold holder—and he said he did. Can you imagine that?"

"I'll give it a go." I shook my head. "No, I can't. He sounds like a fish in a glass case."

"Good-looking, though." Arianne grinned. "And rich. He was wearing a wristwatch and a pocket hunter, and both of them were gold, just like his cufflinks and his shirt studs and his tiepin."

"Very observant of you."

She shrugged. "What can I tell you? I like men who wear gold. It encourages me. Like a red rag to a bull. But it's not the movement. It's the color. And the value, of course. Men who wear a lot of gold bits and pieces are just more generous, I suppose."

"And was he?"

"Gustav? Sure. He tipped me just for lighting his cigarette. And again for sitting with him. At the end of the evening he asked me to meet him the following evening at the Romanisches Café."

I nodded. "Just down from Wittenbergplatz."

"Yes. At eight o'clock. Anyway he was late, and for a while I thought he wasn't coming at all. It was nearer eight twenty-five when eventually he showed up. And he was sweating and nervous. Not at all the smooth-as-silk type he'd been when we were in here the previous night. We talked for a while but he wasn't listening. And when I asked him why he seemed so out of sorts, he came to the point. He had asked me along to the café because he had a job for me. An easy job, he said, but it was going to pay me a hundred marks. A hundred. By now I was shaking my head and telling him I wasn't on the sledge just yet, but, no, he said, it wasn't anything like that, and what did I take him for? All I had to do was wait under the station at Nolli at nine fifteen and give an envelope to a man who would be humming a tune."

"That's nice. What was the tune?"

" 'Don't Say Good-bye, Only Say Adieu.' "

"Zarah Leander. I like that one."

"He even hummed it for me to make sure I knew it. I had to ask the man for a light and then his name, and if he said it was Paul, I was to give him the envelope and walk away. Well, I could tell there was something peculiar about all this, so I asked him what was in the envelope, and he said it was best I didn't know, which didn't make me feel any better about doing it. But then he put five pictures of Albrecht Dürer on the table and assured me that it would be the easiest hundred marks I'd ever earned. Especially in the blackout. Anyway I agreed. A hundred marks is a hundred marks."

"Mm-hmm."

"So I rode the S-Bahn one stop east to Nolli and waited under the station, just like Gustav had told me to do. I was early. And I was scared, but the five Albrechts felt good inside my stocking-top. I had time to think. Too much time, perhaps, because I got greedy. That's a bad habit of mine."

"You and the Austrian corporal."

"I kept on thinking that if I had been given a hundred from Gustav for showing up with an envelope, then I might make at least another ten or twenty from Paul for handing it over. And when eventually he turned up, that's what I suggested. But Paul didn't like that and started to get rough with me. He searched my coat pockets for the envelope. And my bag. He even searched my underwear. Took my hundred marks. And that's when you showed up, Parsifal. You see he wasn't trying to rape me. He was only trying to find his damned envelope."

"Where was it? The envelope?"

"I didn't have it on me when I tried to brolly him. Well, that would have been foolish. I'd already hidden it in some bushes near the taxi rank."

"That was clever."

"I thought so, too. Right up until the moment he punched me."

"Where is it now?"

"The envelope? When I went back the next day to look for it, the envelope was gone."

"Hmm."

She shrugged. "Now I really don't know what to do. I'm scared to go to the cops and tell them. Naturally, I'm worried about what was in that envelope. I'm worried that I've landed myself in the middle of something dangerous." She closed her eyes. "It seemed so easy when we were in the Romanisches Café. Just hand it over in the blackout and walk away. If only I'd done that."

"This Gustav. Have you seen him in here since?"

"No."

"Does anyone else know him?"

"No. It turns out that Magda thought his name was Josef, and that's all she remembers. Am I in trouble, Parsifal?"

"You might be. If you went to the police and told them about this, yes, I think you would be."

"So you don't think I should tell them."

"With a story like yours, Arianne, the police—the real police—are the least of your worries. There's the Gestapo to consider."

She sighed. "I thought as much."

"Have you told your story to anyone else?"

"God, no."

"Then don't. It simply never happened. You never met anyone called Gustav or Josef in this place. And no one ever asked you to be a cutout for them at the S-Bahn on Nollendorfplatz."

"A cutout?"

"That's what you call it when someone wants to give something to someone else without actually meeting them. But that's all right, too, because there was no something. No envelope. You don't even have a hundred marks to show for it, right?"

She nodded.

I sipped the beer and wondered how it and the cigarette could taste so good and how much truth there was in what Arianne Tauber had told me. It was just about possible that Franz Koci had taken a hundred marks out of her underwear, although he'd been carrying only half as much when the cops had found him in Kleist Park. Of course, they could easily have helped themselves to half his cash. And it was just about possible that some Foreign Office type who had an envelope for a Three Kings agent might have been spooked off a meeting and subcontracted the job to a money-hungry girl from the Jockey Bar. Stranger things had happened.

"But I have a question for you, angel. Why are you telling me all this?"

"In case you didn't know, Parsifal's not exactly a common

name around here." She bit her thumbnail. "Look, in spite of what I told you, about getting all that perfume, I'm not the most popular girl around town. There are a lot of people who don't like me very much."

"Sounds like we have a lot in common, angel."

She let that one go. She was too busy talking about herself. That was good, too. To me she looked like a more interesting subject than I was.

"Oh sure, I'm attractive to look at. I know that. And there are a lot of men who want me to give them what men usually want women to give them, but beyond a cigarette and a drink and a tip, and maybe the odd present or two, I don't want anything from anyone. You should know that about me. Maybe you've worked that out already. You seem bright enough. But what I'm trying to say is that I don't have many friends and certainly none that are possessed of what you might call wisdom and maturity. Otto— Otto Schulze—the Fritz who runs this place, I couldn't tell him. I can't tell him anything. He'd tell the Gestapo, for sure. Otto likes to keep in with the Gestapo. I'm almost certain he pays them off with information. Magda, too, I think. And you've met Frau Lippert. So there's no one else, see? My mother is old and lives in Dresden. My brother is on active service. But frankly he wouldn't know what to say or do. He's my younger brother and he looks to me for advice. But you, Parsifal. You strike me as the type who always knows what to say or do. So, if you're interested, there's a part-time job going as my special counsel. It doesn't pay very much, but maybe you can think of me as someone who is in your debt."

"Suddenly I feel every one of my forty-three years," I said.

"That's not so old. Not these days. Just look around, Parsifal. Where are the young men? There aren't any. Not in Berlin. I can't remember the last time I spoke to someone less than thirty. Anyone my age is on active service or in a concentration camp. Youth is no longer wasted on the young because it's wasted on the war instead." She winced. "Forget I said that. I shouldn't have said that. They're fighting for their country, aren't they?"

"They're fighting for someone else's country," I said. "That's the problem."

Arianne looked sly for a moment, as if she'd outsmarted me in a game of cards. "It's not healthy putting your head under a falling ax, Parsifal. You could get into trouble."

"I don't mind a little trouble when it looks like you, angel."

"That's what you say now. But you haven't seen me throwing crockery."

"Volatile, huh?"

"Like my boiling point was on the moon."

"Smart, too. I'm not sure I'm qualified to be your special counsel, Fräulein Tauber. I don't know the boiling point on the moon from my own shoe size."

She glanced down at my feet. "I'll bet you're a forty-six, right?"

"Mm-hmm."

"Then, for a lot of liquids with higher vapor pressures, the boiling point and your shoe size are probably the same."

"If that's true, then I'm impressed."

"Before the war I was a chemistry student."

"Why did you stop?"

"Lack of money. Lack of opportunity. The Nazis like educated women almost as little as they like educated Jews. They prefer us to stay home polishing the hearth and stirring the pot."

"Not me."

She tugged my wrist toward her and checked the time on my watch. "I have to go back to the cloakroom in a minute."

"I could wait but I might need to telephone the Reichsbank to arrange a loan."

"It might be worth it, Parsifal. I finish at two. You could walk me home if you like. Better still you could drive me, if you have a car."

"I have a car. I just don't have any petrol. And I'll gladly walk you home. But I don't think Frau Lippert would approve, do you?"

"I said you could walk me home, not up the stairs. But if ever you did walk me up the stairs, it's actually none of her business. And she knows that, too. The other night, she was just mouthing off. If I hadn't had that sock on the jaw I might have told her to shut up and mind her own business, and she would have. Up to a point. There's nothing in our agreement that says I can't have gentlemen friends in my room for a little quiet conversation. It's hard to hear everything you say in a place like this. You need to speak up. I'm a little deaf."

"Now, you tell me."

"That's because last year I was near Kottbusser Strasse when a tame Tommy went off."

A tame Tommy was what Berliners called an unexploded bomb.

"It blew me through the air. Fortunately I landed in some bushes, which broke my fall. But for a few glorious moments I thought I was dead."

"Why glorious?"

"Haven't you ever wanted to be dead? I have. Sometimes life is just so much trouble. Don't you think so?"

I nodded. "Yes. I've wanted that, too. Quite recently, as a matter of fact. I go to bed wanting to blow my brains out and wake up wondering why I didn't do it. I guess that's why I'm here. You make a very diverting alternative to the idea of self-slaughter."

"I'm glad about that, Parsifal. Hey, I don't even know your name. And I should know something about you if I'm going to let you walk me home, don't you think?"

"My name is Bernhard Gunther."

She nodded and closed her eyes as if trying to visualize my name in her mind's eye. "Bernhard Gunther. Hmm. Yes."

"What does that mean?"

"*Sssh.* I'm trying to connect with it. I'm a little bit psychic, you see."

"While you're there, see if you can't get a fix on where I've left my Postal Savings Bank Book. There's five hundred marks in there I'd like to get my hands on."

She opened her eyes. "That's a solid name, Bernhard Gunther. Dependable. Honest. And wealthy with it, too. I can do a lot with five hundred marks. This is looking good. Tell me, what kind of work does Bernie Gunther do?" She pressed her hands together in supplication. "No, wait. Let me guess."

"It's better that I tell you."

"You don't think I can guess? I'm certain you were in the Army. But now I'm not sure. If you were on leave, then it's been quite a long one, hasn't it? So maybe you were wounded. Although you don't look like a man who was wounded. Then again, maybe you got injured in the head. And that might be why you say you're suicidal. A lot of boys are these days. I mean a lot. Only they don't put that kind of thing in the newspapers because it's bad for morale. Frau Lippert had another lodger who was a corporal in a police battalion, and he hanged himself off a canal bridge in Moabit. He was a nice boy. You know, I might say you were a civil servant, but you're a little too muscular for that. And the suit—well, no civil servant would ever wear a suit like that."

"Arianne. Listen to me."

"You're no fun at all, Gunther."

"I don't want you to get the wrong idea about why I'm here."

"What does that mean?"

"It means I'm a cop. From the Police Praesidium at Alexanderplatz."

The smile dried on her face, as if I'd poured poison in her ears. She sat there for a moment, stunned, immobile, as if a doctor had told her she had six months to live.

I was used to her reaction and didn't blame her for it. There wasn't anyone in Berlin who wasn't deeply afraid of the police, including the police, because when you said "police," everyone thought about the Gestapo, and when you started to think about the Gestapo, it was soon hard to think of anything else.

"You could have mentioned that earlier," she said, stiffly. "Or is that how it works? You let people talk themselves into trouble. Give them enough rope so that they can hang themselves, like my friend."

"It's not like that at all. I'm a detective. Not Gestapo."

"What's the difference?"

"The difference is that I hate the Nazis. The difference is that I don't care if you say Hitler is the son of Beelzebub. The difference is that if I was Gestapo, you would already be in a police van and on your way to number eight."

"Number eight? What's that?"

"You're not from Berlin, are you? Not originally."

She shook her head.

"Number eight Prinz-Albrecht-Strasse. Gestapo headquarters."

I wasn't exaggerating. Not in the least. If Sachse and Wandel had heard even half of her story, Arianne Tauber would have been sitting in a chair with her skirt up and a hot cigarette in her panties. I knew how those bastards questioned people, and I wasn't about to condemn her to that. Not without being damned sure she was guilty. As it happened, I believed at least half of her story, and that was enough to prevent me from handing her over to the Gestapo. I thought she was probably a prostitute. An occasional one. To make ends meet, a lot of single women were. You could hardly blame them for that. Any kind of a living was hard to come by in Berlin. But I didn't think she was a spy for the Czechs. No spy would have volunteered so much to a man in a club she hardly knew well.

"So what happens now? Are you going to arrest me?"

"Didn't I already tell you to forget all about what happened? Didn't I tell you that? There never was an envelope. And there was no Gustav."

She nodded silently, but still I could see she was unable to grasp what I was telling her.

"Listen to me, Arianne, provided you take my advice, you're in the clear. Well, almost. There are only three people who could possibly connect you with what happened. One of them is this fellow Gustav. And one of them is Paul. The man who attacked you. Only he's dead."

"What? You didn't tell me that. How?"

"His body turned up in Kleist Park a day or so after that taxi hit him on Nolli. He must have crawled there in the blackout and died. The third person who knows about this is me. And I'm not about to tell anyone."

"Oh, I get it. I suppose you want to sleep with me. Before you hand me over to your pals in the Gestapo you want to have me yourself. Is that it?"

"No. It's not like that at all."

"Then what is it like? And don't tell me it's because you think I'm special, Parsifal. Because I won't believe you."

"I'm going to tell you why, angel. But not here. Not now. Until then you think about everything I've said and then ask yourself why I said it. I'll be waiting outside at two. I can still walk you home if you want. Or you can walk home by yourself and I give you my word you won't be woken up at five a.m. by men in leather coats. You won't ever see me again. All right?"

6

I went back to the Alex for a while and sat at my desk and wondered if there might be a way of finding Gustav without involving Arianne Tauber. She and only she could have identified him, and for that reason alone, it seemed unlikely that he would ever go back to the Jockey and risk seeing her again. Especially if he was what it seemed he was—almost certainly a spy. More than likely he'd lost his nerve about meeting his Czech contact on Nolli. Possibly he thought he was already being shadowed by the Gestapo, but if they had been tailing him, then surely they'd have picked her up when she met Gustav at the Romanisches Café. If he was under surveillance then the Gestapo would never have risked allowing him to pass information to her. It seemed more likely that Gustav had lost his nerve. In which case, who better than a joy lady to deliver something to his Czech contact? Most of the prostitutes I'd ever known were resourceful, courageous, and above all greedy. For a hundred marks there wasn't a silk in Berlin who wouldn't have agreed to what Gustav had asked. Handing over an envelope in the dark was a lot easier and quicker and, on the face of it, safer than sucking someone's pipe.

"Working late?"

It was Lehnhoff.

"Victor Keil, aka Franz Koci," I said.

"The Kleist Park case. Yeah. What about it?"

"The uniformed fairy that found him under the bushes. Sergeant Otto Macher. Do you know him well?"

"Well enough."

"Do you think he's honest?"

"Meaning what?"

"It's a straightforward question, Gottfried. Is he honest?"

"As far as it goes these days."

"In my book it goes all the way to the altar."

"There's a war on. So maybe not as far as that."

"Look, Gottfried. We're both in the shit-house age group. And I certainly don't want to cause any trouble for you and Sergeant Macher. But I need to know if our dead Czecho was carrying more than just the fifty marks we found on him."

All of the lavatories at the Alex had three numbers on the door, of which two were always 00; and the phrase "shit-house age group" was used to indicate anyone born before 1900 and therefore over the age of forty.

"If you say you're in the shit house, then I believe you," said Lehnhoff. "But from what I've heard around the factory, you're here not because you're ready for your pension, but because you've got vitamin B."

He meant that I had connections with senior Nazis who would keep me better nourished than other men.

"With Heydrich," he added.

"Who told you that?"

"Does it matter? That's the splash on the men's porcelain."

"The Czecho's watch was gone. It wasn't at his apartment when we searched it, and there wasn't a pawn ticket. But I really don't care about that. I'm guessing he had at least five Albrechts on him when he was first found in the park. There were only fifty on him by the time I made his acquaintance. I need to know if I'm right about that. You don't have to say anything. Just nod or shake your head and we'll say no more about it."

Lehnhoff's head remained still. Then he grinned. "I can't help you. I just don't know. But even if I did, what makes you think I'd tell you?"

I stood up and came around the desk. "I don't like threatening other men with my vitamin B. I much prefer it if people pay attention to my natural authority. Me being a commissar'n all."

"That won't work, either, sir."

Lehnhoff was still grinning as he left my office.

I picked up my coat and followed him out onto the landing. Cool air was drifting up the enormous stairwell. Down on the ground floor there were raised voices, but that was normal in the Alex. Even at the best of times the place was like a zoo full of all kinds of wild and noisy animals. But up on the third floor, things were quieter. The blackout curtains were drawn and most of the lights were off. At the other end of the landing was an abandoned floor polisher. It looked a lot like me. The raised voices on the ground floor became a little more urgent and someone cried out with pain. Someone was working overtime and it gave me an idea.

"Hey, Gottfried," I said, catching up with him, "you know what they used to say about this place?"

Lehnhoff stopped at the top of the stairs and looked at me with open contempt. "What's that?"

"Be careful on the stairs."

I hit him in the stomach, hard enough to bend him in two and fold him over the balustrade so that he could empty his fat gut into the stairwell. If it was my lucky day some Nazi would slip on Lehnhoff's soup and break his collarbone. Holding him by the collar, I pushed him down so that his feet tipped off the shiny floor, and then slammed my forearm across one of his kidneys. He yelled out with the pain of it, but that was fine because nobody ever paid much attention to the sound of pain at the Alex. It was one more background noise, like the sound of a typewriter or a telephone ringing in an empty room. I could have slugged Lehnhoff all night until he was groaning for his pastor, and to anyone's ears it would have been just another night at police headquarters.

"Now," I said, bending close to Lehnhoff's waxy ear, "do I get an answer to my question or would you like to go downstairs? Three flights at a time?"

"Yes, yes, yes. Okay. God. Please." His subsequent answers sounded exactly like a cry for help. "We took a hundred marks off him. Me and Macher. Sixty for me and forty for him. Please."

"In twenties?"

"Yes. Yes. Twenties. Yes. Pull me up, for God's sake."

I pulled him back off the balustrade and dumped him on the linoleum, where he lay curled and twitching and whimpering, as if his mother had just delivered him onto the Alex floor.

He gasped. "What the hell—"

"Hmm? What's that?"

"What the hell difference does it make to you, anyway? A hundred fucking marks."

"It's not the money. I don't care about that. It's just that I didn't have the time or even the inclination to wait until you were ready to answer my question. You know something? I think I've been affected deeply by working in an environment where, within the context of a police interrogation, violence is now endemic."

"I'll get you for this, Gunther. I'll make a fucking complaint. Just see if I don't."

"Hmm. I wouldn't rush into that, if I were you. Remember. I've got vitamin B, Gottfried." I twisted the hair on his scalp so that I could tap the back of his skull against the balustrade. "I can see in the dark. And I can hear everything you say from a hundred miles away."

THE JAZZ LOVERS OUTSIDE the Jockey Bar had called it a night and several smart-looking Mercedes cars were parked out front with drivers who were impatient to take their masters home in comfort and safety—or as safe as could be managed with most of the headlights taped up. There was a rumble in the sky but it wasn't the RAF. I could feel a breeze in the air, and the breeze had an edge of moisture that was the vanguard of something heavier. Minutes later it started to rain. I moved into an inadequate doorway and buttoned my coat tight against my neck, but it wasn't long before it started to feel more like a shower curtain and I cursed my stupidity for not bringing along the nail brush and the shard of soap that I kept in my desk drawer. But an umbrella would probably have been better. Suddenly, walking a prostitute home, even a pretty one, looked like a bad idea in a whole novel full of miserable ideas by some miserable French writer. The sort of novel that gets turned into an even more miserable movie starring Charles Laughton and Fredric March. And, reminding myself why I was there—she was the only person who had met Franz Koci, whose homicide I was supposed to be investigating—I pulled my hat down over my ears and pressed myself hard into the doorway.

Ten minutes went by. Most of the cars had driven away with their passengers. It was two fifteen. A kilometer to the west of where I was standing, the Führer, purported to be a bit of a night owl, was probably putting on his pajamas, combing his mustache, and cleaning his teeth before sitting down to write his diary. At around two twenty, the door of the Jockey Bar opened and, for a brief moment, an obtuse triangle of dim light fell on the patent-shiny sidewalk— long enough for me to see a woman wearing a raincoat and a hat and carrying a man's umbrella. She looked one way and then the other before glancing at her watch. It was Arianne Tauber.

Abandoning my inadequate refuge, I walked quickly forward and presented myself in front of her.

"You look like a widow's handkerchief," she said.

"It's only what happens when air turns back into water. You're a chemist. You should know that."

"And you should know I changed my mind about letting you walk me home."

"Looks like I got wet for nothing, then."

"That's precisely why I've decided to walk you home, copper. All that water dripping off your hat. If we move your head the right way we can probably fill a couple of glasses. So it's probably lucky that I managed to steal a half bottle of Johnnie Walker to go with it. That's the only reason I'm late. I had to wait for the right moment to lead the raiding party on Otto's bar."

"With a pitch like that I might just allow you to walk me home and then up the stairs."

"Well, we can hardly drink it in the street."

It's quite a walk from Martin-Luther-Strasse to Fasanenstrasse and it was fortunate that the rain eased soon after we began; even so, we were obliged to stop a couple of times and take a nibble off her bottle. Amundsen wouldn't have approved of breaking into our supplies so soon after setting off from base camp, but then he had sled dogs and all we had were soaking wet shoes. By the time we reached my apartment, the half bottle of Johnnie Walker was only a third, which is probably why we took off our clothes and, it being wartime when these things seemed to happen a little more quickly than of old, we went straight to bed, and after a few minutes of animal magic to remind us both of happier times before God got angry with the people who stole the fruit of his favorite tree, we resumed our earlier conversation with small glasses in our hands and, perhaps, a little less front. It's pointless trying to maintain a persona concealing one's true nature from the world when your damp clothes are lying in a hurried heap on the floor.

"I never slept with a cop before."

"How was it?"

"Now I know why cops have big feet."

"I hate to sound like a cop so soon after—"

"You *are* going to arrest me."

"No, no."

"I won't come quietly."

"So I noticed. No, Arianne, I've been thinking about your job at the Jockey Bar and wondering if you should give it up or not. In case Gustav does go back there looking for you."

"And what did you conclude, Commissar?"

"That if the Gestapo had arrested him and brought him back to the bar to look for you, then you'd be in trouble."

"True. But even if I did leave the club, they wouldn't have a problem finding me. Otto has all my details. My work book number, my address, everything. No, if I left there, I'd also have to leave my room and go underground. Which is impossible. That sort of thing takes money and connections."

"That's the very same conclusion I came to myself. As I see it, there are two other possibilities. One is that he assumes you handed over the envelope, as agreed, and never comes back at all. He gave you that envelope to give to Paul because he was scared to give it to Paul himself; and that could mean he's too scared ever to return to the club and ask you anything more about it. The other possibility is that he does come back, and if he does, you find an excuse to telephone me at the Alex and I come along and arrest him."

"Conveniently leaving me out of it, right?"

I nodded and drank some more of the scotch. It was the first proper liquor I'd tasted since coming back from Belorussia. Normally I don't drink scotch. But this tasted just fine. Like some fiery drink of the gods that might have been gathered from a hive of immortal bees. My own sting was gone, at least for the moment.

But after the defilement of my flesh, I was beginning to feel divine again.

"Conveniently leaving you out of it."

"You said Paul was found dead in Kleist Park. But you didn't say any more."

"No, I didn't."

"How do you know it was him? I was as close to him as I am to you now and I'm not sure I would have recognized him again."

"It was him, all right. His injuries were those of a man who'd been hit by a car. And it's not like there were any other unreported traffic accidents in that area that night."

"So who was he?"

"Do you really want to know?"

"I'm not sure. Maybe. Maybe not. Maybe you should decide, Gunther."

I asked myself how much she ought to know, and when I told her it was mainly because I wanted to see how she would react. Despite our being in bed together—maybe because of it—I wasn't yet satisfied that she was as innocent as she had led me to believe. But even if she did turn out to be rather more culpable than I had previously supposed, I couldn't imagine myself serving her up cold to the Gestapo.

"The man you were paid to meet at Nolli, he was really a Czech called Franz Koci who was working for the Three Kings."

"You mean those terrorists who were in the newspapers earlier this year?"

"Yes."

"Now I am scared." She closed her eyes and lay back against the pillow, then sat up abruptly and stared at me with wide eyes. "You know what that means, don't you? It means that Gustav must be some sort of spy. For the Czechs."

"I'd say that was a pretty good guess."

"What am I going to do?"

"You might try to remember some more about Gustav. And if that doesn't happen, I might tie you over a table and beat it out of you myself. Like the Gestapo."

"Do they really do that? I've heard stories."

"All of them are true, I'm afraid."

"Maybe I should go underground, after all." She shook her head and shivered. "It must be bad enough to have someone hurt you to make you tell them something you know; but to have someone hurt you when you've got nothing you can tell them. That doesn't bear thinking of."

"And that's precisely why I want you to tell me all about Gustav. Once again. From the very beginning. Everything you remember and everything you might have forgotten. Your best chance of disappearing from this picture is to paint another. Of him."

There's a little red warning card with a hole in the middle that the Ministry of Propaganda likes you to slip over the tuning dial of your radio. "Racial comrades!" it says. "You are Germans! It is your duty not to listen to foreign radio stations. Those who do so will be mercilessly punished!" Now, me, I'm a good listener. A big part of being a good detective is knowing when to shut up and let someone else do the talking. Arianne liked to talk—that much was obvious—and while she told me nothing new about Gustav, she told quite a lot about herself, which was of course the main point of the exercise.

She was from Dresden, where she'd gone to university. Her husband, Karl, also a student from Dresden, had joined the German Navy in the summer of 1938 and had been killed aboard a U-boat in February 1940. Three months later, her father, a commercial traveler, had been killed in a bombing raid during a business trip to Hamburg.

Naturally I checked up on all of this later. Exactly as Arianne had described, her fiancé's boat, U-33, had been sunk by depth charges from a British minesweeper in the River Clyde, in Scotland.

Twenty-five men, including Karl and the boat's commander, were lost. Her younger brother, Albrecht, had joined the Army in 1939 but now he was with the military police. Her father had worked for the pharmaceutical works in Dresden and often did business with E. H. Worlée, another chemical company, in Hamburg. Soon after Herr Tauber's death, Arianne had come to Berlin to work for BVG—the Berlin Transport Company—as a secretary to the director of Anhalter Station. But she had quit this job—a good one—because, she said, he couldn't keep his hands off her.

His was a predicament with which I strongly sympathized. I couldn't keep my hands off her, either.

7

Planting evidence was hardly uncommon at the Alex. For a lot of detectives lacking the skills or the patience to do the job properly, it was the only way they could ever secure a conviction. I'd never done it myself, but there's a first time for everything, and in the absence of the evidence that was legally held by the Gestapo in the death of Franz Koci, I decided to "find" some new evidence that hitherto was held only by me. But first I had to make Lehnhoff's earlier on-the-scene inquiry seem like what it was: incompetent, only more so, and when I reviewed his case notes, I discovered that no fingertip search of the area in Kleist Park where Koci's body was discovered had ever been conducted. So

I telephoned Sachse at Gestapo headquarters to prick his ears with this new "information."

"I thought you told me that all of the evidence at the scene of the crime had been collected."

"I did. It was."

"Like hell. With a homicide, especially an important homicide like this one, it's standard practice to have ten or fifteen police officers on their hands and knees in a line to comb the general area. Or at least it was when this department had real police working here. Real police who did real police work. But there's no record of a fingertip search of the ground where Koci's body was found."

"But looking for what?"

"Evidence. What evidence, I don't know. I can't tell you what it might be. But I think I'd recognize it when I saw it."

"You really think that park's worth another look?"

"Under the circumstances, yes I do. Between you and me, Inspector Lehnhoff—the first investigating detective—is lazy and dishonest, so it wouldn't have been your fault if the ground wasn't properly searched. I suppose you just took his word for it that things had been done properly."

I was saying half of this in case Lehnhoff decided to say anything about my assaulting him.

"Well, yes, I did."

"I thought so. All right. You weren't to know. But under the circumstances, you'd better organize a search yourself. Commissioner Lüdtke has told us all that budgets at the Alex are tight. I don't want him coming down on my neck about the cost of this."

"I'll organize it immediately."

"Good. Please let me know if they find anything."

Of course I knew exactly what they were going to find in Kleist Park. I knew because I'd already put it there myself. And when later on that same day Sachse appeared in my office with a paper bag containing a switchblade, I made a big show out of looking surprised.

"This is made by Mikov," I said, examining the switchblade carefully. "That's in Czechoslovakia, isn't it? I mean Bohemia and Moravia."

"Yes."

"That would fit with our friend Franz Koci, wouldn't it?" I leaned back in my chair and frowned a frown that could have made it big in silent movies. "I wonder . . ."

"What?"

I made another big show of thinking hard. I walked around my office, which contained several filing cabinets, a lot of empty ashtrays, and on the wall a nice picture of Adolf Hitler. The picture had been put there by the previous occupant, and though I hated it, for me to have taken it down would, in the eyes of the Gestapo, have made me look like Gavrilo Princip.

I opened one of the filing cabinets. This was as full as the Prussian State Library and contained unsolved cases and reports going back years. Very little of what was in there had anything to do with me, and for all I knew, Philipp Melancthon's report to the Diet of Worms was one of the older files at the back of the drawer. But I knew what I was looking for. I forced a gap and tugged out a gray folder with Geert Vranken's name on the corner.

"Geert Vranken. Aged thirty-nine, a foreign railway worker from Dordrecht, in the Netherlands. Educated at The Hague University. Murdered earlier this month. His body, what remained of it, was found on the railway line just south of Jannowitz Bridge after being struck by a train to Friedrichshagen."

"What about it?"

Sachse sat down on the corner of my desk, folded his arms, and then checked his hair. It was still as neat as a field of wheat and approximately the same color, and I briefly wondered if it ever looked any different in a high wind or underwater. Probably not.

His head could have been found on the roof of the Pintsch factory, like Vranken's, after a train had gone over his neck and there still wouldn't be a hair out of place.

"I was the investigating officer, that's what. And while it's not uncommon for people to get hit by trains in the dark, it is uncommon to find that they had already sustained multiple stab wounds. I examined the torso myself and I seem to remember that the contour of the wounds was not unlike the shape of this Bohemian switchblade."

"How can we find out for sure?"

"Got a car?"

"Of course."

"Good. You can drive me out to the Charité. Let's hope that they haven't incinerated the body."

SACHSE PULLED UP at the corner of the Charité opposite the Lessing Theater, where Ida Wüst was playing in a show called *The Main Point Is Happiness.* I couldn't disagree with that.

"How about it, Werner? Shall I go in and get us a pair of tickets while we're here?"

Sachse smiled thinly and shook his head.

"Not an Ida Wüst fan, huh? You surprise me."

"That old trout? You must be joking. She reminds me of my mother-in-law. But the other one's all right. Jane Tilden."

"She's a bit too wholesome for my taste." I opened the car door but Sachse stayed put. "Aren't you coming in?"

"You don't need me in there, do you?"

Sachse was already looking a little green, and after hearing me relate my favorite but strictly after-dinner anecdotes from the gay world of forensic science, I couldn't blame him for not wanting to come into the Pathological Institute. This, of course, was the intention behind these gruesome stories. I hardly wanted the mortuary attendant asking me any awkward questions in front of Werner Sachse about why I was back there with the same knife to check the same wounds in the same body.

"Strictly speaking," I said, "there should always be two officers present when a body is examined; however, on this occasion, perhaps that won't be necessary. Nothing ever quite prepares you for the sight of a body that's been chewed up by a railway locomotive."

Sachse nodded. "Thanks, Gunther. You're all right."

Chuckling sadistically—the idea of a squeamish Gestapo man just struck me as funny—I went into the hospital and along to the morgue, where I found the same attendant and, having established that Vranken's dismembered body was still safely stored there, informed him that the investigation was now a Gestapo matter and that in no circumstances was the body to be released for burial or incineration without first clearing it with me.

As always, mention of the Gestapo worked an almost magical effect, akin to uttering "open sesame," and the attendant signaled his total compliance with a nervous bow. Of course there was no need to see or examine Vranken's body again. I already knew what I was going to tell Werner Sachse: that Franz Koci had murdered Geert Vranken. And, feeling pleased that I had managed to reopen what was now a proper murder case, I made my way back to the car.

A good humor never lasts long in Berlin. The smell of the war wounded in that hospital was asphyxiating. Dying men lay in dusty wards like so much left luggage, while to walk through a hallway or public corridor was to negotiate an obstacle course of rickety old wheelchairs and dirty plaster casts. And if all of that wasn't bad enough, I came out of the hospital and encountered a little squad of Hitler Youth marching down Luisenstrasse—most likely from a trip to see the National Warriors' Monument in the Invaliden Park—their throats full of some stupid warlike song and quite oblivious to the German warrior's true fate that was to be found in the not so glorious charnel house nearby. For a moment I stood and watched these boys with a kind of horror. It was all too easy to think of them as carrying the infection of Nazism—the brown-shirted bacilli of death and destruction and the typhus of tomorrow.

Feeling more somber than before, I tapped on the window of the Horch-built Audi. It's a useful courtesy to observe with a man sleeping in his own car when he happens to be carrying a loaded automatic.

Sachse sat up straight, lifted the tip of his black felt hat, and opened the passenger door.

"Any luck?"

"Yes. If you can call it that. The Dutchman was stabbed by the Czech, all right. Franz Koci's knife fitted those stab wounds like they'd been cut for it by a good tailor."

"Well, you're the expert."

"The question is, why? Why would a Czech spy stab and kill a Dutch railway worker?"

8

After this "breakthrough"—that's what Sachse called it, anyway—the investigation stalled again, as investigations usually do. I wasn't too worried about that. Detective work is almost always a long game, unless the newspapers get involved, and then it's still a long game, only you have to pretend that it's not. This job isn't only a matter of paying attention to detail, it's also about knowing what to ignore as well as whom. It's about reading the newspapers and staring into space and learning to be patient and to put your trust in your experience, which tells you that something nearly always turns up. Yes, sir, the investigation is going very well. No, sir, there's nothing we could be doing that we haven't done already. Good morning, anything new on the Franz Koci case? No new leads as yet. Good night. Collect your pay, go home, and do your best to forget all about it, if you can. A lot of police work is police idle, police baffled, police at breakfast, police at lunch, police drinking coffee—if there is any coffee—and always police staring out of the window, assuming there is one. And it all adds up to the same thing: that, mostly, being a detective is about coping with boredom and the huge frustration of knowing that it isn't ever like it is in books and movies. Other things have to take place before something else can happen. Sometimes these are other crimes. Sometimes they're things other than crimes. And sometimes it's hard to know the difference—for instance, when a new law is passed, or when a top policeman is promoted. That's jurisprudence for you, Nazi style.

The new law was the yellow star, which made a big difference when it finally came into practice on September 19. The day before, there were just people on the streets of Berlin. Ordinary people. You might say they were my fellow Berliners. The next day, there were all these people wearing yellow stars, which made me realize just how many Jews were living in Berlin and, at the same time, what a terrible thing it was to treat our fellow citizens this way. Now and again there were even small demonstrations against the wearing of the yellow star. Not by Jews but by gentile Germans in favor of the Jews. People talked about "the yellow badge of honor," and the stoic way the Jews endured their fate did not fail to impress even the most fanatical of Nazis. Except of course the fanatical Nazi who had signed this new police law into being; and he was on my mind a great deal after Saturday, September 27, when he was promoted Reichsprotector of Bohemia and Moravia. There was no way that the man who was my boss, Reinhard Heydrich, would ever have been impressed with the way Jewish Germans conducted themselves.

When I heard that Heydrich was on his way to Prague, I was glad—although not, of course, for him. I was glad he was to be gone from Berlin, where there always existed the possibility that he might hand me some special task, as had happened at least twice before. And, for a day or two, I even managed to relax. I took Arianne to the Lido at Müggelsee and then to a show at the Schlosspark Theater in Steglitz. Somewhere in the day I even managed to ask her about Geert Vranken.

"Never heard of him."

"He was a foreign worker from Dordrecht, in the Netherlands."

"Dordreck? No wonder he came to Berlin."

"Not Dordreck. Dordrecht."

"Why ask me?"

"Because I think he may have been murdered by your friend, Paul."

"Who?"

"Franz Koci. The Czecho that Gustav asked you to meet on Nolli Platz."

Arianne rolled her eyes. "Oh, him. I'd only just managed to forget all about that business." She uttered a profound sigh and with her fist smacked the wicker beach chair we were sharing. "What happened to him? This Dutchie."

I told her how Geert Vranken had died; and I told her about Franz Koci's switchblade.

"That's really awful. And you mean to tell me that the poor man is still lying in the mortuary at the Charité like last week's one-pot dinner?"

I nodded.

"What about this family?"

"I wrote to his wife, telling her what had happened."

"That was big of you."

"I didn't have to do it. In fact I was almost ordered not to do it. But I thought someone should. Like you, I felt sorry for her. Besides, I was hoping that his wife might write back, with some more information. Something that would help me to find her husband's murderer."

"You didn't tell her—"

"No, no. I just said there'd been an accident. And that because of wartime regulations, it was impossible for his body to be sent back. But that I'd see to it, personally, that he got a decent burial."

"And will you? I mean, that sounds expensive."

"As a matter of fact I'm hoping to persuade the Gestapo to pay for it."

"How are you going to do that?"

"By lying. I shall tell them that the mortuary needs the space, which is true; and also that it's best that Vranken's remains are not cremated, in case we need to examine the body again, which is not. Something like that. I'm really quite a good liar when the occasion demands it."

"I don't doubt it, Gunther. And the widow? Have you heard back from her?"

"Not yet. And I probably won't. Would you write to some Nazi bastard who was occupying your country?"

We were both silent for a while the way you are on a beach. On the blue water there were lots of little white boats that looked as if they were made of paper. We watched the boats and children building sand castles and some girls playing volleyball. The beach was crowded with people who, like us, figured it could be the last day of summer and were worried we might be in for another hard winter, like the last one, when temperatures fell as low as minus twenty-two degrees Celsius. This, of course, was just one of many things we Berliners had to worry about following the overthrow of Kiev. The German High Command had issued a victory communiqué announcing that the Army was now in charge of 665,000 Soviet prisoners. This seemed like a fantastic figure, and there were some who thought it meant that the war in the East was all but won; but there were many others, like myself, who thought that there were probably a lot more Soviet soldiers where those 665,000 men came from.

Eventually, Arianne said, "I've been thinking of going back to Dresden. To visit my mother."

"Good idea."

"You could come with me if you like. It's only two hours on the train. I'll probably stay there for a couple of weeks, but you might like to stay for the weekend." She shrugged. "You'd enjoy Dresden. It's not like Berlin, where there's no room. My mother has a huge apartment in Johann-Georgen-Allee, overlooking the park. And of course it's much safer than Berlin. I don't think there's ever been an air raid."

She was wearing a blue Lastex swimsuit, which was like a dress and showed off her legs, which looked lovely to me. I was trying to keep my eyes on her face as she talked, but it was difficult when all I wanted to do was lay my muzzle on her lap and have her play with my ears and pull my tail.

"I am supposed to be investigating a murder," I said, eventually. "Two murders, if you count Geert Vranken. However, neither one of them is paying out right now, and I am owed some leave. So, maybe, yes, I could use a holiday. Only I'm going to have to clear it with the commissioner. He worries when I'm not around. I'm the last real cop in Berlin. When I go, it's just the two sentries out front of the Alex and the cleaning lady. So I'll let you know, angel. Tomorrow, probably."

9

"I'm afraid that's quite impossible, Bernie."

I shifted uncomfortably in Lüdtke's office. I felt about ten years old, a schoolboy again, in trouble with his headmaster.

"Would you mind telling me why, sir?"

"I was about to. I've just had a telephone call from an SS major called Dr. Hans-Achim Ploetz."

"Never heard of him."

"In Prague." Lüdtke grinned. "Yes, I thought that would shut you up. Major Ploetz is the chief adjutant to General Heydrich. It seems that your presence is required in Bohemia and Moravia. Or perhaps it's just Bohemia. I'm not sure." He shrugged. "Whichever one Prague is in is where you are requested to go."

I felt a sudden chill on the back of my neck, as if I'd run my finger along the edge of the blade of the falling ax at Plotzensee. Heydrich had that effect on people, which was probably why he was nicknamed "the Hangman."

"Did Major Ploetz explain why I'm needed in Prague, sir?"

"It seems that the general is planning some sort of weekend with friends, at his country house outside Prague. To celebrate his appointment as the new Reichsprotector of Bohemia. I had no idea that you and General Heydrich were on such cordial terms, Bernie."

"No, sir. Nor had I."

"Oh, come now. You might not wear a scary badge on your lapel, but everyone at the Alex knows you've got vitamin B. Even the footballs handle you with care."

Many Gestapo officers were fond of wearing leather coats and hats; and since many of them were also better fed than the rest of us and hence fatter, too, they were known as "footballs." But sadly, kicking one was not an option.

"Perhaps I'll have my own adjutant telephone the general's adjutant and inform him that I will have to decline the invitation," I said.

"You do that."

"What about the case I'm working on? This Czech spy who got himself killed."

"You told me it was a traffic accident, didn't you? Happens every day. And spies are apparently no exception."

"Yes, but I'm pretty sure that he murdered that Dutch foreign worker, Geert Vranken. You remember. The fellow who got himself hit by a train after receiving multiple stab wounds."

"I'm sure he'll be waiting for you when you get back from your weekend with the general."

Lüdtke looked as if he was enjoying my discomfort. He knew the truth about my dislike for the Nazis but it didn't stop him from savoring my dilemma: for me not to be a Party member and yet still be in such apparent high favor with Heydrich was amusing to him. It amused me, too, which is to say it stopped me from thinking about much else.

"Dr. Ploetz, you say?"

"Yes." Lüdtke leaned back in his chair and folded his hands behind his head, as if he were about to surrender. "I hear Prague's very nice at this time of year. I've often fancied going there with the wife. She collects glass, you know. And there's a lot of glass in Prague."

"That should keep the Nazis happy. They like smashing glass. Here, maybe you should go instead of me."

"Oh no." Lüdtke smiled. "I wouldn't know what to say to a man as important as the Reichsprotector of Bohemia. My God, I should be surprised if he even knew I existed."

"Any man who can persuade Berlin detectives to wear women's clothes in order to catch a murderer is certain to have been noticed upstairs."

"It's kind of you to say so, Bernie. But of course I had lots of help. Remember Georg Heuser?"

"Yes."

"Georg Heuser was one of my best detectives on the S-Bahn murder case. Good man, is Georg. Of course, he lacks your subtlety and experience, but he's a promising young policeman. And of more use here than where he is now."

"And where is that?"

"In a Special Action Group somewhere in Belorussia."

I didn't reply. Suddenly going to Prague didn't seem so bad, after all. Not when they were still sending "good" men to Special Action Groups in Belorussia. Just thinking about Georg Heuser and what he was probably going through in Minsk, or Pinsk, or Dnepropetrovsk, or any one of a hundred Jew towns where innocent people were being murdered in the thousands, made me feel that I was much better off than I realized. And all talk of an S-Bahn murderer seemed laughable when one of our own investigating detectives now seemed likely to chalk up more victims in twenty-four hours than Paul Ogorzow had managed in one murderous year.

Lüdtke played with the rocker blotter on his desk for a moment, as if trying to measure something.

"You hear stories," he said finally. "About what is happening out east. In Belorussia and Latvia, for example. The police battalions. Special Action Groups and what have you. You were there,

Bernie. What is the truth about what's happening? Is it true what they're saying? That people are being murdered? Men, women and children? Because they're Jews?"

I nodded.

"My God," he said.

"I think you once said that whenever I came in here it was like rain coming in at the eaves. Now you know why. Since I came home there hasn't been a day when I didn't feel ashamed. And the nights are worse."

"My God."

"That's the third time you've mentioned God, Friedrich-Wilhelm. And I've been thinking that there must be a God because, after all, the Leader is always mentioning Him and it's inconceivable he could be wrong about that. But what we've done to the Jews, and what we're still doing to the Jews, and, I think, what we seem intent on doing to the Jews for a good while longer, well, He's not going to forgive that in a hurry. Perhaps not ever. In fact, I've a very terrible feeling that whatever we do to them, He's going to do to us. Only it'll be worse. Much worse. It'll be much worse because He's going to get the fucking Russians to do it."

"I HEAR PRAGUE is very nice at this time of year. I've often wanted to go there." Arianne shook her head. "I really can't imagine why I haven't been already. After all, Prague is only a couple of hours on the train from Dresden. And my mama's a German-speaking Czech from Teplitz. Did I tell you that? She moved to Dresden when she met my papa. Not that she ever really thought of herself as a Czech. Nobody does in Teplitz. At least that's what my mama says." She paused. "Maybe I could go and see my brother. His unit is stationed near Prague."

We were at Kempinski's Haus Vaterland on Potsdamer Platz, a department store of cafés and restaurants that described itself as "the jolliest place in Berlin" and that was as ersatz as the coffee we were drinking in the Grinzing Café, which with its diorama of Old Vienna and the Danube River was itself pretty ersatz. Of the several bars and cafés in Vaterland, Arianne much preferred the Wild West Bar's log-cabin walls, American flags, and the picture of Custer's last stand but immediately outside its door was an amusement machine with a light gun on which you could shoot at pictures of aircraft, and the city's young antiaircraft gunners were fond of using it for their boisterous practice. This particular form of entertainment was too like the real thing for my money, and so we sat in the Grinzing and hugged each other fondly in sight of a *trompe l'oeil* of the Austrian capital city with miniature bridges, mechanical boats, and an electric train set while a little orchestra played Strauss waltzes. It was like being a giant or a god, which, in Germany, usually amounts to the same thing. Arianne was smaller than me by a head, and while that didn't make her Freia to my Fasolt, she was very much a goddess of feminine love. I'd seldom had a lover as expert as Arianne, and after the depressing horrors of Belorussia, which, whenever possible, I was keen to put out of my mind, perhaps I was falling for her. Hell, I had fallen for her. Since meeting her I hadn't thought about killing myself. Not once. I knew she was riding for herself, but I could hardly blame her for that. The whole damned country was addicted to its own selfish pursuits. So I heard her out as she made her play and probably smiled a fond, indulgent sort of smile as she went about it. Because while there was a part of me that still didn't trust her, there was an even larger part that simply didn't care. Not anymore. I was in Gaza, bound with new ropes and fresh bowstrings, with my hair in knots and my head in her lap. Sometimes it just happens that way.

"Have you got a passport?"

She nodded. "When I was working for BVG, my boss told me

to get one so I could accompany him on a business trip to Italy. I knew what I was in for and if we'd ever actually got there I might have let him sleep with me, only his wife found out that I was going and then I wasn't going, and then I was out of a job. It's a very common story."

"You'd need a visa, of course."

"Sure. From the Police Praesidium on Alexanderplatz. Isn't that convenient, you working there and everything?"

"I don't know. It's possible you might need to produce some certification concerning the military importance of your journey. In which case—well, there is no military importance, angel. Not unless we count the restoration of my own morale. But somehow I don't see them buying that one."

Arianne shook her head. "No, you only need that kind of certification if you're planning to take the express train." Smiling, she added, "You forget. I used to work for BVG. I know all the rules and regulations that affect the railways. No certification of a journey's relevance is required for any other train. If we take the regular service between Anhalter Station and Prag Hibernerbahnhof Station, there won't be a problem. I could probably remember the timetable if I put my mind to it."

"I don't doubt it. But look, angel, I'm not sure where I'll be staying or what I'll be doing. You might find yourself on your own for longer than you'd like. For longer than I'd like, if it comes to that. It could even be dangerous."

"I'll go and see the sights when you're not around. That shouldn't be too difficult to do. German's now the official language in Prague. And it's not like I'll be wearing a uniform. So I can't see how I'm likely to get into any trouble. Or how it could possibly be dangerous." She frowned. "I think you're just saying that because you don't want me to come with you."

"I wasn't thinking about the danger you might be in from the

Czechos," I said. "Frankly, they're the least of our problems. No, there's something far more dangerous in Prague than the damned Czechos."

"And what's that?"

"The new Reichsprotector of Bohemia and Moravia, that's what. General Reinhard Heydrich."

SOMEONE ONCE SAID there's no fool like an old fool in love. But middle-aged fools aren't any less foolish. I walked home and thought some more about taking Arianne with me to Prague. No matter how smart you are, sometimes you just have to sit down and lay out a balance sheet to help you decide on something. On the credit side, Arianne was a potential liability; on the debit side, she gave me a lot of pleasure, and not all of it horizontal. They say that if, in every transaction, you can identify what you received, where it came from, and what it cost, then you have debits and credits mastered. But what they don't say is that sometimes you just figure the world owes you a little bit extra, and to hell with the consequences. In truth, that's how most people handle life's book-keeping. If you believe Prince Hamlet, conscience makes cowards of us all; but I can attest that it's just as likely that conscience, especially a guilty one, can make you just a little bit reckless.

10

I got down to Berlin's Anhalter Station about an hour before the train was due to depart so that I could meet Arianne and make sure that we both got a seat in a compartment. The newspaper vendors were shouting about the greatest victory in all military history at Kiev, and now and then about some smaller Italian air success against the British at Gibraltar. A squadron of pigeons up in the rafters of the station roof must have been listening because they flew south across the station concourse in formation, as if in honor of our wonderful armed forces and their brave Italian allies.

The station was busy. Nowadays Anhalter was always busier than Lehrter or Potsdam: Germans were not traveling west toward RAF targets such as Hamburg and Cologne if they could help it. South was better and southeast was better still. Even the pigeons knew that much.

The train filled. Among the other passengers with a seat in our compartment was an old Jew, easily identified by the yellow star recently sewn onto the left breast pocket of his suit. Nothing else about him was Jewish according to the filthy caricature of a Jew you saw in the newsreels or on the front page of *Der Stürmer*, and prior to the nineteenth of September and Heydrich's new police law I should have assumed the old man was just another Berliner.

Except that he was without question a brave one: the Knight's Cross with oak leaves he wore on a ribbon around his neck was eloquent proof of that, and probably a clever way to offset the stigma of the yellow star.

By now people were standing in the corridor, and a man wearing the uniform of a Labor Corps leader loudly demanded that the old man give up his place to "a German." From his substantial girth, his relationship with real work looked tenuous, to say the least.

Normally I didn't interfere in these matters; maybe it was the sight of the Knight's Cross around the old man's neck—maybe it was just that, like a lot of other Berliners, I didn't like the yellow star—but I was feeling more querulous in the face of Nazi bullying.

"Stay where you are," I told the Jew, and stood up to face down the Labor leader.

His face reddened like a Muscovy duck as he tried and failed to lift his chest above the polished brown belt around his waist.

"And who the hell are you to interfere?"

It was a fair question. I wasn't in uniform. That was in my suitcase and, for once, I was almost regretting not wearing it. But I had the next best thing in my pocket: my warrant disc. I showed it to him in the palm of my hand and it had the usual effect of cowing the man and the rest of the carriage into respectful silence.

"Do you see a sign that says this carriage is forbidden to Jews?"

The Labor leader glanced around, redundantly. There was a small printed panel that read *Attention! The Enemy Is Listening!* but nowhere was there an anti-Semitic sign of the kind sometimes seen on park benches or at public baths. Even I was surprised about that.

He shook his head.

I pointed at Arianne. "This woman worked for BVG until about a year ago."

"That's right," she said. "I was secretary to the director himself."

"Is there anything in the BVG railway rules and regulations that says a Jew must give up his seat to a German?"

"No. There isn't."

"So there," I said. "Let that be an end of it. Go away and keep your ignorant mouth shut." I might also have mentioned the decoration around the old Jew's neck, but I didn't want anyone in that compartment thinking that this was the only reason I was interfering on his behalf.

There was a murmur of approval as the Labor leader barreled his way out of the compartment and down the carriage. I sat down.

"Thank you, sir," said the old man, tipping his hat.

"Don't mention it," I said, and tipped my own in return.

Someone else said, quietly, "No one likes that yellow star."

By now the old man was looking thoroughly bewildered, as well he might be, and he could reasonably have asked any of us how it was, if none of us cared for the yellow star, we had allowed Heydrich's police order to happen. If he had, I might have suggested a better question: how had we allowed Heydrich to happen? There was no easy answer to a question like that.

The old man got off the train in Dresden, which was a relief to everyone. The sight of the word "Jew" emblazoned on a man of such obvious valor made all of us feel thoroughly ashamed of ourselves.

Despite what had been said about the yellow star, no one in our compartment—no one at all—talked about the war. The injunction on the wooden wall that the enemy might be listening was more effective than might have been imagined. And since there was little else on anyone's mind but the war, this meant that none of the other passengers in our compartment said very much. Even Arianne, who liked to talk, was silent for most of the journey.

The train traveled north of the Elbe until Bad Schandau, where it passed over a bridge onto the south bank, then east and south again until Schöna, where it halted to allow several customs officers to board. Everyone—myself included, until I flashed my beer-token—was obliged to leave the train and have their luggage searched in the customs shed. None of my fellow passengers protested. After eight long years of Nazism, people knew better than to complain to authority. Besides, these officers were backed by twenty or thirty SS who stood thuggishly on the platform, ready to see off any trouble.

The customs officers themselves were surprisingly courteous and polite. They did not bother to search Arianne or her bags when I informed them that she was traveling with me. If they had, I wonder what they might have found.

While the rest of the passengers were in the customs shed and we were alone in the compartment, she looked at me strangely. "You're an odd one, Parsifal. I can't figure you out."

"What do you mean?"

"The way you stuck up for that old Jew back there. Jesus, I thought you were supposed to be a Nazi."

"What ever gave you that idea?"

"I don't know. Maybe it's the company you keep. We don't see much of General Heydrich in my circle."

"He's not an easy man to disappoint."

"I can imagine."

"Can you? I wonder. I wasn't always his creature. Even before the Nazis took over, I was out of the police, because of my politics. Which is to say that, like most people who supported the old republic, I didn't really have any politics except I wasn't a Nazi and I wasn't a Red. But that was no good, see? Not for the cops. So I left; they'd have kicked me out anyway. Then, in 1938, not being a Nazi made me seem like good police again. I wasn't about to chalk someone up for a crime just because they were Jewish. That was useful to Heydrich, so he ordered me back into Kripo. And I've been stuck there ever since. Worse than that, if I'm honest. Suddenly, when war was declared, if you were in Kripo you were also in the SS; and when we attacked Russia—"

I shook my head. "Well, from time to time I'm useful to him in the same way a toothpick might be useful to a cannibal."

"You're worried he might eat you, too. Is that it?"

"Something like that."

"Perhaps if more people stood up to Heydrich, the way you stood up to that fat Labor leader?" She shrugged. "I don't know."

"You don't know Heydrich. People don't ever stand up to Heydrich for very long. Most often, they end up standing in front of a firing squad. If they're lucky."

"You're a bit like Faust, I suppose. And Heydrich is your Mephistopheles."

I nodded. "Except that I haven't had any of the pleasures of the world out of the deal. I didn't even get to seduce a beautiful and innocent girl. Gretchen, isn't it?"

"No. Arianne."

"You're hardly innocent."

"But I am beautiful."

"Yes. You are beautiful, angel. There's no doubt about that."

11

An hour later we were moving again and quickly through Bohemia, although from the number of Nazi flags and banners and German troops we saw, you would scarcely have been aware of this. And almost every Czech town we passed through had a new German name, so that it felt less like visiting a foreign country, or even an autonomous territory—which, strictly speaking is what a "protectorate" amounts to—and more like a colony.

We reached Prague in the late afternoon. According to my 1929 Austrian Baedeker—for some reason this edition included a section on Prague, as if it were still a city in the old Austro-Hungarian Empire—the hotel was just around the corner from Hibernerbahnhof, so we decided to walk there and, holding Arianne's bag and mine, I led the way through a tall archway and short colonnade of Doric pillars into a square entrance hall with a glass roof and a peeling maroon-and-gold plaster architrave that resembled something out of an abandoned villa in Pompeii. The hall was full of field gray uniforms, some of which eyed Arianne hungrily, like wolves. I didn't blame them in the least. She had a figure like a snake charmer's pipe. Arianne herself was not unconscious of this effect and, smiling happily, she put an extra couple of notes into the swaying and seductive melody of her walk.

It was less than a hundred meters to the end of the street where the Imperial Hotel was situated. The outside of the building was gray and quite unremarkable, but inside the place was a shrine to art nouveau. On the face of it this seemed at odds with the hotel's obvious popularity with the German Army, which isn't well known for its interest in art except of course when they're stealing it from some poor Jew for Göring's personal collection. On the walls of the small but impressive entrance-lobby was a creamy-colored ceramic relief featuring six classically dressed ladies exercising their pet lions. I knew they were classically dressed because they were wearing little gold circlets with asps on their heads and because they had bare breasts—a fashion of which generally I approve.

Breasts of women are a little hobby of mine, and while I know *why* I enjoy looking at them and touching them, it continues to elude me why I seem to like looking at them and touching them as much as I do.

As soon as I saw the hotel entrance-lobby and the huge café with its temple-tall mosaic pillars, I thought of the Ishtar Gate at Berlin's Pergamon Museum, and I suppose this might have been one reason the Imperial was a local favorite with the German Army. Then again, it might just have been because the hotel was also expensive. The Wehrmacht likes expensive hotels, and if it comes to that, then so do I. Since I first worked as the hotel detective at the Adlon, I have come to realize that I am very easily pleased: usually the best is good enough. Either way, the Imperial's café was full of soldiers, and their off-duty laughter, their off-color jokes, and their better—better than Berlin—cigarette smoke.

Our fifth-floor corner room had two windows. From one side there was a fine view of the southeast of Prague, which was mostly spires and smoking chimneys; from the other, to the west, you could see the rooftop immediately opposite, which had one of those pepper-pot domes made of oxidizing copper. It looked like a large green samovar.

Almost immediately we went to bed, which seemed like the sensible thing to do, as I had no idea of how soon Heydrich would summon me to his country house or for how long, and strenuous sex was something that had been on our minds ever since the train had left Berlin—although, to be more precise, it had probably been on my mind more than hers. Either way, she didn't have to be persuaded, very much. It was love, or at least a good imitation of it, on my part at least.

And then there was life, which of course is love's nemesis, sliding under the door in the shape of a brown envelope.

I rolled off Arianne's naked body and walked across the room to collect it.

Arianne rolled onto her belly, lit only her second cigarette of the day, and watched me read the note.

"Mephistopheles?"

"I'm afraid so. His driver will collect me first thing tomorrow morning, in front of the hotel."

"That certainly gives us plenty of time to do all kinds of things. Who knows, we might even find time to see the sights. I hear the Charles Bridge is worth a look."

"Is that what you'd like to do?"

"Not right now." She blew smoke at the ceiling and then gave me a narrow-eyed look. "Right now I just want some more of what I came for." She put down her cigarette and, lying back on the bed, opened her arms and then her thighs. "Everything else, you know, is just tourism, and I can do that on my own."

I threw Heydrich's note aside, climbed back onto the bed, and crawled between her thighs.

"But for this," she said, "I need help."

12

The general's driver was an SS sergeant who told me his name was Klein. He was a large, heavy man with fair hair, a high forehead, and an expressionless face. I soon learned he was also tight-lipped. When you worked for the Reichsprotector of Bohemia and Moravia, there was a lot to be tight-lipped about.

The car was a dark green Mercedes 320 convertible, and with its less than discreet number plate—SS-4—it was what Klein drove when Heydrich was not on official or state duties. For those, I soon learned, there was a larger model, a Mercedes 770. The 320 had an extra spotlight mounted on the front fender in case the general had to stop and interrogate someone at the side of the road. There was no flag on the wing, but that hardly made me feel any less obvious or insecure. Both of us were in uniform. The top was down. There was no armed escort. We were in enemy territory. To me it felt like visiting an Indian Thuggee village wearing a red coat and whistling "The British Grenadiers." And noting with some amusement my obvious discomfort, Klein explained that the general scorned any escort as a sign of weakness, which was why he preferred him to be driven around Prague with the top down.

"And how often do you drive him around Prague?"

"Between Prague Castle and the general's country house? Twice a day. Regular as sunrise."

"You're joking."

"Nope."

"With one of the Three Kings at liberty, that seems unwise to me."

We set off and I shrank back into the front passenger seat as a tall man standing beside the road snatched off his battered felt hat out of respect for who—but more probably what—we were. There was a lot of that in Prague. Because the Nazis liked this kind of thing. But I didn't like it at all, any more than I liked driving around with a three-color target painted on my chest; taking out my pistol, I worked the slide and dropped it into the leather pocket on the inside of the car door, from where it might be easily and quickly retrieved in an emergency.

Klein laughed. "What's that for?"

"Just ignore me, Sergeant. I was in Belorussia until the end of August. In Belorussia there are lots of Ivans who want to kill Germans. I assume the same holds true for almost any conquered country. Except perhaps France. I never felt unsafe in France."

"So why feel unsafe here?"

"To my ignorant ears at least, the Czech language sounds a lot like Russian. That's why."

"Then let me reassure you, sir. To attack this, or the general's other car, SS-3, would be to risk the most severe retribution. That's what the general says. And I believe him."

"But what do you think?"

Klein shrugged. "I think this is a fast car and the general likes me to drive fast."

"Yes, I noticed."

"I think you'd have to be damned lucky to ambush this car. And that, in the long run, would be very unlucky for the Czechos."

"And for the general, I'd have thought. Possibly you, too, Sergeant. Really, yours is not much of a threat, because it seems to me as if their bad luck is predicated on yours. It's like saying that if you drown, you'll make sure you take them with you. When they're dead, so are you."

We drove about fifteen kilometers northeast of the city center to a small village called Jungfern-Breschan. The Czechos called it Panenské Břežany, which is probably Czech for a very quiet village that's surrounded by a depressingly featureless landscape—just a lot of flat, recently plowed, and very smelly fields. The village itself was rather more quaint and picturesque as long as your idea of what was quaint and picturesque included a few checkpoints and the odd detachment of motorized SS. Anyone foolish enough to attack Heydrich's car would discover that the countryside afforded them little cover from these soldiers. A team of assassins at Jungfern-Breschan would have been caught or killed within minutes. Even so, I had to wonder why Heydrich had chosen to live out here, in the middle of nowhere, when he had at his disposal in the center of Prague a castle the size of the Kremlin, not to mention a handful of elegant Bohemian palaces. Maybe he was worried about defenestration. There was a lot of that kind of thing in Prague. I wouldn't have minded pushing Heydrich or any number of Nazis out of a high window myself.

We turned off the main highway and Klein steered the Mercedes down a gently sloping road that wound around to the right and then the left. There were trees now, and the air was strong with the smell of freshly mown grass and pine needles, and after the gray misery of Prague this felt like a place where it might be easier for Heydrich to escape from the cares of the world, even the ones he himself had inflicted or was planning to inflict. At Jungfern-Breschan, he might get away from it all, just as long as he didn't mind the several hundred SS stormtroopers who were there to protect his privacy.

A handsomely baroque pink stucco house came into view on our right. Behind a gated and guarded archway I counted six windows on the upper floor. It looked like a hunting lodge but I couldn't be sure. I'd rarely been hunting myself, and never for anything more elusive than a missing person, a murderer, or an errant wife, and it was hard to comprehend how anyone wanting to shoot a few pheasants also needed a matching Russian Orthodox chapel and a swimming pool in the grounds to be able to do it. Of course, it's always possible that if I'd prayed a bit more and learned to swim a bit better, I might have bagged the odd snipe or two myself.

"Is that General Heydrich's new house?"

"No. That's the Upper Castle. Von Neurath continues to live there. For the moment, anyway."

Konstantin von Neurath had been the Reichsprotector of Bohemia until Hitler decided he was too soft and gave the job to his blond butcher; but before that von Neurath had been the German foreign minister—a job now held by the most unpopular man in Germany, Joachim von Ribbentrop.

"There's an Upper Castle and a Lower Castle," explained Klein. "Both of them were owned by some Jewish sugar merchant. But when the Jew bastard took off in 1939, the estate was confiscated. The main house is the Lower Castle, farther down the hill. It's a nicer house."

"Doesn't the general mind? That the place used to be lived in by Jews?"

"Sir?"

"You've seen the movie newsreels," I said. "Those people carry diseases, don't they? Like rats."

Klein shot me a look as if he wasn't quite sure if I was serious, and decided, wrongly, that I was. To be fair to him, my sarcasm had a cautious ambivalence about it since coming back from Belorussia.

"No, it's all right," he insisted. "This merchant, he only owned the house since 1909. Originally, the house was owned by a German aristocrat who lost the place to the bank, who sold it to the

Jew at a knockdown price. And before either of them, the estate was owned by Benedictine monks."

"Well, you can't be less Jewish than a Benedictine monk, now, can you?"

Klein grinned stupidly and shook his head.

I was toying with the idea of asking how a man with a name like Klein got to be in the SS at all, let alone driving for Heydrich, when the larger gates of the Lower Castle came in sight. In front of the gateposts were a pair of stone statues that would have given any animal lover a moment's pause. One statue depicted a bear being torn to bits by a pair of hunting dogs; the other, a similarly beleaguered wild boar. But you could see how that sort of thing would have been appreciated by Heydrich, who was certainly the incarnation of Nature red in tooth and claw.

Beside the wild boar an SS soldier stepped out of his sentry box and came smartly to attention as our car turned into the gateway. At the end of a drive about fifty meters long was the Lower Castle itself. It was a modest little place, but only by the standards of Hermann Göring, or Mussolini, perhaps.

This "castle" was actually a late-nineteenth-century French-style château, but no less impressive for that, with sixteen windows on each of two well-proportioned floors, front and back. Unlike the pink stucco Upper Castle, the Lower Castle was canary yellow with a red roof, a square-tower portico painted white, and a central arched window about the same size as a U-Bahn tunnel. On the immaculate lawn was yet another piece of stone statuary: an enormous stag and two deer who were running away from the house. I took one look at the number of SS patrolling the grounds and felt like galloping away myself. With a couple of females in season for frolicsome company I might even have made it over the high wall.

Klein drew up at the front door and switched off the 320's three-liter four-stroke engine. As it cooled, it ticked away as if a family of mice were living underneath the two-and-half-meter-long hood.

For a moment I just sat there, looking up at the house, listening to the soothing coo of some pigeons and, it seemed, to the sound of someone not too far away who was shooting at them.

"Executions?" I said, retrieving my pistol from the door pocket.

Klein grinned. "Hunting. There's always something to shoot around here."

"Something, or someone?"

"I can get you a gun if you'd care to go out and bag something for the pot. We eat a lot of game here at the castle."

"Well, I always say, if you can't play the game properly, eat it. That reminds me. Who do I give my food coupons to?"

The Lower Castle didn't look like a food-coupon sort of place, but I said it anyway, just for the fun of it.

"You can forget about that sort of thing for a while. This is not like Berlin. There are no shortages of anything. The general lives very well out here in the countryside. Cigarettes, booze, chocolate, vegetarian. Anything you want. Just ask one of them."

Klein nodded in the direction of an approaching SS valet wearing a white mess jacket who opened my door and came smartly to attention.

"I'm beginning to see why he lives here. We're not just outside Prague. We're outside what counts as normal as well."

I stood up, returned the Hitler salute, and followed the valet inside the house.

The main hallway was two stories high, with a wrought-iron gallery and a large, ornate brass chandelier that looked like Dante, Beatrice and the Heavenly Host of Angels waiting around for an appointment with Saint Peter. Behind the heavy oak door was a long-case clock the size of a beech tree and which I quickly learned was about as good at keeping time. There was a big, round walnut wood table with a bronze of a mounted Amazon fighting a panther.

The panther was wrapped around the horse, which looked like a mistake when you took into account the Amazon's breasts. Then again, the Amazon had a spear in her hand, so maybe the panther knew what he was doing. There are some women who, no matter how good-looking they are, are best to leave well alone.

Across the hall and down a short flight of marble steps was a large room with tie-side Knoll sofas and a hardwood coffee table that might once have been a small Caribbean island. The only reason one might have assumed this was a room was if one assumed as well that somewhere farther than the human eye could see were more walls and windows and a door or two. There was a big, empty fireplace with brass fire dogs and a cast-iron screen that belonged on the door of a jail. Above this was a mantelpiece with a muscle-bound Atlas at each corner, and on the mantel itself several framed photographs of Hitler, Heydrich, Himmler, and a strongly featured blonde I assumed was Heydrich's wife, Lina. In another picture she and Heydrich were dressed in Tyrolean costume and playing with a baby; they all looked very German. And it was difficult not to think of those Atlases as two poor Czechs groaning under the burden of their new masters. Above the mantel was a large and unnecessarily well painted portrait of the Leader, who seemed to be staring up at the Lower Castle's gallery as if wondering when on earth someone was going to come down and inform him exactly what he was doing there. I had exactly the same feeling myself.

As my eyes gradually adjusted to the size of the place I saw, in the distance, a set of French windows and through them a lawn, some shrubberies and trees, and the clear blue sky that was the inevitable and very pleasant corollary of having no neighbors.

A tall butler wearing a tailcoat and a wing collar glided silently into the hall and bowed, giving me time enough to get a good look at his hair, which, like the deferential expression on his face, seemed to have been painted on his head. The Iron Cross first-class ribbon on his coat lapel was a nice touch, reminding everyone wearing a uniform that he, too, had done his bit in the trenches. He had a thick, jowly face and an even thicker beef soup of a voice.

"Welcome sir, to Jungfern-Breschan. I am Kritzinger, the butler. The general presents his compliments and asks you to join him for drinks on the terrace at twelve thirty p.m." He lifted one arm in the direction of the French windows, as if he had been directing traffic on Potsdamer Platz. "Please let me know if there's anything I can do to make your stay here more comfortable. Until then, if you'll come this way, I'll show you to your quarters."

My room, in the north wing, was larger and better appointed than I'd been expecting. There was a good-sized bed, a secretaire desk with three ebonized drawers for the clothes I had brought from the Imperial, a table chair, and a leather armchair that stood next to a fireplace that was laid but not lit. In the window was a folding tray table with a princely range of alcoholic drinks, chocolate, newspapers, and American cigarettes, and as soon as Kritzinger had made himself scarce, I set about throwing away my johnnies and filling my cigarette case. With a drink in my hand and a decent cigarette in my mouth, I inspected my principality in more detail.

On the desk was a Brumberg table lamp with a parchment shade, and on the floor a dull maroon Turkish kilim. There were some towels on the end of my bed and the door had a key and a bolt, for which I was grateful. Absurdly so. When you're in a house that's already full of murderers, it's perhaps foolish to think that locking your door is going to keep you safe. There were bars on the windows of the lower floor, but not on those of the upper floor. The window in my room, which had some sturdy brass bolts, had a fixed windowpane and two casements that opened out onto the back garden. There was a roller blind for summer and some thick red curtains for when the weather turned colder, as, in that part of the world, it always does.

I poked my head outside. The ground was about five or six

meters below the window ledge. At the center of a circular bed of flowers, a sprinkler was a whirling dervish of water and rhythm. Beyond that was a gravel path lined with neatly trimmed bushes and then a thick clump of trees. And on the lawn was another stone group of escaping deer, which was perhaps a pair to the one in the front garden.

I lay on my bed and finished my drink and smoked my cigarette. These did little to calm me. Being under the same roof as Heydrich made me nervous. I got up and poured myself another drink, which helped, but only a little. Whatever he wanted, I knew it wouldn't sit well with my already badly bruised conscience, and I resolved that when eventually he got around to explaining what it was, I would tell him, as politely as I could, to go to hell. There was no way I was ever going back to Belorussia to perform some loathsome act of genocide, and it really didn't matter if that meant being sent to a concentration camp. I wasn't the same as any of those other bastards in uniform. I wasn't even a Nazi. Perhaps they needed to be reminded of that. Perhaps it was time I repeated my allegiance to the old republic. If they were looking for an excuse to throw me out of the SD, then I would hand them one. Arianne was surely right: if more people stood up to Heydrich the way I'd stood up to the Labor leader on the train, then maybe things would change. More people would be dead, too, including myself, but that couldn't be helped. Lately that didn't seem so bad. That's what I told myself, anyway. It might have been the schnapps. And of course I wouldn't know for sure until the time came. But I knew it was going to take some courage on my part because I was also afraid. That's the only way I know that you can distinguish being brave from being stupid.

"THAT'S RATHER BEAUTIFUL, don't you think?"

I was looking at a dazzling modern picture of a dark-haired *femme fatale*. She was wearing a fabulous long dress, which seemed made of golden Argus eyes, all set against a radiantly primordial golden background. There was something terrifying about the woman herself. She looked like some remorseless Egyptian queen who had been made ready for eternity by a group of economists who were slaves to the gold standard.

"Unfortunately it's a copy. The original was stolen by that greedy fat bastard Hermann Göring and is now in his private collection, where nobody but him can see it. More's the pity."

I was in the Lower Castle library. Through the window I could see the back garden, where several SS and SD officers were already collected on the terrace. The officer speaking to me was about thirty, tall, thin, and rather effete. He had white-blond hair and a dueling scar on his face. The three pips on his black collar patch told me he was an SS-Hauptsturmführer—a captain, like me; and the monkey swing of silver braid on his tunic—properly called an aiguillette, but only by people who knew their way around a dictionary of military terms—indicated he was an aide-de-camp, most likely Heydrich's.

"Are you Dr. Ploetz?" I asked.

"Good God, no." He clicked his heels. "Hauptsturmführer Albert Kuttner, fourth adjutant to General Heydrich, at your service. No, you'll know when you meet Ploetz, it will feel like someone left a freezer door open."

"Cold, huh?"

"I've met warmer glaciers."

"How many adjutants does he have?"

"Oh, just the four. A man for each season. There's myself. Captains Pomme and Kluckholm. And Major Ploetz, who's the chief adjutant. You'll have the great pleasure of meeting them all while you're here."

"I can't wait."

Kuttner smiled a knowing smile, as if he and I were already occupying the same forbidden radio frequency. "And you, I assume, must be Captain Gunther." He shook his head. "The Berlin accent. It's quite unmistakable. By the way, the general doesn't go in for the Hitler salute very much, while we're here at the castle."

"That suits me. I don't go in for Hitler salutes much myself."

"Yes. The general likes to keep things very informal. So mess rules apply. No belts worn." He nodded at my crossbelt. "That kind of thing."

"Thanks," I said, unbuckling the crossbelt I was wearing.

"Also, it's fine to introduce yourself with your SS rank but, after that, do try not to use SS ranks when describing yourself or a brother officer. Army ranks or surnames save time. The general's very keen on saving time. He often says that while we delay, time does not, and that lost time is never found again. Very true, what?"

"He's always been very quotable, the general. You must try to write some of these sayings down. For the sake of posterity."

Kuttner shook his head. It seemed he wasn't quite on my own frequency, after all.

"That wouldn't do at all. The general hates people writing down what he says. It's an idiosyncrasy he has."

I smiled. "It's evidence, that's what it is."

Kuttner smiled back. "Yes, I see what you mean. Very good. Very good."

"I guess that's why he has four adjutants," I added. "To help keep everything off the record."

"Yes, I hadn't thought of that. But you could be right."

I turned back to the golden picture in front of us. "Who is she, anyway?"

"Her name is Adele Bloch-Bauer and her husband, Ferdinand, used to own this house. A Jew, which makes you wonder why Göring likes her so much. But there it is. Consistency is not his strong suit, I'd say. It's a nice copy, of course, but I think it a great pity that the original isn't in the house, where it truly belongs.

We're trying to persuade the Reichsmarshal to give it back, but so far without much success. He's like a dog with a bone when it comes to paintings, I believe. Anyway, one can easily see why he likes it so much. To say that Frau Bloch-Bauer looked like a million marks hardly seems to do her portrait justice. Wouldn't you agree?"

I nodded and allowed myself another look, not at the painting but at Captain Kuttner. For a man who was Heydrich's adjutant, his free and frank opinions seemed to veer toward the dangerous. A bit like my own. It was clear we had more in common than just a uniform and a keen appreciation of modern art.

"It's different," I allowed.

"Superficially stylish, perhaps. But somehow even a copy is deeper than the gold paint, which seems almost to have been spilled onto the canvas. Eh?"

"You sound like Bernard Berenson, Captain Kuttner."

"Lord, don't say that. At least not within earshot of the general. Berenson's a Jew."

"What happened to her anyway?" I lit a cigarette. "To the golden lady in the picture?"

"Sad to say, and rather ingloriously, given how she looks in this painting, the poor woman died of meningitis in 1925. Still, that might turn out to be just as well, when one considers what is happening to Jews in this country. And in her native Austria."

"And Ferdinand? Her husband?"

"Oh, I've no idea what happened to him. And I don't much care, quite frankly. He sounds like your typical grasping Jewish merchant, and he quite wisely cleared off the minute we walked into the Sudetenland. But I do know that the artist—another Austrian named Gustav Klimt—died at the beginning of the influenza epidemic in 1918, poor fellow. But he was a frequent guest here, I believe. Adele was rather fond of old Klimt, by all accounts. Perhaps a bit too fond. Funny to think of them all here, isn't it? Especially now that General Heydrich owns the house. *O quam cito transit gloria mundi.*"

I nodded but said nothing. While the eccentric young adjutant seemed to be a cut above the average SD automaton, I wasn't in the mood to mention the loss of my own wife to the influenza epidemic: if Klimt had been an early victim, my wife had been one of the very last to die of flu, in December 1920. Besides, there was something just a bit unpredictable about Captain Kuttner that made me wonder how someone like Heydrich could tolerate him. Then again, the general also managed, somehow, to tolerate me, and that spoke either of his enormous tolerance—which seemed improbable—or his enormous cynicism.

Kuttner tried and failed to stifle a yawn.

"The general working you late, is he?"

"Sorry. No, actually I'm just not sleeping very well. Hardly at all, if I'm honest."

"He has the same effect on me. I've hardly slept a wink since I received his kind invitation to Prague. And it's not from excitement, either."

"Really?" Kuttner sounded surprised.

"Really."

"You surprise me. Actually he's been very understanding of my situation. Very understanding. He even referred me to his own doctor. He gave me something called Veronal, which is quite effective. For sleeping. Although you have to be careful not to mix it with alcohol."

"Then I'd better make sure I never take any." I grinned. "I'm usually very careful never to let anything stand in the way of my drinking. But what I meant was that the general's reputation goes before him. He's not exactly Mohandas K. Gandhi, is he? And I might sleep a little better, knowing exactly why the hell I'm here. I don't suppose you can shed any light on that, can you? In the same thoughtful and well-informed way that you have illuminated this picture for me."

Kuttner scratched the dueling scar on his cheek. He seemed to do it when he was nervous, which was often.

"It was my understanding that you and the general were friends."

"If you mean like 'a friend in need is a friend to be avoided,' then, yes, we're friends. But I guess the friends we have are probably the friends we deserve."

"You do surprise me, Commissar Gunther."

"Well, maybe you've put your finger on it, Captain. Maybe I'm supposed to be the licensed jester here, to make everyone else but the general feel uncomfortable. Knowing Heydrich as I do, I can easily see how that might amuse him."

"I can assure you that what you say simply cannot be the case. Most of the people here this weekend are the general's most intimate friends. And he's gone to considerable trouble to make sure that everyone enjoys himself. Good food, excellent wine, fine brandies, the best cigars. Perhaps it's just you who is supposed to feel uncomfortable, Commissar."

"That is always possible. The general always did like what the English call a Roman holiday. Where one man suffers for the pleasure of others."

Kuttner was shaking his head. "Please let me reassure you, Gunther. I was joking, just now. Your fears are entirely without foundation. The general was most anxious that you should be comfortable. He chose your quarters himself. He chose everyone's quarters. Including my own. I've known the general for quite a while now, off and on, and I can attest to his generosity and thoughtfulness. He's not at all the capricious, cruel man that you seem to know. Really."

"Yes, I'm sure you're right, Captain." I nodded at the *femme fatale* in gold. "All the same, I wonder if the unfortunate sugar merchant's wife would agree with you."

IT WAS ONE OF THOSE early October afternoons that made you think winter was just a word and that there was no earthly reason why the sun should ever stop shining. The flowers in the Lower Castle's well-tended beds were mostly pink dahlias, white asters, and red marigolds, providing a riot of autumn color—which was the only kind of riot that the SS was likely to tolerate. The lawn was as green and smooth as a python's eyeball. Crystal glasses clinked, heels clicked, and somewhere someone was playing a piano. A soft breeze in the trees sounded like an enormous silk dress. They had turned off the sprinklers, but there was strawberry cup with real strawberries and delicious Sekt, so I managed to get nicely wet all the same.

About eighteen of us went in for lunch. With only another four we could have tossed a coin for kickoff. The white tablecloth was as stiff as a sail on a frozen schooner and there was enough silver on it for an army of conquistadores. Otherwise things were informal, as Captain Kuttner had promised, and I was glad we had abandoned cross belts, as the food was as spectacular as it was plentiful: pea soup with real peas and bacon, liver dumplings with real liver and real onions, Holstein schnitzel with real veal, a real egg, and real anchovies served with a real Leipziger everything. I hardly had room for the real strudel and the real cheese that followed. The wines were equally impressive. There was a box on the table for food coupons, but no one was paying any attention to that, and I figured it was just for show. I looked at it and wondered about the two Fridmann sisters in the apartment beneath mine back in Berlin and how they were getting on with the canned food I'd given them, but mostly I just kept on filling the hole in my face with food and wine and cigarette smoke. I didn't say much. There wasn't much need to say anything very much. Everyone paid close attention to Heydrich's table talk, which was the usual Nazi twaddle, and it was only when he started talking about the stupidity of trying to turn Czechs into Germans that I gave my jaws a rest and let my ears take over:

"People of good race and good intentions, they will be Germanized. Those we can't Germanize and educate to think differently from the way they think now, we'll have to put up against the wall. The rest—that's potentially at least half the population of Bohemia and Moravia—will have to be moved out and resettled in the East, where they can live out their miserable days in Arctic Labor camps. However, whenever we can, we must act with fairness. When all is said and done, the Czechs should be made to see the advantages of cooperation over opposition. And when the current state of emergency has ended, I will increase the local food ration and do everything in my power to hunt down black-market profiteers."

There was a lot more of this guff, and I looked at the fat faces of my fellow officers to see if anyone felt the same way about it that I did, but I saw only consent and agreement. Probably they looked at me and thought the same thing.

Among the faces there was only one, apart from Heydrich's long, thin witch doctor's mask, that I recognized, and this belonged to the former foreign minister and ex-Reichsprotector, Konstantin von Neurath. At almost seventy, he was the oldest person at the table and easily the most deserving of respect. Not that his ambitious young successor, Heydrich, accorded him much of this. From time to time he would pat the old man on the hand like a pet dog and speak to him in a louder voice, as if the baron were deaf, although it was quite plain to anyone who had talked to him that there was nothing at all wrong with his hearing. I suspected that von Neurath was present only to make the new Reichsprotector's triumph complete.

Heydrich avoided conversation with me until well after we had risen from the table and were out on the terrace again with brandies and cigars—or in my case, coffee and cigarettes. It was there that he caught my eye and, having walked me down the Upper Castle's back garden, finally explained the point of my being there.

"You remember our conversation at my office in Berlin, the day we defeated the French. In June 1940."

"I remember it very well. How could I forget the day when Germany defeated France? So that's what this is all about."

"Yes. Again, someone is trying to kill me."

I shrugged. "Any number of Czechos must want you dead, sir. I assume that we're not discussing one of them."

"Naturally."

"Has there been a recent attempt on your life?"

"You mean, am I imagining this?"

"All right, then. Are you?"

"No. There was an attempt made to kill me just days ago. A serious attempt."

"When, where and how?"

"At the Wolf's Lair. Hitler's own field headquarters, in East Prussia. Yes, I thought that would surprise you. As a matter of fact I was surprised myself. It was September twenty-fourth. I had been summoned to Rastenburg to be told by Hitler that he was appointing me as von Neurath's successor, here in Bohemia. Well, that's the when and where. The how is that someone tried to poison me. Toxicologists in the SD's laboratories are still trying to isolate the particular substance that was used. However, they're inclined to believe that it may have been a protein-based toxin called botulinum. From Latin *botulus*, meaning 'sausage.'"

"That sounds especially lethal, for a German."

"It's a bacterium that often causes poisoning by growing in improperly handled meat. I might have assumed it was just a simple case of food poisoning were it not for the fact that some of our

SS doctors have been trying to synthesize it and other antibiotic compounds, such as sulfanilamide. As a means of treating wound infection. But also as a compound neurotoxin. Or to put it another way, as a poison."

"Perhaps it was a simple case of food poisoning," I said. "Have you considered that possibility?"

"I've considered it. And I've rejected it. You see, mine was the only food that was contaminated. Fortunately I wasn't hungry and didn't eat. Instead I fed the food off my plate to Major Ploetz's dog, which subsequently died. Obviously the Leader could not have been the target, because he is vegetarian. Naturally, all inquiries that could be made without alarming the Leader were made; and all of the foreign workers at the Wolf's Lair were replaced, as a precaution. But so far, nothing has been discovered that sheds any light on who was responsible for the incident. And there I feel we have to leave the matter. At least as far as Rastenburg is concerned. As I say, I have no wish to alarm or embarrass the Leader. But here in Prague I am able to take other precautions. You, Gunther, are to be one of these precautions, if you agree."

"So you want me to do what? Be your food taster?" I shrugged. "You should have mentioned this before lunch. I'd have sat beside you."

Heydrich shook his head.

"Keep a lookout for someone who might be trying to kill you? Is that it?"

"Yes. In effect I want you to be my personal bodyguard," said Heydrich.

"You mean you have four adjutants and no bodyguard?"

"Klein, my driver, is quite capable of pulling out a gun and shooting at some witless Czecho. As am I. But I want someone around me who understands murder and murderers, and who can handle himself to boot. A proper detective who is trained to be suspicious."

"The Gestapo isn't known to be naïve, in my experience."

"I want someone who is usefully suspicious as opposed to officious."

"Yes, I see the difference."

"And since I can't offer the position to Hercule Poirot, naturally I thought of you."

"Hercule Poirot?"

Heydrich shook his head. "A fictional detective created by an English lady novelist. It doesn't matter. You're obviously not a reader. He's very popular. And so is she."

I shook my head. "You know that most bodyguards are supposed to care about what happens to their employers, don't you?"

Heydrich grinned. This didn't happen very often, and when it did, his youngish, beaky face looked more like a nasty schoolboy's.

"Meaning you're not qualified, is that it?"

"Something like that."

"I can get any number of yes-men from the SD," said Heydrich. "The trouble is, will they be honest with me? Will they tell me unpalatable truths? What I need to know? And can I trust them?"

"It's true, sir. Without a gun in my hand, you're not an easy man to contradict."

"You I've known for five years. I know you're not Himmler's man. I know you're not even a Nazi. I know you probably hate my guts. But while you almost certainly dislike me, I don't believe you would actually murder me. In other words, I can trust you, Gunther; trust you not to kill me; and trust you to tell me those unpleasant truths that others would shrink from. That seems to me essential for what I need from a bodyguard.

"Of course, in many ways you're a fool. Only a fool would continue to remain in the police without joining the Party. Only a fool would remain sentimental about the Weimar Republic. Only a fool could fail to see that the new Germany cannot be resisted. But I have to admit, you're a clever and resourceful fool. I can use that. Most important of all, you're a damned good policeman. If you become my detective, you'll have a room here at the Lower Castle, your own car, and an office at Hradschin Castle, in the city. From time to time you'll even get to see that charming little whore you brought with you from Berlin. What's her name? Arianne, isn't it?"

That surprised me, although I suppose it ought not to have done; not much happened in Prague that Heydrich didn't know about.

"Frankly, I'm not at all sure what she sees in you. The sort of woman who goes to the Jockey Bar is usually looking for someone with a bit more vitamin B than you have, Gunther. Of course, that particular disadvantage will be quickly remedied if you agree to take this position. Suddenly your status will be improved. You'll forgive me for saying so, but this is an important job."

Throughout our conversation Heydrich's long, thin pianist's hands were deep in the pockets of his uniform's riding breeches, and this seemed to make his bandy horseman's legs even more U-shaped than normal. Now he pulled them out, and from the pocket of his fart catcher—an SD service tunic covered with so many gold and silver badges it looked more like a priest's reliquary—he produced a small silver cigarette case and offered me one. "Smoke?"

"Thank you, sir."

Finding a match, I lit us both.

"So what do you say?"

"Just how honest do you want me to be, General? Imprudently honest? Unflinchingly honest? Or just brutally honest? And what's in it for me apart from some more vitamins in my otherwise lousy diet? One of those opinion reflectors on your breast pocket if I manage to keep you alive? Or a one-way ticket on the partisan express if I don't?"

"Whenever we're alone you can say whatever the hell you want.

At least on matters concerning my personal security. In fact I'm counting on it. On everything else—politics, government, racial policy—your stupid republican opinions are of no interest to me and you'll have to keep your trap shut. As for what's in it for you, I should have thought that was obvious. You'll have free board and lodging, of course. And look around. We Germans live well here in Bohemia. Better than in Berlin. Good food, good wine, plenty of cigarettes and women—should your tastes run to more than one woman at a time. I know mine do. It's all to be had here in Prague. And if I am unlucky enough to be murdered by our own side, all I ask is that you present the evidence to Arthur Nebe or Walter Schellenberg. Between them, they'll find some way of putting it in front of Martin Bormann."

"All right, General. But here's my price. That you have to listen, now, to some of those stupid republican views that you mentioned. The ones regarding politics and government and racial policy you said are of no interest to you. I'll say my piece and you listen. And when I've done, I'll do what you ask. I'll be your detective."

Heydrich's eyes narrowed. I preferred his profile. When you saw his profile it meant he wasn't looking at you. When he looked at you, it was only too easy to feel like the helpless prey of some deadly animal. It was a face without expression behind which some ruthless calculation was in progress. He flicked away his half-smoked cigarette and glanced at the Rolex on his wrist.

"All right. You've got five minutes. But it won't do any good, you know. When the panzers have finished their work in Russia, what you say now will seem quite irrelevant. Even to you, Gunther. Even to you. We'll make a Nazi of you yet."

AFTER LUNCH Heydrich and Generals Frank, Henlein, Hildebrandt, and von Eberstein, a couple of colonels, and three of the adjutants convened a meeting in the castle library, leaving me and some others to amuse ourselves. Which is probably overstating what I was likely to do.

I was feeling tired, due to a combination of good wine and the adrenaline that was still in my blood after telling Heydrich what I really thought about his aim of Germanizing the Czech population, as well as several words on what was happening in Belorussia. True to his word, Heydrich listened for exactly five minutes, after which he walked silently back to the house, leaving me feeling like a novitiate toreador who has just taunted his first bull. Perhaps I was still a little suicidal. It's the only possible explanation for what I'd done.

For a while I contemplated returning to my room and having a sleep; I also contemplated returning to the Imperial Hotel and spending what remained of my life with Arianne, but I was unable to find Klein or anyone who could organize me a car and, mindful of the warm sunshine, I went for a walk in the castle grounds instead.

Naturally, I was unnerved by how much Heydrich already seemed to know about Arianne. But, more important, I was already regretting my candor with him, which I attributed to the amount of alcohol I had consumed during lunch. And I asked myself how long it would be before a couple of SS guards came and fetched me for execution at some pit that even now was being dug in the adjacent forest. That was surely one advantage of living in the countryside: there was always plenty of space to bury a body.

Half convinced that this was to be my fate, I found myself heading out of the front gates, smiling a nervous smile at the stone-faced sentry and then setting off up the fairy-tale road in the general direction of the Upper Castle. This wasn't exactly an escape, but I needed to be away from my so-called colleagues.

Thinking about escape, I got to wondering about Ferdinand Bloch-Bauer, the Jewish sugar merchant whose estate this had once been. Were the statues placed at the gates by him, or by the aristocrat who had owned the house before? And where was he now? England? America? Switzerland? Or was he one of those unfortunate Czech Jews who'd fled to France, thinking it was safe there, only to find it overrun with Nazis in 1940? Time would tell who had been luckier—Ferdinand or his late wife, Adele.

Farther along the quiet road, the Orthodox chapel came into view, and as I rounded the bend I saw the matching pink gateway of the Upper Castle and, walking toward me, another SS officer—a general whom I recognized from lunch but whose name eluded me. I wasn't wearing a cap or belts, and neither was he, which meant I was able to forgo a salute. All the same, I came to attention as he got nearer. I'd irritated enough SS generals for one day.

Even in uniform, this general was a poor example of the master race. A bespectacled Himmler type with thinning hair, with a wide mouth and a double chin, he was one of those pale, bloodless Nazis that reminded me of a very cold fish on a very white plate. Nevertheless, he smiled and stopped to talk, rippling his fingers in the air as though playing the upper register of a church organ as he tried to remember who I was.

"Ah, yes, now, you're—"

"Hauptsturmführer Gunther, sir."

"Yes. Now I have it. You're the police commissar from Berlin, are you not? The Kripo detective."

"That's right, sir."

"I'm Jury, Dr. Hugo Jury. No reason why you should remember me, either, especially after a lunch like that, eh? I'll say one thing for our new Reichsprotector—he knows how to entertain. That's the best lunch I've eaten in God knows how long."

Jury was an Austrian, his accent—or rather his vocabulary—unmistakably Viennese.

"Walk with me for a while if you will, Captain. I'd like to hear more about the exciting life of a real Berlin detective."

"If you like, sir. But there's not much to tell. I'm forty-three years old. I got my school certificate but didn't go to university. The war got in the way, and then there didn't seem to be much call for a degree when there was a more urgent call to make a living and earn some money. So I joined the police and got married to a woman who died almost immediately afterward. Influenza, they called it, but these days I'm not so sure. A lot of different illnesses got swept into that bin by a lot of overworked doctors and by some who were maybe not so much overworked as just inexperienced or even incompetent."

"And you'd be absolutely right to have doubts. I should know. You see, I'm not one of these legal doctors we seem to be overrun with these days. I'm a medical man. I took my degree in 1911, and chances are that I was one of those overworked, inexperienced, and very possibly incompetent doctors you were talking about. During the influenza epidemic I remember sleeping for less than four hours a night. Hardly a recipe for good medical care, is it? Throughout the twenties I was a specialist in tuberculosis. TB's one of those infectious diseases that present a lot of symptoms that are common to influenza. Indeed, I've sometimes thought that what we thought was a flu virus was actually pneumonia brought on by a massive outbreak of TB. But that's another story."

"I'd like to hear it sometime."

"If I may ask, how old was she? Your wife?"

"Twenty-two."

"I'm sorry. That's young. Very young. And you've never remarried?"

"Not so far, sir. Most women don't seem to find my being a Berlin detective as exciting as you."

"I've been married for almost thirty years and I can't imagine what I'd have done without my wife, Karoline."

"You'll forgive me for saying so, sir, but I can't imagine you're an SS general because you're a doctor, sir."

"No. I'm the district leader of Moravia. And head of the Party

Liaison Office in Prague. Before the war I was deputy leader of the Nazi Party in Austria. And if all of that sounds important, well, it isn't. Not any longer. Not since General Heydrich took over. I had hoped to persuade the Leader to break up the protectorate in order that Moravia could become a separate state. Which is really what it's always been. But that isn't going to happen. Or so I've been told. I had also hoped to be able to discuss the matter with Heydrich, but one of his minions told me that this wouldn't be possible. Which leaves me rather wondering why I bothered to come along on this little weekend. Under the circumstances, I'm surprised that I was asked at all."

"That makes two of us, sir. General Heydrich and I were never what you might call close. Then again, one hesitates to decline such an invitation."

"Quite so."

By now we were about halfway back down the road to the Lower Castle, and during our stroll no traffic had passed us, not even a man on a bicycle or a horse. Somewhere in the distance, shots were being fired; presumably one of Heydrich's guests was trying to bag something for the pot. There were certainly plenty of pheasants about. Up ahead we saw Captain Kuttner standing in the Lower Castle gateway; seeing us, he threw down his cigarette and ran toward us.

He was light on his toes; but there was also something vaguely girlish about his elbows-out way of running.

"I loathe this little bastard," murmured Dr. Jury. "This is the cunt who told me I wasn't going to be able to have any time with General Heydrich." Jury let out a sigh. "Just look at him. Little fucker."

"Hmm."

"Like all of the general's henchmen, he's a bit of a golem. Except that he's a German, of course. The original Golem of Prague was—"

"Jewish. Yes, I know."

"Like his master." Dr. Jury smiled. "Rabbi Loew, that is. Not General Heydrich."

Kuttner clicked his heels and bowed a curt little bow. "General," he said. "Captain. I regret forgetting to inform you both that for security reasons if you leave the grounds of the Lower Castle, you will need a password to get back in."

"And that is?" asked Dr. Jury.

"Lohengrin."

"Very appropriate."

"Sir?"

"The new king has assembled all of the German tribes in order to expel the Hungarians from his dominions," said Dr. Jury. "That's the plot of Wagner's opera. Or at least, that's how it begins."

"Oh. I didn't know. Unlike you, sir, I don't go to the opera very often. In fact, hardly at all."

"Hmm. Waste of a life."

"Sir?"

"You seem to be as ignorant as you are stupid," said Jury. Then he smiled at me, bowed slightly, and said, "Nice talking to you, Captain Gunther."

He walked quickly down toward the sentry box and then, having uttered the password, passed through the gate, leaving me alone with Captain Kuttner.

"Bastard," said Kuttner. "Did you hear what he said? How unbelievably rude."

"I wouldn't let it bother you, Captain. I don't much like opera, either. Especially Wagner. There's something about Wagner that's just too piss-German, too fucking Bavarian for a Prussian like me. I like my music to be every bit as vulgar as I am myself. I like a bit of innuendo and stocking-top when a woman's singing a song."

Kuttner smiled. "Thanks," he said. "But the real reason why

Dr. Jury likes opera so much is every bit as vulgar as you describe. Rumor has it that he's been having an affair with a young singer at the Deutsche Oper in Berlin. Rather an attractive creature by the name of Elisabeth Schwarzkopf. And that would be vulgar enough were it not for the fact that she's also singing a duet with Dr. Goebbels. At least that's what General Heydrich says."

"Then it must be true."

"Yes, that's what I thought."

"General Heydrich always knows our dirtiest little secrets."

"Oh God, I hope not."

"Well, he certainly knows mine," I said. "You see, after lunch we went for a short walk in the castle grounds and I made the mistake of reminding him exactly what they are, just in case he'd forgotten."

"I hardly think that can be true. Not if he's appointed you as his new bodyguard." Kuttner lit a cigarette. "Is it true? That you're going to be his detective?"

"I had thought I might have been arrested by now. So it would seem so."

"Congratulations."

"I'm not so sure about that."

"You're right, it won't be easy. But he's fair, you know. And a good man to have on your side. I don't know what would have happened to my SS career if he hadn't taken me on. By the way, how's your stomach for flying?"

"Not good."

"What a pity. The general insists on flying himself to Berlin and Rastenburg. Frankly, I'm always terrified. He thinks he's a much better pilot than he really is. He's had several crashes."

"That's a comforting thought." I shrugged. "Perhaps we'll get lucky and end up in Scotland. Like Hess."

"Yes. Quite." Kuttner laughed. "Still, I hate to think what would happen if we ever flew into some real trouble."

"As a matter of fact, that's what I was doing just now. Looking for trouble. I thought I'd get out of the house and scout the area."

Kuttner winced, noticeably.

"The lie of the land, so to speak," he said.

"Yes. Generally, trouble sort of comes looking for me, so I don't have to venture too far. I've always been lucky that way."

"Quite a few of us in the SS have been lucky that way, don't you think?" Kuttner sighed a faint sigh of regret. "With trouble. Frankly, I've had a bit of a rough summer."

"You've been east, too, huh?"

Kuttner nodded. "How did you know?"

I shrugged. "I look at you and maybe I see something of myself."

"Yes. That must be it."

"Where were you posted?"

"Riga."

"I was in Belorussia."

"How was that?"

"Loathsome. And Riga?"

"The same. And really quite unnecessary, a lot of it. You go to war, you expect to kill people. I was almost looking forward to it, to being in action. When one is young, one has such romantic ideas of what war is like. But it was nothing like that, of course."

"No. It never is."

Kuttner tried to smile, but the part he needed inside himself to make the smile work properly was broken. He knew it. And I knew it.

"It's an odd state of affairs, don't you think, when a man feels guilty for doing his duty and obeying orders?" He took a sharp drag of the cigarette he was smoking as if he hoped it might suddenly kill him. "Not that guilt even begins to cover the way I feel."

"Believe me, Captain, I know exactly how you feel."

"Do you? Yes. I can see that you do. It's in your eyes."

"And that's the reason you're not sleeping?"

"Can you?" Kuttner shook his head. "I don't think I'll ever sleep, properly, again. Not ever. Not in this life."

"Talk about it now, if it makes you feel any better."

"Does it make you feel any better? To talk about it?"

"Not much. I talked about it once, quite recently, to an American journalist. And I felt a little better about it. I felt that it was at least a start."

Kuttner nodded and then dredged up something from his memory. I didn't have to wait long.

"When you mentioned scouting the area, it made me think of something. Something awful. We were on our way through Poland. This was before our assignment in Riga. We had stopped at a town called Chechło. It's a broken-down, shit-on-your-shoes, nowhere sort of place with a lot of drooling peasants whose tongues are too big for their mouths. But I don't suppose I shall ever forget it now; not for as long as I live. We had been burning down Polack villages for no real reason that I could see. Certainly there was no military necessity in it. We were just throwing our weight around like brutes. Some of my men were drunk and nearly all of them were animals. Anyway, we came across a troop of Polish boy scouts. The oldest of them couldn't have been more than sixteen and the youngest perhaps as young as twelve. And my commanding officer ordered me to put all of them up against a wall and shoot them. Shoot them all. They were in uniform, he said, and we have orders to shoot anyone in uniform who hasn't surrendered. I said they were just schoolboys who didn't know any better because they didn't speak German, but he didn't want to know. Orders are orders, he said, get on with it. I remember their mothers screaming at me to stop. Yes, I'll always remember that. I wake up sometimes, still hearing them beg me to stop. But I didn't. I had my orders. So I carried them out, you see. And that's all there is to it. Except it isn't, of course. Not by a long way."

After several stiff drinks I can talk to anyone, even to myself. But mostly I was drinking so that I could talk to Heydrich's other guests. I like to talk. Talking is something you need to do if you're ever going to encourage a man to talk back at you. And you need a man to talk a little if he's ever going to say something of interest. Men don't trust other men who don't say much, and for the same reason they don't trust men who don't drink. You need a drink to say the wrong thing, and sometimes saying the wrong thing can be exactly the right thing to say. I don't know if I was expecting to hear anything as romantic as a confession to an attempted murder, or even a desire to see Heydrich dead. After all, I felt that way about him myself. It was just talk, a little bread on the water to bring the fish around. And the alcohol helped. It helped me to talk and to anaesthetise myself against the more revolting chat that came my way. But some of my colleagues were just revolting. As I glanced around the library it was like looking at a menagerie of unpleasant animals—rats, jackals, vultures, hyenas—who had sat for some bizarre group portrait.

It's hard to say exactly who was the worst of the bunch, but I didn't speak to Lieutenant Colonel Walter Jacobi for very long before I was itching all over and counting my fingers. The deputy head of the SD in Prague was a deeply sinister figure, with—he told me—an interest in magic and the occult. It was a subject I knew a little about, having investigated a case involving a fake medium a few years back. We talked about that and we talked about Munich, which was where he was from; we talked about his studying law at the universities of Jena, Tübingen, and Halle—which seemed like a lot of law; and we even talked about his father, who was a bookseller. But all the time we were talking I was trying to get over the fact that with his Charlie Chaplin mustache, wire-framed glasses, and praying-mantis personality, Jacobi reminded me, obscenely, of what might have resulted if Hitler and Himmler had been left alone in the same bedroom: Jacobi was a Hitler-Himmler hybrid.

Equally unpleasant to talk to was Karl-Hermann Frank, the tall, thin SS general from the Sudetenland who'd been passed over to succeed von Neurath as the new Reichsprotector. Frank had a glass eye, having lost the real one in a fight at school in Carlsbad, which seemed to indicate an early propensity to violence. It was the right eye that was fake, I think, but with Frank, you had the idea he might have changed it around just to keep you guessing. Frank had a low opinion of Czechs, although as things turned out, they had an even lower opinion of him: five thousand people filled the court-yard of Pankrác Prison in the center of Prague to see him hanged the old Austrian Empire way one early summer's day in 1946.

"They're a greedy barbarous people," he told me candidly. "I don't feel the least bit Czech. The best thing that ever happened to me was to be born in the German-speaking part of the country, otherwise I'd be speaking their filthy Slavic language now, which is nothing more than a bastardized form of Russian. It's a language for animals, I tell you. Do you know that it's possible to speak a whole sentence in Czech without using a single vowel?"

Surprised at this startling display of hatred, I blinked and said, "Oh? Like what, for example?"

Frank thought for a moment and then repeated some words in Czech that might or might not have had some vowels, only I didn't feel like looking inside his mouth to see if he was hiding any.

"It means 'stick a finger through your throat,'" he said. "And every time I hear a Czech speak, that's exactly what I want to do to him."

"All right. You hate them. I get the picture. And losing your eye at school like that must have been pretty tough. It explains a lot, I guess. I went to a pretty tough school myself and there are some boys I might like to get even with one day. Then again, probably not. Life's too short to care, I think. And now you're in such an important position, sir—the police leader in Bohemia, effectively the second most powerful man in the country—well, that's the part I don't understand at all, sir. Why do you hate the Czechs so much, General?"

Frank straightened absurdly. It was almost as if he were coming to attention before answering—an effect enhanced by the fact that he was wearing spurs on his boots, which to me seemed an odd affectation, even in Heydrich's country home, which had stables, with horses in them. Pompously, he said, "As Germans it's our duty to hate them. It was the failure of the Czech banks that helped to precipitate the financial crisis that brought about the Great Depression. Yes, it's the Czech bankers we can thank for that disaster."

Resisting my first instinct, which was to shiver with disgust as if Frank had vomited onto my boots, I nodded politely.

"I always thought that was because our economy was built on American loans," I said. "And when they came due, our own German banks failed."

Frank shook his head, full of gray hair combed straight back so that the top of his head seemed in a line with the tip of his longish nose. It wasn't the biggest nose in the room as long as Heydrich was around, but at the same time you wouldn't have been surprised to see it pointing out the way at a crossroads.

"Take it from me, Gunther," he said. "I do know what I'm talking about. I know this damnable country better than anyone in the fucking room."

Frank spoke with some vigor and he was looking at Heydrich as he did, which made me wonder if there was not some grudge he nursed for his new master.

I was glad when Frank walked away to fetch himself another drink, leaving me with the impression that spending an eternity with men like Heydrich, Jacobi, and Frank was the nearest thing to being in hell that I could think of.

But the Knight's Cross with Oak Leaves and Berries—for that

matter the whole damned tree—for the curling turd of the evening went to Colonel Dr. Hans Ulrich Geschke, a thirty-four-year-old lawyer from Frankfurt on the Oder who was chief of the Gestapo in Prague. While studying in Berlin, he'd seen my name in the newspapers, and in spite of our differences in rank, this was a good enough reason for him to try to make common cause with me. Which is another way of saying he need someone to patronize.

"After all," he explained, "we're both policemen, you and I, doing a difficult job, in very difficult circumstances."

"So it would seem, sir."

"And I like to keep abreast of ordinary crime," he said. "Here in Prague we have to deal with more serious stuff than some Fritz slicing his wife up with a broken beer bottle."

"There's not so much of that around, sir. Beer bottles are in rather short supply in Berlin."

He wasn't listening.

"You should come in and see us very soon, at the Peček Palace. That's in the Bredovska district of the city."

"A palace, eh? It sounds a lot grander than the Alex, sir."

"Oh no. To be quite honest with you, it's hard to see how it was ever a palace except in some dark corner of Hades. Even the executive rooms have very little charm."

Geschke's was a waxwork's expressionless face. Captain Kuttner had said that at the Peček Palace Geschke was known as "Babyface," but this could only have been among people who knew some very frightening babies with dueling scars on their left cheeks. Geschke was one of those factory-manufactured Nazis they turned out like unpainted Meissen porcelain: pale, cold, hard, and best handled with extreme care.

"I haven't seen much of the city yet," I said, "but it does seem rather infernal."

Geschke grinned. "Well, we do our best in that respect. So long as they fear us, they do what they're told. We mustn't let these

Czechos make fools of us, you see. We have to be the master in our own house, so we can't afford to overlook any wrong. We really can't. You let them get away with one thing, there will be no end to it. But tell me, Gunther. In the Weimar Republic, when you had a suspect at the Alex and he refused to cooperate, what did you do? How on earth did you manage?"

"We never hit anyone, if that's what you're driving at, sir. We weren't allowed to. The Prussian Police Regulations forbade it. Oh, some cops smacked a suspect around now and then, but the bosses didn't like that. We got results because we got the evidence. Once you have the evidence, it's hard for a man not to sign a confession. Find the evidence and everything else follows. We were good at that: finding evidence. The Berlin Detective Service was, for a while, the envy of the world, and its backbone was the police commissars."

"But weren't you at all frustrated by the stupidities of Prussian justice? Sometimes it seemed absurd that penal servitude for life rarely ever lasted longer than twelve years. And that so many criminals deserving of their death sentences were reprieved by the Prussian government. For example, those two Jews, Saffran and Kipnik. Remember them?"

I shrugged. "Honestly? I can think of many others I'd like to see under the falling ax before those two. Why, just a few months ago there was the S-Bahn murder case. Fellow named Paul Ogorzow, who killed six or seven women and tried to kill as many more again. Now, *he* deserved his fate."

"Is it true that he was a Party member?"

"Yes."

"Unbelievable."

"Lots of other people thought so, too. That's probably why it took so long to catch him. But what you were saying is absolutely right. We can't afford to overlook any wrong. Especially when it's a wrong committed by our own, don't you think?"

"Ah, now there speaks a true policeman."

"I like to think so, sir."

"Well, if there's anything I can do to help you, Gunther, in your new capacity as the general's personal detective, then please let me know." Geschke raised his glass and bowed. "Anything to help General Heydrich and keep him safe for the new Germany."

"Thank you, sir."

I glanced around the room and tried to picture which, if any, of the general's guests might actually try to poison him, and found that in the new Germany it wasn't so hard. In a room full of murderers, anything seemed possible.

ABOUT HALFWAY THROUGH this unforgettable evening Major Dr. Ploetz, Heydrich's first adjutant and number one myrmidon, turned on the library radio so that we could listen to Hitler's speech from the Sportpalast, in Berlin.

"Gentlemen, please," he said, while the radio was warming up. "If I could ask you to be silent."

"Thank you, Hans-Achim," said Heydrich, as if he, and not the Leader, had been at the microphone. And then solemnly, as the sound of the Sportpalast crept into the room, he intoned: "The Leader."

It was typically thoughtful of Heydrich. I suppose he thought it would be a treat for those of us who were feeling a little homesick. And it was: a bit like hearing my mother reading the old story of how the bad boy Friedrich terrorized a lot of animals and people. It remained to be seen if the Third Reich's ranting answer to bad Friedrich might yet be bitten by the same dog that had eaten the naughty boy's sausages, but for me, at any rate, there was always the hope that he would be. It was hard to think of a treat half as enjoyable as the idea of the Leader being bitten by a greedy dog. His own, perhaps.

In the corridor outside the library a man was on the telephone, and I poked my head out of the door to see who among Heydrich's guests had dared to make or take a call in the middle of Hitler's speech. Whoever he was I certainly didn't blame him. Even at the best of times the Leader was always too loud for me. Probably he'd honed his oratorical skills in the trenches, during bombardments.

Not that you couldn't have heard every rasping word of the broadcast in the corridor. The radio was an AEG Super Orchestra as big as a Polish peasant's barn, and with the speech playing at full volume, there was no chance of not hearing it almost anywhere in the house. Probably you could have heard the speech at the center of the earth.

"No, you did the right thing in calling me here, Sergeant Soppa."

The man speaking was Oskar Fleischer, head of the Gestapo's Resistance Section in Prague—the same man who had been taunted so infamously by one of the Three Kings.

"All right, I'll be there in half an hour. Just don't let the bastard die until I get there. He did? So it was him, after all."

Fleischer caught my eye and turned his back on me.

"No, no, I'm perfectly certain he'll want to know. Yes, of course I'll tell him. I'll do it right now. Yes. Good-bye."

Fleischer replaced the telephone and, grinning excitedly, scribbled something on a piece of paper before handing it to Captain Pomme and then running upstairs, two steps at a time.

I lit a cigarette and drifted out into the corridor next to Captain Pomme.

"Good news?" I asked.

"I should say so," the adjutant said, and went back into the library without further eludication.

I was about to follow when I glanced out the window above the telephone and had a good view of Heydrich's other adjutants—Kuttner and Kluckholm—standing under the flagpole on the front lawn. Although the window was open, I couldn't hear what was said—not with the radio in the library so loud—but it was plain that a heated argument was in progress, indeed that the two men were on the edge of exchanging blows. I was about to go outside and play Saturday-night policeman when Kuttner angrily came up the drive toward the gatehouse. A moment later Fleischer, wearing belts and his cap, galloped downstairs again and went straight out the front door as a car drew up and then took him away in a furious spray of gravel.

A little disappointed that I was not going to break up a fight between two SS officers, I turned my attention back to what was being broadcast in the library.

Hitler's speech was the traditional opening of the Winter Relief Campaign. This was the Nazi Party's annual charitable drive to provide food and shelter for the less fortunate during the coming winter months and was as near as it ever got to real socialism. Failure to donate was not an option. People who forgot to donate were quite likely to find their names in the local newspaper. Or sometimes worse.

Hitler's oratorical style for the Winter Relief speech was calculated to impress rather more than the actual content, and usually it wasn't so much what he said as the way he said it. But my normal reaction was that it was a little like listening to Emil Jannings recite a bit of cudgel verse, Caruso singing a song from a Silly Symphony, or Mark Antony eulogizing a dead cat. This year it was different, however, as it soon became clear that there was more at stake than a few fat Germans going hungry in January. As well as the more predictable bromides about the glory of giving and being generous—something that was second nature to us Germans, of course—the Leader proceeded to make an announcement concerning the beginning of "the great decisive battle of the coming year," which would be devastating to the enemy.

Now, many of us in that library and in the country at large

were already under the impression that "the great decisive battle" was already as good as won. We had certainly been told as much by Dr. Goebbels on several previous occasions. But here was Hitler more or less admitting that he'd bet the family silver on what was yet to happen, that he'd gambled all of our futures on something that was not a cast-iron certainty; and the upshot was that anyone listening to him now was left inescapably with the distinct idea that things in the East were not going entirely to plan for our hitherto invincible armed forces.

When the speech and the thunderous applause that greeted it in the Sportpalast had finally concluded and the AEG radio was at last turned off by Major Dr. Ploetz, it was immediately apparent that several others in that library had the same thought as I: someone in the government—Hitler himself, perhaps?—had woken up to the painful reality of just what Germany had undertaken to do in Russia. And this being the Third Reich, of course, which was based on lies, it meant that things were probably much worse than we had been told.

Our somber faces told the same grim story. Indeed, General von Eberstein, who was some big noise in the SS general staff, may actually have muttered some desperate imprecation to a God, who was certainly someplace else, if anywhere at all. General Hildebrandt, who was Heydrich's equivalent rank in Danzig, merely hurled his cigarette into the fireplace as if he were as disgusted with it as he was with everything else.

This might have been what prompted Heydrich to say a few words, to resurrect our visible lack of enthusiasm. More likely it was Fleischer's handwritten note that Captain Pomme had handed him a few minutes earlier. Heydrich himself was grinning as if he'd just eaten the last slice of honey cake.

"Gentlemen," he said. "If I could have your attention for just a few more minutes. I've been given a note by Criminal Commissar Fleischer of the Gestapo, which contains some excellent news. As most of you know, since May of this year we've had two of the Three Kings—Josef Balabán and Josef Mašín—in custody at Pankrác Prison, here in Prague. These are, of course, two of the three leaders of Czech terrorism here in Bohemia. However, the third king—Melchior, as we like to call him—has eluded us. Until now. It seems that one of our two prisoners—I don't know which, but somehow I feel sure that his name must be Josef—has agreed to cooperate with our inquiries and finally has revealed that Melchior's real name is Václav Morávek, formerly a captain in the Czech Army. We have already begun a search for him here in Prague and at his hometown of Kolín, near Losány, and it is now expected that we shall shortly make an arrest."

I felt oddly sick. It seemed that while we'd been stuffing ourselves with veal Holstein and Leipziger everything, a brave man had been tortured into revealing the name of the most wanted man in the Third Reich.

"Bravo," said one of my brother officers, an Abwehr major named Thümmel.

Others present applauded this news, which seemed to please Heydrich no end, and there he might, and perhaps should, have left the matter. But, full of his own importance, Heydrich continued to talk for several more minutes. He was not, however, a public speaker. Self-conscious and calculating, he lacked Hitler's common touch and rhetorical flourish. His voice was pitched too high to inspire men; worst of all, he used a string of big German words where one or two smaller ones would have worked better. Of course, this was typical of the Nazis, for whom language was often used to mask their own ignorance and stupidity—which they possessed in an inexhaustible supply—as well as to give their words the placebo effect of authority; like a doctor who has an impressive Latin name for what is wrong with you, but sadly not a cure.

Fortunately for everyone present, Captain Kuttner and Kritzinger the butler appeared with champagne and a tray of Bohemian glass flutes, and before long there was something of a party atmosphere in that library. I drank a glass without much pleasure, and when I thought I was unobserved, I slipped out to the terrace and smoked a cigarette in the darkness. It felt like somewhere I belonged—a crepuscular world of creatures that hooted and howled and where one might hide to avoid larger predators.

After a while I glanced through the leaded library window and, seeing no sign of Heydrich, I decided I might sneak off to bed. But I had not reckoned on Heydrich's study being immediately at the top of the first flight of stairs; the doors were open and he was seated behind his desk, signing some papers under the cold bespectacled eye of Colonel Jacobi. Insouciantly I headed toward the north-wing corridor and my room, but if I had hoped not to catch the general's eye, I was quickly disappointed.

"Gunther," he said, hardly looking up from his signature file. "Come in."

"Very well, sir."

Entering Heydrich's study in the Lower Castle at Jungfern-Breschan, I had the distinct feeling that I was in a smaller, more intimate version of the Leader's own study at the Reich Chancellery, and this would have been typical of Heydrich. Not that there was very much that was small or intimate about that room. The ceiling was about four meters high, and there were marble relief columns on the walls, a fireplace as big as a Mercedes, and enough green carpet on the floor for a decent game of golf. The refectory-style desk had more glass protecting its smooth oak surface than a good-sized shop window. On this were a marble-urn lamp, a couple of telephones, a leather blotter, an inkstand, and a brass model of a plane—quite possibly the same Siebel Fh 104 he used to fly himself to and from Berlin. In the arched window was a bronze bust of the Leader, and behind a throne-sized desk chair was a green silk wall hanging with a gold German eagle holding on to a laurel wreath enclosing a swastika, as if it were something worth stealing.

Heydrich put down his fountain pen and leaned back in the chair.

"That girl back at your hotel," he said. "Arianne Tauber. Have you called her to tell her you won't be coming to see her tonight?"

"Not yet, sir."

"Then don't. Have Klein drive you into Prague. I think I will be safe enough tonight, don't you?"

"If you say so, sir."

"Oh no. In the future it's for you to say so. That was rather the point of your appointment. But I'm sure you'll get the hang of it. Meet me at Peček Palace tomorrow morning at ten o'clock. I have a meeting there to coordinate the arrest of this Morávek fellow."

"Very well, sir. And thank you."

I may even have clicked my heels and bowed my head. Working for Heydrich was like being friendly with a vicious tomcat while you were looking around for the nearest mouse hole.

13

Arianne was pleased to see me, of course, although not as pleased as I was to see her, in our bed, alone, naked and willing to use her body to help divert my thoughts from Heydrich, Jungfern-Breschan, the Three Kings, and Peček Palace. I told her nothing of my worries. Where Heydrich was concerned, it was best to know very little, as I myself was beginning to discover. What did

I tell her as, exhausted by our lovemaking, we lay intertwined like two primitive figures carved from the same piece of antler horn? Only that my duties kept me out of Prague, in Jungfern-Breschan, otherwise I should certainly have visited her at the Imperial Hotel before now.

"That's all right," she said. "Really, I'm quite happy here on my own. You've no idea how nice it is just to sit and read a book or to walk around the city by myself."

"I do," I muttered. "I can imagine, anyway."

"I left a message for my brother. And there are plenty of other Germans in Prague I can talk to. As a matter of fact, this hotel is full of Germans. There's a very beautiful girl in a suite on the same floor as us who's having an affair with some SS general. And she's a Jew. Doesn't that sound romantic?"

"Romantic? It sounds dangerous."

Arianne shrugged that off. "Her name is Betty Kipsdorf and she's utterly sweet."

"What's his name?"

"The general? Konrad something. He's more than twice her age but she says you really wouldn't know it." She laughed. "On account of the fact that he used to be a gymnastics teacher."

I said I didn't know who that could be. And I didn't. I wasn't exactly on first-name terms with any SS generals, even the ones I knew.

"He's very vigorous, apparently. For a general. Me, I always say that if you want a job done, and done properly, it's a captain you want. Not some effete flamingo with clockwork heels."

Flamingos were what the ranks called officers of the general staff, a reference to the red stripes on their trouser legs.

"What do you know about flamingos?"

"You'd be surprised who we get through the doors of the Jockey Bar."

"No. But I'm still surprised that you'd prefer a captain to one of them."

"And perhaps a little suspicious."

"That's probably no fault of yours."

"We'd get on like a house on fire if you weren't a cop, don't you think so, Parsifal?"

"These are the times we live in, I'm afraid. All sorts of things make me suspicious, angel. Two aces in a row. Double sixes. A sure thing for the state lottery. A kind word or a compliment. Venus rising from the sea. I'm the kind of Fritz who's apt to look for a maker's mark on the scallop shell."

"I might get insulted if I knew what any of that was about. After all, there's a little part of you that's still in me."

"Now it's my turn to get insulted."

"Don't be, Gunther. I enjoyed it, a lot. I think that maybe you underestimate yourself."

"Perhaps. I might even call it an occupational hazard, except that, so far, it's helped to keep me alive."

"Is staying alive so very important to you?"

"No. Then again I've seen the alternatives, and at close quarters. In Russia. Or twenty years ago, back in the trenches."

She gave me a little squeeze, the kind that feels like a wonderful sort of conjuring trick and that doesn't need any limbs. Whenever a woman holds me tight like that, it's the best argument there is against the solipsistic idea that one can be truly certain only of the existence of one's own mind.

"How much more suspicious would you get if I said I'd fallen for you, Gunther?"

"You'd have to say it a lot for me to believe it might be true."

"Maybe I will."

"Yeah. Maybe. When you've said it the first time we can review the situation. But right now it's just a hypothetical."

"All right, I—"

She paused for a moment, uttering a sigh that was as unsteady as a whippet's hind leg as I nudged up deep against the edge of her latest thought.

"Go on. I'm listening."

"It's true, Parsifal. I'm falling for you."

"You're a long time in the air, angel. By now anyone else would have hit the ground." I nudged into her again. "Hard."

"Damn you, Gunther."

Her breath was hot in my ear, except it sounded cold and erratic, like someone laughing silently.

I prompted her a little more and said, "Go on. Let's hear what it sounds like."

"All right. I love you. Satisfied?"

"Not by a long way. But I will be, if this keeps up."

She hit me on the shoulder but there was pleasure on her face. "You sadistic bastard."

"I'm a Nazi. You said so yourself. Remember?"

"No, but you're also rather wonderful, Gunther. All the more so because you don't realize it. Since Karl, my husband, there have been other men. But you're the first man I've cared anything about since he died."

"Stop talking."

"Go ahead and make me."

I didn't say anything. Conversation between us had become unnecessary. We didn't need speech to act out a story that many others had told before. It wasn't original but it felt like it was—an almost silent film that seemed both familiar and new. We were still performing our own highly stylized homage to German expressionism when the telephone on the bedside table rang.

"Leave it," I said.

"Is that wise?"

"It sounds like trouble."

It stopped ringing.

When our own motion picture finished, she got up to fetch one of my cigarettes.

I rolled onto my back and stared out the window at the little pepper-pot dome on top of the building opposite.

The telephone started to ring again.

"I told you," I said. "It always rings again when it's trouble. Especially first thing in the morning, before breakfast."

I picked up the receiver. It was Major Ploetz, Heydrich's first adjutant. He sounded shaken and angry.

"A car is coming to pick you up and bring you back here, immediately."

"All right. What's up?"

"There's been a homicide," said Ploetz. "Here, at the Lower Castle."

"A homicide? What kind of homicide?"

"I don't know. But you should be outside your hotel in fifteen minutes."

And then he hung up.

For one glorious moment I allowed myself to hope it was Heydrich who was dead. That one of those officers and gentlemen of the SS and the SD, jealous of Heydrich's success, had shot him. Or perhaps there had been a machine-gun attack by Czech terrorists while Heydrich was out for his early-morning ride in the countryside around Jungfern-Breschan. Perhaps even now there was a horse lying on top of his lifeless body.

And yet surely if it had been Heydrich who was dead, Ploetz would have said so. Ploetz wouldn't ever have used the phrase "a homicide" for someone as important as his very own general. The victim had to be someone of lesser importance or else Ploetz would have said "Heydrich has been murdered" or "The general has been murdered" or "There's been a catastrophe, General Heydrich has been assassinated." A homicide didn't begin to cover the lexicon that would probably be used by the Nazis if ever Heydrich was unfortunate enough to meet with a well-deserved but premature death.

"Is it?"

"Is it what?" I answered her absently.

"Trouble," said Arianne.

"I have to go back to Jungfern-Breschan, immediately. There's been a death."

"Oh? Who?"

"I don't know. But I'm sure it's not Heydrich."

"Some detective you are." She shrugged. "Well, it certainly won't be the gardener who's dead if they want you to go back immediately. It must be someone important."

"I can dream, I suppose."

FIFTEEN MINUTES LATER I was washed and dressed and standing outside the Imperial Hotel as a black sedan drew up. The driver wearing an SS uniform—it wasn't Klein—stepped smartly out of the car, saluted, opened the door, and pulled down the middle row of seats because two men wearing plain clothes were already seated in the back.

They were well-fed, hefty types, probably the kind who couldn't run very fast but who could hand out a beating without breaking the skin on their knuckles.

"Commissar Gunther?"

The man who spoke had a head as big as a stonemason's bucket but the face carved on the front of it was small, like a child's. The eyes were cold and hard, even a little sad, but the mouth was a vicious tear.

"That's right."

A grappling iron of a hand came across the back of the seat.

"Kurt Kahlo," said the man. "Criminal assistant to Inspector Willy Abendschön, from Prague Kripo."

He looked at the other man and grinned, unkindly.

"And this is Inspector Zennaty, of the Czech police. He's only along for the sake of appearances, aren't you, sir? After all, technically speaking, this is a Czech matter, isn't it?"

Zennaty shook my hand but he didn't say anything. He was thin and hawklike, with shadowy eyes and a hairstyle that looked like an extension of a short stubbly beard.

"I'm afraid our Czecho friend doesn't speak much German, do you, Ivan?"

"Not very much," said Zennaty. "Sorry."

"But he's all right, is our Ivan." Kahlo patted Zennaty on the back of the hand. "Aren't you, Ivan?"

"Very much."

"Mr. Abendschön would have attended himself," said Kahlo, "but almost everyone in Prague is now looking for this Morávek fellow. General Heydrich has made his apprehension the number one police priority in the whole of the protectorate."

I nodded. "So who's dead? They didn't say."

"One of General Heydrich's adjutants. A captain named Kuttner, Albert Kuttner. Did you know him at all, sir?"

"I met him for the first time yesterday," I said. "How about you?"

"I only met him a couple of times. To me, one adjutant looks like another."

"I'd expect this one might look a bit different now, don't you?"

"Good point." Kahlo's eyebrows were almost permanently at an angle, like a sad clown's, but somehow he managed to raise them even farther up his forehead.

"How about you?" I asked Zennaty politely. "Did you know Captain Kuttner?"

"Not very much," said Zennaty.

Kahlo grinned at this, which helped persuade Zennaty to stare out of the window. It was a kinder view than Kahlo's sneering, ugly mug.

We drove east for a while, to Kripo headquarters in Carl Maria von Weber Strasse, where Zennaty briefly left the car and Kahlo informed me he had gone to fetch an evidence box. He and Zennaty had been across the river at the Justice Ministry when Abendschön, Kahlo's boss, had telephoned, telling him to pick me up and then go to Jungfern-Breschan.

After a few minutes Zennaty returned and we drove north again.

To see Prague in the autumn of 1941 was to see a crown of thorns with extra points, as painted by Lucas Cranach. A city of church spires it certainly was. Even the spires had smaller spires of their own, the way little carrots sometimes grow bigger ones. These lent the unfeasibly tall Bohemian capital an unexpectedly sharp, jagged feel. Everywhere you looked it was like seeing a Swiss halberd in an umbrella stand. This sense of medieval discomfort was accentuated by the city's omnipresent statuary. All over Prague there were statues of Jesuit bishops spearing pagans, heavily muscled Titans stabbing each other with swords, agonized Christian saints horribly martyred, or ferocious wild animals tearing each other to pieces. To that extent Prague appeared to suit the cruelty and violence of Nazism in a way Berlin never did. The Nazis seemed to belong here—especially the tall, spindly figure of Heydrich, whose austere, pale features brought to mind the face of a flayed-alive saint. The red Nazi flags that were everywhere looked more like blood dripping down the buildings that they hung on; the polished bayonets on German rifles at sentry points across the city glittered with an extra steely edge; and goose-stepping jackboots on the cobbles of the Charles Bridge seemed to have a louder crunch, as if beating down the hopes of the Czechs themselves.

That was shameful if you were a German but worse if you were a Czech, like the impotent Inspector Zennaty. Worst of all if you were one of Prague's Jews. Prague was home to one of the largest communities of Jews in Europe, and even now there were still plenty of them left for the Nazis to kick around. Kick them around they duly did, and it remained to be seen if the legendary Golem that was reputed to dwell in the city's Old-New Synagogue would, as legend supposed, emerge from the attic one night and climb down the outside wall to avenge the persecution of Prague's Jews. Part of me hoped that he had already put in an appearance at Jungfern-Breschan and that Captain Kuttner's unexplained death was just the beginning. If things were anything like the silent movie called *The Golem*, which I'd seen not long after the Great War, then we Germans were in for some fun.

TWENTY MINUTES LATER the car stopped outside the front door of the Lower Castle and we went inside.

Kritzinger, the butler, ushered Kahlo, Zennaty, and me upstairs to Heydrich's study, where he was waiting, impatiently, with Major Ploetz and Captain Pomme. Heydrich and Pomme were wearing fencing jerkins, and from their flushed and still-perspiring faces it was clear that it had not been long since they had finished their absurd sport.

Since I was the only one wearing a uniform, I saluted and then introduced Kahlo and Zennaty.

Heydrich looked coldly at Zennaty. "You can wait downstairs," he told the Czech policeman.

Zennaty nodded curtly and left the room.

"You took your time getting here," said Heydrich, sourly.

The remark appeared to be directed at me, so I glanced at my watch and said, "I received the call from Major Ploetz in my hotel just forty-five minutes ago. I came as quickly as I could, sir."

"All right, all right."

Heydrich's tone was testy. There was a cigarette in his hand. His hair looked disheveled and uncombed.

"Well, you're here now, that's the main thing. You're here and you're in charge, d'you hear? You're the experienced man in this situation. Incidentally, I don't want that fucking Czech involved at all. D'you hear? This is a German matter. I want this thing investigated quickly and discreetly, and solved before it can reach the ears of the Leader. I've every confidence in you, Gunther. If any man can solve this case, it's you. I've told everyone that you enjoy my complete confidence."

"Thank you, sir," I said, although this wasn't at all how I felt or indeed what he meant. I wasn't about to enjoy Heydrich's confidence for any longer than he took to say it.

"And that I expect everyone to cooperate fully with your inquiry. I don't care what you ask and who you upset. D'you hear? As far as I'm concerned, everyone in this house is under suspicion."

"Does that include you, sir?"

Heydrich's blue eyes narrowed, and for a moment I thought I'd gone too far and that he was going to bawl me out. I was relieved he wasn't holding a sword. I had gone too far, of course, and it was clear the two adjutants thought so too, but for the moment, neither man was prepared to protest my insolence. Unpredictable as always, Heydrich took a deep breath and nodded, slowly.

"I don't see why not," he said. "If it helps. Anything that will get this sorted out as quickly as possible, before my tenure in this position descends into farce and I become a fucking laughingstock in Berlin."

He shook his head and then stubbed out his cigarette, irritably.

"That this should happen now when we're just about to put paid to UVOD."

"UVOD?" I shook my head. "What's that?"

"UVOD? It's the Central Leadership of Home Resistance," said Heydrich. "A network of Czech terrorists."

He leaned down on the desk with both fists and then hammered the glass surface hard enough for the model plane to shift several centimeters nearer the lamp. "Damn it all."

I lit a cigarette and drew down a lungful of smoke, and blew it back at him hard, hoping it might distract him a little from what I was about to say and the way I meant to say it.

"Why don't you take it easy, General? This isn't helping me and it's certainly not helping you. Instead of beating up the furniture and biting my head off, why don't you or whoever else has the best grip on the story tell me exactly what happened here? The whole once-upon-a-time in a town called Hamelin. And then I can do what I do."

Heydrich looked at me and I sensed he knew I was taking advantage of him. Everyone else was looking at me too, as if surprised that I should dare to speak to the general in this way; but just as surprised that he should continue to hold off shouting me back into my shell. I was a bit surprised about that myself, but sometimes it can be interesting just how wide the door can open.

For a moment he bit his fingernails.

"Yes. You're absolutely right, Gunther. This isn't getting us anywhere. I suppose, well, it's a great shame, that's all. Kuttner was a promising young officer."

"Yes, he was," said Pomme.

Heydrich looked at him strangely and then said, "Why don't you fill in some of the details for the commissar?"

"Yes, sir. If you wish."

"Mind if I sit down?" I said. "Like any copper, I listen better when I'm not thinking about my feet."

"Yes, please, gentlemen, be seated," said Heydrich.

I picked a chair in front of the Leader's bust and almost

immediately regretted it. I didn't care for Hitler staring at the back of my head. If ever he learned about what was at the back of my mind, I was in serious trouble. I reached into my fart catcher's pocket and took out my officer's diary. It was more or less the same kind of diary the Gestapo had found on Franz Koci's dead body in Kleist Park.

"If you don't mind," I said to Pomme, "I'll make some notes."

Pomme shook his head. "Why should I mind?"

I shrugged. "No good reason." I paused. "Whenever you're ready, Captain Pomme."

"Well, Albert, that's to say Captain Kuttner, was supposed to awaken me at six o'clock this morning. As usual. He awakens me, or Major Ploetz, or Captain Kluckholm, because it's our job to awaken the general at six thirty. I suppose that's just the pecking order. Him being the fourth adjutant, you understand. However, this was no longer a satisfactory arrangement. Kuttner was never a good sleeper, and lately he has been dosing himself with a sleeping pill, which meant he started to oversleep in the morning. This made me late, and that made the general late. This morning was fairly typical in that respect. And, anticipating some sort of a problem, I managed to awaken myself at six and then went to see if Kuttner was awake. He wasn't; or so it seemed at the time. I knocked on the door several times, without success. Again, that wasn't so very unusual. When he's taken a pill, it can be a while before he can be roused. But after ten minutes I was still knocking without a reply and, well, I suppose I began to worry a little."

"Couldn't you just have gone in there and shaken him awake?" I asked.

"I'm sorry, Gunther, I didn't make myself clear. He always locked his door. He was quite a nervous person, I think. Something to do with what happened to him in Latvia, he said. I don't know. Anyway, the door was locked, and when I bent down to take a look through the keyhole, I saw that the key was still in the lock."

Pomme was a handsome little martinet, not much more than thirty years old, lugubrious, with a wide but narrow-lipped mouth. In his white fencing jerkin he resembled a nervous dentist.

"Having failed to awaken Kuttner, I quickly awoke the general and then went to find Herr Kritzinger, to see if there was perhaps some other means of gaining entry to Kuttner's room."

"What time was this?" I asked.

"It would have been about six forty-five," said Pomme. He glanced at the butler, the only man in the room who remained standing, for verification.

The butler looked at me. "That is correct, sir," he said. "I went to find the spare key. I keep spare keys for all of the doors in my safe. I noticed the time on the clock on my mantelpiece when I was opening the safe. I went back upstairs with the room keys, but I was unsuccessful in using the spare to push the key out of the lock so that I could open Captain Kuttner's door from the outside."

I considered telling him about the key turners we'd used at the Hotel Adlon for just such a situation but it hardly seemed relevant now.

"I then instructed one of the footmen to go and find the gardener," said Kritzinger, "and have him fetch a ladder to take a look through the window and perhaps open it from outside the house."

"Meanwhile I resumed knocking on the door," explained Pomme, "and calling Captain Kuttner's name. And by now I was late for my fencing bout with the general."

Heydrich nodded. "Every morning I fence with one of the adjutants before breakfast. Kuttner was the best—he was outstanding with the saber—but, of late, he had too much on his mind to be competitive. This morning when I arrived at the gymnasium there was no sign of Pomme, so I went to look for him, and met the footman who'd been sent to fetch the gardener. When I asked him if he'd seen Captain Pomme he explained the situation. That would have been around six fifty-five. So I went to see if I could assist, and found Pomme still knocking on Kuttner's door. It was now seven o'clock, I suppose. I also became a little concerned for Kuttner's safety. The fact is, he'd been rather depressed of late. And I ordered Pomme and Kritzinger to break down the door. Which they proceeded to do."

"That can't have been very easy," I said. "The doors here are thick."

Instinctively Pomme rubbed his shoulder. "It wasn't. It took us all of five or ten minutes."

"And when the door was open, what did you see?"

"Very little," said Pomme. "The curtains were drawn and the room was quite dark."

"Was the window closed or open?"

"Closed, sir," said Kritzinger. "The general ordered me to pull back the curtains so that we could see, and I noticed then that the window was closed and bolted."

"Then I called Kuttner's name," said Heydrich. "And, hearing no reply, I approached the bed. It was immediately clear to us all from his position that something was very wrong. He was still wearing his uniform, and his sleep seemed abnormally sound to me. What with the sound of the door coming down and our voices, it didn't seem right that he shouldn't even stir. So I pressed my fingers on the side of his neck to look for a pulse, and I noticed straight away that his skin was cold to the touch. Colder than it ought to have been. And then I noticed that there was no pulse. No pulse at all."

"Have you been trained to take a pulse like that?" I asked.

Heydrich frowned. "Why do you ask?"

"It's a straightforward question, sir. You'd be amazed how many dead men turn up fit and well after someone has taken their pulse and pronounced them dead."

"Very well, yes, I have. During my Luftwaffe training at the Werneuchen Aerodrome, in 1939, I received basic training in first aid. And again in May 1940. That was in Stavanger." He shook his head. "There's no question about it, Gunther. The man was quite dead. That would have been at approximately ten minutes past seven."

Kritzinger was nodding.

"What happened next?" I asked him.

"The general ordered me to telephone for an ambulance."

"Where did you call?"

"The Bulovka Hospital is the nearest," he said. "It's on the northeast outskirts of Prague, about ten kilometers away."

"I drive past it every morning," said Heydrich.

"A Czech doctor called Honek attended," said Kritzinger. "In fact he's still downstairs."

"And what did you do?" I asked Pomme.

"General Heydrich told me to go and fetch General Jury right away."

"Why?"

"Because he's a doctor, too," said Pomme.

"Yes, I remember now. He was a specialist in tuberculosis, I believe. Before he joined the SS." I nodded. "So you went to fetch him. What happened then?"

"I'm afraid he was feeling rather the worse for wear after last night. It was at least another fifteen minutes before he was dressed and on the scene."

I looked at Heydrich. "Meanwhile, sir, you were still in the room with Kuttner, isn't that right?"

"Yes."

"What did you do while you were waiting for Dr. Jury?"

"Let's see now. I opened the window, to get some air. I was feeling a little queasy for some reason. No, that's not fair. He was a friend of mine. I lit a cigarette, to calm my nerves. But I tossed the end out of the window when I was finished. The crime scene is substantially uncontaminated." He shook his head and then ran a thin hand through his short hair. "I can't think of anything else. After a while Dr. Jury turned up with Pomme. The doctor was, as Pomme says, very hungover. But not so hungover that he was incapable of pronouncing poor Kuttner dead. After that I had Ploetz call you and the local police right away. At approximately seven thirty."

"Where's Dr. Jury now?" I asked.

"In the library, sir," said Kritzinger. "With Dr. Honek. He asked for a pot of strong black coffee to be brought to him there."

"Has Dr. Honek examined the body?"

"No," said Heydrich firmly. "I decided that there was no urgency about doing so. I thought it might be better if he waited until you had had a chance to examine the body yourself."

I nodded. "I'll do that now, if I may."

"Of course," said Heydrich.

"Mr. Kritzinger," I said, "would you ask Dr. Jury to join us in Captain Kuttner's room?"

"Yes, sir."

"Captain Pomme? Perhaps you'd like to lead the way."

I stood up and looked at Kahlo, the criminal assistant from Prague Kripo. "You'd better fetch the evidence kit that Zennaty brought," I said.

"Right you are, sir."

"General? If you'd care to join us?"

Heydrich nodded. "Major Ploetz? You'd better inform the rest of my guests of what has happened. And that they will be required to answer the Commissar's questions before anyone is allowed to leave. And that includes everyone at the Upper Castle."

"Yes, sir."

KUTTNER'S ROOM WAS on the same floor as mine, but was in the south wing and overlooked a little glass winter garden. On the pink-papered walls were some pictures of English hunting scenes, which made a welcome change from the Czech ones, with which I was more familiar. The fox, who appeared to be smiling, must have believed he stood a good chance of escaping from the hounds, and that was all right with me. Lately I'm the kind of antisocial type who cheers when the fox makes a clean getaway.

Before I looked at the body I made my way around the room, noting a large pile of books by the bed and a bottle of Veronal beside a water carafe on the desk. The screw cap was still off the bottle. There were several pills on the floor but, oddly, the bottle was upright. Kuttner's belts and the holster containing his Walther automatic were hanging on the back of his chair.

Heydrich saw me pick up the open bottle of Veronal. "Until I realized the true nature of his injuries I assumed that the Veronal was the culprit," he said. "It was only when Dr. Jury opened the tunic of his uniform to examine Captain Kuttner that we realized he'd suffered a lethal wound to his abdomen."

"Mm-hmm."

Kuttner lay at an angle across the bed, as if he'd collapsed there. His eyes were closed. One of his arms lay neatly alongside his torso; the other was sticking straight out at a right angle to the rest of his body, like a dead Christ. Well, half of a dead Christ, anyway. But both hands were unscathed and empty. There were four buttons on his captain's fart-catcher tunic, with three unbuttoned from the top. He was wearing a white collarless shirt, unbuttoned at the neck, and no tie. It was easy to see how anyone could have missed the fact he'd been shot. Only when lifting the flap of the tunic could you see the blood covering the shirt. He was still wearing his riding breeches, and just one boot. The monkey swing—his adjutant's braided rope—was off his top button but still attached to the right epaulet. He looked like a man who had been shot while still undressing.

"Has anyone been over the floor yet?" I asked Heydrich. "To look for evidence?"

"No," said Heydrich.

I nodded at Kahlo, who without complaint dropped onto his hands and knees and began to look for a bullet shell or perhaps something as yet unimagined.

I collected the P38 from Kuttner's holster, sniffed the barrel, and then checked the magazine. The gun was dirty and not well maintained, but clearly hadn't been fired in a while.

"Your conclusions?" asked Heydrich.

"Beyond the fact that he was shot in the torso and that it hardly looks like a suicide I don't yet have any," I said.

"Why do you think it doesn't look like a suicide?" asked Pomme.

"It's unusual to shoot yourself and then neatly replace the weapon in the holster," I said. "Especially when you weren't being neat about so much else. If you were going to shoot yourself, you would take off both boots or neither of them. Quite apart from that, his own pistol has a full magazine and hasn't been fired in a while."

I shrugged.

"Then again, there is no other gun in the room. But all the same, it's hard to imagine that he was shot, and then he returned to his room, locked the door, lay down on the bed, took off one boot, and then quietly died. Even if that's what it looks like."

"What I can't understand," said Heydrich, "is why nobody seems to have heard a shot."

"Well, we don't know that until we ask everyone," I said.

"I can ask around if you like," offered Pomme.

"What I mean," Heydrich said firmly, "is that the sound of a shot would surely have raised the alarm. Especially here, in a house full of policemen."

I nodded. "So the chances are that somehow the shot was muffled. Or someone did hear the shot and either chose to ignore it or thought that it was something else."

I went to the open window and put my head outside.

"Today I can't hear anything," I said. "But yesterday when I arrived here, at around the same time, someone was out there shooting birds. Rather a lot of birds."

"That would have been General von Eberstein," said Captain Pomme. "He likes to shoot."

"But not this morning," I observed.

"This morning he has a hangover," said Pomme. "Like General Jury."

Kahlo stood up. "Apart from all of these pills, there's nothing on this floor, sir," he said. "Not so much as a blood spot."

"What? Nothing at all?" I frowned.

"No, sir. I'll organize a more thorough search, after the body's gone. But this floor is clean, sir." He shook his head. "It's a mystery. Maybe he shot himself, threw the gun out of the window, closed it again, and then collapsed on the bed and died."

"Good thinking," said Heydrich, sarcastically. "Or maybe Captain Kuttner was just shot by a man who could pass through solid walls."

"You'd better check outside, anyway," I told Kahlo.

He nodded and left the room.

Heydrich shook his head. "That man is an idiot."

"How well do you know this house, General?"

"You mean, are there any false walls and secret passages?"

"Perhaps."

"I haven't the faintest idea. I've not been here for very long at all. Von Neurath had the house before I did. He knows this place much better than me, so you'd better ask him that."

Absently I drew open Kuttner's drawers and found several shirts, a toilet bag, some underwear, a shoe cleaning kit, some *Der Führer* magazines, a clay pipe, a book of poems, and a framed picture of a woman.

"Can I ask von Neurath something like that?"

"As I told you already, Gunther, I expect everyone to cooperate. No matter who or what they are."

"Thank you, sir." I smiled. "Do I have to be polite? Or can I just be myself?"

"Why change the habit of a lifetime? You're the most insubordinate fellow I know, Gunther, but sometimes that yields results. It might, however, be a good idea if, while you were conducting your investigation, and practicing your habitual impertinence, you wore civilian clothes. So that you can't be accused of something that would get you court-martialed in a uniform. Yes. I think that might be best. Have you any civilian clothes with you?"

"Yes, sir. They're in my room."

"Good. And that reminds me, Gunther. You'll need a suitable space from which to conduct your investigations. You can use the morning room. See to it, will you, Captain Pomme?"

"Yes, Herr General."

"Pomme will be your liaison officer for the inquiry. For SD, SS, Gestapo, or military matters, go through him. Anything else, speak to Kritzinger. Come to think of it, he's the real Lower Castle expert, not von Neurath."

Kritzinger bowed his head in Heydrich's direction.

General Jury appeared in the doorway, breathing heavily. He was perspiring and looked pale, as if he really did have a severe hangover. He closed his eyes for a moment and let out a sigh.

"Ah, Jury, you're here."

Heydrich was trying to keep the smirk out of his voice but without success; it was obvious that he was enjoying the other general's hangover as another man might have taken pleasure at watching someone slip on a banana skin.

"What else would you like to know about the captain?" Jury asked biliously. "Beyond the fact that he's dead and that there appears to be a gunshot wound in his abdomen, I can tell you very little, without examining his body in the morgue. And it's been many years since I did that kind of thing."

"What made you think it was a gunshot wound?" I asked. "Rather than a knife wound?"

"There's what looks like a neat bullet hole in his shirt," explained Jury. "Not to mention a neat hole on his body. And yet there's very little blood on the captain's torso. Or, for that matter, elsewhere. It's rare in my experience that a man who is stabbed doesn't bleed more. I saw no blood on the floor or in the bed. But it was only an educated guess. And I could yet turn out to be wrong."

"No, I think you're right," I said. "He was shot, all right."

"Well, then, Commissar," he said stiffly, "I fail to see the need for the question. Indeed, I'm inclined to consider it impertinent. I am a doctor, after all."

I decided to let Jury have it between his oyster eyes. In his present, crapulous state—assuming it was for real—he was weak and vulnerable, and it might take a while to find him like that again. Besides, I thought it important that I make a very early test of Heydrich's declaration that I enjoyed his full confidence and that he didn't care what I asked or indeed who I upset, just as long as I solved the case. If Heydrich stood by and let me bully General Jury, then it would surely send out an early message to other senior officers in the Lower Castle that I was to be taken seriously.

"All right," I said. "You're a doctor. But that doesn't mean you didn't kill him. Did you kill him?"

"I beg your pardon."

"You heard me, Dr. Jury. Was it you who shot Captain Kuttner?"

"If that's your idea of a joke, Commissar Gunther, then kindly take note of the fact that no one in this room is laughing. Including myself."

This wasn't quite true. Heydrich was smiling, almost as if he approved of my putting Jury on the spot in this way, which at least told me he was serious about my investigating the murder.

"I can assure you it's no joke, sir. Yesterday afternoon, when we talked on the road up to the Upper Castle, you told me that you hated Captain Kuttner."

"Nonsense," spluttered Jury.

"You told me you thought he was a cunt. And that you detested him. That was before you went on to describe Captain Kuttner as General Heydrich's golem."

Jury colored with embarrassment.

"Golem," said Heydrich. "That's an interesting choice of words. Remind me, Gunther. What exactly is a golem?"

"A sort of creature created long ago by a local Jewish mystic called Rabbi Loew, sir. To do his bidding on behalf of Prague's Jews."

Jury was still protesting his innocence, but for the moment, Heydrich ignored him.

"If Captain Kuttner was the golem, then I suppose that makes me comparable to this Jewish mystic. Rabbi Loew."

"That was certainly my impression, sir."

"General Heydrich, sir," said Jury. "I can assure you that I meant nothing of the sort. Commissar Gunther is entirely mistaken. In no way did I mean to compare you to . . . that person."

"Leaving that aside for a moment," I said, roughly, "why did you detest Captain Kuttner?"

Jury advanced on Heydrich. Though I was the one asking the questions, all of his answers were directed, a little desperately, at the Reichsprotector.

"It was an entirely private matter," he insisted. "And nothing at all to do with the captain's death. It's true I did dislike the man. However, if the commissar is suggesting that it was a reason for killing him, then I really must protest."

"A man has been murdered," I said. "An officer of the SS, in circumstances that compel investigation, regardless of personal feelings. I'm afraid there is no such thing as a private matter in a situation like this, General Jury. You know that as well as anyone else. This is now a criminal investigation, and I'll decide if your reason for disliking Kuttner was sufficient reason to kill him."

"And who made you judge and jury, Captain?" demanded the doctor.

"I did," said Heydrich. "Commissar Gunther is one of the most competent detectives in Kripo, with an admirable forensic record. He is only doing the job that I have asked him to do. And doing it rather bravely, I think."

"Can I see your gun, Dr. Jury?"

"What?"

"Your pistol, sir. I notice you're wearing it, this morning. May I examine it, sir?"

Jury glanced at Heydrich, who nodded firmly.

"I'm not sure why I put on my belts this morning," he muttered. "I suppose it was because I was suddenly roused from sleep by Captain Pomme. I mean, I wouldn't normally—"

He unbuttoned his holster and handed over the Walther P38, standard issue for most SS officers unless, like me, they were anything to do with the criminal police, in which case they were given the PPK. He checked the safety, ejected the magazine quickly, and placed both in my hands. It was an impressively competent display for a man who was a doctor and SS bureaucrat.

I inspected the breech, which was empty, sniffed the barrel, and then glanced at the single-stack magazine in the palm of my hand.

"Only three rounds," I said. "And it's been fired. Recently."

"Yes. I did some shooting practice with my gun yesterday afternoon. In the woods near the Upper Castle. It was just to keep my hand in. It's my belief that one cannot be too careful, what with all these Czech terrorists from UVOD running around."

"And are you a good shot, sir?"

"No. Not good. Competent, perhaps."

I nodded at Kuttner's body. "Obviously we won't know the kind of gun that was used to kill the captain until a postmortem has been performed. However, I'm afraid I will have to keep your weapon for now, sir."

"Is that really necessary?"

"Yes. I may need to try to match the bullet that killed Captain Kuttner with a bullet fired from your gun. What were you using for target practice yesterday?"

"Songbirds. Pigeons."

"Hit anything?"

"No."

"Did anyone see you? Baron Neurath, perhaps?"

"I don't know. You'd have to ask him, I suppose."

"I will."

"I didn't kill Captain Kuttner," he repeated.

I said nothing.

"But I think that perhaps I could explain my opinion of him to you and the general in private."

"I think that's an excellent idea, Hugo," said Heydrich. He glanced at Kritzinger and Pomme. "Gentlemen. If you would excuse us for a moment, please."

The butler and captain left the bedroom. I closed the door as best I could, given the fact that it had been broken in. I stayed there for a moment, running my fingers over the splintered wood and broken brass work while Jury blustered his way through an explanation of why he had disliked the dead man.

"The matter is a delicate one, involving a lady I know. She is a woman of probity and reputation, you understand. However, the other day I overheard Captain Kuttner talking about her in a way I considered extremely distasteful. I'm sure you'll understand if

I don't mention her name or the specific details of the scurrilous gossip that was being relayed." Jury cleared his throat nervously, removed his glasses, and started to polish the lenses with a handkerchief. "But I can assure you it was not the sort of thing one would expect to hear from an officer and gentleman."

"It's true," admitted Heydrich. "Kuttner had an unfortunate tendency to be indiscreet. Even outspoken. I had occasion to speak to him about this."

I nodded. "Exactly whom did Kuttner tell about your affair with this little opera singer?" I asked him bluntly.

"Well, I really must protest." Jury proceeded to give me a look as if he wished it was me lying on the bed with a bullet hole in my torso.

"What was her name again? Elisabeth something. Elisabeth Schwarzkopf, wasn't it?"

"Suppose we just leave her name out of this," said Jury.

"All right. Suppose we do. Only that's going to make it a little difficult to try to clear your name, General. You see, I'll need to speak to this other officer that Kuttner was speaking to. About your friend. Who was he?"

Jury bit his lip. This took some doing, given how thin it was. "Major Thümmel," he said.

"And, by the way, you were right," I said. "Captain Kuttner was a gossip. He told me the same thing. About you and Fräulein Schwarzkopf and Dr. Goebbels. Kuttner seemed to think that there might be some other reason behind the minister's patronage than just her singing."

"You are impertinent, Captain Gunther."

"There's no question about that, sir. The question is what else was said. And whether any of that is enough of a motive for murder."

"Need I remind you that you are speaking to a general?"

"You can sit on the highest branch if you want, sir. But it certainly won't stop me from shaking the tree. And I can shake it quite hard if I have to. Hard enough to dump you on your backside."

"I'm afraid Gunther is right, Hugo," said Heydrich. "This is really no time to be sensitive. I must have this situation cleared up as soon as possible if I am to avoid any embarrassment. That's embarrassment to me and my office, you understand, not to you, Hugo. I can't allow anything to get in the way of an early conclusion to this unfortunate matter. Even if that does mean us riding roughshod over your feelings and quite possibly your whole future, too, if you refuse to cooperate with the commissar's inquiry."

Heydrich looked at me now.

"The fact is, Gunther, that Captain Kuttner heard this story from me. It was I who told him about General Jury's affair with Fräulein Schwarzkopf. I'm sorry, Hugo, but everyone in Berlin knows what's been going on. Except perhaps the Leader, and your wife, Karoline. Let us hope that she above all people can remain in ignorance of all this.

"But, Herr Commissar, I think that the part of the story at which poor General Jury will have taken most offense relates not to her talents in the bedroom, which I assume are considerable, but to her talent as a singer. I'm afraid it's true, Hugo. If the Fräulein was really any good as a soprano, she'd be singing with the Berlin State Opera and not the German Opera. And you may not know it for sure, but the commissar is quite right that she has been sharing her sexual favors with the minister of propaganda. I have the incontrovertible proof of that, which at some future stage I would be happy to show you. So there's no need to get on your high horse about all of this. You've both been fucking her and that's all there is to it. I mean, how else do you think she was made a principal soprano so soon after joining the chorus? It was Goebbels who fixed that for her. In return for services that she rendered to him horizontally."

Jury's cheeks were now quite red and his hands were fists. I wondered if that showed a man who was angry enough to kill a brother officer in cold blood.

"I don't care for your manners, General Heydrich," said Jury.

"That is of small account to me, Hugo." Heydrich paused. "Well, how about it? Did you kill Captain Kuttner?" He paused. "If you did, then I promise that we can arrange things so as to avoid too much of a scandal. You can resign quietly and go back to your loyal wife, Karoline. Perhaps you can even pick up your medical career again. But I can promise that if you deny it and it turns out to be you, after all, who murdered the captain, then it will go very hard for you. We have plenty of filthy prison cells in Terezín Castle, where even a distinguished man such as you can be forgotten for years, right up until the moment when I sign his death warrant and have him hanged the old Austro-Hungarian way: by strangulation from a pole."

"I didn't kill him," Jury insisted, and then, with a short click of his heels and a bow of the head, he abruptly left the room.

"I hope you enjoyed that capricious demonstration of your new powers," said Heydrich. "I know I did."

A few seconds later there was a knock on the open door. It was Kurt Kahlo.

"I searched underneath the window, sir," he told me. "Nothing. But I found this lying on the floor farther down the corridor. I marked the spot, so don't worry."

He placed a small brass object in my hand.

"What is it?" asked Heydrich.

I held up the object in my fingers. It looked like a metallic cigarette end.

"Unless I'm very much mistaken, sir, it's a shell case from a Walther P38."

HEYDRICH TOSSED the shell case back to me.

"Well, Gunther, much as I should like to stay and observe you destroy the character of another of my guests, I do have urgent business to attend to. The rather more urgent matter of finding Václav Morávek."

"Yes, of course, sir."

"I've told Major Ploetz that no one is to leave until you've had a chance to question him. No one, apart from him and me and Klein, my driver."

"Thank you, sir."

"I shall see you this evening, when you can tell me of the progress you've made."

"All right, sir."

When Heydrich was gone, I opened Captain Kuttner's tunic and pulled up his bloody shirt to inspect the bullet wound, and was surprised to find not one but two holes, both in the center of his chest and each about the size of the nail on a man's little finger. Kahlo was searching the floor again. I didn't say anything about there being two gunshot wounds. After a minute or so I turned the dead man onto his side so that I could inspect his back.

"There's no exit wound," I said, carefully using the singular. I rubbed my hand up and down the dead man's back. "But sometimes you can find the bullet just underneath the skin. I've seen bullets just fall out of people who'd been shot, after which they can end up just about anywhere. But I think this poor sonofabitch is still carrying metal."

I pushed Kuttner onto his back again and stood up.

"Show me where you found that shell case."

Kahlo led the way out of Kuttner's bedroom and in the corridor outside, pointed to a box of matches on the floor that he'd used to mark the spot where he'd discovered the shell casing.

"All right," I said. "You cut along to the morning room and make it look as much like an interview room as possible. On second thought, no. Leave it as it is. But we'll need pencils and paper, a jug of water, some liquor, some glasses, a fresh pot of coffee every hour, a telephone, some cigarettes, and a typewriter."

"Yes, boss."

"And tell Dr. Honek that the ambulance men can remove the body to the hospital. And have him arrange an autopsy, will you? Today, if possible."

"Yes, boss."

I glanced back to Kuttner's door, about twenty meters away, and once Kahlo had gone, dropped onto my hands and knees and made my way slowly along the corridor. After a few minutes a door opened, and out of a bedroom stepped the only officer in the Lower Castle who wasn't a member of the SS or the SD. He was wearing the uniform of a major in the German Army.

"You look how I feel," he observed.

"Hmm?"

"Last night. I drank far too much. But on top of all that was the champagne, which never agrees with me in the best of times. Still, under the circumstances I didn't want to turn it down. We were celebrating after all, weren't we? All the same, I do regret it now. Woke up with a bit of a head this morning. I felt like I wanted to curl up and die."

"You have to be alive to feel like that, I suppose."

"What's that? Oh yes. I heard one of the adjutants got Stalin's greatcoat. A terrible business."

Stalin's greatcoat was a coffin.

"Which one was he? All of these adjutant fellows sort of look the same to me."

I found what I was looking for: the second shell casing. I stood up and found myself facing a man of about the same age as me.

"Captain Kuttner."

He shook his head as if he couldn't remember him. "And you're the detective fellow, from Berlin, aren't you? Gunther, isn't it?"

"That's correct, sir."

"I suppose that accounts for why you're crawling around the place on your hands and knees."

"I do quite a lot of that anyway, sir. Even when I'm not hunting for evidence. I like to drink, you see, sir. That is, when I can get it."

"There's no shortage of it here, Gunther. If this keeps up I shall need a new liver. Major Paul Thümmel, at your service. If there's anything I can do to help, just let me know. Major Ploetz says that you want to interview everyone who was staying here last night. Fine by me. Just say when. Always glad to help the police."

I pocketed the little shell casing. "Thank you, sir. Perhaps we could speak later on. I'll have Captain Pomme contact you to arrange a time."

"Sooner the better, old man. Ploetz says that none of us can leave the house until we've given a statement. Frankly, it all sounds a bit excessive. After all, it's not like any of us is going to run away, is it?"

"I think it has rather more to do with remembering details that might seem unimportant anywhere else. In my experience, it's always better if you can interview witnesses as close to the crime scene as possible."

"Well, you know your job, I suppose. Just don't interview people in alphabetical order, that's all. You'll find that puts me last, I think."

"I'll certainly bear that in mind, sir."

INVESTIGATING THE MURDER of one young SD officer who had almost certainly participated in the murders of hundreds, perhaps thousands, of Latvian Jews, Gypsies and other "undesirables" struck me as absurd, of course. A mass murderer who'd been murdered. What was wrong with that? But how many had I killed myself? There were the forty or fifty Russian POWs I knew about for sure—nearly all of them members of an NKVD death squad. I'd commanded the firing squad and delivered the coup de grâce to at least ten of them as they lay groaning on the ground. Their blood and brains had been spattered all over my boots. During the Great War there had been a Canadian boy I'd put the bayonet into when it was him or me, only he died hard, with his head on my shoulder. God knows how many others I'd killed when, another time, I'd taken over a Maxim gun and squeezed the trigger as I pointed it at some brown figures advancing slowly over no-man's-land.

But it seemed that Albert Kuttner's death mattered because he'd been a German officer and a close colleague of General Heydrich's. That was supposed to make a difference, only it didn't. At least not to me. Investigating a murder in the autumn of 1941 was like arresting a man for vagrancy during the Depression. But I did what I was told and started to go through the motions the way a proper policeman would have done. What choice did I have? Besides, it kept my mind off what I knew was happening out there, in the East. Most of all, it kept my mind off the growing sense that I'd been to the worst place on the planet, only to realize that the worst place of all was inside me.

"I'VE PREPARED A LIST of everyone who stayed at the Lower Castle last night and therefore who you will want to interview," said Major Ploetz.

He handed me a sheet of neatly typed, headed notepaper.

"Thank you, Major."

We were in the morning room. With its greenish silk chinoise wallpaper, the room felt like an extension of the garden and a little more natural than the rest of the house. There were a couple of big sofas facing each other like very fat chess players across a polished wooden coffee table. In the window was a grand piano, and in the fireplace, a fire that cheered the room. On either side of the marble fireplace was a mosaic of picture frames featuring Heydrich and his family. Kahlo was inspecting these, one at a time, as if looking to judge a winner. Now wearing my civilian clothes, I was seated on one of the sofas, smoking a cigarette.

"Here is your mail, Commissar, forwarded from the Alex in Berlin. And here is a copy of Albert Kuttner's SD personnel file. The general thought it might help you to get a better sense of the man and what he was like and—you never know—perhaps why he was killed. The personnel files of everyone staying here this weekend are being sent over from Hradschin Castle this morning."

"That's very efficient of you, Major."

It was easy to see why Ploetz was Heydrich's chief adjutant. There was no doubting his efficiency. With his lists and memoranda and facts and figures Hans-Achim Ploetz was a real electric Nazi. Before the war I'd been to a town called Achim. It was near Bremen, in a nice part of the country that, in its natural state, is mostly moorland. But there was nothing natural about Hans-Achim Ploetz, and in that respect at least, Dr. Jury was right: all of Heydrich's adjutants were a bit like the Golem of Prague.

Outside the morning room window a Mercedes drew up and Heydrich's driver got out and opened the passenger door expectantly.

Ploetz saw him out of the corner of his eye.

"Well, I'd better go and tell the general that our car is here," he said. "If there is anything you want, just ask Pomme."

"Yes. I will."

Then he was gone and Kahlo and I were standing at the window, peering around the heavy drapes like two comedians getting ready to take a curtain call. The convertible's top was down and the engine was purring smoothly like some green metal dragon.

Ploetz climbed aboard first and sat in the rear. Heydrich sat up front with the driver, as if that might help him to control the car, despite the fact someone else was at the wheel. He was just like that, I guess. As we watched them drive away, there was no sign of an armed escort.

"So what do you make of it, sir?"

"Bloody fool," I muttered.

"How's that, sir?"

"Heydrich. The way he drives around the city like he's invulnerable. Like Achilles. As if daring the poor bastards to come and have a go."

"The Czechos are just mad enough to do it, too."

"You think so?"

Kahlo nodded.

"How long have you been in Prague?"

"Long enough to know that the Czechos have got guts. More than we like to give them credit for."

"Kurt, isn't it?"

Kahlo nodded.

"Where are you from, Kurt?"

"Mannheim, sir."

"How did you become a cop?

"I'm not exactly sure. My dad was a car worker at the Daimler-Benz factory. But I never much fancied being stuck in a factory myself. He wanted me to become a lawyer, only I wasn't clever enough, so becoming a cop seemed like the next best thing."

"So what do you make of it?"

"It's a puzzle, sir. A man is found shot dead inside a first-floor bedroom that's locked from the inside. The windows are bolted and there's no murder weapon present. Down the corridor there's a spent nine-millimeter Parabellum round on the floor, so clearly a gun was fired at some time between the hours of midnight and, say, five o'clock this morning. And yet you'd also expect someone to have remarked on that, because a P38 wasn't picked as the Army's choice of firearm because it's so bloody quiet. They can't all have been so pissed they didn't hear anything. The staff weren't pissed. Not with Kritzinger in charge. Why didn't they hear something? And not just a gunshot, either. I can't imagine Kuttner standing on the landing upstairs and saying nothing as someone is about to shoot him. Me, I'd have shouted 'Help' or 'Don't shoot,' or something like that."

"I agree."

"Kuttner was under the influence of a sleeping pill," he said. "Maybe he didn't realize quite how much peril he was in. Maybe it was dark and he didn't see the gun. Maybe he was shot outside, and because he was drugged, he didn't realize the severity of his injury. So he comes back in the house, goes back to his room, locks the door, lies down, and dies. Maybe."

I shook my head. "You've got more maybes there than Fritz bloody Lang."

"I know," he said. "Frankly, I wouldn't know where to start with this one, sir. However, I'm keen to learn from someone who does, such as you. That is, if General Heydrich is to be believed. Anyway, you have my full cooperation, sir. Just tell me what to do and I'll do it, with no questions asked."

"Questions are good, Kurt. It's obedience I have a problem with. In particular, my own."

Kahlo grinned. "Then I think yours should be an interesting career, sir."

I opened Kuttner's SD file and glanced over the details of the dead man's short life.

"Albert Kuttner was from Halle an der Saale. Interesting."

"Is it? I can't say I know the place."

"What I mean is, Halle is where Heydrich is from."

"So he could be taking this personally."

"Yes. True. Kuttner was born in 1911. That makes him seven

years younger than Heydrich. His father was a Protestant pastor at a local church. But instead of pursuing a career in the Church, or in the Navy—like his boss—"

"Heydrich was in the Navy? I didn't know that."

"It's said he got kicked out of it for conduct unbecoming when he knocked up some admiral's daughter. But don't tell anyone I said so."

"This admiral's daughter. Is that the present Frau Heydrich?"

"No. It's not."

"So he is human, after all."

"I wouldn't go that far."

"Kuttner studied law at the Martin Luther University of Halle-Wittenberg and the Humboldt University of Berlin, where it seems he was a brilliant student. He received his doctorate of law in 1935 and worked for the ministries of justice and the interior before joining the SD."

"So far, so predictable."

"Hmm. Near the top of his class in officer school. Highly praised by everyone who assessed him; he was being groomed for one of the top jobs in Berlin. In May this year he was transferred to the Einsatzgruppen and ordered to Pretzsch, where he was assigned to Group A and sent east. Nothing unusual about that. Lots of decent men have been sent east. Decent men and some lawyers. On June 23, he and the group were ordered to proceed to Riga, in Latvia, to help with 'the resettlement of the indigenous Jewish population.'"

"Resettlement. Yes, I know what that entails."

"Good. It will save me having to explain the distinction between 'resettlement' and 'mass murder.'"

"Am I to assume that your appreciation of the distinction is based on personal experience, sir?"

"You are. But please don't assume that I did a good job. There are no good jobs out east. Albert Kuttner didn't take to his work any more than I did. Which is why he felt guilty. Like me. And why he wasn't sleeping."

"Thus the Veronal in his room."

I turned the page in Kuttner's file and read on a little before speaking again.

"That guilt appears to have manifested itself for the first time just three weeks into his tour of Latvia, when he put in for a transfer to the Army. But the request was refused by his commander, Major Rudolf Lange. Well, that hardly surprises me. I knew Rudolf Lange when he was with the Berlin police. The cat never stops catching mice. He was a bastard then and he's a bastard now. Reason given for refusal of request for transfer: personnel shortages. But a week later he puts in for another transfer. This time he's given an official reprimand. For conduct likely to damage morale."

"It's a dirty job, so someone has to do it, right?"

"Something like that, I suppose."

I turned another page in Kuttner's file.

"By August, however, Albert is back in Berlin, facing a disciplinary inquiry. It seems he threatened a superior officer with a pistol—it doesn't say whom, but I hope it was Lange; I've often wanted to stick a gun in that fat fucker's face. Kuttner's placed under close arrest, but not close enough, because he then attempts suicide. No details on that, either. But he's sent back to Berlin for that disciplinary inquiry. A so-called SS court of honor. Only the disciplinary inquiry is suspended. No reason given."

"Do you think Heydrich might have pulled some strings?"

"That's what it looks like, because the next thing is that Albert is on the general's staff in Berlin. Lighting his cigarettes, booking seats at the opera, and fetching coffee."

"Now, that is a good job," said Kahlo.

"You don't strike me as an opera fan."

"Not the opera. The cigarettes." His eyes were on my cigarette. "The tobacco ration being what it is."

"Sorry." I opened my cigarette case. "Help yourself."

Kahlo took one, lit up, and then puffed with obvious satisfaction. Holding the cigarette in front of his eyes, like a rare diamond, he grinned happily.

"I'd forgotten how good a cigarette can taste," he said.

"There's a page missing from this file," I said. "In my own SD file there's a page headed 'Personal Remarks.' I've only ever seen it upside down, but it's full of things my superiors have said about me, like 'insubordinate' and 'politically unreliable.'"

"You read good upside down." Kahlo grinned. "I'm a bit of a beefsteak Nazi myself, sir. Brown on the outside but red in the middle. Although I'm not as rare as my old dad. Being a car worker, he was red all the way."

"Mm-hmm."

I handed Kahlo the file.

"It's not much to go on," he said, flicking through it.

"Let's see what we can find out for ourselves."

I picked up the telephone and asked the Lower Castle switchboard to connect me with the Alex in Berlin. A few minutes later I was able to speak with the Records Division. I asked them if they had a file on Albert Kuttner. They didn't. So I had them run a check on his address, which was always something you could do in Berlin because it wasn't just individuals who generated records in Prussia, it was places, too. The Prussian State Police were nothing if not thorough. And a few minutes later Records called back to tell me that flat 3, 4 Pestalozzistrasse, in Charlottenburg was home to another man besides Albert Kuttner.

And when I had the Records people check him out, I started to believe I had something.

"Lothar Ott," I said, reading aloud my notes of these several telephone conversations. "Born Berlin, February twenty-first, 1901. Two convictions for male prostitution, one 1930, the other 1932. Not only that, but his previous address was number one

Friedrichsgracht, near Berlin's Spittelmarkt. That won't mean much to a cop from Mannheim but to a bull from Berlin it means a lot. Until 1932, number one Friedrichsgracht was a notorious homosexual club called the Burger Casino. Either the late Captain Kuttner was very tolerant of homosexuals or—"

"Or he was maybe a bit warm himself." Kahlo nodded. "I mean, you wouldn't live with someone like that unless you were, would you?"

"What do you think? You met him."

"You're asking if Kuttner struck me as the type? I dunno. A lot of officers strike me that way. It's possible, I suppose. He could have been the type. You know, a bit fastidious. A bit too careful about his appearance. A bit too much cologne on his hair. The way he walked. Now I come to think of it, yes, I can see it. When he shrugged, it looked just like my brother's daughter."

"I agree."

"Someone ought to give this other fellow, Ott, a knock and see how he takes the news that Kuttner's dead."

"That's an idea."

So I telephoned the Alex again and explained Kahlo's idea to an old friend in Kripo called Trott, who promised to go and see Lothar Ott and give him the bad news in person and then report back on the show.

As soon as I replaced the receiver, the telephone rang. Kahlo answered it.

"It's Dr. Honek," he said, handing me the candlestick. "Calling about the autopsy."

I took the phone.

"This is Gunther."

"I managed to find someone to perform an autopsy on Captain Kuttner," said Honek. "Today. Like you asked me, Commissar. In view of the circumstances, Professor Hamperl, from the Pathological Institute of the German Charles University in Prague, has agreed to carry out the procedure at four o'clock this afternoon. He's most distinguished."

"Where?"

"At the Bulovka Hospital."

"All right. We'll be there at four."

After I hung up, Kahlo said, "We? What's this 'we'? You don't want me there, do you?"

"You said you were keen to learn, didn't you?"

"Yes, but, well, the thing is, I've never seen an autopsy before."

"There's nothing to it. Besides, we have a distinguished professor to perform the autopsy."

"I don't know," he said, anxiously. "I mean, dead people. I don't know. They look like they're dead, right?"

"It's best that way. When they look alive it puts the pathologist a bit off his knife." I shrugged. "It's your choice. Now let's have a look at that list of names that Major Ploetz gave us. I think some of them look like they're people."

Those present at the Lower Castle on the night of 2nd/3rd October 1941 included the following:

SS-Obergruppenführer Reinhard Heydrich

SS-Obergruppenführer Richard Hildebrandt

SS-Obergruppenführer Friedrich Karl Freiherr von Eberstein

SS-Gruppenführer Konrad Henlein

SS-Gruppenführer Dr. Hugo Jury

SS-Gruppenführer Karl Hermann Frank

SS-Brigadeführer Bernard Voss

SS-Standartenführer Dr. Hans Ulrich Geschke

SS-Standartenführer Horst Böhme

SS-Obersturmbannführer Walter Jacobi

SS-Sturmbannführer Dr. Hans-Achim Ploetz

Wehrmacht Major Paul Thümmel

SS-Hauptsturmführer Kurt Pomme

SS-Hauptsturmführer Hermann Kluckholm

SS-Hauptsturmführer Albert Kuttner

SS-Unterscharführer August Beck

Staff:

SS-Sturmscharführer Gert Kritzinger, Butler

SS-Oberscharführer Johannes Klein, Chauffeur

SS-Unterscharführer Hermann Kube, Chef

SS-Rottenführer Wilhelm Seupel, Assistant Chef

SS-Rottenführer Walther Artner, Senior Footman

SS-Stürmann Adolf Jachod, Senior Footman

SS-Stürmann Kurt Bauer, Footman

SS-Stürmann Oskar Fendle, Footman

SS-Helferinnen Elisabeth Schreck, Secretary to Heydrich

SS-Kriegshelferinnen Siv Elsler, Assistant Secretary to H.

SS-Kriegshelferinnen Charlotte Teitze, Maid

SS-Kriegshelferinnen Rosa Steffel, Maid

SS-Kriegshelferinnen Liv Lemke, Maid

Bruno Kopkow, Head Gardener

Otto Faulhaber, Assistant Gardener

Johannes Bangert, Assistant Gardener

Upper Castle Personnel:

SS-Gruppenführer Konstantin von Neurath

The Baroness von Neurath, Marie Auguste Moser von Filseck

SS-Hauptsturmführer Eduard Jahn

SS-Oberscharführer Richard Kolbe, Butler

SS-Rottenführer Richard Miczek, Chef

SS-Sturmmann Rolf Braun, Footman

SS-Kriegshelferinnen Anna Kurzidim, Maid

SS-Kriegshelferinnen Victoria Kuckenberg, Maid

For obvious reasons it is recommended that you conduct your interviews at the Lower Castle in strict order of seniority. For reasons of security and confidentiality, please confine all interviews to the morning room. Interviews at the Upper Castle should be conducted by arrangement with the baron's adjutant, SS-Hauptsturmführer Eduard Jahn. A safe will be provided for your use in the morning room. All documents pertaining to this inquiry should be placed in it when not in use, for reasons of confidentiality.

> *Signed*
> *SS-Major Dr. Hans-Achim Ploetz, Adjutant*
> *to SS-Obergruppenführer Heydrich*

My eyes slid off the page and landed on the floor with a loud sigh.

"If one were to assume that anyone at the Lower Castle might have had the opportunity and the motive to kill Captain Kuttner," I said, "that leaves us with thirty-one suspects."

"Christ," muttered Kahlo. "That's at least one for every day of the month."

"Thirty-nine, including the personnel at the Upper Castle with von Neurath. It's only a short walk from there to the Upper Castle, so I don't see how they can be excluded."

"And God knows how many if we include all of the SS up at the guardhouse."

I grunted.

"Do you want to include them?"

"How many are in the garrison?"

"At least two hundred."

"I don't want to include them, no. No. But I hardly see how I can exclude them, given the possibility that Albert Kuttner may have been warm. A bit of rough trade with an enlisted man in the woods might have been just his beer. The first thing we have to do—"

"You mean apart from interviewing the senior ranks."

I paused.

"So far no one's complained about being kept waiting by you," said Kahlo. "But it won't be long."

I nodded. "All right. While I start with the formal interviews, the first thing you have to do is to try and speak to everyone informally and get a sense of Kuttner's movements last night. Who was the last person to see him alive and at what time? That kind of thing. Now, I saw him at about nine o'clock, when he was having a fairly heated discussion in the garden with one of the other adjutants—Captain Kluckholm, I think. Then about half an hour later, after Heydrich had made a speech, he appeared in the library with some champagne. So you might start with that in mind. I want times and places. And see if you can't get a plan of the house. That way we can start plotting his various positions."

"Yes, I suppose that might help."

"Any suggestions of your own will be gratefully considered."

"Then a clairvoyant with a crystal ball couldn't do any harm. Strikes me that's the only way we're going to find a murderer who walks through locked doors and shoots people without making a sound."

"You make me begin to wonder what I'm doing here, Kurt."

"By the way, sir, if you don't mind my asking. What *are* you doing here? What I mean is: all this damned cauliflower. It's like a market garden in this house."

He was referring to the oak-leaf collar patches that distinguished SS generals, brigadiers, and colonels from lesser mortals.

"What's it all about? What's the reason for it?"

"You ask some pretty good questions for a man who promised to work for me, no questions asked."

"So what's the answer?"

"I believe General Heydrich wanted a quiet weekend with friends to celebrate his appointment as the new Reichsprotector of Bohemia."

"I see."

"You sound surprised. But not as surprised as I was to be asked along on this jaunt. The general and I, we've grown apart, you understand. Schiller once wrote a pretty good poem to his friends. When I was at school we were obliged to learn all five verses. I used to think he said all there was to say about what friendship means in Germany. Only I don't remember a verse covering the kind of friend I have in General Heydrich. Goethe did it better, I think. You know? What happens when Mephistopheles invites you over for real coffee and American cigarettes."

Even as I said it Arianne came into my mind; it was she who

had made the comparison between Heydrich and Mephistopheles on the train from Berlin; ever since then I'd been wondering just how long I had to work for Heydrich before my soul was forfeit.

"Oh yeah," said Kahlo. "Temptation. And temptation like real coffee and American cigarettes. Well, that's very tempting."

"I figure that the alternative is worse. I can't answer for why all the cauliflower is here, but that's why I'm on board. Because the general asked me to dance. Because he doesn't like it when you say no."

"All right. I'll buy that."

"Good. Now, let's see what we can do about getting a bead on the invisible man."

SS-OBERGRUPPENFÜHRER Richard Hildebrandt was the higher police leader in Danzig and commander of a large unit of SS stationed in West Prussia. In the event that citizens of Berlin rose up against Hitler, Hildebrandt would be in charge of suppressing that particular revolution.

Born in Worms in 1897, he was an old friend of Heydrich's. Smooth, neat, fastidious, and of only average height, he had the look and manner of a prosperous businessman. Certainly he had the best tailoring of any officer who was staying at the Lower Castle. On his left breast pocket he wore a Knight's Cross of the War Merit Cross with Swords—a silver Nazi medal that had nothing to do with the proper Knight's Cross, and everyone who'd seen proper combat thought of this decoration as a substitute Iron Cross; but I suppose a general has to have some kind of furniture on his tunic if people are ever going to listen to him. But the gold Party badge he wore next to the faux Knight's Cross was the real hallmark of his sterling Nazi status and near untouchability. That little gewgaw occupied pride of place on his uniform and was the cynosure of anyone who knew what was what in Nazi Germany.

He sat down on the sofa opposite me, lit a cigarette, and crossed his legs. "Will this take long, Commissar?"

"Not long, sir."

"Good. Because I have some important paperwork I need to get through."

"How well did you know Captain Kuttner?"

"I didn't know him at all. Until I arrived here the day before yesterday I had perhaps spoken to him twice, and only on the telephone."

"How did you find him?"

"He struck me as efficient. Well educated. Diligent. As one might expect of an officer working for a man like General Heydrich."

"Did you like him?"

"What kind of stupid question is that?"

"A fairly easy one, I'd say. Did you like him?"

Hildebrandt shrugged. "I did not dislike him."

"Can you think of any reason why someone would want to kill him?"

"No, and my own opinion is that a Czech must have committed the crime. There are Czechs working here, in the house and grounds. My advice, Commissar, would be to start by questioning them, not senior generals in the SS."

"My apologies, Herr General. I was led to believe by Major Ploetz that I should conduct these interviews in strict order of seniority, so as not to keep anyone important—such as yourself—hanging around."

Hildebrandt shrugged. "I see. My apologies, Commissar."

I shrugged back.

"However, I still fail to see why senior ranks should be questioned at all. In my opinion, my word should be good enough."

"And what word is that, sir?"

"That I had nothing at all to do with this man's death, of course."

"I don't doubt it, sir. However, it is not the point of this interview to find out if you murdered Captain Kuttner. The immediate purpose of this inquiry to build a detailed picture of the man's last few hours. And having done so, to identify some genuine suspects. You do see the difference."

"Of course. Do you take me for an idiot?"

I didn't answer that. "You were with us all, in the library, to listen to the Leader's speech, were you not?"

"Naturally."

"And then to hear Heydrich's speech."

Hildebrandt nodded impatiently. He took a last puff of his cigarette and then extinguished it in a heavy glass ashtray that lay on the table between us.

"Do you remember Captain Kuttner bringing in some champagne after that?"

"Yes."

"Did you stay to celebrate very long?"

"Yes. I confess I drank rather too much, I think. Like everyone else, I have a bit of a headache this morning."

"Yes, sir. Only I have a bigger one. I have to solve this murder. That won't be easy. You do see that, don't you? At some stage it's possible I'm going to have to accuse a brother officer of killing Kuttner. Perhaps even a senior officer. I think you might try to be a little more understanding of my position, sir."

"Don't tell me my duty, Commissar Gunther."

"With the scary badge in your lapel? I wouldn't dream of it, sir."

Hildebrandt glanced down at his gold Party badge and smiled. "You mean this, don't you? I've heard that's what some people call it. Although I can't imagine why anyone would be scared of this."

"It means that you joined the Party very early on, doesn't it?"

"Yes. In my case it was 1922. The following year I took part in the Munich putsch. I was right behind the Leader as we left the beer hall."

"You must have been very young, sir."

"I was twenty-six."

"If you don't mind my asking, what happened to you, sir? After the putsch failed."

His eyes misted over for a moment before he answered.

"Things were difficult for a while. Very difficult. I don't mind telling you. Apart from the harassment I received at the hands of the police, I was short of money and I had little choice but to go and work abroad."

He seemed relieved to be talking about something that had nothing to do with Kuttner; relaxed, even, which, momentarily, was my intention.

"Where did you go?"

"America. There I tried my hand at farming for a while. But after that failed I became a bookseller, in New York."

"That's quite a switch, sir. Did you fail at being a bookseller, too?"

Hildebrandt frowned.

"Or did you come back to Germany for another reason, sir?"

"I came back because of the wonderful things that were happening in Germany. Because of the Leader. That was 1930."

"And you joined the SS when, may I ask?"

"Nineteen thirty-one. That is when I first met Heydrich. But I don't see what any of this has to do with the death of Captain Kuttner."

"I'm coming to that, if you'll bear with me. I suppose you must have a high regard for the standards of the SS, having joined as early as 1931."

"Yes, I do. Of course I do. What kind of a question is that?"

"Do you suppose that Captain Kuttner lived up to those standards?"

"I'm sure he did."

"Are you sure he did, or do you suppose he did?"

"What are you driving at, Gunther?"

"If I told you that Captain Kuttner was a practicing homosexual, what would your reaction be?"

"Nonsense. General Heydrich would never have tolerated such a thing. I've known him long enough to be quite sure of that."

"What if General Heydrich didn't know about it?"

"There are no secrets from Heydrich," said Hildebrandt. "You should be aware of that. And if you're not, you soon will be. What he doesn't know probably isn't worth knowing."

"Would it surprise you if I told you that there are some things even Heydrich doesn't know?"

"Nonsense," he repeated. "This whole line of questioning is nonsense, Commissar. Kuttner was artistic, at worst. But we don't condemn a man for enjoying good music and appreciating good paintings."

"With respect, I don't think it is nonsense, sir. Kuttner was living with a man in Berlin. A man with convictions for male prostitution. A man who used to frequent a notorious homosexual bar called the Burger Casino, dressed in a schoolboy sailor suit, and who used to take his clients to a nearby pier on the river in order to have sex with them."

"Rubbish. I just don't believe it. And I think it very poor taste on your part to malign a fellow officer who is no longer in a position to defend himself from that kind of defamation."

"Let us assume for one minute that I'm right about this."

"Why?"

"Please, sir. Indulge me for a moment."

"Very well."

"What would your opinion be of a man like that?"

"My opinion?"

"Yes, sir. What do you think of an SS captain who shares his bed with a male prostitute?"

Hildebrandt's smooth face darkened. The lips tightened and the jaw turned pugnacious.

"I mean, sir, it's said it was Ernst Röhm's homosexuality that was one of the reasons the Party turned on him, why he was executed."

"That's probably true," admitted Hildebrandt. "Röhm was a degenerate. As were some of the others. Edmund Heines. Klausener. Schneidhuber. Schragmüller. They were loathsome specimens and richly deserved their fate."

"Of course they did."

I wasn't sure they had deserved their fate, not all of them. Erich Klausener had been the leader of the police department at the Prussian interior ministry in Berlin and not a bad fellow at all. But I wasn't there to debate with Hildebrandt.

"Do you think that sort of thing should be tolerated in the SS?"

"Of course it shouldn't. And it isn't tolerated. Never has been."

"Do you think it brings dishonor to the SS? Is that why?"

"Certainly it brings dishonor to the SS, Commissar Gunther. What a fucking question. It's obvious. If the man was, as you say, homosexual—although I still don't believe Kuttner was—then I'd go further than that. Such a man should be put in front of a firing squad. Like Röhm and those other queers. It's the pansies and the Jews who almost destroyed Germany during the Weimar Republic."

"Oh, surely," I said.

"Who continue to threaten the moral fiber of our country. We are cultivating increasingly healthy blood for Germany and it must be kept pure. As the father of three children myself, two of them boys, I say it quite emphatically. If such a man were under my command I should not hesitate to denounce him to the Gestapo. Not for a minute. No matter how serious the consequences."

"Well, of course," I said, "I know it's illegal under paragraphs one seventy-four and one seventy-five of the Criminal Code. But I thought that homosexuals could be sent to prison for only up to ten years. So let me get this straight. There are extra punishments that apply to such people in the SS, is that right? Like being shot, as you say. I assume you would know, sir."

He lit another cigarette.

"As a matter of fact, I do know. And in the strictest confidence I will tell you what happens. In the SS we have about one case of homosexuality a month. When they are uncovered, by order of the Reichsführer-SS himself they are degraded, expelled, and handed over to the courts; following completion of the statutory punishment, which you mentioned, they are then sent to a concentration camp, where they are most often shot while attempting to escape."

"I see."

"Personally, I can't see the need for the camp. If it was up to me, it would be the commanding officer who would shoot such a man. Summarily."

"So if you had absolute incontrovertible proof that Captain Kuttner was a homosexual, and he'd been your junior officer, you'd have shot him yourself. Is that right?"

"Absolutely."

"Thank you, General. That will be all, sir. I do appreciate your candor in this matter."

Hildebrandt paused. "Are you playing games with me, Commissar?"

"I was merely testing a theory, sir."

"And what theory is that?"

"Only that it's quite possible he wasn't murdered by a Czech, after all, as you insisted earlier. But by another German. I daresay you're not the only man who thinks Kuttner was probably murdered by a Czech. It's a common enough prejudice we Germans have: a suspicion of other lesser races. Take Berlin's S-Bahn murderer, this summer. Paul Ogorzow. Remember him?"

"Yes."

"Before he was caught, everyone thought the murderer was a foreign worker. But Paul Ogorzow was a German. Not only that, he was a Party member. Not as early a member as you, sir, but I think he joined well before Hitler became Reich chancellor."

I shrugged. "When it comes to murder, I like to keep an open mind."

Hildebrandt got up to leave. He straightened his immaculate riding breeches, which were the expensive kind—with the suede inside legs, as if he actually went riding—and moved toward the morning room door.

"By the way, sir. How did you find living in America?"

"I beg your pardon?"

"Did you enjoy living in America, sir?"

"Yes. I did."

"I'd love to work in a foreign country. So far it's been France, Bohemia, and Belorussia. And I didn't much like Belorussia. And I certainly didn't like the work."

Hildebrandt remained silent.

"Neither did Captain Kuttner," I said. "Did you know that?"

"No."

"Yes. He told me that himself. It bothered him. A lot. Made him feel disgusting."

"There's no doubt that it's difficult work," said Hildebrandt. "Not everyone is suitable for this kind of duty. However, there's no shame in that, I think. No shame for you anyway, Commissar."

"Thank you, sir. I'll try to bear that in mind."

I HAD ABOUT THIRTY MINUTES before my next appointment in the morning room, so I went upstairs to search Kuttner's room. I wanted to do this without anyone else looking over my shoulder just in case I found something interesting that I had to show Ploetz or Heydrich or whoever else took it upon themselves to scrutinize my work.

But Kuttner's bed had already been stripped. The sheets and blankets lay in a heap on the floor. The window had been opened wider than before and the room was full of the scent of freshly cut grass. The gardener at Jungfern-Breschan was forever tending the lawns. Outside the window the motorized lawn mowers were already at work.

Seated on the end of Kuttner's bed was a girl of about twenty-five. She had blond hair and a handkerchief in her hand and was wearing a sleeveless gray pinafore and a regulation SS black dress—the one with the big floppy collar trimmed with white piping. She was an SS-Helferinnen: a helper and, in this case, a maid.

I watched her silently from the doorway for several minutes. And, not noticing me, she didn't move except, now and then, to press the handkerchief to her nose, as if she had a head cold. Finally my curiosity could no longer be contained and, clearing my throat, I advanced into the dead man's room.

Abruptly the helper stood up and looked the other way—at least she did until I caught hold of her arm.

"I'm sorry, sir," she said. "I didn't mean any harm coming in here. Mr. Kritzinger sent me to strip the bed, and I was just overcome for a moment at the thought of that poor man being murdered."

She was older than I had first supposed and not particularly good-looking—too thin and highly strung for my taste. Her skin was clear as tissue paper and you could see the little blue veins at the side of her forehead like the maker's mark on good porcelain. The mouth was wider and sadder than it ought to have been, perhaps, but it was her big eyes I was really interested in, because they were red and full of tears.

"I'm Commissar Gunther."

"Yes, sir. I know who you are. I saw you when you arrived here yesterday."

She gave a little curtsy.

"I'm investigating Captain Kuttner's murder."

She nodded. She knew that, too.

"Did you know him?"

"Not really, sir. We talked a few times. He was kind to me."

"What did you talk about?"

"Nothing really, sir. Nothing important. It was just incidental talk, you might say. Idle conversation about nothing very much."

"It's all right. I'm not going to tell anyone. I'm just trying to get the handle on what kind of a fellow he was. Maybe when I've done that I'll have a better grip on why someone killed him." I pointed at the bed where she'd been sitting. "Can we sit down and talk? Just for a minute."

"All right."

She sat down and I sat beside her.

"Albert was a very sweet, gentle man. Well, he was more of a boy, really. Such a handsome boy. I can't imagine anyone wanting to hurt him. Let alone kill him. He was thoughtful and considerate, and very sensitive."

"You liked him, then."

"Oh yes. Much more than some of these other officers. He was different."

"He certainly was."

Thinking I might have sounded insincere, I added, "I liked him, too." Even as I said this I realized for the first time since hearing about Kuttner's death that I really had liked him. Probably it was mostly the fact we had both shared a terrible experience in the East; but more than that, I had also liked his wit and candor, which bordered on the indiscreet.

To that extent at least Kuttner reminded me of myself, and I wondered if I had started to take his murder a little more personally than seemed appropriate.

"Go on."

She shook her head. "I don't want to get in any trouble."

"I can promise you that you won't. But if there's anything you know that sheds any light on what happened here last night, then I think I need to know about it, don't you? General Heydrich is very determined that I find out who murdered the captain. And the only way that is going to happen is if I persuade people like you to have confidence enough in me to tell the truth."

"All right, sir."

"Good. What's your name?"

"Steffel. Rosa Steffel."

"Well, Rosa, why don't you tell me what happened?"

"Last night," she said, "when all of the officers started to go to bed, he insisted on helping me collect up the glasses, even though I could see he was dead tired."

"That was kind of him," I said. "What time was that?"

"It must have been after one o'clock. I heard the clock chime in the hall. Some of the cauliflowers were still up, of course, swigging brandy in the library. And one or two were drunk. One in particular. I wouldn't like to say who he was, but he got a bit too familiar with me, if you know what I mean. You see, there's something about this uniform. When some of the cauliflowers get drunk, they think we're little better than camp followers, and they take liberties with us. This particular officer touched my breasts, and he tried to put his hand up my dress. I didn't care for it and told him so; but he's my senior officer and it's not easy trying to put a man in his place when he's a general. It was Captain Kuttner who came to my assistance. Rescued me, if you like. He told the general off, in so many words. The general was furious and swore a lot at the captain and told him to mind his own effing business. But Captain Kuttner was wonderful, sir. He ignored the general and escorted me back below stairs before the general could touch me again."

I shook my head. "Some of these SS generals are loathsome," I said. "I've just come out of a rather rough meeting with General Hildebrandt. And he really put me back in my shell. Was it he who touched you?"

"No."

I sighed. "Rosa. Please. I'm in a real spot here. One of these men—yes, maybe even one of these cauliflowers—murdered a man in cold blood. Right here in this room. The room was locked from the inside and the window was bolted, which means that this investigation is already difficult. Don't make it impossible. You need to tell me who it was who touched you last night."

"It was General Henlein."

"Thank you."

"What happened when Captain Kuttner escorted you below stairs, Rosa?"

"We talked a bit. Like we usually did. About nothing much, really."

"Tell me one of the things you used to talk about, Rosa."

She shrugged. "Prague. We talked about Prague. We both agreed that it's very beautiful. And we also talked about our hometown."

"You're not from Halle an der Saale, too?"

"Sort of. I'm from Reidesburg, which is just outside Halle."

"It seems as though everyone but me is from Halle. General Heydrich is from Halle, do you know that?"

"Of course. Everyone knows about the Heydrichs in Halle. Someone else here is from Halle; at least that's what Albert told me, but I'm afraid I don't remember who that is."

"What else did he tell you?"

"That he went to the same school as the general. The Reform-Real-Gymnasium. My brother Rolf went there, too. It's the best school in town."

"Sounds like they had a lot in common. Albert and the general."

"Yes. He said things had been difficult for him lately. But that the general had been very kind to him."

The idea of Heydrich being kind was not something I felt like contemplating. It was like hearing that Hitler liked children, or that Ivan the Terrible had owned a puppy.

"Did he elaborate on any of that? On why things had been difficult? On exactly how the general had been kind to him?"

Rosa looked at her handkerchief as if the answer lay crushed inside its sodden interior.

"Albert made me promise not to tell anyone about it. He said that people in the SS were not supposed to talk about such things. And that it might get me into trouble."

"So why was he telling you about it?"

"Because he said he had to tell someone. To get it off his chest."

"Well, he's dead now, and so is that promise, I think."

"I suppose so. But do *you* promise not to tell anyone that I spoke about this with you?"

"Yes. I promise."

Rosa nodded. And hesitantly she gave voice to what Kuttner had told her.

"He said he was in our Latvian provinces during the summer and that Germany had done terrible things there. That lots of people, thousands of people, had been killed for no other reason than that they were Jews. Old men, women, and children. Whole villages full of defenseless people who had nothing to do with the war. He said that at first he carried out his orders and commanded the firing squads that murdered these people. But after a while, he'd had enough and refused to have anything more to do with these killings himself. Only this landed him in trouble with his superior officers." She shook her head. "It seemed unbelievable to me, but when he talked about it, he started to cry, and so I couldn't help but believe him at the time. I mean a man—especially an officer—he doesn't cry for nothing, does he? But now I don't know. Do you really think it can be true what he told me, Commissar Gunther? About the killings?"

"I'm afraid it's true, Rosa. Every word of it. And not just in Latvia. It's going on everywhere east of Berlin. For all I know it's even going on here in Bohemia. But he was wrong about one thing. Within the SS and the SD, it's an open secret what's been going on in the eastern territories. And just to put your mind at rest, I'm almost certain it wasn't his talking about this that got him killed, but something else."

Rosa nodded gratefully. "Thank you, Commissar. I was worried about that."

"Tell me something. When Captain Kuttner intervened on your behalf, with General Henlein, you said the general swore at Albert."

"That's right."

"Did he threaten him?"

"Yes."

"Can you remember his exact words?"

"Perhaps not exactly. As well as a lot of horrible words I don't want to repeat, the general said something along the lines of 'I'll remember you, Kuttner, you worthless little coward.' And 'I'll make you pay for this, just see if I don't.'"

"Did anyone else hear that besides you, Rosa?"

"Mr. Kritzinger. General Heydrich. They must have heard it.

And I suppose some of the others, too, but I don't remember their names. In their uniforms they all look the same to me."

"I have the same problem. And that's partly why I took mine off. Sometimes when I'm playing detective it's necessary to put myself apart from everyone else. But frankly I hope I never have to put the uniform on again."

"You're beginning to sound a lot like Albert."

"I suppose that's why I liked him."

"You're a strange one, too, Commissar. For a policeman."

"I get a lot of that. Remember that wild kid they found walking around Nuremberg during the last century? The one who claimed he'd spent his early life alone in a darkened cell?"

"Kaspar Hauser. Yes, I remember. He ended his days in Ansbach, didn't he? Everyone knows that old story."

"The only difference between me and Kaspar is that I have a terrible feeling I'm going to end *my* days in a darkened cell. So, for that reason alone, it might be best if you made me a promise not to tell anyone that we've had this conversation."

"I promise."

"All right, you can run along now. I'm going to search Albert's room."

"I thought you already did."

"What do you mean?"

"I mean that the other two adjutants, Captains Kluckholm and Pomme, were here already when I came in to strip the bed. They'd emptied the drawers into some cardboard boxes and took them away."

"No, that was nothing to do with me. However, they probably wanted to collect Albert's personal effects to send back to his parents. The way your pals do when you catch the last bus home."

"Yes, I expect so."

But Rosa Steffel didn't sound any more convinced of this than I was.

ON THE WAY BACK to the morning room I found Kritzinger winding the long-case clock. I looked at it and checked my wristwatch but the butler was shaking his head.

"I wouldn't ever set your watch by this clock, sir," he said. "It's running very slow."

"Is that well known in the house?" I was thinking of the approximate times that had been given to me in Heydrich's study earlier on.

"Generally, yes. The clock urgently needs to see a clockmaker."

"There must be plenty of those in Prague. This city's got more clocks than Salvador Dalí."

"You would think so, sir. But so far my own inquiries have revealed that all of them seem to be Jews."

"A Jew can't fix a clock?"

"Not in this house, sir."

"No, I suppose not. That was naïve of me, wasn't it? This is an interesting time we live in, wouldn't you say? Even if it is always the wrong one."

I glanced at the gold pocket watch in Kritzinger's hand.

"How about your watch, Herr Kritzinger? Can that be relied upon?"

"Yes, sir. It's a Glashütte and belonged to my late father. He was a stationmaster, on the railways in Posen. A good watch is essential for a railwayman in Prussia, if the trains are to run on time."

"And did he? Get the trains to run on time?"

"Yes, sir."

"Me, I always thought it was the Leader who did that."

Kritzinger regarded me with polite patience. "Was there something I could help you with, sir?"

"According to that Glashütte of yours, Kritzinger, what time did the party in the library fold last night?"

"The last gentlemen went up to bed just before two, sir."

"And they were?"

"I believe it was General Henlein and Colonel Böhme."

"I believe General Henlein made himself a late-night snack out of Captain Kuttner. Is that right?"

"I'm not sure what you mean, sir."

"Sure you do. The general cut the captain off at the tops of his boots, didn't he?"

"I believe the general might have said something to the captain, yes, sir."

"Didn't he threaten him?"

"I wouldn't like to say, sir."

Kritzinger snapped the lid shut on the gold pocket watch and dropped the timepiece into his vest pocket. It was an impatient action, quite at odds with his general demeanor, which was always to be of service even when it was in the face of the provocation I offered, like asking him apparently frivolous or trivial questions that bordered on the impertinent or the unpatriotic.

"I can understand that. Nobody likes a *Petzer*. Especially when the *Petzer* is the butler. In relation to their employers and perhaps their guests, too, good butlers are expected to behave like the three wise monkeys, right?"

Kritzinger's head bowed almost imperceptibly. "That describes my position vis à vis my superiors, only up to a point, sir. As you suggest, I am obliged always to observe. But I never judge. One must always guard against such unnecessary distractions in service."

"Particularly now, I'd have thought. Working for General Heydrich."

"I really couldn't say, sir."

"Herr Kritzinger? I respect you. And I wouldn't ever try to bully a man who wears an Iron Cross ribbon on his lapel. The way I figure it, you probably won yours the same way I won mine: in hell. Fighting a real war against real soldiers who fought back, most of them. So you'll know that I'm not likely to be a man who makes idle threats. But this is a murder inquiry, Kritzinger, and that means I'm supposed to behave like a very nosy fellow and take a peep between the pots on everyone's window ledge. I don't like doing it any more than you do, but I will do it even if I have to throw every fucking pot through your window. Now, what did General Henlein say?"

The butler stared at me for a long moment, blinking with silent disapproval, like a cat in an empty fishmonger's.

"I can assure you, I do appreciate your position. There's no need for profanity, please, sir."

I sighed and thumbed a cigarette into my mouth.

"I think there's every fucking reason for profanity when someone is murdered. Profanity helps to remind us that this isn't something that happened politely and with good manners, Kritzinger. You can polish the silver on this all you want, but a man was shot last night, and every time I put a cigarette near my mouth I can still taste his blood on my fingers. I see a lot of bodies in my line of work. Sometimes it looks like I brush it off, but 'fuck' is what I still say to myself every time I see some poor bastard with a leaky hole in his chest. It helps to focus on the true profanity of what happened. Do I have to swear more loudly and twist your face in my hand while I'm doing it or are you going to heave it up? What did General Henlein say to Captain Kuttner?"

Kritzinger colored and then glanced around nervously.

"The general did threaten the captain, sir."

"With what? A blanket bath? A kiss on the cheek? Come on, Kritzinger, I'm through dancing with you."

"General Henlein had taken a fancy to one of the maids, sir. Rosa. Rosa Steffel. She's a good girl and she certainly did not encourage him. But the general had consumed a little too much alcohol."

"You mean he was drunk."

"That's not for me to say, sir. But I do believe he was not quite himself. He made a pass at Rosa, which left the girl embarrassed, and I would have intervened had not the captain done so first. This earned him a reprimand from General Henlein. More than just a reprimand, perhaps. He was abusive. But I recall it wasn't just General Henlein, sir, who spoke so violently. Which is another reason, perhaps, I did not interfere sooner. Colonel Böhme had something to say as well, and between them they straightened the unfortunate captain's tie for him."

"Give me some verbs here, Kritzinger. What were they going to do to him when they were sober?"

"I do believe that the general called the captain a filthy coward and said he'd make him pay for his damned interference. Then the colonel came in with his two pfennigs' worth. He accused Captain Kuttner of insubordination and of being a Jew lover."

"What did Captain Kuttner say to that?"

"Mostly nothing at all, sir. He just took it as you might have expected, given their difference in ranks." Pointedly, he added, "The way a butler might have to take abuse from one of his employer's more uncouth and loutish houseguests."

That made me smile. It was easy to see how Kritzinger had won his Iron Cross.

"Colonel Böhme also mentioned something about sending Captain Kuttner to the eastern front, where his cheek and insubordination would receive short shrift from his commanders. Captain Kuttner replied—and I believe I'm quoting him here—that 'it would be a privilege and an honor to serve with real soldiers in a real army commanded by real generals.'"

"He said that?"

"Yes, sir. He did."

"Good for him."

"I thought so, too, sir."

"Thank you, Herr Kritzinger. I'm sorry if I was loutish with you."

"That's all right, sir. We both of us have jobs to do."

I glanced at my wristwatch again and saw that I had five minutes before I was supposed to see General von Eberstein in the morning room.

"One more thing, Kritzinger. Did you see Captain Kuttner before he went to bed?"

"Yes, sir. It was after two. By my watch. Not this clock."

"How did he seem?"

"A little depressed. And tired. Very tired."

"Oh?"

"I remarked upon it. And wished him a good night."

"What did he say to that?"

"He gave a bitter sort of laugh, and said that he thought he'd probably had his last good night for a long while. I confess this struck me as an unusual thing to say, and when I asked him what he meant, he said that the only way he would sleep would be if he were to take some sleeping pills. Which he intended to do."

"So you had the impression that he hadn't yet taken them?"

Kritzinger paused and thought about this. "Yes. But as I say, he certainly didn't look like a man who needed sleeping pills."

"Because he looked so tired already?"

"That's right, sir."

"Did you see him drink very much last night?"

"No. He hardly drank at all. He had a glass of beer in his hand before he went to bed, but now that I come to think of it, that was all I saw him drink the whole evening. He seemed to be a most abstemious sort of person, if I'm honest."

"Thank you. By the way, I should like to have a plan of the house, with an indication of who was in each of the bedrooms. Is that possible?"

"Yes, sir. I'll see to it."

"All right, Kritzinger. That'll be all for now."

"Thank you, sir. Will you be lunching with everyone, sir?"

"I really hadn't thought about it. But I missed breakfast and now I find I'm ravenously hungry, so, yes, I will."

SS-OBERGRUPPENFÜHRER Friedrich Karl von Eberstein was chatting with Kurt Kahlo when I came into the morning room. He was a genial type for an aristocrat.

"Ah, Commissar Gunther, there you are. We were beginning to think you'd forgotten me."

He was early and he knew it, but he was also a general, and I wasn't yet ready to start contradicting him.

"I hope I haven't kept you waiting for long, sir."

"No, no. I was just admiring General Heydrich's grand piano. It's a Blüthner. Very fine."

He was standing right in front of the instrument—which was as big and black as a Venetian gondola—and touching the keys, experimentally, like a curious child.

"Do you play, sir?"

"Very badly. Heydrich is the musical one. But of course it runs in that family. His father, Bruno, was something of a star at the Halle Conservatory. He was a great man and of course a great Wagnerian."

"You sound as if you knew him, sir."

"Bruno? Oh, I did. I did. I'm from Halle an der Saale myself."

"Someone else from Halle. That's a coincidence."

"Not really. My mother was Heydrich's godmother. It was I who introduced the general to Himmler and set him on his way."

"Then you must feel very proud of him, sir."

"I do, Commissar. Very much so. He's a credit to his country and to the whole National Socialist movement."

"I had no idea that you and he were so close."

Von Eberstein came away from the piano and stood beside me in front of the fire, warming his backside with conspicuous enjoyment.

He was in his late forties. On his gray tunic was an Iron Cross, first and second class, indicating he'd been given it twice, no small feat, even for an aristocrat. Still, there was a pious air about him—a bit like a hypocritical priest.

"I like to think of him as my protégé. I'm certain he wouldn't mind my saying that."

The way he said this made me think that Heydrich just might mind his saying that.

"How about Captain Kuttner?" I asked. "He was from Halle, too. Did you know him well?"

"Well enough. His father I know rather better. We were in the Army together. During the last war. Pastor Kuttner was our regimental chaplain. But for him I'm not sure I'd have fared as well as I did. He was a tremendous comfort to us all."

"I'm sure."

Von Eberstein shook his head. "It's a great pity that this happened. A great pity."

"Yes. It is, sir."

"And you're quite certain it was murder and not suicide?"

"Of course we'll have to wait for the autopsy this afternoon to be completely sure. But I'm more or less certain, yes."

"Well, you know your business, I suppose."

"Why do you mention suicide?"

"Only because of what happened to Albert in Latvia. He tried to kill himself there. Or at least threatened to kill himself."

"Exactly what did happen? I'm still a little unclear about that."

"I believe he suffered a nervous breakdown, brought on by the difficulty of his war assignments. I mean, of course, the evacuation of the Jews in the eastern territories. Not everyone is equal to the tasks that have been set before us as a people."

"I wonder if you might be a little more specific, sir. Under the circumstances I think I should know all there is to know."

"Yes, I agree with you, Commissar. Perhaps you should."

Von Eberstein proceeded to explain, using words and phrases that made the whole filthy business of murdering thousands of people sound like an engineering job, or perhaps an exercise in crowd control after a large game of football. It was typical of the Nazis that they should call a spade an agrarian implement, and as I listened to one weasel word after another, I felt I wanted to slap him.

"Responding to fundamental orders issued in Berlin, Lieutenant Kuttner was assigned the task of tactically coordinating the activities of a special detachment of SS that was made up of units of Latvian auxiliary police. Throughout the summer this same detachment carried out many extensive special actions in and around the Riga area. Principally, Kuttner's function was to perform a rudimentary census for the purpose of apprehending communists as well as identifying provincial Jews. After the census, Jews were ordered to assemble at a given location, and from there they were evacuated. It was later found that some of these evacuations were carried out with unnecessary brutality, and this seems to have occasioned feelings of guilt and depression in poor Kuttner. He started drinking heavily, and, following one protracted bout of drinking, he threatened a superior officer with his pistol. Subsequent to that, he tried but was prevented from shooting himself. Because of these incidents he was sent home to face a court-martial."

"Well, that's clear enough," I said, and watched Kahlo cover the smile on his face with a hand and its cigarette.

"Yes, it was an unfortunate business and might have severely blighted what was a very promising career. Albert was a brilliant young lawyer. But the Reichsführer is not an insensitive man and fully understands the problems that are sometimes provoked by these special actions. I talked it over with him at some length—"

"I'm sorry, sir," I interrupted. "To clarify what you said just now. You mean you discussed Lieutenant Kuttner's case with Reichsführer Himmler, on an individual basis?"

"That's right. He and I agreed that it should not be held against a man that he was too sensitive for such psychologically arduous duties. Given his legal talents, it was a waste of a fine mind just to allow him to be cashiered without a second chance to redeem himself. Consequently, Heydrich agreed to take Kuttner onto his personal staff; if he had not, then I would certainly have done so. Captain Kuttner was far too able an officer to let go."

"You were referring to Lieutenant Kuttner, sir. This is only a few weeks ago and yesterday he was a captain. Am I to understand that not only was there no court-martial, but that Lieutenant Kuttner was promoted to captain upon joining General Heydrich's staff?"

"For reasons of administrative efficiency it's usually best if adjutants are all of an equal rank. It saves any petty bickering."

"If you don't mind my saying so, sir, but Kuttner was lucky to have that kind of vitamin B. I mean, to have two patrons who can count the Reichsführer-SS as a friend."

"Yes. Perhaps."

"How long have you and Reichsführer Himmler been friends, sir?"

"Oh, let's see now. I joined the Party in 1922. And the SS in 1925."

"That explains the gold Party badge," observed Kahlo. "It seems as if you've been part of the movement since the very beginning, sir. If I'd had the good sense you had, then I might be something better than a criminal assistant now. No disrespect intended, sir."

"Oh, I wasn't always so resolute in my devotion to the Party."

"Go on, sir." Kahlo grinned.

"No, really. There was a time—after the failure of the beer hall putsch and the despairing of our cause—when I even left the Party."

Von Eberstein wagged a finger at Kahlo.

"So you see, we all make mistakes. For three years I was—"

He paused and looked thoughtful for a moment.

"Well, I was doing other things."

"Like what, sir?"

"It doesn't matter now. What matters now is that we find the person who murdered Captain Kuttner. Is that not so, Commissar?"

"Yes, sir."

"Have you any ideas on that score?"

"I've got plenty of ideas, sir. We Germans have never been short of those. But mostly what I know is limited by the terms in which the mind can think, which means it's probably best I don't try to explain what those ideas are. Not yet, anyway. What I can tell you is that not everyone liked the young captain as much as you and General Heydrich. And I'm not talking about the Czechs, sir. I figure that, given half a chance, they'd shoot any one of us wearing a German uniform. No, I'm talking about—"

"Yes, I know what you're talking about." Von Eberstein sighed. "No doubt you've heard about that unfortunate incident in the library last night. When General Henlein spoke with unnecessary harshness to Captain Kuttner."

"I'm not saying it demonstrates a motive for murder, but when you've seen men murdered for no motive at all, as I have, it gives pause for thought. Henlein was drunk. He was armed. Clearly he didn't like Kuttner. And he certainly had the opportunity."

"All of us had that, Commissar. You've a difficult job to do here and no mistake. But I've known Konrad Henlein ever since

I was the police president of Munich. And I can tell you this: he's no murderer. Why, the man used to be a teacher in a school."

"What kind of teacher?"

"A gymnastics teacher."

"So he's the one," I said, thinking of the girl in the suite at the Imperial Hotel—the one Arianne had spoken to.

"What?"

"I was just thinking. The gym teacher at my school was a regular sadist. Now that I come to think of it, I can't imagine a man who was more likely to murder someone than him."

Von Eberstein smiled. "I'm sure that Henlein isn't like that. Indeed I'm confident that none of the senior ranks here in Heydrich's own house could have committed such a heinous crime."

But I didn't share his confidence.

"When this is all over, Commissar, when you have—as I'm sure you will—solved the crime, I believe we'll find that the solution is much less remarkable than we might suppose right now. Isn't that usually the case?"

"I might agree with you, except for the very singular circumstances of this particular case. Most murders are simple, it's true. Simple, sordid, violent crimes of passion, greed, or most likely alcohol. This isn't anything like that. There appears to be no love interest here. Nothing was stolen. And if the murderer was drunk, then he was an unusually thoughtful drunk who was very careful not to leave a trace of his presence in Captain Kuttner's room. It's only an opinion at this stage, however, I have the feeling that someone is playing a game here. Possibly to embarrass General Heydrich."

"It's true there are those who are jealous of Heydrich," admitted von Eberstein.

"Possibly to embarrass all of you."

"In which case I wonder that you can write off the Czechs as possible culprits quite so quickly, Commissar. Perhaps you've forgotten how fond the Three Kings were of teasing the local Gestapo. One of them even left a provocative and embarrassing message in poor Fleischer's coat pocket. And it strikes me that this is just the sort of stunt they might pull. Especially now, when their organization is under threat. If I were you, I'd be trying to examine the backgrounds of the house staff in closer detail. They may be in the SS, but some of them have a German Czech background. I wouldn't be at all surprised if that throws up something that wasn't found when they were checked the first time."

"General von Eberstein's got a point, sir," said Kahlo. "It could be them thumbing their noses at us. Just like before. And nothing would give those bastards more pleasure than to have us chasing our own tails."

I grinned. "That's what it feels like, doesn't it?"

"I DON'T BELIEVE IT," said Kahlo. "*Krautwickel.* I thought that was it after the potato soup. That had real bacon in it. And real potatoes, too. But this is even better. I haven't had *Krautwickel* since the war started. If this keeps up, sir, I might just have to kill someone myself just so that we keep this investigation going for a good while longer."

"That's as good a motive for murder as any I've heard today," I said. "I may even have to put you down on my list of suspects after that remark."

We were in the dining room, but with Heydrich and Ploetz and some Gestapo officers away in pursuit of Václav Morávek, there were fewer of us for lunch at the Lower Castle than there had been for dinner. At my direction, Kahlo and I were seated at the opposite end of the table from everyone else; not because I disliked their company—which of course I did—but mostly because I wanted to avoid discussing the case with any of them. Besides, I hoped that our position at the table would set us apart and help to remind the cauliflower that a murder investigation was being conducted. Doubtless that suited Dr. Jury very well, and probably General Hildebrandt, who, following their interviews, now regarded me as they would a large and verminous dog.

Another reason I wanted to sit apart from the SS cauliflower was to give myself a chance to get to know Kurt Kahlo, whom to my surprise I liked more than anyone I had ever expected to like at Heydrich's house.

"Why do they call Mannheim the checcurboard?"

"Because it's the most regularly built city in Germany, that's why. The city center is divided into one hundred and thirty-six neat squares and the blocks of houses are distinguished only by letters and numerals. My dad used to live at K-Four. He was a factory foreman at Daimler but he got hit hard by the inflation. Me and my brother had to go to work to help supplement the family income and so that we could stay on at school, if that doesn't sound like a contradiction."

"You married?"

"Five years, to Eva. She works at a local hotel."

"Which one?"

"The Park."

"Any good?"

"Too pricey for me."

"I was in the hotel business for a while. I was the house bull at the Adlon."

"Nice."

"How does Eva like the hotel business?"

"She likes it. The guests can be a bit much sometimes. Especially the English, at least when they were still coming to Germany. They used to try it on a bit, and give themselves airs, you know?"

"Sounds a lot like this place."

"Yeah." Kahlo looked sideways at the cauliflower. "How'd you come to know General Heydrich?"

"The way you know a dangerous dog. Most of the time I just cross the road or walk the other way when I see him coming. But sometimes he corners me and I have to humor him or end up badly bitten. Really, I'm like one of those four animals on his way to the town of Bremen. A donkey, probably. And, like the donkey, I'd just like to live without an owner and become a musician."

"What instrument do you play?"

"Nothing, of course. Whoever heard of a donkey that could play a musical instrument? But I seem to be in the robbers' house, all the same; just like in the story."

Kahlo grinned. "It's not what you'd call a relaxing place, is it? Some of these bastards would frighten Himmler himself." He shook his head. "I almost feel sorry for Captain Kuttner."

"Almost?"

"I met him, remember?"

"What did you think of him?"

Kahlo shrugged. "Hardly matters now, does it? He's dead."

"If you think that's going to save you from telling everything to your barber, you're wrong."

"All right. I thought he was an arrogant little prick. Like all these fucking adjutants, he thought he was more than just his master's voice. He turned up at Kripo headquarters here in Prague a few days ago, demanding this and that and as soon as possible. My boss, Willy Abendschön, had to deal with him, and that meant to some extent I did, too. A right little cunt he was."

"A few days ago?"

"Monday. Heydrich wanted a report on something."

"Specifically?"

"OTA transmission intercepts. OTA is the codeword for all the intercepts."

"You mean radio broadcasts to the British, by the Czechos."

"No, no. That's what made this interesting. The Czechos were *receiving* broadcasts, and what's more, from somewhere in the

Fatherland. Intelligence tip-offs. Abendschön reckoned that the Czechos were sending the information on, to Beneš, in London, so that he could boost his standing with Churchill and the Tommy intelligence community."

"A Czech spy in Germany."

Kahlo shook his head. "No, a *German* spy in Germany. As I'm sure you know, there's nothing worse than that. I'm not entirely privy to all of this, you understand, sir; it goes well above my pay grade. But here in Prague the word on the cobbles is that there's a high-level traitor in Berlin who's behind the OTA transmissions; who's been feeding the Czechos with top-grade information about Reich policy on a number of things. Heydrich wanted everything we had on OTA so that he could hand it all over to a special search group he's setting up inside the SD. The Traitor X Group, it's called, or VXG, for short. Catching Morávek, the third of the Three Kings, is just half the game. You catch him, then you stand a better chance of identifying traitor X."

"Yes, I see. I think I'm going to need to know more about Kuttner's movements in the days leading up to his death."

"Very good, sir. But right now all I've got are his movements in the hours leading up to his death."

"Let's hear them."

We sat back in our chairs as the SS waiters cleared away. Kahlo found his notebook and flicked through several pages until a wet thumb found his place. He was about to read when the waiters returned with dessert. Kahlo's eyes were out on stalks.

"That's mish-mash," he said, groaning with anticipated pleasure. "With real cherry sauce."

I tasted the sauce. "Actually, it's cranberry," I said.

"No," he breathed.

"I'll eat while you talk."

Kahlo looked at his shredded pancake pudding, licked his lips, and hesitated. "You won't finish all that sauce, will you, sir?"

"No, of course not. Now, let's hear it."

Reluctantly, Kahlo started to read out his notes.

"Yesterday lunchtime you know about because you were here. According to Elisabeth Schreck, Heydrich's secretary, at three p.m. Kuttner made a couple of telephone calls. One to Carl Maria Strasse—sorry, sir, that's Kripo HQ—and one to the Peček Palace, Gestapo HQ. At around four, you saw him again, sir, on the road to the Upper Castle. At five he spent an hour in General Heydrich's office. I don't yet know what that was about. Then he went to his room: Kritzinger saw him go through the door. At eight o'clock there were drinks in the library, and then all of you listened to the Leader's speech on the radio. Fleischer's telephone call from Gestapo headquarters was put through just after nine, and that's when you saw Kuttner outside, having an argument with Captain Kluckholm. Do you know what that was about, sir?"

"Not yet."

"Kuttner helps to bring some champagne into the library after the speech, and after that, things are understandably vague. Just after one a.m. there is some sort of altercation between Kuttner and General Henlein and Colonel Böhme. I'm not quite sure what that was about."

"General Henlein made a pass at one of the maids. Her name is Rosa Steffel. Kuttner was her champion."

"I see. Then he's in Heydrich's office for a while with the general and Colonel Jacobi." Kahlo lowered his voice. "He's the one whom I find to be the most sinister of the lot."

"Then Kritzinger sees Kuttner just before two and wishes him a good night. Says he seemed dog tired."

Kahlo made a note of that and then continued reading his notes.

"At six o'clock this morning Kuttner fails to awaken Captain Pomme, as arranged. Nothing new there. He often overslept because he was taking sleeping pills. At six thirty Pomme says he's still knocking on Kuttner's door, trying to awaken him. At six forty-five Pomme goes to fetch Kritzinger to see if there's some other means of opening the door, which is locked from the inside. There isn't. Kritzinger tells one of the footmen to go and fetch a ladder and see if he can't get in from the outside."

"And did he?"

"Yes. But the ladder was locked up and the footman had to go and fetch the gardener, so it was seven fifteen a.m. by the time he brought it around to the window. Coming back a bit, though: at seven a.m. Heydrich is also outside Kuttner's door, and that's when he tells Pomme and the butler to break it down. Entering the room, they find Kuttner dead and Captain Pomme is dispatched to fetch Dr. Jury. Jury arrives in the room just as the footman arrives with the ladder."

"We shall want to speak to that footman. Maybe he saw something."

"His name is Fendler, sir."

"Then at seven thirty I get the call from Ploetz in my room at the Imperial. And at eight thirty we viewed the scene of the crime."

"What were you doing at the Imperial anyway? Why weren't you staying here in your room, sir?"

"I was sleeping. What do you know about Veronal?"

"It's barbital. Sleeping pills. Take too many and you don't wake up. That's about it, really."

"Ever use them yourself?"

"The wife did. She'd been working nights at the Park and couldn't sleep in the day. So the doctor gave her some Veronal. But she didn't care for the stuff at all. They always left her feeling like she'd been coshed."

"Strong, then."

"Very."

"Kuttner goes to bed at around two a.m., having told the butler that he intended to take some sleeping pills. Nobody sees him enter his room."

"I'm not sure if I'd take sleeping pills, knowing I had to be up at six," observed Kahlo. "Then again, you do get used to them, so it's possible he didn't see that as a problem."

"Which may be why he doesn't undress for bed. He's still dressed when we found him."

"Looked like he took one boot off and then got tired. Or dead. So then maybe he was shot before he entered his room."

"In the corridor." But I was shaking my head even as I said it. "Sure. After he's shot—and, by the way, nobody hears the shot—"

"Perhaps the murderer used a sound suppressor."

"For a P38? Hasn't been invented yet. So after he's shot in the corridor and no one hears a thing, he staggers along to his room without mentioning it to anyone or shouting for help, locks the door carefully behind him, as you do when you've just been shot, lies down on the bed just to get his breath back, removes a boot, and then dies sometime between two and five thirty a.m."

"It's a mystery, isn't it?"

"No, not really. I solve this kind of case all the time. Usually in the penultimate chapter. I like to keep the last few pages for restoring some sort of normality to the world."

"You know what I reckon, sir? I reckon that if you solve this case, Heydrich will probably promote you."

"That's what I'm worried about."

"And then you won't ever get to Bremen to live there without an owner."

"Shut up and eat your mish-mash."

KAHLO'S MENTION OF the Traitor X Group and a top-level spy in Germany who had been transmitting information to the Czechos got me wondering about Arianne and her friend Gustav, the man she claimed to have met in the Jockey Bar.

A smooth type with a thin prick accent and spats. Or so she

had described him. A civil servant with a gold cigarette holder and a little gold eagle in his lapel. A man whose nerves had prevented him from meeting Franz Koci, a former lieutenant of Czech artillery and possibly one of the last members of the Three Kings group operating in Berlin—at least he had been until a collision with a taxicab in the blackout had terminated his career as a spy.

Was it possible that Gustav and Heydrich's traitor X were one and the same person?

Arianne struck me as an unlikely sort of spy. After all, hadn't she confessed to being Gustav's unwitting courier *before* I had told her that I was a cop? And, having told her I was a commissar from the Alex, what kind of spy was it who, instead of disappearing the very next day, chose to begin a relationship with someone who very probably ought to have seen it as his duty to inform the Gestapo about her? What kind of spy was it who was prepared to risk so much for so little? After all, I was privy to no secret information she could have passed to anyone. Surely she was just what she seemed to be: a good-time girl with a dead husband and a brother who was a kennel hound with the Field Military Police. I'd checked him out, too. What else did she want but a chance to see a bit of what life had to offer before the Nazis turned her into yet another dutiful little German wife producing children for her first-class rabbit medal—the Honor Cross for the German Mother?

All the same, now that I knew about the local SD's VXG, it had become very obvious that bringing Arianne along to Prague for my own pleasure had helped put her in considerable danger; and it seemed imperative that she return to Berlin as soon as possible.

It was while deciding to send Arianne back to Berlin I remembered Major Ploetz had given me a letter forwarded from the Alex. Sitting in the morning room with a coffee and a cigarette, awaiting the next senior officer on my list, I read it.

The letter was from a girl I knew in Paris; her name was

Bettina and she worked at the Hotel Lutetia. I'd stayed there during my posting to the French capital. I had fixed her up with a better job at the Adlon and she was writing to thank me and to tell me that she would be coming to Berlin before Christmas. She hoped to see me then. She wrote a lot of other things besides, and since I didn't get many letters, least of all from attractive girls, I read it again. I even passed it under my nose a couple of times, as it seemed to be scented—then again, that might have been my own imagination.

I was reading the letter a third time when Kahlo ushered General Henlein into the morning room.

Henlein wore round metallic-framed glasses that flashed in the firelight like newly minted coins. His hair was dark and wavy, but the wave was on the ebb flow. His mouth was sulky, and to look at he was not unlike Dr. Jury. It was hard to connect this forty-three-year-old from Maffesdorf and the leader of the Sudeten German movement with the vigorous gymnastics teacher described by Arianne's girlfriend at the Imperial.

Kahlo handed me the plan of the house that Kritzinger had given him, and while Henlein made himself comfortable I glanced over it briefly and, for the moment, noted only that Henlein had occupied the room immediately next to Captain Kuttner's.

Kahlo sat down on the piano stool. Henlein, seated on the sofa opposite me, picked some fluff off his breeches, checked the cutlery on his tunic lapel—another War Merit Cross with swords—and smiled nervously several times. He had good teeth, I'll say that for him; they were the only vigorous-looking thing about him.

"Let me say something before we go any further." He spoke quietly, as if he were used to being listened to. "It's no secret that I was blue last night. I think we all were, after the Leader's speech and the good news about the Three Kings."

He paused for a moment, as if waiting for me to agree with

him; but I didn't say anything. I just lit another cigarette and let him hang there.

Momentarily discomfited, he swallowed noticeably and then continued, "Toward the end of the evening I believe I may have made certain remarks to the unfortunate Captain Kuttner that I now regret. They were spoken in the heat of the moment and under the influence of alcohol. I have never been much of a drinker. Alcohol does not agree with my constitution. I try to keep myself fit, you understand, as all of us should who are in the SS. It is an elite, after all, and a higher standard is expected of us. Not just physically, but in matters of behavior, too. Consequently, it seems to me that my own behavior was not all that it could have been. And in retrospect the poor captain was quite right to remonstrate with me. Indeed, it is very much to that officer's credit that he did so.

"Of course when I heard what had happened I was shocked and saddened. I deeply regret this brave young officer's passing and also the fact that I was unable to apologize to him in person. In my own defense I should like to reiterate that it is quite out of character for me to behave in such an inappropriate fashion. But the circumstances of his death being what they are, I feel it is incumbent on me to state, upon my word as a German officer, that I did not shoot Captain Kuttner. Nor do I have any knowledge of his death. After returning to my own room at around two o'clock this morning, I have very little knowledge of anything except that I went to bed and awoke with a filthy hangover. It was after nine when Major Ploetz informed me of what had happened and explained that you were handling the official inquiry at the request of General Heydrich. And let me assure you, Commissar Gunther, that I will cooperate with your investigation in any way I can. I'm sure that this can't be easy for you."

"I appreciate your candor."

Almost to my amusement, Henlein got up to leave. I let him get as far as the door before throwing a grappling hook after him.

"However, there are a few questions I should like to ask you."

Henlein smiled again. This time the smile was sarcastic.

"Do I take it that you intend to cross-examine *me*?"

You would have thought he was Hitler himself the way Henlein pronounced that personal pronoun.

I shrugged. "If that's what you want to call it. But look here, I'm only taking you at your word. You just offered to cooperate with my investigation in any way you can. Or am I mistaken?"

"I know what I said, Commissar Gunther," he said, crisply, his glasses flashing angrily as his head moved with jerky indignation. "I assumed that my word as a German officer—and not just any German officer—would suffice."

He straightened a little and put his fists on his hips as if challenging me to knock him over. I wouldn't have minded punching him on the nose at that, if only to find out for myself how vigorous he really was.

"You're quite right, sir." I paused to achieve the full amount of mockery that was implied in my next remark. "That was an assumption, I'm afraid. And it isn't correct. As you also said yourself, General Heydrich has authorized me to handle an official inquiry, and that does necessitate my asking a lot of questions, some of which might very well sound impertinent to a man of your high standing. But I'm afraid that can't be helped. So perhaps you'd like to sit down again. I'll try not to keep you too long."

Henlein sat down and regarded me with some disfavor.

"According to a plan I have here of all the officer accommodations in the Lower Castle, which has been prepared by Herr Kritzinger, you were in the room right next door to Captain Kuttner."

"What of it?"

I smiled patiently. "Whenever a man is murdered I usually go and speak to his neighbors to ask if they heard or saw anything suspicious, that's what of it."

Henlein sighed and then leaned back against the cushion and made a little steeple out of his fingers, which he tapped together with a pedant's impatience.

"Weren't you listening? I already said. I went to bed, drunk. I saw nothing and heard nothing."

"You're sure about that?"

Henlein tutted loudly. "Really, this is too much. I had assumed Heydrich had chosen you because you were a detective. Now I find you're nothing but a stupid policeman."

I was getting tired of all this. I was tired of a lot of things, but being made to feel I was lucky to breathe the same air as the regional governor of the Sudetenland was close to the top of the whole tiresome heap. I decided to take Heydrich at his word and dispense with good manners; for me this was never particularly difficult, but when I let go I took even myself by surprise.

I sprang to my feet and, coming around the back of the sofa Henlein was sitting on, I pushed my jaw into his face.

"Listen, you pompous shit curl, a man was murdered in that room. And in case you'd forgotten while you were sitting behind your nice desk on that lazy fat arse of yours, guns make loud noises when you pull the trigger." I clapped my hands hard in front of his nose. "They go 'bang' and 'bang' and 'bang,' and other people are supposed to do something about that noise when they hear it."

Henlein was coloring now, his lips quivering in anger.

"So don't give me 'What of it?' and make like you were a hundred miles away with a cast-iron alibi. You were right next door to a man you had earlier threatened in front of several witnesses. That's just a brick's width away from being in the same room with him, see? So you may be a senior officer; you might even be a gentleman, for all I know; but you're also a goddamn suspect."

"How dare you speak to me like that, Commissar Gunther?"

"Ask me that again," I snarled back.

"How dare you speak to me like that?"

He stood up with the look of a man who was about to challenge me to a duel.

"I've a very good mind to punch you on the nose," he said.

"I suppose that counts as brave coming from a man with that kind of tinfoil on his chest." I pointed at his War Merit Cross. Flicking his Party badge with my forefinger, I said, "Well, I'm not scared."

"I am going to make a point of breaking you, Commissar. I am going to take great pleasure in making sure that by the time this weekend has ended, you will be directing traffic on Potsdamer Platz. I've never been insulted like this in all my years as a German officer. How dare you?"

Henlein walked toward the morning room door.

"That deserves an answer, General. I'll tell you how. You see, I know all about your little friend on the top floor of the Imperial Hotel. Betty, isn't it? Betty Kipsdorf? Apparently you and she get along very well. And why not? She's a real sweet girl, from what I hear."

Henlein had stopped in his tracks as if commanded to do so on a parade ground by a particularly tough drill sergeant.

"I haven't seen her myself but my source tells me she thinks you're very vigorous. Somehow I doubt she means that you and she like to go for energetic walks in the countryside. And I do wonder how our host will greet the news that dear Betty is a Jew."

He turned slowly and then sat down on a chair by the door, like a man awaiting a doctor's appointment. He took off his glasses and turned several shades of white before settling on the color of a goat's cheese that seemed to reflect the greenish wallpaper.

"Yes. Sit down. Good move, General."

"How did you find out?" he whispered.

For one glorious moment I thought I was about to hear a confession of murder.

"About the girl."

"You idiot, I'm a cop, not a brass monkey. If you're going to keep a joy lady in a hotel, then make sure she's the kind of girl who can keep her peep shut."

It was good advice. I hoped I was paying attention to it myself.

The spectacles in his hand were trembling. Four years later, while being held by the Americans at the military barracks in Pilsen, Konrad Henlein would use the glass in those spectacles to cut open his veins and kill himself. But for now they were just a pair of harmless, trembling specs. Then he started to cry, which was tough because I'd put him through all of that without the least suspicion he'd shot Captain Kuttner. You get a feel for these things: Henlein was a lot of things—a pompous ass, a Nazi agitator, a womanizer—but he wasn't a murderer. It takes a lot of nerve to pull the trigger on a man in cold blood, and if his tears proved anything, it was that he didn't have what it takes.

"Relax. We're not going to tell anyone, are we, Kurt?"

I went over to the piano and offered Kahlo a cigarette. He took one, stood up, and lit us both.

"No, sir," he said. "Your little secret is quite safe with us, General. Provided, of course, that you cooperate."

"Of course. I'll do anything you want. Anything. But I am telling you the truth, Herr Commissar. I didn't kill the captain. It's as I told you. I was drunk. I went to bed around two. Even that's a blur, I'm afraid. I'm only aware of what I said to the unfortunate captain because one of my brother officers drew it to my attention this morning. I feel terrible about what happened. But the first I knew that Captain Kuttner was dead was when Major Ploetz came and told me this morning. I'm not the type of person to kill anyone. Honestly. I'm almost a vegetarian, like the Leader, you know. It's true I do have a gun. It's in my room. But I am certain it's never been fired while it's been in my possession. I can fetch it now if you like and then perhaps you can check for yourself. I believe that we have scientists in police laboratories who can determine such things."

Somewhere during the course of Henlein's miserable, pleading speech I stopped listening. I stared at the keys of the piano for a moment and then out the window, all the while wondering what the hell I was doing with my life. At least the cigarette tasted good. I'd reacquired a taste for good tobacco, and I told myself that when this was all over and Heydrich had Kuttner's murderer, I was probably going to have to get used to the ration line again, and three johnnies a day. Because I had the strong feeling that finding Kuttner's killer was going to impact upon my becoming Heydrich's bodyguard, after all. I couldn't see how I was going to keep a job like that when I'd finished insulting all of his closest colleagues; at least, that was my earnest hope.

Then Kahlo was talking again, and Henlein was answering him, and it was another moment or two before I realized that the subject had changed. We were no longer speaking about Captain Kuttner or even Betty Kipsdorf but something entirely different.

"Your friend Heinz Rutha," said Kahlo, "the furniture designer. He hanged himself in prison, didn't he? In 1937, wasn't it?"

"Yes," said Henlein.

"Because he was queer, too."

"I wouldn't know about that."

"Is that why you decided to work for Admiral Canaris and the Abwehr? Because of what happened to your friend? Because you held the Nazis responsible for that?"

"I don't know what you're talking about."

"But maybe not just Canaris, eh? Maybe because of that you went to work for the British. Maybe you're a British spy. Maybe you've always been a British spy, General Henlein. You help to destabilize the Czech Sudetenland for Hitler while all the time you're really working for the Tommies. Good cover, I'd have thought. I mean, it doesn't get better than that, does it? Frankly, I can't really say that I blame you. The way you were passed over first by Frank and then by Heydrich, you've every reason to feel aggrieved, haven't you, sir? So, how about it? Are you spying for the Tommies?"

"Please." Henlein looked desperately at me. "I really don't know anything about this."

"Neither do I," I said.

"I'm no more a spy than I am a murderer."

"Says you," said Kahlo.

"That's quite enough," I told Kahlo.

"Suppose we let the Gestapo find out," persisted Kahlo. "Suppose we were to hand you over to Sergeant Soppa. You've heard of him, haven't you, General? He's the specialist they brought in to question the Three Kings. I haven't seen him in action myself, but apparently he uses this technique he calls the bascule. They strap you onto a wooden board, just like the one they use on a guillotine—"

"Thank you, General Henlein, that will be all for now, sir."

Kahlo was still speaking, only now I was talking over him. Not only that, but I had Henlein by the arm, and I was steering him out to the door of the morning room.

"If there's anything else you think we need to know, then please don't hesitate to contact me, sir. As for your friend at the Imperial, my advice would be to get her out of there. Find somewhere else for your trysts. An apartment, perhaps. But not a hotel, General. If I know about Betty, it won't be long before someone else does, too."

"Yes, I understand. Thank you, Herr Commissar. Thank you very much indeed."

Henlein glanced uncertainly at Kahlo and then he was gone.

I closed the door behind him and, for a moment or two, Kahlo and I faced each other in awkward silence.

"What the hell was all that about?"

"You heard."

"I guess I did at that."

"You had him on the ropes." Kahlo shrugged. "It seemed a pity not to take advantage of that, sir. I thought that there might never be a better opportunity to ask him some questions that needed asking."

"It's those questions that I'm interested in, Kurt. You see, I thought I was supposed to kick the ball. Only it turns out that you're allowed to pick it up and run with it. That makes me wonder what kind of game we're playing here."

Kahlo looked sheepish. "We're on the same side, sir. That's all that matters, isn't it?"

"Actually I wonder about that, too. This VXG. The Traitor X Group you mentioned. The one that Heydrich was setting up to find the high-level spy who's been giving information to the Czechos. You wouldn't be part of that group, would you, Kurt?"

"Didn't I say?"

"You know you damn well didn't."

"I should have thought it was obvious after what I told you over lunch about the VXG. About how Captain Kuttner came down to Kripo HQ to brief us about it. How would I have known about those OTA radio intercepts if I wasn't part of the group? That stuff is highly sensitive. By rights I shouldn't have told you about that at all."

"So what else haven't you told me?"

"Frankly, I thought that enjoying General Heydrich's confidence as you do, you knew about traitor X yourself. That you knew that and that you knew—"

"What?"

"That everyone in this house is under suspicion."

"Of being traitor X?"

"Yes, sir. I assumed you would certainly know that much, at least."

I shook my head. "Let me get this straight. Everyone in this house is suspected of being a spy for the Czechos."

Kahlo nodded. "I don't think you are. And I know I'm not. And I'm damned sure Heydrich isn't. Or his three adjutants. Everyone else, well, there's a question mark against everyone else, yes." He shrugged. "I'm sorry, sir. I really thought you knew about all this."

"I didn't."

"Well, that's hardly my fault, is it? I just do what I'm fucking told. It's up to Heydrich what he tells you, not me. I'm just a criminal assistant." He kissed his cigarette and continued: "Maybe it slipped his mind. Maybe he assumed that I would tell you. Which I have."

"When we were discussing a possible motive for someone murdering Captain Kuttner—"

"No, sir," he said firmly. "You never discussed that with me. You discussed that with General Henlein."

"Well, don't you think you might have mentioned it before now? In passing? I mean, if someone suspects you of being a spy, then that would be a pretty powerful fucking motive for murder, don't you think? Maybe Kuttner was onto someone in this house. Maybe that's why he was killed. But why should I have to know about that? I'm just the investigating detective. Jesus, I feel like a parrot with a cloth over my cage."

"Try to look at it from my point of view, Commissar. Kuttner turns up at Prague Kripo on Monday. Several of us are picked out to join Heydrich's Traitor X Group. But Kuttner tells us that on no account are we to talk about this to anyone. It's all top secret, he says. Anyone opens his pie hole about this group to anyone, the reward is a ticket on the partisan express. Then he gets killed and you're in charge of the investigation. Heydrich's clever dick. That's what Ploetz says. Christ, that's what everyone says. And the way you speak to the general. Like you had a special license. How am I to know that you're not fully in the picture, sir? I'm used to being told this but not that, see? I'm just a foot soldier, sir. All this fucking cauliflower, I'm not familiar with it. And I'm certainly not used to hearing them getting roughed up by a mere captain like you."

"Everyone in the house?" I repeated dumbly.

"More or less. Like I said, it's everyone except me and you and the adjutants. And Heydrich, of course. There's a list, see. Of suspects. I haven't got a copy myself, but I can remember who was on it. And Henlein's name was certainly one of them."

I poured myself a cup of coffee and sipped it thoughtfully.

"Hildebrandt?"

Kahlo nodded.

"But he's an old friend of Heydrich's," I said. "To say nothing of the fact that he's an old friend of Hitler's. Von Eberstein? What about him? Is he suspected, too?"

Kahlo nodded again.

"But how? How can they be under suspicion? That little gold Party badge is supposed to mean something."

"I only know what I've been told. And that's not everything. Hildebrandt is a suspect because for two years, from 1928 until 1930, he was in America. While he was there he went bankrupt as a farmer, but someone paid off all his debts and then helped to set him up as a bookseller in New York. The suspicion in the SD is that it was the British Secret Service. And that it was them who persuaded him to return to Germany and join the SS in 1931 to spy for the British.

"Von Eberstein was a banker after the war and a bit of a weekend Nazi, if you know what I mean. He actually quit the Party after the putsch, which automatically makes him suspect. For three years he had no Party affiliation at all. And during this time he goes from being a banker with the Commerce and Private Bank to running his wife's factory in Gotha, but when that goes belly up his debts are paid off anonymously and he starts a travel agency. That business takes him to London for much of 1927 and 1928. But by 1929 he's back in the Party again. So did the Tommies set him up with the travel agency and train him to operate a radio while he was in London? That's the sort of thing Heydrich wants to know."

Kahlo grinned and wagged his finger.

"You see how easy it is to fall under suspicion? And it doesn't matter who you are or how high up in the Party you have flown. Dr. Jury is a suspect because before he joined the Austrian Nazi Party in 1932 he attended several medical conferences in Paris and London. While he was in Paris he had an affair with a woman who also had an affair with a French colonel in their intelligence service. Also his friendship with Martin Bormann automatically makes him a suspect in Himmler's eyes, since it seems Himmler would love to discredit any friend of Bormann's in the eyes of Hitler.

"General Frank is a suspect because of something his ex-wife, Anna, has told her new husband, Dr. Köllner. He succeeded Frank as the deputy governor of the Sudetenland and has made certain allegations based on what Anna Köllner told him about his loyalty to the Leader. And also because his new wife, Karola Blaschek, is suspected of having contact with several Czech resistance figures. She comes from the local town of Brux, and there's a suspicion that some of her friends and relations in that town may have been part of UVOD. The Home Resistance."

"What about von Neurath? Not him, surely. He was the foreign minister, for Christ's sake."

"Konstantin von Neurath is suspected of being recruited as a British spy as early as 1903, when he served as a diplomat at the German embassy in London, or possibly when he was at the German embassy in Denmark, in 1919. While he was German ambassador to London in 1930 he came under the suspicion of the Abwehr but he was cleared after an investigation; but in 1937 the Abwehr was burgled by a special SS team and certain papers were removed that showed the whole investigation to have been a sham. Subsequent to this, von Neurath joined the Nazi Party for the first time, as a sign of his loyalty. As if he suddenly needed to underline his loyalty. Instead of which it seems to have put him under suspicion."

Kahlo stubbed out his cigarette and helped himself to coffee. But he wasn't yet finished.

"And that's possibly the reason Major Thümmel is suspected of being traitor X. He was in charge of the Abwehr section that was supposed to have investigated von Neurath. He may be a friend of Heinrich Himmler and he may wear a gold Party badge, but he's also a close friend of the Abwehr's boss, Admiral Canaris, who is Himmler's most bitter rival. Heydrich's, too.

"Let's see now. Who else was on that list? Brigadier Voss? He commands the SS officer school at Benešchau. Until 1938, he was in charge of the officers' training school at Bad Tölz, where there's a powerful radio transmitter. When officers from that school were mobilized for the invasion of Czechoslovakia in 1938, someone tipped off the Czech intelligence service about it. Voss was one of only a handful of people who knew the invasion was about to happen. He's also a keen amateur radio enthusiast. Who better to broadcast secrets to the Czechos? He even speaks the language.

"Walter Jacobi was dismissed from the SD in 1937 by his then boss, General Werner Lorenz. I'm afraid I don't know why. In the spring of 1938, he took a holiday in Marienbad, in the Sudetenland. Coincidentally, perhaps or perhaps not, one of the other guests taking the cure at the spa was a retired British naval commander who is currently believed to be the head of an operational Czech section within the British SIS. After his holiday, Jacobi rejoined the SD."

"Guilt by association."

"Possibly."

Kahlo nodded.

"Henlein—well, you heard what I said to him. And Fleischer's been under suspicion for a while now because of his failure to arrest the third of the Three Kings. You probably know as much about that as I do. It's common knowledge that the Czechos were making a fool of him for a while. The rest of the cauliflower, I really don't remember or I don't know. Your guess is as good as mine."

"I doubt that very much," I said. "And by the way, what happened to 'I'm keen to learn' and 'You have my full cooperation' and 'It's a puzzle, sir'?"

"You don't think it's a puzzle?"

"Of course it is. I just don't much like the fact that you've had one of the pieces in your trouser pocket all along."

"And I don't suppose you've ever kept your mouth shut about something?" Kahlo shook his head. "Come on, sir. We both know that saying one thing and thinking another is what this job is all about. Tell me it's not like that for you. Go on."

I found myself silent.

"Tell me that you've told *me* everything. That there's something you're not keeping from me."

Still I didn't answer. How could I when Arianne was back at the hotel? If I'd told him less than half of what I knew about Arianne Tauber, there was no telling what might happen to her.

Kahlo grinned. "No, I thought not. You see, when it comes right down to it, Commissar, I reckon your piss is just as yellow as mine."

I sighed and fetched myself a brandy from the decanter. Suddenly I felt very tired and I knew the brandy wasn't going to help.

"Maybe you're right."

"Look, sir. You want to know what I think? I think we should go through the motions of trying to find Kuttner's killer, just like you were told to do. We ask the right questions, we do our duty, right? Like regular cops. That's all we can do, and it's pointless thinking we can do any more than that. But when it comes right down to it, what does it fucking matter, eh? You tell me. Who cares who killed the bastard? Not me, not you. From what I heard, he did his own fair share of murder out east. And the chances are, he had it coming. Probably we all do. But what's one more murder, eh? One tiny drop in a very tall glass of beer, that's what it is. Take my advice, sir. Don't sweat it. Enjoy the free forage and the booze and the cigarettes. For as long as we can, eh?"

"Maybe."

"That's the spirit, sir. And who knows? Maybe we'll get lucky. Even a blind chicken finds the corn now and again."

I needed a walk and some fresh air after all that information, although it might have been the brandy and the mish-mash. I went around the house to the little Winter Garden that Kuttner's room looked out on. Inside the glasshouse was a fountain shaped like a shrine with a water nymph's head spouting water, and above her a bronze statue of a centaur with a winged cherub on his back. On either side of the fountain was a veritable jungle of sago palms and geraniums. It seemed an odd place to find a centaur or a cherub, but I wasn't surprised at anything anymore. The water nymph could have told me my fortune lay in farming guinea pigs and I wouldn't have batted an eyelid. Anything looked like a better bet than being a detective in Jungfern-Breschan.

A ladder lay on the ground, and, assuming that this was probably the one Kritzinger had ordered Fendler, the footman, to fetch around to Captain Kuttner's window, I spent the next ten minutes propping it up against the wall of the house. Then I climbed up to take a look at the window ledge. But that told me only that the glass roof needed cleaning, that the sun was still strong for the first week in October, and that I was not at all certain to kill myself cleanly if I threw myself from the top. I descended the ladder and found one of the footmen waiting at the bottom.

"Fendler, sir," he said, unprompted. "Herr Kritzinger saw you were out here and sent me to see if I could be of any assistance, sir."

He was not far off being two meters tall. He wore a white mess jacket with SS collar patches, a white shirt, a black tie, black trousers, a white apron, and gray over-sleeves, as if he might have been cleaning something before receiving his order from the butler to wait on me. He was lumpish in appearance, with an expression that suggested he was none too bright, but I'd gladly have changed places with him. Polishing silver or removing the ash from a fireplace looked like more rewarding work than the domestic task I had been set.

"You're the one whom Kritzinger told to fetch the ladder to look in Captain Kuttner's window, are you not?"

"That's right, sir."

"And what did you see, when eventually you got up there? By the way, what time was that, do you think?"

"About a quarter past seven, sir."

I peeled my shirt off the sweat on my chest.

"I was about to ask you why it took so long to fetch a ladder and prop it up against the window, but I think I know the answer to that already. It's heavy."

"Yes, sir. But it wasn't in the Winter Garden like it is now, sir."

"That's right. It was locked up, wasn't it?"

"Bruno, the gardener—Bruno Kopkow—he helped me carry it around here and prop it up."

"How did you know which window to choose?"

"Kritzinger told me it was the room overlooking the Winter Garden, sir. And to be careful I didn't drop it on the glass roof, sir."

"So you prop the ladder up against the window. Then what? Tell me everything you saw and did."

Fendler shrugged. "We—Kopkow and I—we heard a loud

bang, sir, and then, just as I was stepping on the lowest rung, sir, General Heydrich looks out of the window and, seeing me and Bruno, tells us that there's no need to bother coming up now as they had just broken down the captain's bedroom door."

"And what did you say? If anything?"

"I asked him if everything was all right and he said that it wasn't, because it looked as if Captain Kuttner had probably killed himself with an overdose."

"Then what did you do?"

"We took the ladder down and left it where you found it, sir, just in case anyone decided they needed it again."

"How did he seem? The general."

"A bit upset, I suppose. Like you would be, sir. He and the captain were friends, I believe." The footman paused. "I knew he must be upset because he was smoking a cigarette. Usually the general doesn't smoke at all in the morning, and never before he fences, sir. Mostly he only smokes in the evening. He's very disciplined that way, sir."

I glanced up at the window of Kuttner's room and nodded. "I don't doubt it."

"Will there be anything else, sir?"

"No. That's all, thank you."

I went back to the morning room. Kahlo was waiting for me.

"Police Commissar Trott telephoned while you were out, sir. From the Alex. He said to tell you that he went to see Lothar Ott at Captain Kuttner's apartment in Pestalozzistrasse and told him that the captain was dead. Apparently Ott wept like a baby. The commissar's exact words. That would seem to confirm it, wouldn't you say? That the captain was warm?"

I nodded. It only confirmed what I already knew.

"Who'd have thought it?" said Kahlo. "I mean, the fellow seemed quite normal in a lot of ways. Like you or me, really."

"I guess that's the point. That maybe they are just like you or me."

"Speak for yourself, sir."

"I used to think like you. But the Nazis have taught me to think differently. I'll say that for them. These days I say live and let live, and if we can learn to do that, then maybe we can behave like a civilized country again. But I suspect it's already too late for that."

I glanced at my wristwatch. A cheap Bulova, it had two ways to remind me that we had an autopsy to view at the Bulovka Hospital at four, and that only one of them was the time.

"Come on," I said to Kahlo. "We'd better get going. You're about to discover just how like you and me Albert Kuttner really was."

SERGEANT KLEIN had returned from Hradschin Castle in Prague to drive us out to the hospital. He'd read the Leader's Sporspalast speech in the morning newspaper and, instead of depressing him, Hitler's facts and figures had left him feeling optimistic about our prospects in the East.

"Two and a half million Russian prisoners," he said. "No country could ever recover from losing that many men. If that was all, it would be enough; but in addition fourteen thousand Russian planes have been shot down as well, and eighteen thousand of their tanks destroyed. It's hard to imagine."

"And yet the Leader still believes we have a fight on our hands," I remarked.

"Because he's wise," insisted Klein. "He's saying that so as not to raise our hopes in case the impossible should happen. But it's obvious, the Ivans are as good as beaten, that's what I think."

"Let's hope you're right," said Kahlo.

"I hate to think what we're going to do with two and a half

million Russian prisoners if he's wrong," I said. "If it comes to that, I hate to think what we're going to do with them if he's right."

I paused for a moment before adding what was sometimes called "the political postscript"—something that was usually said for the purposes of self-preservation.

"Not that I expect him to be wrong, of course. And I don't doubt that the Leader will be delivering a victory speech in Moscow before very long."

I wanted to bite off the end of my tongue and spit it onto the road.

Set on a hill overlooking the northeast of the city, Bulovka Hospital was a four- or five-story building made of beige-colored stone with a red mansard roof and a greenish little bell tower that stuck up in the air like an infected finger. Built before the Great War, the hospital was surrounded with lush gardens, where recuperating patients could sit on wooden benches, enjoy the many blooms in the flower beds, and generally appreciate the democratic ideals of the sovereign state of Czechoslovakia; at least they could have when there had still been a sovereign state of Czechoslovakia. Like every other public building in Prague, the hospital was now flying the flag of the least democratic European state since Vlad III impaled his first Wallachian boyar.

Klein drew up in front of the entrance. Two men wearing surgical gowns were already waiting for us, which seemed excessively servile until you remembered Heydrich's reputation for obsessive punctuality and ruthless cruelty. One of the men was Honek, the Czech doctor who had attended the crime scene at the Lower Castle earlier that day. He introduced the other man, a handsome German Czech in his early forties.

"This is Professor Herwig Hamperl," said Honek, "who is most distinguished in the field of forensic medicine. He has kindly agreed to take charge of this autopsy."

"Thank you, sir," I said.

Swiftly, as if he wanted us to be gone and out of his hair as quickly as possible, Hamperl muttered a curt "good afternoon" and led the way upstairs and along a wide bright corridor with walls that showed the grimy blank squares where signs and posters written in Czech had been displayed until German became the official language of Bohemia. Hamperl might have been a German Czech, but I soon discovered he was no Nazi.

"Have either of you two gentlemen attended an autopsy before?" he asked.

"Yes," I said. "Many."

"This is my first," said Kahlo.

"And you're feeling nervous about it, perhaps?"

"A little."

"Being dead is like being a whore," said Hamperl. "You spend most of your time on your back while someone else—in this case, me—gets on with the business in hand. The procedure can seem embarrassing, sometimes even a little preposterous, but it is never disgusting. My advice to anyone who hasn't witnessed an autopsy before is to try to see only the lighter side of things. If it starts to seem disgusting, then that's the cue to leave the room before an accident occurs. The smell of a dead body is usually quite bad enough without the smell of vomit to cope with. Is that clear?"

"Yes, sir."

Hamperl unlocked a wooden door with smoked windows and led us into an autopsy suite where a stout-looking body lay under a sheet on a slab. As Hamperl started to draw back the sheet to reveal Kuttner's head and shoulders, I saw Kahlo's eyes widen.

"Jesus," he muttered. "I don't remember his stomach being that big."

Hamperl paused.

"I can assure you it's not big with fat," he said. "The man might be dead, but the enzymes and bacteria in his belly are still very much alive and feeding on whatever still remains in his stomach. Probably last night's dinner. In the process, these enzymes and bacteria produce gas. Here, let me demonstrate."

Hamperl pressed hard on the sheet still covering Kuttner's stomach, which caused the body to fart, loudly.

"See what I mean?"

Hamperl's behavior was a piece of crude theater that seemed intended to make us feel uncomfortable. In a way I didn't blame him for this at all. The Nazis were past masters at making others feel uncomfortable. Doubtless, the professor was just paying us back in kind. A fart from a dead Nazi was as eloquent a comment on the German presence in Czechoslovakia as I was ever likely to hear, or indeed smell. But Kahlo winced noticeably, and then bit his lip as he tried, vainly, to steady his nerves.

Hamperl collected a long sharp curette off a neatly prepared instrument table and held it at arm's length, like a conductor's baton. The light from the abbey-sized windows caught the flat of the curette, and it glittered like a bolt of lightning. Instinctively Kahlo turned away, and, noting his discomfort at the symphony of destruction he was about to begin, Hamperl grinned wolfishly, exchanged a meaningful look with Dr. Honek, and said, "There's one thing you can say about the dead, my dear fellow. They have an extraordinary ability to deal with pain. Any pain. No matter how bad it might seem to you. Believe me, this poor fellow won't feel a thing as I seem to do my absolute worst. Much worse than perhaps you have ever seen inflicted on any human being before. However, do try not to let your imagination run away with you. The most terrible thing that could happen to this man happened several hours before he arrived in this hospital."

Kahlo shook his head and swallowed loudly, which sounded as if a very large frog had taken up residence in his throat.

"I'm sorry, sir," he said to me. "I just can't do this. I really can't."

He covered his mouth and left the room quickly.

"Poor fellow," said Hamperl. "But probably it's just as well he's gone. We need all our attention for the task that now lies before us."

"Surely, that was your intention," I said. "To scare him off."

"Not at all, Commissar. You heard me try to reassure him, didn't you? However, it's not everyone who can witness this procedure with a cool head. Are you sure about yourself?"

"Oh, I have no feelings at all, Professor Hamperl. None whatsoever. I'm like that curette in your hand. Cold and hard. And best handled with extreme care. Just one slip would be most unfortunate. Do I make myself clear?"

"Quite clear, Commissar."

Hamperl threw back the remainder of the sheet covering Kuttner's body and quickly went to work. Having photographed the two entry wounds on the dead man's chest, and then probed them both, first with his finger and then with a length of dowel, he made a Y-shaped incision from Kuttner's porcelain-pale shoulders, across his hairless chest, and down to the pubic area, which, unusually, appeared to have been shaved, and recently, too.

Hamperl remarked upon this.

"Well, you don't see that every day. Not even in my profession. I wonder why he should have done this."

"I've a good idea," I said. "But it will wait."

Hamperl nodded. Then he was cutting through subcutaneous fat and muscle, and the speed of his scalpel was something to behold, with the flesh swiftly shrugged off the bone like the skin of a very large snake; within only a few minutes there was just a mess of intestines and prime rib that might have been the envy of any good Berlin butcher. Especially in wartime.

"There appears to be something lodged at the top of the oropharynx," said Hamperl. He looked up at me and added, "That's the part of the throat just behind the mouth."

He collected a small white object, flicked it off his fingers' ends into a kidney dish, and then held it up for our joint inspection.

"It appears to be a troche, perhaps," he said. And then: "No, this was not designed to dissolve in the throat, but in the stomach. It has hardly dissolved at all. A pilule. A tablet, perhaps."

"He was taking Veronal," I said. "A barbiturate."

"Is that so?" Hamperl's voice was dripping with sarcasm. "Well, then, that is probably what it is. Only it could not have affected him very much in the condition you see it in now. Although this would be quite consistent with a case of overdose, where someone has swallowed several pills all at once, Dr. Honek said there was initially some suspicion that this might have been a barbiturate overdose."

"That's right," I said. "Until I found the bullet wounds."

"Quite."

At an almost imperceptible nod from Professor Hamperl, Dr. Honek stepped forward with a set of surgical bolt cutters and began to cut the ribs, which, under the steel jaws, snapped loudly, like thick twigs, one by one, in order to expose the chest cavity. But there was one he hesitated to cut.

"One of these ribs looks damaged, don't you think so, sir?" asked Honek.

Hamperl bent down to take a closer look. "Chipped," he said. "Like a tooth. But not from a Veronal pilule. Most probably from a bullet."

Honek went back to work. He was even quicker than the professor, and within a couple of minutes Hamperl was slicing through the remains of the diaphragm and reflecting back the whole chest-plate, like the top of a boiled egg, to expose the dead man's heart and the lungs.

"Quite a lot of blood has pooled inside the diaphragm," he murmured.

By now Albert Kuttner was hardly recognizable as a human being. His intestines—most of them—were resting on the upturned palm of his own hand, as if, like the perfect aide-de-camp he had possibly hoped to become, he might assist even in the process of his own dissection.

Hamperl placed the chest-plate on a nearby table, where it lay like the remains of a Christmas goose.

I cleared my nose, noisily.

"Commissar? Are you all right?"

"I'm just trying to see the lighter side of things that you were talking about earlier, sir."

"Good."

But the professor sounded almost disappointed that I was not yet lying on the floor.

"Cutting the pulmonary artery," he said to Honek. "Checking for blood clots. Which we have. Probably a postmortem blood clot." He slashed some more of the lungs and then squeezed the heart. "Feels like something hard in here. A bullet, probably. See if you can find it, will you, Dr. Honek?"

He handed the heart to the other man and got to work with the scalpel again, slashing at the flesh holding what looked like a shiny red football.

"The liver, is it?" I asked.

"Very good, Commissar Gunther. The liver it is." Hamperl laid the liver in another dish before removing the spleen as well.

"Looks like this got hit, too," he said. "It's almost in pieces."

I went over to the table where Honek was still palpating the heart to isolate the bullet, and glanced briefly at the spleen.

"It's a mess, all right."

"That certainly covers all of what's in the medical dictionary," observed Hamperl.

Honek had isolated the bullet. He cut it out and laid it in a separate metal tray like a gold prospector putting aside a precious nugget. This was easier on the eye than watching Hamperl clamp Kuttner's small intestine so that he could haul it out in one block. I'd seen one too many of my comrades in the freezing cold of the trenches with their steaming guts hanging out of their tunics to view that particular sight with any equanimity.

So far we had been there for less than thirty minutes and already the kidneys were being removed.

The second bullet was lodged deep in the spine and took several minutes to gouge out.

When that was done Hamperl asked, "Do you wish me to remove the brain?"

"No. I don't think it will be necessary."

"Then that would appear to be that, for now." He shrugged. "Of course, it will take a while to analyze the organs, the hematology, and the contents of the stomach. Naturally I will test the quantities of Veronal present then."

"At this moment in time I must ask you both not to make any verbal reference to a second bullet," I said. "As far as anyone else is concerned, just the one shot was fired."

"Am I to understand that you plan on using this subterfuge as the basis for some incriminating piece of cross-examination?" said the professor.

"Yes," I said. "I am. You can mention your real findings in your written report, of course."

"Very well," said the professor. "It'll be our little secret until you say otherwise, Commissar."

When both bullets were lying in a tray, I took a closer look. I'd seen enough spent lead in my time to recognize metal from a thirty-eight when I saw it.

"Right now, I'd be grateful if you were to indulge me with your first thoughts, sir."

"All right."

Professor Hamperl sighed and then thought for a moment.

"Both shots seem to have been fired at fairly close range," he said. "Of course I should have to check the shirt for powder burns to give you an accurate distance, but the size of the entry wounds persuades me, strongly, that the shooter could not have been more than half a meter away when these shots were fired. The angle of the entries would seem to indicate that the person who fired the shots was immediately in front of him. The grouping of the shots was tight, as if the two shots were fired in very quick succession before the victim moved very much."

"If the shooter fired at only half a meter's distance, why didn't the slugs go straight through him?"

"One clipped the rib and lost most of its velocity before it penetrated the heart, I shouldn't wonder," Hamperl said thoughtfully. "And the other lodged deep in the spine, as you saw. That's why.

"As I say, we'll have to see how much barbiturate was absorbed by his organs, but on the basis of the organ damage and the amount of blood that was in the diaphragm, I'd say it was the shots that killed him, not the Veronal."

"What do you know about that stuff?"

"Barbital? It's been around for a good while. Almost forty years. It was first synthesized by two German chemists. Bayer sells the stuff as a soluble salt or in tablet form. Ten to fifteen grams would be a safe dose, but fifty or sixty could be lethal."

"That's not much of a margin for error," I said.

"Of course someone using it regularly would soon develop a tolerance of the drug and possibly require a higher dose, which he might easily accommodate without any mishap. But if he left off taking it for a while, it'd be a mistake to start again with a high dose. Possibly might turn out to be a lethal one."

"So it has to be handled with care."

"Oh yes. It's powerful stuff. My own sleep would have to be very disturbed to want to take it myself. All the same, it's a lot better than its predecessor: bromides. There's no unpleasant taste with Veronal. In fact, there's not much taste at all."

"Any side effects?"

"It would certainly affect the heart rate, the pulse, and the blood pressure. And of course that would substantially affect the bleeding. Perhaps there would have been more blood exiting from the wounds if this man hadn't sedated himself. As it is, most of the blood from the wounds was in the diaphragm."

"Anything else?"

"You wouldn't want to mix the stuff with alcohol. It reacts badly in the stomach. I've seen cases of people who mixed it and were choked to death when they vomited in their sleep."

"Thank you."

"Will there be anything else?"

"I believe there's a way that you can find out if he was homosexual."

Hamperl didn't bat an eyelid.

"Ah, yes, I see. The shaven pubic area. Yes, it is unusual for a man to shave himself down there. It might indicate an effeminate inclination, yes. I see what you mean. Intriguing, isn't it?"

"There were other things that make me think he might be homosexual," I added. "Things I can't tell you about. But I would like to know for sure."

"Sometimes," agreed Hamperl, "in a habitual sodomite the anus becomes dilated. It loses its natural puckered orifice and develops a thicker, keratinized skin. Or even becomes like an open shutter on a camera. I assume you're referring to that. Would you like me to take a look?"

"Yes."

"Dr. Honek, would you help me turn the cadaver over, please?"

The two men wrestled the gutted body onto what there was of its front and spread the dead man's buttocks.

After a moment or two Hamperl started to shake his head.

"The anus looks all right to me. Of course, the fact that there has been no apparent interference doesn't indicate that he wasn't homosexual. But I could always swab the anus for semen when I do some of the other tests. And swab his penis for traces of fecal matter."

"Please do that."

Hamperl was trying to conceal a gleeful, triumphant smile. "An SS officer who was homosexual. Perhaps that's why he was murdered. I can't imagine this sort of thing goes down well in Berlin."

Hamperl exchanged a look with Dr. Honek, who was looking equally amused.

"Of course one hears things. About Berlin and transvestism."

I nodded. "All the same, if I were you, I wouldn't mention this, either. The SS doesn't have much of a sense of humor about that sort of thing. It would be a shame to find that out the hard way."

"You'll have my histological report on the organs and my pathological diagnosis in forty-eight hours, Commissar."

"Thanks again."

The professor escorted me to the door.

"So, Commissar, will you be leaving your own body to science, do you think? For medical students to use in the anatomy lab."

I glanced at the shambles that was a man I had been speaking to about a painting by Gustav Klimt at Jungfern-Breschan just twenty-four hours earlier.

"No, I don't think I will."

"Pity. A man as tall as you must have a fine skeleton. I sometimes think that the real fun stuff for our bodies doesn't start until we're dead."

"I'm already looking forward to it."

KAHLO APOLOGIZED AGAIN as Klein drove us away from the hospital.

"You get used to it," I said.

"Not me. Not ever. It was the smell of the ether that really got to me, I think. Reminded me of when my mother died."

"Bad, huh?" said Klein.

Kahlo shook his head, but his expression told a different story, and, seeing it in his rearview mirror, Klein reached into the leather pocket on the inside of the driver's door and took out a silver flask.

"I keep this for cold days," he said, and handed it to me.

"It doesn't get much colder than that," I said. "Not for Captain Kuttner, anyway." I took a bite off the flask, which was full of good schnapps, and handed it back to Kahlo.

"That bastard." Kahlo upended the flask. "That bastard professor was enjoying it, too. My discomfort. Did you hear him, sir? The way he started laying it on. I thought, Fuck this. I'm off. He's having a laugh at my expense."

"That he was," I said. "But a man has to take pleasure in his work where and when he can. Especially in this country."

I bent forward to the floor of the car, lit a cigarette, and handed it back to him.

"There was a time when *I* took pleasure in my work, too. When I was good at it. Those were the days when the Berlin murder squad was the best in the world. When I was a real detective. A professional. What I didn't know about the science of murder wasn't worth knowing. But now"—I shook my head—"now I'm just an amateur. A rather quaint and old-fashioned amateur."

IT WAS FIVE THIRTY in the afternoon, and back in the library at the Lower Castle, irritation and disappointment hung in the air like mustard gas ready to contaminate the lungs of all who were unfortunate enough to breathe it in. SS and Gestapo officers shook their heads and smoked furiously and looked around for someone to blame. Opinions were offered and rejected angrily and offered again until voices were raised and accusations made. There appeared to be several officers in the library, and while ultimately there was only one man whose opinion counted, others were determined not to be held responsible for "the failure."

Kahlo and I had crept into the morning room to avoid being drawn into these recriminations, but left the door wide open so that we could hear and increase our strength, for a wise man is strong and a man who listens at doors increases his strength.

"We let him slip through our fingers," raged Heydrich. "We have at our disposal the most powerful police force ever seen in this city and yet we don't seem to be able to catch one man."

"It's too early to give up hope, sir." This sounded like Horst Böhme, the head of the SD in Prague. His Berlin accent was instantly recognizable to me. "We're continuing to conduct house-to-house searches for Morávek, and even now I'm certain that something will turn up."

"We know his name," said Heydrich, ignoring him. "We know what he looks like. We even know he's somewhere in the city, and yet we can't find him. It's a total bloody failure. An embarrassment."

"Yes, sir."

"An opportunity thrown away, gentlemen," stormed Heydrich. "However, I suppose I shouldn't really be all that surprised, given what happened here in May. At the UVOD safe house in—what was the name of that dumb Czecho street, Fleischer?"

"Pod Terebkov Street, sir," said Fleischer.

"You had them all in your fucking hands," yelled Heydrich. "They were trapped in that damned apartment. And still you managed to let two of them escape. Jesus, I should have you shot for incompetence or for being complicit in their evading capture. Either way I should have you shot."

"Sir," protested Fleischer, "with all due respect, they were thirty meters off the ground. They used a steel radio aerial to slide out of the window thirty meters down to that courtyard. It was covered in blood when we found it. A man's fingers were on the ground."

"Why didn't you have men in the courtyard? Is there a shortage of SS and Gestapo here in Prague? Well, Böhme? Is there?"

"No, sir."

"Fleischer?"

"No, Herr General."

"So this time you would think we could get it right. This time we have a photograph of Václav Morávek. We know the safe house he's been using for the last five months. And what do we find? A note, addressed to me. Remind me of what Morávek's note said, Fleischer."

"I'd rather not, sir."

"It said, 'Lick my arse, General Heydrich.' It's even written in German and Czech, as the law says it ought to be, which is an especially insolent touch, don't you think? 'Lick my arse, General Heydrich.' It would seem that I'm an even bigger prick than you are, Fleischer. You're already a laughingstock after that incident in the Příkopy Bar."

"On that particular occasion you mention, sir, the man was wearing a Party badge on the lapel of his jacket."

"And that makes all of the difference, does it? I wish I had ten marks for every bastard wearing a Party badge I've had to shoot since 1933."

"Someone tipped him off, sir. Morávek must have been told we were coming."

"That much is obvious, my dear Commissioner. What isn't fucking obvious is what we're doing about finding the traitor who might have told him. Major Ploetz?"

"Sir?"

"Who is liaising with the special SD squad that I ordered to be set up? The VXG."

"It was Captain Kuttner, sir."

"I know who it *was*, Achim. I'm asking who it is *now*."

"Well, sir, you haven't said."

"Do I have to think of everything? Apart from my children, who incidentally will be arriving here in less than forty-eight hours, nothing, I repeat nothing, is more important than finding the man behind the OTA transmissions; traitor X, or whatever you want to call him. Nothing. These are the Reichsführer's own orders to me. Not even Václav Morávek and the Three Kings and the UVOD Home Resistance network are as important as that, do you hear?"

Another voice spoke up, but it was one I didn't recognize.

"Frankly, sir, I don't wish to speak ill of the dead, but Captain Kuttner was not a good liaison officer."

"Who's that speaking?" I asked Kahlo.

He shook his head. "Don't know."

"The fact is, Kuttner was arrogant and rude, and often quite unpredictable; and he managed to piss off the local Kripo and Gestapo in double-quick time while he was here."

"Like I said," murmured Kahlo, "he was a prick."

"He did not serve you well, General," continued the same voice. "And now that he's gone, might I suggest, sir, that I handle the liaison with the VXG. I can promise you I'll make a better job of it than he did."

"Very well, Captain Kluckholm," said Heydrich. "If Captain Kuttner was as bad as you say he was—"

"He was," insisted another voice. "Sir."

"Then," said Heydrich, "you had better get yourself over to Peček Palace and then to Kripo and try to smooth over any ruffled feathers and make sure they know what they're supposed to be doing. Clear?"

"Yes, sir."

I heard a chair move, and then someone—Kluckholm, I imagined—clicked his heels and left the room.

"Talking of ruffled feathers, sir." This was Major Ploetz. "Your detective, Gunther, has already managed to upset the whole chicken coop. I've already had several complaints about his manner, which leaves a great deal to be desired."

I nodded at Kahlo. "True," I said. "Too true."

"I agree with Major Ploetz, sir." This was Colonel Böhme, again.

"I suppose you think I should have picked you to handle this inquiry, Colonel Böhme."

"Well, I am a trained detective, sir."

Heydrich laughed cruelly. "You mean you once went on the detective lieutenant's training course at the Police Institute, in Berlin-Charlottenburg, don't you? Yes, I can easily see how that might make anyone think he was Hercule Poirot. My dear Böhme, let me tell you something. We don't have any good detectives left in the SD or in the Gestapo. Within the kind of system that we operate we have all sorts of people: ambitious lawyers, sadistic policemen, brown-nosing civil servants, all, I daresay, good Party men, too; sometimes we even call them detectives or inspectors and ask them to investigate a case; but I tell you they can't do it. To be a proper detective is beyond their competence. They can't do it because they won't stick their noses in where they're not wanted. They can't do it because they're afraid of asking questions they're not supposed to ask. And even if they did ask those questions they'd get scared because they wouldn't like the answers. It would offend their sense of Party loyalty. Yes, that's the phrase they'd use to excuse their inability to do the job. Well, Gunther may be a lot of things, but he has the Berlin nose for trouble. A real *Schnauze*. And that's what I want."

"But surely Party loyalty has to count for something, sir," said Böhme. "What about that?"

"What about it? A promising young SS officer is dead. Yes, that's what he was, gentlemen, in spite of your own reservations.

He was murdered, and by someone in this house, I shouldn't wonder. Oh, we can pretend that it might have been some poor Czecho who killed him, but all of us know that it would take the Scarlet Pimpernel to get past all these guards and to walk into my house and shoot Captain Kuttner. Besides, I flatter myself that if a Czecho did take the trouble to penetrate our security, he would prefer to shoot me instead of my own adjutant. No, gentlemen, this was an inside job, I'm convinced of it and Gunther's the right man—my man—to find out who did it." He paused for a moment. "And as for Party loyalty, that's my job, not yours, Colonel Böhme. I'll say who is loyal and who isn't."

I'd heard enough for the moment. I stood up and closed the door to the morning room.

"Hardly a ringing endorsement," said Kahlo. "Was it, sir?"

"From Heydrich?" I shrugged. "Don't knock it. That's as good as it gets."

I sat down at the piano and fingered a few notes, experimentally. "All the same, I get the feeling I'm being played. And played well."

"We're all being played," said Kahlo. "You, me, even Heydrich. There's only one man in Europe who has his mitts on the keyboard. And that's the GRÖFAZ."

The GRÖFAZ was a derogatory name for Hitler.

"Maybe. All right. Who's next on our list? I have a sudden desire to ruffle some more feathers."

"General Frank, sir."

"He's the one with the new wife, right? The wife who's a Czech."

"That's right, sir. And believe me, she's tip-top. A real sweetheart. Twenty-eight years old, tall, blond, and clever."

"Frank must have some hidden qualities."

"Yes, sir."

"Or better still, some hidden vices. Let's find out which it is."

"DID YOU KNOW Captain Kuttner very well, General Frank?"

"Not very well. But well enough. Ploetz, Pomme, and Kluckholm and Kuttner—" Frank smiled. "It sounds like an old Berlin tailor's shop. Well, they all sort of merge into one, really. That's what you want from an adjutant, I suppose. Me, I wouldn't know, I don't have an adjutant myself. I seem to manage quite well without one, let alone four. But if I did have an adjutant I should want him to be as anonymous as those three are. They are efficient, of course. Heydrich can tolerate nothing less. And, being efficient, they stay out of the limelight.

"I knew Kuttner slightly before his Prague posting. When he was at the Ministry of the Interior. He helped me in some administrative way, for which I was grateful, so when he turned up here I tried to help him out. Consequently he shared a few confidences with me. Which is why I know what I'm talking about.

"Kuttner was the latest addition to Heydrich's stable of aides-de-camp. And that meant that he and Heydrich's third adjutant, Kluckholm, were never likely to get on very well, since the first principle of doing the job well is, I imagine, to make your superior redundant. So Kluckholm resented Kuttner. And feared him, I shouldn't wonder. Well, that's understandable; Kuttner was a clever man. Much cleverer than Kluckholm. He was a brilliant lawyer before he went east in June. Kuttner, on the other hand, felt that Kluckholm tried to keep him in his place. Or even to put him down."

For a moment I pictured the two men arguing in the garden the previous evening. Was that what I had witnessed? Kluckholm trying to put Kuttner in his place? Kuttner resisting it? Or something more intimate, perhaps.

"Was Heydrich aware of this rivalry?"

"Of course. There's not much that Heydrich's not aware of, I'll say that for him. But he likes to encourage rivalry. Heydrich believes it persuades people to try harder. So it wouldn't have bothered him in the least that these two were vying with each other for his favor. It's a trick he's learned from the Leader, no doubt."

"No doubt."

General Karl Hermann Frank looked almost ten years older than his forty-three years. His face was lined and furrowed, and there were bags under his eyes, as if he were another Nazi who didn't sleep very well. He was a heavy smoker, with two of the fingers on the hand holding his cigarette looking as if he'd dipped them in gravy, and teeth that resembled the ivory keys on an old piano. It was difficult to see what a beautiful, twenty-eight-year-old woman saw in this thin, stiff-looking man. Power, perhaps? Hitler might have passed him over in choosing von Neurath's successor, but as SS and police leader of Bohemia and Moravia, Frank was effectively the second-most-important man in the protectorate. More interesting than that, perhaps, was why a beautiful Czech physician should have married a man who, by his own admission, hated Czechs so much. The hatred I'd heard him articulate about the Czechs the day before was still ringing in my ears. What, I wondered, did Mr. and Mrs. Frank talk about after dinner? The failure of the Czech banks? Sentences in the Czech language that didn't use any vowels? UVOD? The Three Kings?

"Sir, when you say there was no love lost between Captains Kluckholm and Kuttner, do you mean to say they hated each other?"

"There was a certain amount of hatred, yes. That's only natural. However, if you're looking for a man who really hated Captain Kuttner—hated him enough to kill him, perhaps—then Obersturmbannführer Walter Jacobi is your man."

"He's the SD colonel who's interested in magic and the occult, isn't he?"

"That's right. And in particular, Ariosophy. Don't ask me to explain it in any detail. I believe it is some occult nonsense that's to do with being German. For me, reading the Leader's book is enough. But Jacobi wanted more. He was forever badgering me to become more interested in Ariosophy until I told him to fuck off. I wasn't the only one who thought his interest in this stuff to be laughable. Kuttner, whose father was a Protestant pastor and no stranger to religious nonsense himself, thought that Ariosophy was complete rubbish, and said so."

"To Colonel Jacobi's face?"

"Most certainly to his face. That's what made it so very entertaining for the rest of us. It happened when they were both at the SS officer school in Prague. That was last Sunday, the twenty-ninth. The day after Heydrich arrived here in Prague. The school asked him to come to a lunch in his honor, and naturally his adjutants accompanied him. Someone, not Kuttner, had asked Colonel Jacobi about the death's-head ring he was wearing—a gift from Himmler, apparently. One thing led to another, and before very long Jacobi was talking balls about Wotan and sun worship and the Masons. In the middle of this, Captain Kuttner burst out laughing and said he thought all of that German folk stuff was 'complete poppycock.' His exact words. For a moment or two there was an embarrassed silence and then Voss—he's the officer in charge at Benešchau and one of the guests here at the Lower Castle and, I might add, an idiot—Voss tried to change the subject. But Kuttner wasn't having any of it and said some other stuff, and that's when Jacobi said it."

Frank frowned for a moment.

"Said what?"

"I'm trying to think of his exact words. Yes. He said something like 'If it wasn't for the fact that you are wearing an SS uniform, Captain Kuttner, I would cheerfully kill you now, and in front of all these people.'"

"You're quite sure about that, sir?"

"Oh yes. Quite sure. I'm sure Voss will confirm it. Come to think of it, he didn't say 'kill,' he said 'shoot.'"

"What did Kuttner say to that?"

"He laughed. Which didn't exactly defuse the situation. And he made some other remark that I didn't understand at the time but which relates to the fact that there had already been some previous bad blood between them. Apparently they knew each other at university. And they were enemies."

"I thought Jacobi was from Munich, sir," said Kahlo.

"He is."

"And that he studied law at Tübingen University," Kahlo added. "At least that's what it said on his file."

"Oh, he did. But he also studied law at the Martin Luther University in Halle. The same as Kuttner. He might not look like it, but Jacobi is only a year or two older than Kuttner was. According to Heydrich, they even fought a duel. While they were students."

"A duel?" Kahlo guffawed. "What, with swords?"

"That's right."

"About what, exactly?" he asked.

"They were in a dueling society. It doesn't have to be about anything at all. That's the whole point of being in a dueling society."

"So it might even have been Jacobi who put the *schmitte* on Kuttner's face?"

"It's possible. You should certainly ask him."

"Given that Jacobi was Kuttner's superior," I said, "then surely Kuttner was being grossly insubordinate when he said what he said. Surely there would be repercussions for saying something like that. Why wasn't Kuttner put on a charge?"

"For one thing, this was the mess and it wasn't a formal occasion. As you may know, there is supposed to be a certain amount of leeway in what officers can say to each other on these occasions. Up to a point. But beyond that, well, that wasn't a problem, either, because Kuttner had vitamin B, of course."

"You mean with Heydrich."

"Of course with Heydrich."

Frank lit a cigarette with a handsome gold lighter before crossing his legs nonchalantly, affording us a fine view of his spurs. Maybe his Czech wife, Karola, liked the dashing cavalry-officer look. This was certainly better than Frank's natural look, which was that of a man recently released from a prison. His bony head, drawn features, strong fingers, sad smile, and chain-smoking were straight out of a French novel.

"What you also have to understand," said Frank, "is that after Kuttner's breakdown in Latvia, and because it was Heydrich and von Eberstein who saved the young man from being cashiered, his brother officers were already cutting him quite a bit of slack. And for Jacobi to have pressed the matter through official channels would have meant taking on Heydrich. And since Heydrich is now the source of all advancement in Bohemia, you would only do that if you were prepared to park your career in the toilet. Jacobi might be a cunt and a complete waxed mustache, but he's not entirely stupid. No, not entirely."

"But is he a killer?" I said. "To shoot a fellow officer in cold blood, that does seem stupid."

Frank's tired eyes tightened, and a few seconds after that a smile arrived on his lean face, like a winning card. "And I thought you were supposed to be a detective."

"It's Jacobi who's keen on the occult, sir, not me. And generally I question witnesses because, more often than not, it turns out to be more reliable than a crystal ball or a set of tarot cards."

Leaning forward in a way that made him seem almost simian, Frank played with a ring on his right hand for a moment and kept on smiling as he enjoyed the superiority of knowing something I didn't, at least for a few seconds longer; it was obvious to both of us that he was going to tell me, eventually, exactly what this was.

"Heydrich thinks highly of you, Gunther. But I'm not so sure."

"To some coppers that might seem like a crushing blow, sir, but I'm sure I'll get over it, with a drink or two."

"I don't mind if I do."

Frank glanced at Kahlo, who went over to the drinks tray.

"Yes, sir? What'll it be?"

"Brandy."

"Me, too," I said. "And have one yourself, why don't you?"

I waited until we were all holding a glass and then toasted the general.

"Here's to getting over our superiors' not thinking as highly of us as we'd like."

Frank knew that was meant for him—that of course he might have been the new Reichsprotector of Bohemia, and not Heydrich, if the Leader had thought more of him. To his credit, Frank took the jab on his chin without blinking, but he took the drink even better, as if swallowing a baby's cordial. I'd seen men drink like that before, and it helped explain how we were both the same sort of age but with different maps on our faces. Mine was all right, I guess, but his looked like the Ganges Delta.

"I think we'd better have the decanter over here, Kurt," I said.

"Good idea," said Frank.

When there was a fresh glassful in his fingers, Frank studied it carefully for a moment and said, "Usually there's a payoff for a good informer, isn't there?"

"Sometimes," I said. "But with all due respect, you don't look like a man who's going to be happy with five marks and a cigarette."

"A favor, Commissar. More than one favor, perhaps."

"What kind of favor?"

"Information. You see, since being passed over for the top job here in Bohemia—as you were kind enough to remind me—I don't hear as well as I used to."

"And you'd like us to be your ear trumpet, is that it?"

Frank looked critically at Kahlo. "I don't know about him. But you'll do for now."

"I see."

"I just want to be kept in the loop, that's all. Right now I'm the last to know everything. It's Heydrich's little way of reminding me he's in charge. You saw the way he dealt with von Neurath the other evening. Well, I get the same treatment." He shrugged. "It's not like I'm asking very much, Commissar. After all"—he poured the second brandy on top of the first and then licked his lips loudly—"it's not like I'm a spy or anything."

Kahlo and I exchanged a swift look.

Smiling, I poured myself another drink. "Are you sure about that, sir?" I kept on smiling, to make him think I might be joking and to keep him listening without taking offense. "Let's look at it logically. A man with an ax to grind like you. I think you'd make a pretty good spy."

Frank ignored me. "Don't change the subject. Not now, when we're making progress. Just tell me this: do we have a deal?"

"To trade information now and in the future? Yes, I think so. I could use a few friends in Prague. Right now I don't have any. Come to that, I don't have any at home, either."

Frank nodded, his eyes glistening.

"All right," he said. "You first. Some information. A sign of good faith."

"Yes. If you like."

"What's the name of this bit of mouse that Henlein has got stashed in the Imperial Hotel? I hear you know all about her."

"Her name is Betty Kipsdorf."

"Is it, now?"

"Now, tell me why you want to know."

"Maybe I just wanted to see if you were prepared to keep your end of the bargain before I told you about Lieutenant Colonel Jacobi's interesting past."

"What, more interesting than fighting a duel with my murder victim? And threatening to shoot him?"

"Oh, this is very much more interesting than that, Commissar. That was merely an appetizer. Here is the main dish.

"Jacobi joined the SA in 1930, while he was still a law student in Tübingen. Nothing unusual about that, of course, but I would suggest that there are not many law students who get themselves arrested for murder in the same week that they graduate.

"Yes, I thought that would catch your breath. In 1932, Jacobi murdered someone in Stuttgart, which is only twenty kilometers from Tübingen. The victim was a KPD cadre, although it seems that might not be the real reason the boy was killed. There was, it seems, some suspicion he was queer and that this was the real motive for the murder. Now, I don't have to tell you of all people what things were like in 1932. In some ways von Papen's government was every bit as right-wing as Hitler's. The Stuttgart prosecutor's office was rather slow in putting together a case against Walter Jacobi. So slow, in fact, that the case was never actually brought because, of course, in January 1933 the Nazis were elected and nobody was interested in bringing a case against a loyal Party member like Jacobi anymore. All the same, it's no wonder he joined the SS and then the SD soon afterward; it was probably the best way of staying out of jail. And of course one of the very first things he did when he achieved a certain position of authority within the SS was to have the papers in the case destroyed. That almost got him kicked out of the SD in 1937, but Himmler stepped in and pulled his nuts out of the nosebag."

"And you were thinking that a good detective might have found that out for himself, sir?"

"Something like that."

"You overestimate me, General. Then again, there's only so much I can find out in less than twelve hours. That's how long I've been on this case. And of course there's a limit to how much I can ask my superior officers without bringing down a charge of gross insubordination on my head."

Frank laughed. "We both know that's not true."

He laughed again in a way that made me think that there were probably a lot of things he found funny that I would have felt very differently about.

"We both know that it suits General Heydrich to have you humiliate us all. Especially at this particular moment as he becomes Reichsprotector of Bohemia. It becomes an object lesson in power for us all. Perhaps to test our loyalty. Hitler admires Heydrich because he suspects everyone of everything. Me included. Me especially."

"And why would he suspect you, General?"

Frank looked at Kahlo almost as if he knew it had been Kahlo who told me about the VXG.

"Don't pretend to be naïve. I'm married to a Czech woman, Commissar. Karola. My first wife, Anna, hates my guts and is married to a man who affects to look like the Leader and now makes it his business to tell lies about me and my new wife. Just because she's German Czech. Between them they have already turned my two sons against me. And now they're doing their best to allege that the only reason my wife married me was because she is a Czech spy and that when I go home at night she persuades me to part with state secrets. Well, it's simply not true. And it's why I didn't think your joke was funny. I'm loyal to Germany and the Party, and one day I hope that I will have the opportunity to demonstrate to the whole world just how devoted to the Leader and the cause of National Socialism I really am. Until then I hope I can count on your help—yes, both of you—to put paid to this baseless innuendo."

He stood up and I shook hands with him and, in my defense, so did Kurt Kahlo. It was Frank's idea, not mine, that we should, and at the time I thought nothing of it—a handshake seemed like a small price to pay for some important information about a potential new suspect. It was another eight or nine months before I realized I'd shaken hands with the man who had ordered the destruction of the small town of Lidice and the murder of everyone in it, in reprisal for the assassination of Reinhard Heydrich.

I GLANCED AT MY WATCH. It was seven o'clock.

"If I wasn't confused before," admitted Kurt Kahlo, "I'm certainly confused now. Every time we speak to someone we find out a little bit more. The only trouble is that it leaves me a little bit less enlightened. It's curious, really. You might even call it a paradox. Even as I think I'm getting a proper grip on this case I find there's something interrupting my thoughts, as though someone had built a wall between the two halves of my brain. Just as I find a big enough chair to stand on and look over at the other side, I forget what I'm supposed to be looking for, anyway. And then, before you know it, I've even forgotten why I'm standing on the chair in the first place."

Kahlo sighed and shook his head ruefully.

"Sorry, sir, that's not helping, I know."

Even as Kahlo spoke I was trying to put up a fight against the rampaging contagion of his utter confusion. In my mind I seemed to hear a lost chord and see some words underneath the palimpsest. An elusive fragment of real insight flashed like a pan of magnesium powder inside the dark chamber that was my skull, and then all was black again. For a brief moment everything was illuminated and I understood all and I was on the cusp of articulating exactly what the problem was and where the solution might lie, and didn't he, Kahlo, know that what he was describing was precisely the intellectual dilemma that afflicted every detective? But the very next moment a gray mist descended behind my eyes, and before I knew it, this same thought that looked like an answer was slowly suffocating like a fish landed by an angler on a riverbank, its mouth opening and shutting, with no sound emerging.

I told him I needed to get away from the Lower Castle so that I might order my own thinking. That's what I also told myself. I'd had enough of them all for one day, and suddenly that included Kahlo, too. I decided that I wanted to go back to the hotel and devote my energies to Arianne for a while and that we could spend our last night together before I sent her home in the morning.

"Ask Major Ploetz to find a car that will take me back into Prague," I said.

Kahlo looked sad for a moment, as if disappointed I was not ready to be honest with him about where I was going.

"Yes, sir."

I did not have long to wait before a car became available, but I was less than pleased to discover that I was to share a ride with Heydrich himself.

"Now you can tell me what conclusions you've come to," he said as Klein steered us left, out of the Lower Castle's infernal gates and onto the picture-postcard country road.

"I haven't any yet."

"I was rather hoping you would have everything wrapped up by this weekend. Before my wife, Lina, gets here."

"Yes. I know. You told me that before."

"And before my guests are obliged to leave. They do have duties to perform."

"Mm-hmm."

"I must say I find it rather odd that you think you can just take the evening off while a murderer remains at liberty in my house. Perhaps I didn't make myself clear this morning. It is urgent that this case is solved before news gets back to Berlin."

"No, you made that perfectly clear, sir."

"And yet you're still going to see that whore of yours."

I nodded. "Tell me something, sir. Do you play chess?"

"Yes. But I don't see what that has to do with this. Or your whore."

"Well, then, you might know that in major tournaments it isn't uncommon for players to get up and leave the board between moves. Reading, sleeping, or indeed any pleasant distraction can refresh the human mind, enabling the player to perform at a higher intellectual level. Now, while I don't expect to do any reading this evening, I do expect my lady friend will provide some very pleasant distractions, after which it's perfectly possible that I may get some sleep. All of which is a long way of saying that I need some time away from you and your house in order to try to make sense of everything I've discovered today."

"Such as?"

Reaching the main road at last, Klein stepped hard on the accelerator, leaving Jungfern-Breschan behind, and we sped toward Prague at almost eighty kilometers per hour, obliging me to raise my voice to answer the general.

"I know of at least three people who are staying at the Lower Castle who hated Captain Kuttner. Henlein, Jacobi, and Kluckholm. I can't yet say if they hated him enough to kill him. They hated him for a variety of reasons, which mostly come down to the fact that Kuttner was insubordinate and clever and perhaps a bit conceited and really not quite the senior officer's toady that a good adjutant ought to be. But there were other reasons, too—probably more important reasons—that might have got him murdered. Principally the fact that he was your liaison officer for the SD's Traitor X Group. If he'd found out something concerning the identity of the traitor, that would have been a pretty good reason for someone to kill him. You might have told me about that yourself, General."

"When?"

"This morning. When we were in your office. When you handed me this case."

"I hardly wanted to broadcast the news about the existence of such a squad in front of my own butler. Besides, I had assumed your criminal assistant would inform you about that. Major Ploetz tells me Kahlo is part of the VXG."

"He assumed it was a secret. I've only just found out about it."

"Well, you know now."

"Is everyone who has been invited to your house under suspicion?"

"Until the traitor is apprehended? Yes. Of course. What a ridiculous question. Oddly enough, Gunther, traitors have a habit of turning out to be the people we trusted most. It would be foolish to assume that there are some people who are simply above suspicion merely by virtue of a long acquaintance with the Leader or me, or their continuing demonstration of Party loyalty. A Czech spy would be no good if he was suspected of being a Czech spy, would he? However, I do agree that this might conceivably have been the reason why Kuttner was murdered. Which makes it all the more imperative that we catch the bastard as soon as possible, wouldn't you agree?"

"I have another reason why he might have been murdered."

"I'm listening."

"Captain Kuttner was homosexual."

"Nonsense. What ever gave you such a ridiculous idea? Let me tell you, I knew Kuttner for more than a decade. And I would have known. It's impossible that I wouldn't have known such a thing."

"Nevertheless, it's a fact."

"You'd better have some damned good evidence for an assertion like that, Gunther."

"I'll spare you the details, sir, but you can take it from me that I would hardly have told you in front of your butler; and I wouldn't mention it now, in front of your driver, unless I was damned sure about what I'm saying. Moreover, I think we can agree that being homosexual, especially in the SS, is, in these enlightened times that we live in, more than enough reason to get you killed. I suspect any number of SS officers would feel entirely justified in shooting that kind of man. Equally, I suspect one or two would have felt quite justified in having Kuttner shot for—what shall we call it, sir?—his dereliction of duty with that Special Action Group in Latvia."

"That's something you should know quite a bit about yourself, Gunther. Perhaps you have asked yourself why you were allowed to leave your own police battalion in Belorussia so easily. If you have not done so already, then perhaps you should."

I nodded. "Arthur Nebe said something to me at the time, by way of an explanation."

"And Nebe takes his orders from me. Wouldn't you agree?"

"Yes, sir."

"You remind me of someone, Gunther. A rather stubborn Belgian by the name of Paul Anspach. He used to be president of the International Fencing Association. After Belgium was defeated, in June 1940, Anspach, who had acted as a military judge advocate, was arrested for alleged war crimes and put in prison. After he was released I had him summoned to Berlin, where I ordered him to surrender the presidency to me. He refused. I can't tell you how irritating that was; however, I admired his courage and sent him home."

"Not even you can always get what you want, General."

"I can, actually. With the help of the Italian president of fencing, I managed to have him stripped of the international presidency anyway. It's pointless being stubborn with me, Gunther. I always get what I want in the end. You should know that by now. That it's not wise to oppose me. In case you didn't understand, that's the point of the fucking story."

"I've never believed it was wise to oppose you," I said. "Even when I was doing it. No more than I think it's wise for you to drive without an escort in an open-top car. You are an invitation to any would-be Gavrilo Princip to have a go. In case you had forgotten, the Archduke Franz Ferdinand of Austria also traveled in an open car."

Heydrich laughed, and although such a thing seemed almost impossible, I found I disliked him even more than before.

"If I should ever gain the impression that my conduct in this respect was wise or ill considered—if ever someone were to attack this car—I would not hesitate to respond with unheard-of violence. I suspect that the population of Prague is well aware of this fact. And while your concern is touching, Gunther, I think it unlikely that I will ever need to take your advice about this."

"Oh, I don't mean to sound like I care what happens to you, sir. Any more than I mean to sound touching. What I mean to say is what your detective ought to say. Your bodyguard. Whatever it is you choose to call me. I don't know a hell of a lot about fencing, but if it's anything like boxing, then a fighter is told to protect himself at all times. That's not weakness, General. Any more than it's weakness to look out for a fellow officer from Halle an der Saale who went to the same school with you."

"It's clear to me by now that not everyone agreed with that."

"Tell me, sir, was Kuttner any good at his job?"

"Insofar as it went."

"Meaning?"

"I have three other adjutants, all of whom are quite competent. I had thought that one more wouldn't make any difference. One is enough for most people, of course. Of course I am not most people. However, the only reason I have four adjutants—correction, three adjutants—is to remind me to delegate more. I have a great problem trusting people to carry out my orders.

"Ordinarily there's nothing any of them do that I couldn't do better myself. But seeing them at my every beck and call reminds me that there are other, more important tasks that require my attention. Having three adjutants makes me more productive, more efficient. Frankly, however, I can't stand the sight of any of them.

Kuttner was at least someone I thought I liked. But adjutants are a necessary evil for a man in my position. Much like yourself."

"I'm flattered."

"That certainly was not my intention."

"Your father knew Kuttner's father. Is that right?"

"Yes. But since you ask, what is more relevant, perhaps, is that my mother gave Albert Kuttner music lessons."

"Is that how you met?"

"I think it must have been. I seem to recall seeing him when I was back on leave from the Reichsmarine. I couldn't have been more than twenty at the time. Kuttner was much younger, of course. I may even have tried to talk Albert into joining the naval academy, just like me. After all, he went to the same school that I did. But his father was less of a nationalist than my own, which might be why he chose to pursue a legal career instead. Not that any of this is relevant."

"I disagree. Finding out everything there is to know about a man who has been murdered and a lot more besides is, in my opinion, always the best way to discover why he was murdered. And once I find out why, it's often a very simple matter to discover who."

Heydrich shrugged. "Well, it's your business. You know best in these matters. You must do what you think fit, Gunther."

About halfway between Jungfern-Breschan and Prague the road ran between recently plowed fields. It was a desolate scene with little in the way of other traffic until, nearing Bulovka Hospital, we encountered an ambulance and, farther on, a tram grinding up a hill that led to the city suburbs. Crossing Troja Bridge, the car slowed and rounded a corner, and a man snatched off his cap and bowed as he caught sight of a German staff car.

It was easier to hear Heydrich now that we weren't going quite so fast, and once again I tried to question him about Albert Kuttner.

"Did you like Albert Kuttner?"

"Is that your way of asking if I killed him?"

"Did you?"

"No. And to answer your other question, no, I didn't like him. Not anymore. Once I did. A while ago. But not lately. He was a disappointment to me. And to some extent he was becoming something of a liability. Since you mentioned Colonel Jacobi, I assume you know the details of what happened there. The quarrel they had. To be frank, Gunther, I am not at all sorry that Kuttner is dead. But my conscience is clear. I gave the man every opportunity to atone for his inadequacies. At the same time I can't have people murdering my staff just because they don't like them. Christ, if you and I were to murder all of the people back at the Lower Castle I didn't like, then we should have hardly anyone left in the local SD: Jacobi, Fleischer, Geschke, von Neurath. I wouldn't shed a tear if any of them caught a bullet."

"That's straightforward enough, I suppose."

"Henlein and Jury are particularly awful, don't you think? Cunts. The pair of them."

"When first we talked, sir. In the garden, yesterday. You mentioned an attempt on your own life. Do you think Kuttner's murder might be related? A case of mistaken identity, perhaps? Kuttner was tall and blond, much like you. His voice and accent were not unlike yours, either."

"You mean, high?"

"Yes, sir. In the dark, who knows? The killer might simply have shot the wrong person."

"The thought had occurred to me, of course."

"In which case I might very well be wasting my time looking for one of our colleagues with a good reason to murder Captain Kuttner, when my energies might be better spent looking for one of them who badly wants you dead."

"Interesting idea. And of my dear friends and esteemed colleagues back at my new home, which of them would you say has the best reason to want me dead?"

"You mean, apart from me?"

"You have an alibi, don't you? You weren't actually in the house at the time when Kuttner was murdered."

"Thoughtful of you to have provided me with one," I said.

"Isn't it?"

"I should have thought that Frank or von Neurath have the best reasons, from a professional point of view. Von Neurath might like to be revenged on you for the sake of it. Although he doesn't strike me as a murderer. But Frank does. With you dead, Frank probably gets your job."

"This is intriguing. Anyone else?"

"Henlein and Jury probably hate you, too, don't you think?"

"Almost certainly."

"And I wouldn't trust Jacobi as far as I could kick him."

"He does make the flesh creep, does he not?"

"Geschke and Fleischer are hardly my idea of good friends, either."

"Not friends, perhaps. But colleagues. And good Nazis. And since we are discussing those among my staff who might hate me, there's Kritzinger, too. I'm not suggesting that he might kill me, but I shouldn't be at all surprised if he hates me. He's an Austrian, from Vienna, and before the war he worked for the Jew who used to run the estate."

"Ferdinand Bloch-Bauer. Kuttner told me."

"After the Anschluss, he and his master fled here from Vienna, hoping to escape the inevitable before Bloch-Bauer finally took off for Switzerland, in 1939."

"But Kritzinger is in the SS. Most of the staff are in the SS, aren't they?"

"Of course. But very few of them were in the SS until the Reich acquired the Lower Castle."

"I thought that's why they were hired. Because you knew you could trust them."

"They are all in the SS because it means the Reichsprotector doesn't have to pay them out of his own pocket, Gunther. Otherwise I should never be able to keep a house as big as that, not on my salary."

That made me sit up a little: Heydrich had never struck me as mean with money; mean-spirited, yes, but not an embezzler. And to be so honest about it, too! Of course, I knew he'd never have told me if Himmler didn't know about it and approve. Which meant that they were all in it. The whole rotten crew. Living high on the hog while the ordinary Fritz went without his beer and sausage and cigarettes.

"Oh, I'm sure Kritzinger is a good German," continued Heydrich. "But it has to be faced, he was devoted to the Bloch-Bauers."

"Then why on earth do you keep him on?"

"Because he's an excellent butler, of course. Good butlers like him don't grow on trees, you know. Especially now that we're at war. I wouldn't expect someone like you to understand what that means, but Kritzinger puts his professional duties as a butler ahead of his own personal opinions, always. He sincerely believes that it is his duty to provide good service and concentrate only on that which lies within his realm, as a butler. If you were to question him he would probably tell you that he wouldn't care to say, or something else that was courteously evasive."

"And yet you said that he might hate you."

"Of course. I have to recognize that it's a possibility. It would be stupid not to consider it. Doing what I do, Gunther, it's wise not to trust anyone. All I ask of people is that they do their duty, and in that respect at least, Kritzinger is beyond reproach." He looked impatient for a moment. "That may be too subtle a distinction for a man like you, but there it is. Such are the dilemmas that afflict everyone who finds himself in a position of great authority."

"All right, General. Whatever you say."

"Yes. It had better be."

When we were still several blocks east of the Imperial Hotel, Klein drew up outside an apartment building with massive, fierce-looking atlantes; Jugendstil windows; and a roof like a Bavarian castle. The portal was covered in mosaic and topped with a decorative filigree balcony. The building looked as if it had been designed by someone whose architectural influences were Homer and the Brothers Grimm. But the address was chiefly remarkable for the absence of any SS or even regular Army sentries, and it was immediately clear to me that this was not an official building.

"What's this place?" I asked.

"The Pension Matzky. A brothel run by the Gestapo for the entertainment of important Czech citizens. It's staffed by twenty of the most beautiful amateur courtesans in all of Bohemia and Moravia. You need a password just to get through the door."

"I bet that keeps the tone up."

"Occasionally I visit the place myself. Or when I wish to reward the men who work for me with something special. And everything at the Pension Matzky is special."

As we were sitting there a furtive-looking man went through the front door; but he was not so furtive that I didn't recognize him. It was Professor Hamperl, the man who had carried out the autopsy on Captain Kuttner.

"Who's he?" I asked. "One of these important citizens of Prague?"

"I really have no idea," said Heydrich. "But I expect so. Incidentally, the password is Rothenburg. Now, ask me why I told you that, Gunther."

"Why did you tell me that?"

"So that you'll be thinking about what you're missing when you see that whore you brought from Berlin. I ask you, Klein, with the thousands of very willing girls there are in this town, can you imagine such a thing?"

Klein grinned. "No, sir."

Heydrich shook his head. "That's like taking an owl to Athens."

"Maybe I just like German owls."

Heydrich smiled his wolf's smile, stepped out of the car, and went inside the pension without another word.

"OH, GOOD. You're back. Now we can go out somewhere."

It was seven forty-five, but a short while later when I looked at my watch, it seemed like it was nine o'clock. With her head in shadow, Arianne was just a naked torso lying on the bed like a piece of marble sculpture. Dominated by light and form, she herself was almost secondary and not a person at all, so that I was reminded, a little, of what I'd seen during my time at the Bulovka Hospital.

I sat down on the edge of the bed and laid my hand on the curving white ski slope that was the summit of her behind, descending the broad field of her thigh to her near-invisible knee.

"It's not that I don't want you here."

"I know you want me, all right," said a disembodied voice. "You've made that perfectly clear. All you do is fuck me."

"It's no longer safe for you here in Prague. I told you. There's a special group of SD that's been set up to look for Gustav. If they had any idea you'd actually met him, no matter how innocently—well, you can't imagine what would happen. At least, I hope you can't imagine what would happen. You're in danger, Arianne. Real danger. That's why you urgently have to go back to Berlin. First thing tomorrow. For your own protection."

"And you. What will you be doing?"

"I'll be going back to Heydrich's house in Jungfern-Breschan."

"Is that his car? The Mercedes you went away in yesterday morning?" She paused. "I followed you downstairs to say good-bye and changed my mind when I saw those other men in the car."

"Yes. That's his car. One of them, anyway."

"What are you doing there, anyway? At Heydrich's house. You don't tell me anything."

"There's nothing to tell. Not yet. I had a couple of rather boring meetings with some very boring generals."

"Including him."

"Heydrich is a lot of things, but he's never boring. Most of the time I'm much too afraid of him to be bored."

Arianne sat up and put her arms about my neck.

"You? Scared? I don't believe it, Parsifal. You're brave. I think you're very brave."

"To be brave you first have to be scared. Take my word for it. Anything else is just foolhardy. And it's not bravery that keeps people alive, angel. It's fear."

She started to cover my head and neck with kisses. "Not you," she said. "I don't believe it."

"I'm afraid of him, yes. I'm afraid of all of them. Afraid of what they might do to me. Afraid of what they might do to Germany. But right now I'm afraid of what they might do to you. That's why I went to the Hibernerbahnhof before I came here and bought you a ticket back to Berlin."

Arianne sighed and wiped a tear from her eye.

"Will I see you again?"

"Of course."

"When?"

"Soon, I hope. But right now everything is confused. You've no idea how confused."

"And sending me back to Berlin makes things simpler?"

"Yes. But I told you, that's not the reason you have to go back home. All the same, I'll sleep a lot sounder knowing you're all right."

She stroked my head for a moment and then said, "On one condition."

"No conditions."

"That you tell me you love me, Parsifal."

"Oh, I love you, all right. As a matter of fact I love you very much, Arianne. That's why I have to send you away. It was a mistake bringing you here, I can see that now. It was selfish of me. Very selfish. I did it for me, and now I have to do this for you, see? I don't in the least want you to go home. But because I love you I really do have to send you away."

Maybe I did love her at that. Only it didn't matter very much one way or another. Not now that she was leaving Prague. And somewhere inside me I knew that I couldn't ever see her again. So long as she knew me she would be in danger because of who and what I was. After she had gone home she would be safe because I was the only person who could connect her with Gustav and Franz Koci. I knew I was going to feel bad about losing her, but this was nothing to how I knew I would feel if ever being with me put her into Heydrich's cold, white hands. He'd gut her for information the way Hamperl had gutted poor Albert Kuttner on the slab at Bulovka.

"I'll always love you," I said, for effect.

"And I love you, too."

I nodded. "All right. Let's go and find some dinner."

14

I couldn't sleep that night, but Arianne had very little to do with that, although she didn't sleep well, either. Sometime before dawn I must have slept a little because I dreamed I had returned to an almost preternatural time and place that was before the Nazis. But this was a recurring dream for me.

We made a desultory attempt at intimacy but our spirits were not in it, hers even less than mine. We washed and dressed and ate some breakfast in the mosaic café downstairs. She seemed depressed and spoke very little, almost as if she were already on the train back to Berlin; but then again, I wasn't exactly gabby myself.

"You seem very quiet this morning," she said.

"I was thinking the same of you."

"Me? I'm fine." She sounded defensive. "I didn't sleep very well."

"You can sleep on the train."

"Yes. Perhaps I will."

Pushing aside the salt and pepper cellars, I tried to take her hand but she pulled it away.

"Don't pretend, Bernie. You look like you can't wait to get rid of me."

"Let's not go over this again, Arianne."

"As you like."

We walked toward the elevator. The boy opened the double doors to admit us to his little vertical world, but just as I was about to follow Arianne inside, the hotel clerk appeared in front of us and handed me a sealed envelope. As the car groaned its way up the shaft I read the note that it contained.

"What is it?" asked Arianne.

"I just lost my ride to Jungfern-Breschan."

She frowned.

"Oh? Why?"

"Heydrich reminding me who's boss, probably."

"You mean you've got no car?"

"That's right."

"Well, how will you get there? It's fourteen kilometers."

"Apparently I will have to walk over to Hradschin Castle and beg a lift there."

The elevator car arrived on the top floor, where we got out.

"That's quite a walk from here," she said. "To the castle. I did it yesterday. At least forty minutes. Maybe more. You should telephone them and make them send a car." She smiled uncertainly. "Then you could spend some more time with me."

I shook my head. "Believe me, I'm in no hurry to get there. Besides, it's a nice day. And the walk will do me good. It will give me some time to think. Now I can see you off at the station."

"Yes. That would be lovely."

On our way along the floor she went into the bathroom, and I went back to the room. I lit a cigarette and lay down on the bed and waited for her.

Arianne was quite a while, although this wasn't unusual. She was always well dressed and well groomed, which was one of the reasons I liked her. There's something very sexy about disassembling something that has taken so long to put together: belt, dress, shoes, suspenders, corset, brassiere, stockings, panties. But when she returned after at least fifteen minutes, she seemed even stiffer than before, as if the paint she had applied to her lovely face were meant not just to enhance her beauty but also to cover her true feelings.

"Actually," she said, a little breathlessly, as she came through the door, "I'd rather you didn't come to the station, if you don't mind. I've just done my makeup and I know I'll cry if you're standing on the platform, waving good-bye. So, if you don't mind, darling, let me go on my own. It's only five minutes' walk. My bag isn't heavy. And I can manage perfectly well on my own."

I didn't protest. Clearly her mind was made up.

And that was it. When I walked out of the hotel and turned right and west to walk to the Charles Bridge and the castle that lay beyond it, I never expected to see Arianne Tauber again, and it was as if a great load had been lifted off my shoulders. I felt, if not carefree, then certainly a profound sense of liberation. Strange how wrong we can be about so much. Being a detective, even a bad one, I should have been used to that: being wrong is an important part of being right, and only time can tell which it turns out to be.

In the Old Town Square, I took a moment to remind myself of that. A few tourists, mostly off-duty German soldiers, had assembled in front of the town hall's astronomical clock to witness the hourly medieval morality lesson involving Vanity, Delight, Greed and Death, which took place in two little windows above the elaborate astrolabe. The off-duty soldiers took lots of photographs of the clockwork figures and checked their wristwatches, but none of them seemed to be learning much. That's the thing about morality lessons. Nobody ever learns anything. We were face-to-face with the past, but none of us seemed to understand that we were also face-to-face with an allegory of our future.

I GOT BACK TO the Lower Castle at around ten o'clock and found Kurt Kahlo waiting patiently for me in the morning room.

"Captain Kluckholm was just here," he said.

"What did he want?"

He handed me a sheet of paper.

"It's a list of Kuttner's personal effects," he said. "Apparently these are available for our inspection in Major Ploetz's office."

I glanced over the list.

Kahlo handed me a brown envelope and, smiling, shook his head.

"He's also given us two tickets each for the circus next Wednesday evening."

"The circus? What the hell for?"

Kahlo nodded. "Prague's Crown Circus. I hear it's very good. Everyone's invited. Even me. It's an outing for the SD and the SS and the Gestapo. Isn't that nice? Mr. and Mrs. Heydrich are going. And so are Mr. and Mrs. Frank. Apparently your lady friend, Fräulein Tauber, is also invited. Whoever she is. I didn't even know you had a lady friend here in Prague."

"I don't. Not anymore. Right now she's on a train back home."

"God, I wish I was."

"Me too."

"Now I understand why you wanted to get away last night. At the time I thought you were headed for the Pension Matzky."

"You know about that, do you?"

"More than you might think. A mate of mine in the local vice squad had to interview the girls. Heydrich set the place up even before he became Reichsprotector."

"He never struck me as the type to pimp for his fellow officers."

"Oh, he's not. The place is a honey trap. It's equipped with listening devices so that he can eavesdrop on important Czechos or the top brass when they come down from Berlin. My mate reckons he's blackmailing half of the general staff. Apparently he's got a similar place planned in Berlin. In Giesebrechtstrasse. If I were you, sir, I'd keep away from both."

"Thanks for the tip. I think I will."

"Don't mention it."

"Anything else?"

There was a second envelope in Kahlo's hand. He handed it over. Inside was a letter from Geert Vranken's father in the Netherlands, thanking me for contacting his daughter-in-law—she was too upset to write herself—and for informing them of his son's "accident"; he also asked me to keep him informed of exactly when and where his son's remains were eventually interred.

"News from home?"

"Not exactly." I put the letter and the circus tickets in my pocket. "Who's our next witness?"

"Brigadier Bernard Voss."

"Remind me who he is."

"In charge of the SS officer school at Beneschau. And everything you'd expect from the commandant of an officers' training school: a real stiff prick. Very probably you could use some uglier words than that. Especially if you're a Czech. In November 1939 some students from the local university organized a demonstration, during which Frank's driver was injured. He shouldn't have been there at all, but that's another story. Anyway, twelve hundred students were arrested and Voss commanded the firing squads that shot several of them. As an example to the rest."

I pulled a face. It was easy to despise a man who'd done something like that. I knew because I'd done something like that myself.

"And Voss once met Hitler," added Kahlo, "which is not so unusual in this house. However, when you talk to him it seems to have been the most important day in his life."

It was easy to believe this after just ten minutes in Voss's company. Hitler he regarded as the modern equivalent of Martin Luther; and maybe he wasn't so far wrong: Luther was another hugely deluded German I regarded with more than a little distaste.

Fortunately for my inquiry, it seemed that Voss was just as

happy to talk about the incident at Benešchau involving Kuttner and Jacobi as he was about the day he met Hitler.

"Captain Kuttner was a highly intelligent young officer, and I was surprised that he should have said what he did. However, I was not at all surprised that Colonel Jacobi should have answered him in that way. But then that's Jacobi for you."

"Where was General Heydrich when this happened?"

"In the dining hall at Benešchau we have a long refectory-style table. I was right next to Jacobi. But Heydrich was at the opposite end of the table."

"Why didn't he sit next to you, sir? Surely that would have been customary."

Voss shrugged. "The general was late. Delayed by some official business."

His voice was about as thick as a recently tarred road.

"Why weren't you surprised that Jacobi should have said what he said?"

Voss shrugged again. He wasn't as tall as he should have been; these days you don't have to look commanding to be in command. But he did look tough for a man of almost fifty, which is about the number of stitches it must have taken to sew up the *schmitte* on his left cheek, and you couldn't argue with an Iron Cross, first class, or the courageous, even foolhardy way he smoked, as if every cigarette were his last.

"It's no secret that he and I don't agree on a number of issues. Still there was no excuse for young Kuttner to be insubordinate like that. That was a surprise. I always thought him a very polite, courteous young man. Always. Ever since I first met him several years ago."

"So you knew him before he came to Prague?"

"Oh yes. He was a cadet officer at the SS Junker School in Bad Tölz when I was the commander there."

"When was that?"

"When I was the commander at Bad Tölz? Let's see now. July 1935 until November 1938. Kuttner was one of the best young officers that was ever produced there. He graduated at the top of his class. As you might have expected. After all, he was a law graduate of some brilliance. And great things were expected of Kuttner. He was certainly being groomed for one of the top jobs in the SS. Yes, it's true he had important connections. But he had considerable ability of his own. If only things hadn't gone wrong for him in Latvia, he'd have been a major by now. With an important desk job in Berlin."

Voss shook his head.

"Of course, he's not the first SS officer that this sort of thing has happened to. I know because I keep up with a lot of the young men who passed through my hands at Bad Tölz. Men like Kuttner. The work is too much to expect anyone to carry out without its having some effects on morale and character. They're only flesh and blood, after all."

It was odd how the same did not seem to apply to the victims of "the work" that Voss described.

"A new approach is needed to the work of evacuation and resettlement. A different solution to the Jewish problem. A better solution. And I've told Heydrich as much. Something is needed that takes into account the humanity of the men we ask to carry out these special actions."

He sounded so reasonable, I had to remind myself that he was talking about mass murder.

"After Bad Tölz, when you next saw Kuttner again—which was when?"

"At the luncheon where the incident we were talking about took place."

"When you saw him again, would you say that he'd changed?"

"Oh yes. Very much. And the change was obvious. To me he looked a nervous wreck. Which is what he was, of course. But still highly articulate. And likable. Yes, I still liked him. In spite of everything. It's a great shame this has happened."

After I finished with Brigadier Voss, Captain Kluckholm appeared in the morning room and explained that Major Thümmel had to be back in Dresden that evening and, with their agreement, he had leapfrogged the list of witnesses ahead of Geschke, Böhme, and Jacobi.

"Is that all right with you, Gunther?"

"Yes. But now that you're here, Captain, I have a couple of quick questions I'd like to put to you."

"To me?"

"To you, yes. Of course. And by the way, thanks for the circus tickets."

"Don't thank me. Thank the general."

"I will." I opened my cigarette case and offered him one.

Kluckholm shook his head. "Don't smoke."

"Hermann, isn't it?" I lit my nail and whistled down the smoke. He nodded.

"Which adjutant are you? First, second, or third? I never can remember."

"Third."

Kluckholm folded his hands at his back and waited politely. He was the tallest and most distinguished of Heydrich's remaining three adjutants. He was also the leanest. His hair was dark and he wore it slightly longer than most other officers in the SD, which added an almost glamorous, film-starrish aspect to the way he looked. A uniform suited him and he knew it. There was a second-class Iron Cross ribbon worn from the second buttonhole on his tunic, and the right angles on the flares of his riding breeches looked as if they'd been put there by Pythagoras. The Spanish-cut top-shaft boots were polished like horse brass and had almost certainly been supplied by an expensive dressage company such as König. I had half an idea that if Heydrich ever accused him of being improperly dressed, Kluckholm would have hanged himself with his own aiguillette.

"Tell me, Hermann. The night before Captain Kuttner was found dead. What did you two argue about?"

"I'm afraid you're mistaken. We never argued."

"Oh, come on. I saw you in the front garden. While the Leader was on the radio telling us how wonderfully things were going for our armies in Russia, you two were at each other's throats, like one of those stone sculptures on the front gate."

"I'm sorry to contradict you, Gunther. You may have seen what you assumed to be an argument, but if you had been privy to our conversation, you would have heard something quite different from an argument."

"So what was it?"

"A gentlemanly discussion."

"Clenched fists. Gritted teeth. Face-to-face, like a couple of boxers at a weigh-in. I think I recognize an argument when I see one."

"Are you calling me a liar, Captain Gunther?"

I let my lips tug at my cigarette for a long second before I answered him.

"No, not at all. But all the same I'm still wondering if the gentlemanly conversation you had that was very different from an argument makes you a suspect in a murder. You hardly liked the man, after all."

"Who said so?"

"You did. Yesterday afternoon, when General Heydrich was biting everyone's ears in the library. I couldn't help but hear your handsome eulogy of Captain Kuttner. I would say I was eavesdropping, except that I imagine your boss left the door open and meant me and some others in the house to hear exactly what was said. There's not much he does that hasn't got a damned good reason behind it. Incidentally, I'm not the only one who's wondering if you were up to putting a bullet in adjutant number four. Some of the other officers aren't exactly slow when it comes to casting aspersions on the characters of their fellow officers. Are they, Kurt?"

"I'm afraid so. But it is disappointing, sir. I thought that among brother officers of the SS and the SD there would be a greater sense of honor and camaraderie. To be honest, there have been times in the last couple of days when this room seemed more like the school principal's office, the number of tales that have been told in here."

"So how about it, Hermann?"

Kluckholm shook his head. "Whatever you heard, Captain Gunther, I can assure you I did not murder Captain Kuttner. Perhaps my language was a little intemperate yesterday in the library. But I had a better opinion of him than perhaps you heard me say."

Kluckholm spoke as if his voice were being recorded on a gramophone disc.

I looked at Kahlo. "Kurt. Would you please close that door?"

Kahlo moved away from the piano and quietly closed the door behind him.

"What are you hiding, Hermann?"

Kluckholm shook his head. "I can assure you, I'm not hiding anything."

"Sure you are, Hermann." I shrugged. "Everyone in this damned house is hiding something or other. Small secrets. Big secrets. Dirty secrets. And you're no exception, Hermann."

"I would rather you did not call me Hermann in that familiar way. I prefer Kluckholm, or Captain Kluckholm. And your suggestion that I'm hiding something is not only nonsensical, it is also insulting." Coloring with irritation and injured pride, Kluckholm moved toward the closed door. "And I am not going to remain here to endure your insinuations."

"Yes, you are, Hermann."

I nodded at Kahlo, who quickly turned the key in the lock and then pocketed it.

Meanwhile Kluckholm looked as if I had just stood on his corn.

"You really are a most vulgar, tiresome fellow, Gunther. Has anyone told you that?"

"Many times. It must have something to do with all the vulgar murders I've investigated. Not to mention all the murders that I myself have been obliged to commit. Of course that hardly makes me unusual in this house. But, like Captain Kuttner, I found there was something about it I didn't like. Which is the reason I'm here now, speaking to you instead of carrying on the good work out east with all the Special Action boys. By the way, how was it that you escaped that particular tour of duty, Hermann?"

"I'm ordering you to unlock that door," Kluckholm told Kahlo.

Kahlo folded his arms and looked sad, as if disappointed that he couldn't obey the order. I didn't doubt that he was more than equal to the task of dealing with Kluckholm if the third adjutant decided to try and get tough with him. Kahlo looked tougher. Kahlo would have looked tough in a bath full of Turkish wrestlers.

"Maybe you had vitamin B, too," I said. "Better still, perhaps you had vitamin A. What's the big name in Berlin that's been helping you to keep your nice polished boots out of the murder pits of Minsk and Riga, Hermann?"

Kluckholm stood immediately in front of Kahlo and held out his hand. "As your superior officer I am ordering you to hand over that key."

"Why don't you sit down and tell us what you're hiding, Hermann? For example, why don't we talk about this list of Captain Kuttner's personal effects? It was you who compiled that, wasn't it?"

"Open that damn door, or you'll regret it."

"The trouble is, I'm afraid, that you left some items off the list. And I don't like it when people try to deceive me. You see, I conducted a very swift search of the room before you tidied up. Which is how I know that this list doesn't include those copies of *Der Führer* magazine that were in Kuttner's drawer."

I felt Kahlo frown at me.

"They're not quite what you think," I told Kahlo. "*Der Führer* is, or rather was, a homosexual magazine. Used to be quite popular with some of Berlin's warmer boys. So were the others in that drawer. *Der Kreise* and *Der Insel*. Lots of naked men playing with medicine balls or doing push-ups on top of each other." I shook my head. "You see the corrupting things I've had to deal with in my career as a police officer, Kurt? It's a wonder I'm not in the cement myself, some of the filth I've seen."

"Lots of bums, was it, sir?"

"Lots. Collector's items now, on the Berlin black market, pornography being so hard to obtain these days. Expensive stuff. For connoisseurs of that kind of thing, you might say."

Kahlo pulled a face that was a pantomime of disgust.

"It's a dirty job, sir. Being a detective."

"Don't tell anyone, Kurt. Not in this house. They'll all want to do it."

Kluckholm had calmed down a bit and was looking a little less inclined to fight Kahlo for the key to the morning room door.

But another minute passed before he turned away and sat down on the sofa.

"Of course," said Kahlo, "it's possible the captain here took those dirty magazines off the list not because he wanted to deceive you, sir, but because he wanted to keep them for himself."

"No," said Kluckholm, loudly.

"I never thought of that, Kurt. Good thinking."

Kahlo grinned, enjoying himself. There wasn't much license to insult senior officers in the Gestapo and SS, and he was going to take full advantage of it now.

"Of course," I said. "He took them to use while he was rubbing his own pipe."

"No," insisted Kluckholm. "No. I was merely trying to safe-guard Kuttner's reputation. Not to mention the reputation of the squadron."

The squadron was what nice well-bred people like Kluckholm called the SS.

"Kuttner wasn't like that, I'm sure of it. He liked women. Those filthy magazines must have belonged to someone else. Per-haps they were already here when the house was taken over. Perhaps they belonged to the Jews who owned the place before von Neurath. After all, as far as I could tell, they were hardly re-cent copies." He shook his head. "Anyway, I talked it over with my own conscience and I decided that it was best to burn them. It was obvious they had no bearing on the case."

"You burned them?"

"Yes, I burned them all. It was quite bad enough that Kuttner should be murdered, but we hardly wanted you questioning his reputation as an officer and a gentleman."

"We? You mean you and Ploetz burned them?"

"Yes. And we certainly didn't want those filthy magazines being sent to his parents in Halle, along with all his other personal effects."

"That much I can understand."

"I doubt that, Gunther. I really do."

"What makes you think he liked women, Hermann?"

"Because he talked about a girl he'd met. A girl here in Prague. That's why."

"This girl have a name?"

"Grete. I don't know her surname."

"She wouldn't be the woman in the framed photograph that's still listed among his possessions?"

"No, that's his mother."

"Maybe this Grete was just his blackface," I said. "To help persuade you that he was as normal as the rest of you."

"Or maybe," offered Kahlo, "he was just dipping his toe into the water, to see if he liked it."

"Or maybe Hermann here is just making it up," I said. "To make his fellow adjutant seem like less of a queer in our eyes than he really was."

"Perhaps he's a bit warm himself, sir. Perhaps he has to give Kuttner an alibi so he can have one, too. Could be that's what they were arguing about. A lover's tiff."

Kluckholm stood up and stared angrily at Kahlo. "I don't have to take that from you." He turned to glare at me. "I don't have to take it from either of you."

"Sit down," I said. "Before I make you sit down."

Kluckholm remained standing.

"By the way," I said. "What other evidence did you destroy when you were burning Kuttner's puppy mags?"

Kluckholm shook his head and sat down. "Nothing," he said. "Nothing at all."

"A diary perhaps? Some love letters? Photographs of the two of you on a nice trip to Rügen Island with all the boys?"

I wasn't interested in any of these, although I might have been if I had ever supposed that they had been among his possessions. There was, however, one more thing I was interested in; something I knew had been in his drawer, because I had seen it.

"What about the pipe?"

"What pipe?"

"There was a broken clay pipe in his drawer. What happened to that?"

"I didn't see a clay pipe. But I fail to see what relevance a broken old pipe might have to anything."

"That all depends," I said. "Doesn't it, Kurt?"

"Depends on what?" Kluckholm asked.

"Depends on what he smoked in it," Kahlo said. "Tobacco. Marijuana. Opium. They say a clay pipe is best for opium, don't they, sir? Clay keeps the heat better."

"That's right," I said. "Opium or marijuana might be just the thing for a man who was having trouble sleeping. Or just to ease the conscience of a man who felt very guilty about what he'd done in Riga."

"Of course," added Kahlo, "you would only throw it away if you suspected that's what it had been used for. You wouldn't throw it away if you thought he'd only used it to smoke tobacco."

"Good point," I said. "Of course, if we still had it we could have tested it in the lab. They might have cleared him of any suspicion on that score. But now we'll never know."

Kluckholm was about to say something and then seemed to think better of it. For a moment his brown eyes met mine pleadingly, as if he wanted me to stop and he really did have some secret he couldn't bring himself to reveal. He took hold of his fist in the palm of his other hand and started to squeeze it, trying to stop it from punching me, almost as if Belshazzar had managed to get hold of the disembodied hand that was interrupting his famous feast.

"Go ahead," I said. "Punch me on the nose. Then we'll have all the excuse I need to beat it out of you. Won't we, Kurt?"

"Just say the word, sir. I'd love to smack this bastard."

Kluckholm regarded us with real hatred before he seemed to shrink into a silence and then a shape that made me think we really would have to beat anything else out of him.

Which effectively meant that the interrogation was over.

"Back at the Alex, when a suspect won't talk, we put him down in the cells to think it over. That's what I'd do with you, Hermann, if we weren't doing this in a nice country house with a good piano and some choice works of art. That's what we'd do if we were doing this back in Berlin. We'd lock you up for the night, if we were doing this the proper police way, not like some bullshit scene in a crappy detective novel by that English lady novelist Heydrich seems to admire so much."

I flicked my cigarette into the fireplace, where it smashed against the chimney wall in a hail of tiny sparks.

"You can go," I said, "but I shall certainly want to speak to you again, Hermann. You can depend on it."

Kluckholm stood up and, without uttering another word, made straight for the door, which Kahlo then unlocked with a deliberate insolence that strongly reminded me of myself.

When the captain was gone, Kahlo went over to the coffee table where I'd left my cigarette case and helped himself.

"Guilty conscience, do you think?" he asked.

"Around here? I'm not sure what that might look like."

"The bastard was shaking like a rice pudding. If he didn't do it, or knows who did it, then I'm a Blue Dragoon."

The Blue Dragoons was the nickname of an Army punishment battalion stationed on the peat-bog moors of the Ems River region. They said that if the damp didn't kill you, the Labor—digging peat in all weathers—was certain to do it.

"That's probably what he's worried about," I said. "Being sent there. Or whatever the SS equivalent of the Blue Dragoons might be. Some lesser circle of hell, probably."

"A firing squad looks like a better bet, if you ask me. He destroys evidence and won't say what he and Kuttner were arguing about? Fuck off. Not to mention his declared dislike of the man. If it was me, I'd arrest him now and tap it out of him with a small hammer."

Kahlo took a fierce drag of his cigarette and then bared his teeth as if he were enduring pain.

"And you know something, sir? Kluckholm might be just as good as it can get for us. In fact, I think he's perfect for it."

"Meaning what, exactly?"

"Only that he's standing right in front of your box camera with a name and number chalked on a piece of board. No, really. You could just as easily snap him for this murder as anyone else."

"You sound so like the Gestapo sometimes that I wonder why I like you, Kurt."

"You're the one with Heydrich's breath in your ear. When you've got a suspect who's suspicious, it's foolish to go and look for someone with a kind face and a good alibi. Come on, sir. Every bull does it now and then, even when they don't have to. And if you ask me, you have to." He paused. "We have to."

I grinned. "It's quite like old times, working with you. You remind me of why I left the police the first time."

"It's your funeral." Kahlo shrugged. "I just hope that I'm only the chief mourner."

"You needn't worry. I'm not about to reach up and pull you in the grave beside me."

"It's not just that."

"What, then?"

"I need to get on. In the job. I can't stay being a criminal assistant for the rest of my bloody life. Unlike you, I've got a wife to support. The only way I'm going to get a promotion is if you deliver someone's head for Kuttner's murder, or if I join one of those SS police battalions in Russia. Come on, sir, you've been there. Everyone says it's the holiday in hell."

I nodded. "That it is."

"It sent Kuttner over the edge. We know that. I don't want that happening to me. I want kids. I want to be able to look them in the eye when they go to bed at night."

"Yes, I can understand that."

"Right, then. So far I've managed to avoid all that resettlement shit. But I don't know how much longer I can do it. I can't afford for you to fuck this case up because you're a bit squeamish about sewing someone into the bag for this, sir."

"So you admit you don't actually think he did it, then?"

"It doesn't matter what I think. What matters is if it will stand up in front of General Heydrich."

"Well, I don't think it will. I agree, Kluckholm's keeping something from us. But if you remember, he said that Major Ploetz was party to the decision to burn those puppy mags. For all we know, he knew about the pipe, too. You can't put a man in front of a firing squad just because he tries to sidestep a few awkward questions."

"No? This is Germany, sir. Remember? It happens every day. Someone has got to go down for this, and if you ask me, it might as well be him. Besides, adjutant or not, he's only a fucking captain, and it's going to be a lot easier pinning a charge on him than on any of the cauliflower. There's not one of these bastards that doesn't have a supply of vitamins that goes all the way to the top."

He had a point. I didn't like it, but what he was saying made a lot of sense.

"Am I interrupting you?"

An officer in Army uniform put his head around the door, and for a moment I failed to recognize him.

"Only Captain Kluckholm said he was going to try to get me bumped up your list, but—peculiar fellow—he wouldn't answer me when I asked him just now if that was all right with you. Seemed rather upset about something. Had a face like thunder." He paused. "Well, is it? All right, I mean? I can come back in a few minutes if you'd prefer, only I was rather hoping to catch this afternoon's train to Dresden. There's quite a lot of work waiting on my desk. The admiral—that's Admiral Canaris—he keeps me pretty busy these days, I can tell you."

"I'm sorry. Major Thümmel, isn't it?"

"That's right."

"You'd better come in."

"Good of you," he warbled.

Paul Thümmel advanced into the morning room. He moved

with flat-footed nonchalance, like a golfer approaching a putt he expected to sink without any trouble, and sat down on the sofa recently vacated by Hermann Kluckholm.

"All right here, am I?" He smoothed his hands along the silk cushions like a schoolboy and then leaned back, comfortably. "I haven't been in this room," he added, looking around. "Very cozy. Although maybe a bit too feminine for my taste. Not that I have any. At least that's what my wife says. She gets to choose the wallpaper in our house, not me. I just pay for it."

Thümmel was about forty. He had dark hair, which, like almost everyone wearing a German uniform, he wore very short at the sides, so that what was on top of his skull resembled a little cap. His face was sharp and he had a very pronounced hook nose that seemed to be trying its best to meet his equally prominent chin halfway. He was friendly and as smoothly confident as one might expect of a man wearing a gold Party badge, a first-class Iron Cross, a decent cologne, and a silver wedding band.

"Any suspects yet?"

"It's still a little early for that, Major."

"Hmm. Bad business all around. Leaves an unpleasant taste in the mouth to think that some fellow sitting next to you at dinner might have cold-bloodedly murdered some other fellow you knew."

"Have you anyone in mind?"

"Who me? No." Thümmel crossed his legs, took hold of the shin of his boot, and hugged it toward himself like an oar in a two-man scull. "But fire away with your questions, Commissar, all the same."

"Are you feeling better today?"

"Hmm?"

"The hangover?"

"Oh, that. Yes. Fine, thanks. I'll say one thing for Heydrich, he keeps a spectacular cellar. Himmler will be jealous when I tell him."

That was a little heavy-handed, I thought. Just as he was doing so well creating an easygoing impression of himself, he had to go and spoil it by mentioning Himmler, with whom he was quite probably familiar. I looked at Kahlo, who rolled his eyes eloquently, as if to suggest that Kluckholm was wasting my time—that Thümmel was one of the people with a kind face and a good alibi he had been talking about.

"Nevertheless, I shan't be at all unhappy to go back to Dresden. I don't feel at all comfortable here in Bohemia. Nothing to do with the Reichsprotector's hospitality, of course. But there's something about this country that makes you feel as if you might get your head bashed in on your way to church, like poor old King Wenceslas. Or that one might be defenestrated by a bunch of malodorous Hussites. Awkward, stinky mob, the Czechos. Always were. Right the way through history. Always will be. If you ask me, the general's got his work cut out with these bastards. You were in Paris before this, I hear."

"That's right, sir."

"Well, I don't have to tell you how different Prague is from Paris. The Frenchies are nothing if not pragmatic. They know what side their bread is buttered on, for now. But the Czecho is a very different kettle of fish. He's a real festering sore, is your average Czecho. You mark my words, Commissar, there's going to be a lot of blood spilled here if we're ever going to hold on to this country."

He frowned.

"Sorry. Rattling on like a milkmaid as usual. You want to talk about poor old Captain Kuttner, don't you? Not my opinion of the Czechos."

"I found a spent cartridge on the landing in front of your door. From a P38. Which would seem to indicate that a shot must have been fired in that vicinity. On the morning of the murder did you hear a shot fired?"

"You mean in the house. Not outside. Seems to me there's always someone shooting something out there. No, I didn't hear a thing. Mind you, that night I slept like a pickled marmot after all the booze I'd consumed. Slept right through until about—let's see now—well, it must have been about seven o'clock in the morning when I heard a couple of loud bangs. I got up to see what the commotion was about, and Captain Pomme, I think, explained to me that he and the butler had been obliged to batter down Kuttner's door, on account of how they thought he must have taken an overdose of Barbital. At least that's what I think he said. So I wandered along to see if I could help and heard Dr. Jury say that the poor fellow was dead. There was nothing I could do, of course, so I went back to bed. Stayed there until just about nine. Had a wash, dressed, came out my door again, and there you were, crawling around on the floor, looking for that bullet casing. Frankly, I've been racking by brains ever since for a reason why anyone would have killed him. Not to mention how. The room door was locked and bolted from the inside, wasn't it? Window bolted? And no murder weapon yet found. A regular mystery."

I nodded.

"I even had a look about the dead man's bedroom last evening, in search of some inspiration. I'm not trying to show the hen how to lay an egg and all that, but while I was there I found several floorboards underneath the rug that were loose. Loose enough to pull up. There was a good space underneath them. Easily big enough for a decent-sized man to have hidden there. And it occurred to me that the murderer, with a sufficiently cool head, might have been lurking in there all the while that you were all in the room, on top of him, so to speak. Of course, he would have to have devised a means of replacing the floorboards on top of his place of concealment and then pulling the rug back. With a couple of lengths of fishing line, perhaps. Yes, that's what I'd have used if it had been me in there. With a couple of strategically placed nails on the baseboard, you could have wound the rug in as easily as a venetian blind."

I looked at Kahlo, who shrugged back at me.

"Sorry." Thümmel smiled ruefully. "I just sort of thought you ought to know. Really, I wasn't trying to make you look a fool or anything, Commissar Gunther."

"Actually, sir, I seem to be managing that particular task perfectly well on my own."

I sighed and stared up at the ceiling, where, immediately above, Kuttner's room was situated.

"Why didn't I think of that?"

"You can't think of everything. Such an investigation as you are trying to conduct in this house would try the patience and ingenuity of any mortal man. And, look here, I am not saying that is where the murderer was hiding. I am merely suggesting it as a possibility, although not a strong one, I think."

He shrugged.

"However, I will say this. In the Abwehr we are constantly impressed by the resourcefulness and imagination of the enemy. Especially the Tommies. Desperation is the father of innovation, after all." He sighed. "I do not say that is how it was done, Commissar. I say only that is how it could have been done."

I nodded. "Thank you, sir."

"Don't mention it, Commissar. I certainly won't. If you receive my meaning."

"We had better go up there and take a look for ourselves."

We all three stood up and moved, simultaneously, for the morning room door.

"By the way, Major Thümmel," I said, remembering the letter I had received from Berlin that morning. "Does the name Geert Vranken mean anything to you?"

"Geert Vranken?" Thümmel paused for a moment and then shook his head. "No, I don't think so. Why, should it?"

"There was a murder investigation in Berlin this summer. The S-Bahn murderer? Vranken was a foreign worker on the railways who was interviewed by the police as a potential suspect, and he mentioned a German officer who might be prepared to stand as a character witness for him."

"And you think that was me?"

"I just received a letter from his father in the Netherlands and he said that his son had met a Captain Thümmel, in The Hague, before the war, in 1939."

"Well, there are you are, Commissar. It must be another officer called Thümmel. Last time I was in The Hague was 1933. Or maybe '34. But certainly not in 1939. In 1939, I was stationed at our embassy in Paris. You know, Thümmel is not an uncommon name. The maître d' at the Adlon Hotel is called Thümmel. Did you know that?"

"Yes, sir. I do know that. You're right, it must be another officer called Thümmel."

Thümmel grinned cheerfully. "Besides, I'm hardly in the habit of giving guest workers a character reference." He nodded upstairs. "But I don't mind showing you those loose floorboards, Commissar."

AFTER THÜMMEL HAD LEFT Kuttner's bedroom, Kahlo climbed into the space in the floor and waited patiently while I replaced the boards. Then I took them up again.

Kahlo climbed out, covered in dust.

"Well, it's possible, all right," I said. "But hardly probable."

"Why do you say that, sir?"

"The amount of dust on you. If someone had been hidden there on Friday morning, I'd have expected a little less dust than there is in there now. Or at least, was, until you got in there."

I handed Kahlo the clothes brush I'd picked up from the top of the dresser.

"Lucky it's not a good suit," I said.

Kahlo growled an obscenity and began to brush off his jacket and trousers.

"Depends on how much dust was down there before, doesn't it?" he muttered.

"Maybe."

"And with all of the cauliflower still pissed in their rooms, any one of them might have hidden himself in there, and no one would have been any the wiser."

"I've looked at the rug, too, and I can see no means whereby someone could draw the rug back over the boards while he was hidden down there. No fishing line; no nails on the baseboard."

"Perhaps," said Kahlo, "the murderer has been back in here and removed them."

"Perhaps. Anyway, if the murderer did manage to conceal himself down there, that puts Kluckholm in the clear. Immediately after the murder, he was here in the room, remember? With you and me."

"Pity. But I still like him for it. And like you said yourself, it's hardly probable, is it? That the killer would have hidden in here." Kahlo shook his head. "No, you're right. Kluckholm must have done it some other way. It might just be that he turned himself into a bat."

I grinned and shook my head. "He couldn't have done it that way, either. The window was closed, remember?"

"So the general says. We all assume that because he's the general, his evidence is one hundred percent. What if he made a mistake about that? What if the window was open, after all?"

"Heydrich doesn't make mistakes about things like that."

"Why not? He's only human."

"Whatever gave you that impression?"

Kahlo shrugged.

"It'll be lunchtime soon," he said. "You could ask him then."

"Why don't you ask him yourself?"

"Yeah, sure. I meant what I said about that promotion, you know."

He handed me the clothes brush and then turned around.

"Do you mind, sir?"

I brushed the worst of it off his jacket and thought of Arianne brushing off my own jacket the previous day. I liked that she had been so particular about my appearance, straightening my tie, adjusting my shirt collar, and always picking my trousers off the floor and tucking them under the mattress so that they might keep the crease. It was a caring touch I was already starting to miss. By now she was probably across the Bohemian border and back in Germany and a lot safer than she was in Prague. I knew what Thümmel had been talking about; there was something about Prague that I didn't care for at all.

"I'm looking forward to lunch," said Kahlo. He was sniffing the air like a big hungry dog. "Whatever it is smells good."

"Everything smells good to you."

"Everything except this case."

"True. Look, you go ahead to lunch. I'm going to stay here for a while."

"And do what?"

"Oh, nothing much. Stare at the floor. Listen to that crow outside the window. Shoot myself. Or perhaps pray for some inspiration."

"You're not going to miss lunch, are you?"

Kahlo's tone made this sound serious, as if I really were planning to shoot myself. Which wouldn't have been so very far from the truth.

"Now I come to think of it, that's a good idea," I said. "Eating has a habit of interfering with my thinking. In that respect it's almost as bad as beer. If I fast for a while, maybe I'll be given a vision as to how this murder was done. Yes, why not? Maybe if I starve myself like Moses for forty days and nights, then perhaps the Almighty will just come and tell me who did it. Of course he might have to set the house on fire to get my full attention, but it'll be worth it. Besides, I'm pretty sure I have a head start on Moses in one respect."

"Oh? What's that?"

I opened my cigarette case. "A smoke. A very small burning bush from whence a great deal of wisdom can be imparted. I reckon any one of those saints could have saved themselves a lot of time and discomfort with a simple cigarette."

After Kahlo had left me alone with my angst I sat on the edge of Kuttner's mattress and lit one, and when I'd had enough of looking at my cigarette's little mystic trail of holy inspiration, I decided to take a look around the house. With more or less everyone now gathered in the dining room, I was able to go where I pleased without having to furnish an explanation of what I was doing. Besides, I wasn't sure there was an explanation for what I was searching for. All I knew was that I needed an idea—any idea—and to have one fast.

Hearing a loud cheer downstairs in the dining room gave me my first idea. It wasn't much of an idea but it had at least the merit of being practical. An experiment. An empirical test of an assumption I and everyone else had made right from the very beginning of the case.

I went along to my own bedroom and fetched the Walther PPK from my bag. Back in Kuttner's room, I closed the door as best I could, racked one bullet into the chamber, fired the weapon twice in quick succession, and then sat down to wait for whatever might happen. But if I had expected the shots to summon the arrival of a concerned group of officers in Kuttner's room, I was wrong. A minute passed, then two; after five minutes I was quite certain that no one was coming, because no one had heard the shots. Of course this told me only that Kuttner might easily have been shot without anyone hearing or bothering to investigate the shots, but that still felt like something. It was one assumption I'd made that could easily be proved to have been false. And where there was one, there might easily be another.

I went back to my room and replaced the gun in my bag before heading out and along the landing, with its blackamoor figures, the hunting-style leather chairs, the decorative Meissen, and the less decorative framed photographs of Hitler, Himmler, Goebbels, Göring, Bormann, and von Ribbentrop. It was a home away from home if you lived at the Berghof.

I was familiar with the more attractive parts of the Lower Castle, including the library, the dining room, the billiard room, the winter garden, the conference room, and the morning room; but there were other parts of which I knew nothing or that felt forbidden. Heydrich's study certainly seemed out of bounds, even to someone who was supposed to be Heydrich's detective. Outside the door, I paused for a moment, knocked, and then, hearing no one and expecting to find the door locked, I turned the thick brass handle. The door opened. I went inside. I closed the heavy door behind me.

The room—one of the largest in the house—was quiet and cool; it felt more like a sepulchre than a study. I walked around for a good minute before retracing my footsteps, which, like a ghost's, were completely silent in that room, as if I hardly existed at all. Heydrich could have arranged that, of course, and only too easily. As easily as emptying out the crystal ashtray on the desk, which looked very clean and brightly polished. One of Kritzinger's duties, perhaps?

I don't know that I expected to find anything. I was just being nosy, but like any detective I felt I had the license to indulge this tendency, which only feels like a vice when it is accompanied by something more venial, such as envy or greed. There was nothing in there I really coveted, although I had always wanted a nice desk with a comfortable office chair, but maybe this furniture was a little too grandiose for my purpose. All the same, I sat down, spread my hands along the Reichsprotector's desk, leaned back in his chair, glanced around the room for a moment, handled some of the books on his shelves—mostly popular fiction—looked over his many photographs, inspected the blotter for some recent correspondence—there wasn't any—and then decided I was very glad I wasn't Reinhard Heydrich. Not for all the world would I have changed places with that man.

The leather desk diary was full of appointments and not much else. There were many previous meetings at the Wolf's Lair in Rastenburg, at the Berghof, at the Reich Chancellery; and future evenings at the circus—strangely, that was underlined—a day at Rastenburg, a weekend at Carinhall, a night at the Deutsches Opernhaus, a December conference at an SS villa in Grosser Wannsee, followed by Christmas at the Lower Castle. As Heydrich's detective would I be required to go to all of these places? Rastenburg? The Reich Chancellery? The thought of actually meeting Hitler filled me with horror.

I searched the wastepaper-bin underneath the desk and found only a sock, with a hole in it.

There were no office drawers for me to search. If Heydrich had secret files, they were certainly kept somewhere secret. I looked around the room.

The safe, I decided at last, was behind the portrait of Hitler; and so it was; but I wasn't about to try to open it; even my impertinence had its limits. Besides, there were things I really didn't want to know. Especially the secret things that Heydrich knew.

The heavily lined curtains looked as if they belonged in a

theater and might easily have afforded me a hiding place if someone were to come into the study. The big windows were as thick as
my little finger and quite possibly bulletproof, too. Behind the curtains were a couple of machine pistols and a box of grenades; Heydrich wasn't leaving much to chance. If anyone attacked him in his
house, he clearly intended to defend himself to the last.

But did I want him or one of his adjutants to catch me in there?
Perhaps. Being thrown out of his office might also have resulted in
my being thrown off the case and sent back to Berlin in disgrace,
which seemed like an outcome devoutly to be wished for. But it
didn't happen, and finally, after I'd been in there for almost fifteen
minutes, I got up and went out onto the landing, still unobserved.

The next door along from Heydrich's study was a suite of
rather more feminine rooms—doubtless these had been set aside
for Lina Heydrich—where, among the rose-patterned sofas, elegant chairs, and long mirrors, was a dressing table as big as a Mes-
serschmitt.

I went downstairs and managed to creep unnoticed past the
open door of the dining room, which was full of cauliflower; nearer
the back garden I put my head around the door of a playroom, and
then a nursery.

As yet I had no knowledge of the extensive servants' quarters
in the basement, so I descended a narrow flight of stairs and walked
along a dimly lit corridor that seemed to serve as the spine and nervous system of the house. Even on a sunny day like this one, the
stone-flagged basement corridor felt more like the lockup at the
Alex, although it smelled a lot better. Kahlo was right about that.

In the big kitchen several cooks were hard at work preparing
the next course of lunch, which was being served by waiters whose
faces were more familiar. They regarded me with suspicion and
alarm. Fendler, the footman I'd spoken to earlier, who happened to
be smoking a cigarette near the back door, came over and asked me
if was lost. I said I wasn't, of course, but a little deterred by the

horrified looks I was getting, I was about to return upstairs and get some lunch after all when, at the farthest, dimmest end of the corridor, a door opened and an SS sergeant whom I was certain I'd never seen before came out, carefully closed the door behind him, and went into the room opposite.

In the moment before the door closed I saw a brightly lit, busy room containing what looked like a telephone switchboard, and, thinking that this was as good a time as any to introduce myself in person—there was another call to the Alex I wanted to place—I went along the corridor and opened the door.

Immediately, a burly-looking SS corporal jumped up from a wooden bench, threw down his newspaper, and blocked my way. At the same time he kicked another door shut behind him, but not before I caught a glimpse of several large tape recorders and, seated in front of them, some more SS men wearing headphones.

"I'm sorry, sir," said the corporal, "but I'm afraid you can't come in here."

"I'm a police officer." I showed him my warrant disc. "Commissar Gunther, from the Alex. General Heydrich has given me the run of the house to investigate a murder."

"I don't care who you are, sir, you can't come in here. This is a restricted area."

"What's your name, Corporal?"

"You don't need to know that, sir. You don't need to know anything about what happens in here. It doesn't concern you or your particular investigation."

"My *particular* investigation? That's my call, Corporal, not yours. What is this place anyway? And what happens behind that door? It looks like Deutsche Grammophon in there."

"I'm afraid I'm going to have to insist that you leave, sir. Right now."

"Corporal, did you know that you're obstructing a police officer in the execution of his duty? I have no intention of leaving until I have a full explanation of what's going on in here."

By now voices were raised, my own included, and there had been a certain amount of chest-on-chest pushing and shoving. I was angrier at myself than at the corporal—frustrated at having missed finding the loose floorboards before and now irritated to discover what looked to me like a listening post for eavesdropping on the houseguests—only the corporal didn't know that, and when someone appeared behind me in the door I had just come through and I turned around to see who this was, the corporal hit me. Hard.

I didn't blame him. I didn't blame anyone. Like raising your voice and arguing and pointing, blaming people is not something you can do when you're heading down through the black hole that suddenly appears beneath your shoes. Dr. Freud didn't give it a name and, strictly speaking, you only know what being unconscious really means when a thug with a hardwood fist like a Zulu's knobkerrie has used this same lethal object to hit you expertly on the back of the neck, as if trying to kill a large and argumentative and rather gullible rabbit. No, wait, I did blame someone. I blamed myself. I blamed myself for not listening to the eavesdropping SS corporal in the first place. I blamed myself for missing the trick with the floorboards in Kuttner's bedroom. I blamed myself for taking Heydrich at his word and thinking I really did have the run of the house to pursue my investigation. But mostly I just blamed myself for thinking it was even possible to behave like a real detective in a world that was owned and run by criminals.

I DON'T SUPPOSE I was unconscious for longer than a couple of minutes. When I came to, I could have wished it had been a lot longer. Another thing you can't do when you're unconscious is feel sick or have a splitting headache or wonder if you should dare to move your legs, in case your neck really is broken. Ignoring the severe pain of opening my eyelids, I opened my eyelids, and found myself staring down the blunderbuss barrel of a large brandy balloon. It was a big improvement on a real blunderbuss or the pistol that these circumstances usually produce. I took a deep, heady breath of the stuff and let it toast my adenoids for a moment before taking the glass from the hand that was holding it in front of me and then pouring all of the contents carefully—tipping my head meant moving my neck—down my throat.

I handed the glass back and found it was Kritzinger who had taken it from me.

I was in a neat little sitting room with a window onto the basement corridor, a small desk, a couple of easy chairs, a safe, and the chaise longue I was lying on.

"Where am I?"

"This is my office, sir," said Kritzinger.

Behind him were two SS men, one of whom was the corporal who had argued with me a few minutes before. The other was Major Ploetz.

"Who hit me?"

"I did, sir," said the corporal.

"What were you trying to do? Make a bell ring?"

"Sorry about that, sir."

"No, don't apologize. Kritzinger?"

"Sir?"

"Give this boy a piece of sugarloaf. I reckon he won it fair and square. The last time I got hit like that, I was wearing a pointy hat and sitting in a trench."

"If only you'd listened to me, sir," said the corporal.

"It looked to me as if that's exactly what *you've* been doing." I rubbed the back of my neck and groaned. "To me and everyone else in this house."

"Orders are orders, sir."

Ploetz put his hand on my shoulder. "How are you feeling, Captain?" He sounded oddly solicitous, as if he really did care.

"Really, sir," insisted the corporal. "If I'd known it was you, sir—"

"It's all right, Corporal," Ploetz said smoothly. "I'll handle things from here."

"Sure, Doc, sure," I said. "You can pretend there's a perfectly innocent explanation for all that recording equipment, and while you're at it, I'll pretend I'm a proper detective. Right now the only thing I am absolutely certain of is the quality of that brandy. Better pour me another, Kritzinger. I pretend better when I've had a drink."

"Don't give him any," Ploetz told Kritzinger. And then: "Your tongue is quite loose enough as it is, Gunther. We wouldn't want you to say something to your own detriment. Especially not now that you're in the general's good books."

I ignored this. It didn't sound right. Clearly the blow on the back of my neck had affected my hearing.

"That's right, Doc. We've got to be careful what we say. What is it the sign says? Attention! The Enemy Is Listening. Well, they are. And they're pretty good at it, too. Aren't you, boys? What were you listening to anyway? And don't tell me it was the Leader talking about the Winter Relief. Something in the meeting room? Something in the bedrooms? Maybe you've got a recording of Kuttner getting shot. That might come in useful. For me, anyway. Something in the morning room? Me, perhaps? Only what would be the point in that? I don't mind calling you all crooks and liars to your ugly faces. Just see if I don't."

Ploetz moved his head in the direction of the door and the two SS men started to leave.

"Look, Gunther," Ploetz said, "I think it might be better if you returned to your room and had a lie-down. I'll inform the general of what's happened. Under the circumstances, he'll want to know you're all right."

At this moment a lie-down looked very appealing.

Ploetz went outside while Kritzinger helped me to my feet.

"Are you all right, sir? Would you like me to help you back to your room?"

"Thanks, no, I'll manage. I'm used to it. It's an occupational hazard for a policeman, being hit. It comes from sticking my nose in where it's not wanted. I should know better by now. It used to be that a detective could turn up at a country house, question everyone, find some recognizable clues, and then arrest the butler over chilled cocktails in the library. But it hasn't worked out like that I'm afraid, Kritzinger. I'm afraid you won't be getting your big moment when everyone realizes what a clever fellow you've been."

"That is disappointing, sir. Perhaps you would care for another brandy, after all."

I shook my head. "No. I expect Dr. Ploetz is right. I do talk too much. It comes from not having any answers. I don't suppose you know who shot Captain Kuttner."

"No, sir."

He smiled a fleeting smile and then scratched the back of his head awkwardly.

"Pity."

"You understand, sir, that there are lots of things in this house I prefer not to hear, but if these things had included a shot, or perhaps a snippet of conversation that might shed some light on his unfortunate death, then I should certainly tell you, Commissar. Really I would. However, I am certain there's nothing I can tell you."

I nodded. "Well, that's very good of you to say so, Kritzinger. I really think you mean that. And I appreciate your saying it."

"Really?" The smile flickered on again for just a second. "I wonder."

"No, I do."

"I flatter myself that perhaps I know your own independent cast of mind. One can't help but hear things in a house like this."

"So I noticed."

"Consequently, I know you believe that I think in a certain way, only, for what it's worth, I don't. I never have. I am a good German. Like you, perhaps, I don't know what else to be. But unlike you, I am not a courageous man, if you follow me."

"That Iron Cross ribbon in your buttonhole says otherwise, Mr. Kritzinger."

"Thank you, sir. But that was then. I think things were simpler in that war, were they not? Courage was perhaps easier to recognize not only in oneself but in others as well. Well, I was younger then. I have a wife now. And a child. And long ago I concluded that the only practical course of action available to me was simply to do as I'm told."

"Me too."

I headed for the stairs a little unsteadily. It had been a very German conversation.

As I passed the dining room I noticed that lunch was finishing. Seeing me, Heydrich made his excuses to the other cauliflower and, smiling, nodded toward the drawing room.

It wasn't every day that Heydrich smiled at me. I followed him, and he led me to the French windows and out onto the terrace, where he offered me one of his cigarettes and even condescended to light it for me. He did not smoke one himself. And he seemed oddly cheerful, considering that Václav Morávek continued to elude the Gestapo. I had only ever seen him like this once before, and that had been in June 1940, after the French capitulation.

"Major Ploetz told me what happened to you below stairs," he said, almost apologetically. "I should have informed you about the SD listening station, but really, I've had so much on my plate. As if I didn't have enough to do here in Bohemia with the Three Kings and UVOD and traitor X. Reichsmarshal Göring has tasked me to submit to him a comprehensive draft as to how we can sort out the way the Jews are being handled in all new territories under German influence. Well, I'm sure I don't have to tell you what things are like in the East. It's nothing short of chaos. But that's hardly your concern.

"But to come back to traitor X: as you know, all of the guests in this house were under suspicion in that respect. However, by a simple process of elimination, our intelligence analysts had narrowed down the search for the traitor's identity to one of six or seven officers. Consequently, everything these men said on the least of subjects was of interest to us. Which is why some of the rooms in the Lower Castle have concealed microphones, just in case one of them should let something important slip."

"You mean, like the Pension Matzky."

Heydrich nodded. "You know about the microphones, do you?" He grinned. "Yes, like the Pension Matzky."

"And do these rooms here include the morning room?"

"Yes, they do."

My stomach turned over for a moment; not for my own sake—as far as Heydrich was concerned, I was a hopeless case—but for Kurt Kahlo's. I started to rack my brains for anything he had said that might have been interpreted as evidence of his disloyalty.

"So you've heard everything that was said in there?"

"No, not me personally. But I've read some of the transcripts."

"Kuttner's room?"

"No. My fourth adjutant was hardly important enough to have rated that level of surveillance." Heydrich made a face. "Which is a pity, because if he had been, then of course we would now know who it was who pumped two bullets into his chest."

I let out a weary sigh and tried to put some sort of tolerant, understanding face on what had just been revealed to me.

"In my book, a traitor is a traitor. I can easily see why you should wish to employ every method at your disposal in order to catch him. Including secret microphones. But I just hope you'll excuse some of Criminal Assistant Kahlo's looser talk in the morning room. You can blame me for a lot of that. He's a good man. I'm afraid I've been a bad influence on him."

"On the contrary, Gunther. It's thanks to you and your unconventional, not to say insubordinate methods that the traitor has now been revealed. In fact, everything has worked out exactly as I had hoped it would. You, Gunther, have been the catalyst that changed everything. I don't know whom to congratulate more: myself for having the inspiration of bringing you here in the first place, or you for your own stubbornly independent cast of mind."

I felt my face take on an expression of disbelief.

"Yes, it's quite true. It seems that we owe you everything in this matter, Gunther. Which makes it all the more unfortunate that your immediate reward should have been to be knocked unconscious by one of our more robust colleagues in the SD. For which, once again, I offer my sincere apologies. You were after all merely doing your job. A job well done. For even as we speak the traitor is under close arrest and on his way to Gestapo headquarters in Prague."

"But who was it? The traitor."

"It was Major Thümmel. Paul Thümmel, of the Abwehr."

"Thümmel. He's a man with a gold Party badge, isn't he?"

"I did say it would turn out to be someone who was apparently above reasonable suspicion."

"But he's also a friend of Himmler."

Heydrich smiled. "Yes. And that is something of a bonus. The acute embarrassment that this particular association will cause the Reichsführer will be a great pleasure to behold. I can't wait to see Himmler's face when I tell the Leader. For that same reason, however, it's by no means certain that we'll make any of this stick against Thümmel. We shall, of course, do our best."

I nodded. "I'm beginning to understand. It has something to do with that letter I received this morning from the Netherlands, doesn't it?"

"It does, indeed. You asked Major Thümmel if he was the same Captain Thümmel who was in The Hague in 1939. He denied it, of course. Now, why? Why would that be of any interest to you? But this was a lie. It was a matter of only a few minutes to check through a record of his military and diplomatic service. When Thümmel was a captain in 1939, he passed through The Hague on his way to an embassy appointment in Paris. We know he was in The Hague because he visited our military attaché at the German embassy. But while he was in The Hague we also think he met secretly with his Czech controller, a man named Major Franck. Franck and Thümmel shared a Dutch girlfriend named Inge Vranken. I shall want to see your letter, of course, but it rather looks as if Inge Vranken was your friend Geert's little sister.

"We suspect Thümmel has been spying for the Czechos since as early as February 1936. For a long time he was using a radio transmitter to send messages here, to Prague. As you are aware we were intercepting some of that radio traffic; what we called the OTA intercepts. The Czechos called him A54. Don't ask me why. Call sign, probably. The radio messages were forwarded by courier to the Czech government in exile in London. That went on for quite a while. But then Thümmel began to get scared. He stopped using the radio transmitter altogether. And for all intents and purposes it looked as if he had closed up shop, thus narrowing our chances of getting him.

"We suspect that UVOD despaired of having lost their best agent. Not least because his material had put the exiled Beneš government in London in very good odor with Winston Churchill. No more intelligence meant no more operational scraps from the top table. So the UVOD people set out to reestablish contact with him in Berlin, in person; and for a while that did the trick. But with the net closing in, he lost his nerve for that, too. Frankly, I think he's been expecting this for a while."

"But why? Why would an old Party comrade—a man with the confidence of Hitler—why would such a man spy for the Czechos? Why spy at all?"

"That's a good question. And I'm afraid I don't yet know the answer. He's still denying everything, of course. It's likely to be several days before we have any idea of the reason behind his treason, or even the full extent of his treachery."

Was it possible that Thümmel had been Gustav? For a moment I pictured Thümmel in the hands of the local Gestapo and wondered how long it might take them to beat "the full extent of his treachery" out of the man.

"Surely it won't take your people that long."

Heydrich shook his head. "Actually it will. As I said, Thümmel has vitamin B. We shall have to question him quite carefully. Himmler would never forgive me if I had him tortured. In the short term at least we can but hope that close interrogation will find holes in his story."

"I understand."

Heydrich nodded, silently.

"Well," he said. "Good work, Gunther. As my personal detective you are off to a flying start, I think."

He was heading back through the French windows when I spoke again.

"What I don't entirely understand, General, is why you murdered Captain Kuttner."

Heydrich stopped and turned slowly on the heel of his shoe.

"Hmm?"

"It was you who killed your own adjutant. That I am certain of. I know how you did it. I just don't know why you did it. I mean, why bother to murder him when you had ample opportunity to have him court-martialed? No, I don't understand that. Not entirely. And I certainly don't understand exactly why you had me go to all the trouble of investigating a murder that you yourself had committed."

Heydrich didn't say anything. It seemed he was waiting for me to do some more talking before he said anything. So I did. It felt as if I was talking my own neck into a noose, but it was hard to imagine it being any more painful than it was now.

"Of course, I have a few ideas on that score. But first, if you'll permit me, sir, let me deal with how you killed him."

Heydrich nodded. "I'm listening."

"I see you haven't denied it."

"To you?" Heydrich laughed. "Gunther, there are about three people in the world to whom I ever need to justify myself, and you're not one of them. Nevertheless, I should like to hear your explanation of the solution to the crime, as you see it."

"On the night before he was murdered, you gave Kuttner a dose of Veronal, which he unwittingly drank in a glass of beer. It was the only thing Kuttner drank that night, as he knew to avoid mixing the drug with alcohol. But I bet you persuaded him to have just the one. Everyone else was celebrating, after all. And what an honor to be served by you. I should have thought beer was perfect for your purposes. It wasn't so alcoholic that he might refuse. And of course beer is bitter, so Kuttner wouldn't ever have tasted the significant dose of the drug with which you'd doctored it.

"But doctor it you certainly did. Kritzinger reports seeing Kuttner looking very tired at around two. So the drug was already taking effect. But Kuttner didn't know that, so when he got back to his room he took his regular dose of Veronal and actually passed out with one of the pills still in his throat. Which accounts for how he had only one boot off. My guess is that you wanted him to sleep extra soundly, although why you didn't just do him in with an overdose, I'm not sure. Possibly you wanted to make sure he was indeed dead, and there is, as you must know, always something uncertain about an overdose. It's amazing just how much people can swallow without dying. But a bullet is much more certain. Especially when it's fired point-blank at the heart.

"In the morning, you let Captain Pomme and Kritzinger try to rouse him before making sure that you were on the scene to authorize them to break down the door. And, being a general, naturally you were first into the bedroom, which meant you were also the one who was able to take charge and examine Kuttner's drugged body and pronounce him dead. Naturally, they took your word for it, General. You're not an easy man to contradict, sir.

"Judging by his appearance, of course, that he was still alive was hardly probable. He was half dressed from the night before, and there was an open bottle of Veronal on the bedside table, so everyone assumed that the obvious explanation was the correct one: Kuttner had taken an overdose, possibly intentionally—after all, most of his fellow officers were aware he'd had some sort of breakdown—and was dead. No one suspected that he had been shot because the fact is he hadn't been shot. Not at that moment. At that moment he was only unconscious.

"Having ordered Kritzinger to call an ambulance and Captain Pomme to fetch Dr. Jury, you were now alone in the room with the captain's unconscious body. Dr. Jury's room is in the other wing of the house, so you knew Pomme would take several minutes to return with him. Apart from the telephone in your office, the nearest telephone is on the ground floor, so Kritzinger was far away, too. All the same, you probably waited a few minutes just to make sure that no one was around before closing the door as best you were able. There was now plenty of time for you to produce a gun from inside your fencing jerkin, pull aside his tunic, and coolly fire two shots in rapid succession into Kuttner's body at close range, killing him instantly. Because he was still wearing his tunic, the gunshot wounds were not immediately obvious to anyone who had already seen the body. Moreover, these wounds didn't bleed much, either, because Kuttner was lying on his back. Not to mention the convenient effect that the extra Veronal would have had on the dead man's blood pressure."

Heydrich listened patiently, still denying nothing. Folding his arms, he placed a thoughtful finger across his thin lips. He might have been considering some plan for the evacuation of Prague's Jews.

"You put the gun back inside your jerkin. Then you opened the window, to help ventilate the room a little more, just in case someone caught a whiff of the shots. When you opened the window, that's when you saw the footman, Fendler, with the ladder; you told him that the ladder was no longer required; that poor Kuttner was dead of an overdose, because, after all, you were obliged to pay lip service to what at that moment everyone else believed.

"Then you did a quick search on the bed and the floor for the spent brass. You wanted to pick this up so that you could help muddy the waters and add to the mystery that was bound to attach to a murder in a room locked from inside. That might have taken a while. They're elusive things when you need to find them in a hurry. Of course, if someone had entered the room you would have given some excuse about looking for clues. After all, there were pills on the floor. You were just picking them up. You are a policeman, after all. Maybe it was you who chucked them there for effect. Set dressing, so to speak. But to me it never seemed right that the Veronal bottle remained upright on the table when there were pills on the floor.

"Having found the two spent brass cartridges, you flung them along the corridor, lit a cigarette to help conceal the smell of the two shots—although, as I discovered for myself a little while ago, it isn't particularly noticeable, and certainly no more noticeable than the noise of two shots. I fired my own pistol in Kuttner's room while you were all eating lunch and, of course, no one noticed a thing. Most people assume a noise like that is something else, something a little less dramatic. A car backfiring. A vase of flowers knocked over. A door slammed by a careless footman. Of course you already know that. I'll bet you even conducted a similar experiment yourself when you were planning this whole thing.

"It was about then that Captain Pomme and Dr. Jury arrived in the room. Dr. Jury was a good choice. For one thing Jury was possibly still drunk, and at the very least badly hungover, and he probably didn't even notice that the dead man was still bleeding, only that he'd been shot. Again no one was about to suspect your own first version of events. Besides, there was now an even bigger mystery in front of everyone's eyes, which is how a man could be found shot dead in a room locked on the inside with no murder weapon on the scene. It's a useful thing, mystery. Any stage conjurer knows the value of misdirection. You draw attention to what one hand is doing while the other hand does the dirty work.

"People do love a good mystery, don't they? You included, General. Perhaps you more than most. On your bookshelves I found a well-read copy of a detective novel by that writer you mentioned to me when I arrived here: Agatha Christie. It's a novel called *The Murder of Roger Ackroyd*. And I only had to flick through it for a few minutes to see that the book contains certain similarities with this case. A body in a locked room. Only that person, Roger Ackroyd, isn't dead at all—not in the beginning. And it's the person who supposedly finds the body—Dr. James Sheppard, isn't it?—who turns out to be the murderer. As indeed you are. In fact, I wouldn't mind betting that's where you got the idea in the first place.

"But my neck and my head hurt and I just can't figure out why. Why would you murder your mother's favorite piano pupil? It couldn't be that, could it? Jealousy? No, not you. That would be much too human of you, General Heydrich, sir. No, there has to be some other reason. Something much more important than personal revenge."

I paused and lit another cigarette.

"Well, don't stop there," said Heydrich. "You're doing so well and I have to confess I'm actually quite impressed. This is more than I had expected of you, Gunther." He nodded firmly. "Keep going. I insist."

"For old times' sake, you'd rescued Albert Kuttner's career. That was oddly sentimental of you. And quite out of character, if you don't mind my saying so, sir. Or perhaps you did it at someone else's request. Kuttner's father. Your mother, perhaps."

"You'd best leave my mother out of this, Gunther, if you don't mind."

"Gladly. You'd rescued Albert Kuttner's career only to discover that, as you told me yourself, he was a disappointment. More than just a disappointment, he'd become something of a nuisance, even an embarrassment. Kuttner was insubordinate. For example, there was that scene at the officers' training school with Colonel Jacobi. And what was worse, you had found out he was quite possibly homosexual, too. After what happened to Ernst Röhm and some of his warmer friends in the SA, that was too much. Did you worry that you might be tainted with an association like that? I wonder. In Germany it's one thing to be suspected of being a Jew, as you are, and quite another to be suspected of being soft on homosexuals. Even then, however, you could have sent Kuttner quietly back to Berlin. To one of those nice private clinics in Wannsee, where top Nazis go to dry out or be weaned off drugs. Some of them even claim they can cure you of homosexuality. So you must have had an important reason to murder him in cold blood like that. There must have been some sort of gain in it for you. But what?"

"Excellent. You're almost there."

Heydrich lit a cigarette and looked very amused, as if I were telling him a very funny story. It made me suspect that he had a better punch line than the one I had written myself. But I was in too far now to stop.

"Everything you do has a reason, doesn't it, General? Whether it's murdering Jews or murdering your own adjutant."

Heydrich shook his head. "Don't get sidetracked," he said. "Keep to the point."

"But why have me investigate the murder? At first I assumed it was because you thought I wasn't up to the job; that you wanted me to screw up; but that was too obvious. You could have picked anyone for the job. Willy Abendschön from the local Kripo is a good man, I hear. Clever. Efficient. Or you could have picked someone more pliable than either of us. Unless of course that was exactly what you wanted. Someone who doesn't care about his future in the SD. Someone who is just pigheaded enough to ask the difficult questions that the cauliflowers might not care to answer. Someone for whom advancement and promotion are not issues. Me. Yes, that must be it. You picked me to handle the investigation of Kuttner's murder because you really wanted me to search for your spy. You used the murder of Kuttner as a pretext for a secret spy hunt."

"Now you're onto it," said Heydrich.

"You couldn't risk some flat-footed idiot questioning all of your spy suspects about being traitor X, or A54, or whatever he's called; not without putting them on their guard. But if I questioned them all about something else, something serious that necessitated their being detained here, then all of them might relax, more or less, since each knew he was innocent of murder. And of course my conversations with them were being recorded, transcribed, picked over by your own SD analysts for something small—an inconsistency, perhaps. A clue. Real evidence. You didn't know exactly what it was, but you thought you would recognize it when you saw it. And you're right. That's all a clue really is. I have to hand it you, sir; it's clever. Utterly ruthless, but clever."

Heydrich clapped his hands three times. To me his congratulations sounded almost ironic, but there seemed to be some genuine appreciation in them.

"Well done. I underestimated you, Gunther. I've always assumed that as a policeman you were the more muscular type. Tough, resourceful, and irritatingly dogged, but hardly intellectual. It seems I was wrong about that. You have a much better brain than I gave you credit for. I had hoped you might uncover the spy, it's true. But I did not expect you would also solve the murder. That has been a real bonus. But now I really am intrigued. I want to know. I must have made a mistake. Exactly how did you conclude that it was I who shot Captain Kuttner?"

"Sorry to disappoint you. It wasn't anything clever, at all."

"Oh, come on. You're being unnecessarily modest."

"Actually, you told me yourself. Just a few minutes ago. Only I and the doctor who carried out the autopsy knew that Kuttner had been shot twice. Even Jury didn't notice that. And I kept it secret in the hope that eventually the real killer would mention two shots when everyone else believes that it was just the one shot that killed him."

Heydrich frowned. "Is that all?"

To my delight he sounded disappointed.

"What else is there? I'm not one for crossword puzzles, General. Or detective novels. Actually, I really can't stand them. Me, I'm just a plain, old-fashioned cop. And you described me rather well a moment ago when you said I was irritatingly dogged. I don't have the better brain you gave me credit for. These days I wouldn't know what to do with it. You see, sir, most murders aren't complicated. People just think they are. The same goes for the detection process. There are no great scenes of revelation. There's just the small stuff. And that's where I come in. Really, if detective work was as difficult as it seems in the books, then they wouldn't let cops do it."

"Yes, I take your point." Heydrich sighed. "But now I have another question. And perhaps you should answer this one more carefully."

I nodded.

"What do you think you're going to do about it?"

I didn't answer. I didn't know. What could I do against a man of Heydrich's standing and authority?

"What I mean is, are you intending to try to arrest me, perhaps? To make a scene?"

"You murdered someone, General."

"You're right, of course. And I did regret having rescued Kuttner's career. I could have lived with his behavior in and after Latvia. What happened to him there is by no means unusual, and is of course why Reichsmarshal Göring has charged me with finding a better solution to this problem. I could even have lived with his behavior toward Colonel Jacobi. The two of them have some history, it seems; however, Jacobi is a prick and frankly anyone who gets the better of that man is to be admired rather than condemned.

"But I was shocked when Berlin's Gestapo informed me that my own adjutant was probably homosexual. Not that he was very obvious about it; indeed I was so skeptical that I sent him along to Pension Matzky, where, I'm afraid to say, he disgraced himself with a girl called Grete. When he failed to perform with her, unfortunately she mocked his inadequacy and earned herself a beating. He was very apologetic about it afterward; he even sent her some flowers as compensation; most bizarrely he then seems to have adopted an entirely opposite opinion of the poor girl and decided that he felt some romantic attachment for her. I'm sure there are medical explanations for his mental state. But if there are, I have no time for them. That was when I decided to get rid of him. I dislike men who are violent to women almost as much as I dislike men who are unreliable.

"Anyway, if I had sent him back to Berlin in disgrace, it wouldn't have been long before he disgraced himself again and, more important, disgraced his family in Halle. I couldn't have that.

I am very fond of those people. Fond enough to want to spare them any further pain. So, I thought it was better for him to be quietly murdered by me in a way that could easily be hushed up rather than allow his family to endure the public disgrace that would follow his being sentenced to some SS punishment battalion. Indeed, it already seems to me much more probable that at some stage in the hopefully not too distant future, Captain Kuttner will become an unfortunate victim of Václav Morávek, and be shot by him while heroically trying to assist in the Czech terrorist's arrest. We may even have to award him a posthumous decoration. That's a story that should play well at home, don't you think?"

"Why not? He is as good a Nazi hero as any others I can think of."

Heydrich smirked. "Yes, I thought you might approve. You were wrong about one thing, however. I couldn't ever have wasted so much time searching for my spent brass on the floor of Kuttner's room. So I had the gun inside a sock, so that it could be fired without any of the spent brass being ejected onto the floor or on the bed. It all stayed safely inside the sock. Until I threw it into the corridor.

"Anyway, having decided to kill him—it was, as you say, *The Murder of Roger Ackroyd* that gave me the idea of how to do it—I then wondered if I might put his death to some useful purpose. If I could rely on you to be your usual awkward self and pose a lot of awkward questions to people like Henlein, Frank, von Eberstein, Hildebrandt, Thümmel, and von Neurath, whom we've had our doubts about for some time. And you came up trumps. Nothing you've said can spoil what I'm feeling now. And you'll no doubt be pleased to discover that you will have advanced my reputation even further. The apprehension of traitor X will put me in very good odor with the Leader. Ever since the invasion of Poland, the traitor has been a thorn in our side. No more. And my triumph will be complete just as soon as the third of the Three Kings is in my hands. You see, now that I have Thümmel, it can't be very long before everything is neatly wrapped up."

"Hardly," I said. "I'm not about to let you get away with murder, General."

"We're getting away with it every minute," murmured Heydrich. "I thought you knew that."

"Kuttner had it coming for all I know, but even in the SS there are standards that have to be adhered to. Military discipline. Due process. Probably it will cost me my job. Even my life, but I can at least try to bring you down."

"You're a fool if you think you can bring me down. But then I think you know that already, don't you? It's certainly true, you can cause a bit of trouble for me, Gunther. Himmler won't thank me for exposing Paul Thümmel; and naturally the investigation will have to be entirely above reproach. Very possibly that will involve you. In which case I can hardly have you shot or sent to a concentration camp. No, I can see I'm going to have to provide you with a better, more urgent reason than your loyalty to me, one that will make sure you keep your mouth shut about all of this."

I shook my head. "I don't think that's going to happen, sir. Not this time."

"Do try to be sporting about this, Gunther. At least let me try."

"If you like."

Heydrich threw away his cigarette and glanced at his wristwatch.

"We'll go straight to Gestapo headquarters. There, if you wish, you can make out your own report, in as much detail as you like. Peček Palace is the proper place to bring charges against me. That is, if I can't provide you with a better reason than simple self-preservation."

"I daresay you have people there who can persuade anyone to do anything."

"Oh, you misunderstand me, Gunther. You weren't listening,

perhaps. I said I was going to give you a much better reason to keep your mouth shut than self-preservation, and I meant it. You're quite safe from that sort of thing, I can assure you. I'm going to give you something much more compelling than violence against your person, Gunther. Shall we?"

I nodded, but something told me that I had already lost. That this was one murderer who was almost certain to get away quite unscathed.

IT WAS THREE THIRTY in the afternoon when Heydrich and I got into the Mercedes with Klein and started out for the center of Prague. No one said very much, but it was obvious that Heydrich was in a good humor, humming a pleasant-sounding melody that was the very opposite of the threnody playing inside my own thick skull.

Nearing the railway line that led west to the Hibernerbahnhof, we overtook a horse-drawn hearse headed south, for the Olšany Cemetery. The mourners walking behind looked at Heydrich with baleful eyes, as if somehow they held him responsible for the death of the person they were escorting to church. For all I knew that was true, and the sight of his distinctive SS car must have been like catching a glimpse of the grim reaper himself. I could feel the hate following us like X-rays, and despite Heydrich's overbearing confidence that he was invincible, it was clear to me that the hatred directed at him could just as easily have been a hail of machine-gun bullets. An ambush was the best way to kill Heydrich, and once you were in that car, anything might happen. If it had happened right then and there, I wouldn't have minded that much.

By the time we reached the outskirts of the city, what little confidence I had of making something stick to Heydrich had faded. Optimism has its limits. I was an idealist, and ahead of me lay an unpleasant, possibly painful, even fatal demonstration of just where idealism could get me. A jail cell. A beating. A train ride to the concentration camp being built around the fortress of Terezín. A bullet in the back of the head. Heydrich might have assured me I was safe, but I had little confidence in his assurances; thoughts of my own peril overpowered any other ideas of just what the man sitting in front of the car—whose own mind seemed more preoccupied with Schubert and his trout—had in store to deflect me from any attempt to bring charges against him.

So we drove on to what promised to be some sort of final reckoning between us.

Peček Palace, formerly a Czech bank, was part of a government area that was home to several tall and rusticated gray buildings, any one of which could have been Gestapo headquarters. But the real HQ was easy to spot at the end of the street, surrounded as it was with checkpoints and bedecked with two long Nazi banners. It was a grim, granite edifice that was a near copy of the Gestapo's central HQ in Berlin's Prinz-Albrecht-Strasse, with huge cast-iron lamps that belonged on an ogre's castle, and a Doric-columned portico that might have seemed elegant but for the several SS men grouped out front, easily recognizable with their leather coats, pig-knuckle faces, and pugilist's manners. None of them gave the impression that they would turn a short hair to see a defenestrated Czech crash onto the black cobbles in front of their cold eyes. Five stories above the street the balustrade featured stone vases that resembled giant funeral urns. Certainly it wouldn't have surprised the Czechs to be told that this was what these were used for. After three years of occupation, the Gestapo at Peček Palace had acquired the most fearsome reputation in all of Europe.

Klein stopped the car at the entrance and the guards came to attention. I followed Heydrich through the wrought-iron doors and up a short, shiny limestone staircase illuminated by a large brass chandelier. At the top of the stairs were some glass double doors lined with green curtains, and in front of these were two SS guards, a pair of Nazi flags, and between them a portrait of the Leader—the one by Heinrich Knirr, which made him look like a queer hairdresser. To the left was a reception area, where I presented my identification and endured the awl-like scrutiny of the uniformed NCO on duty.

"Tell Colonel Böhme to come and fetch us," Heydrich told the NCO. And then to me: "I'm lost in here."

"A common experience, I imagine."

"Böhme is the one who thought he could solve Kuttner's murder," said Heydrich.

"Are you going to tell him or shall I?"

"Oh, I know you find it hard to credit, but I take a lot of vicarious pleasure in your solving Kuttner's murder. I mean I can admire it as a piece of reasoning. And I'm very much looking forward to seeing the expression on his stupid Saxon face."

"I'd been kind of looking forward to that myself. Böhme was the other officer who straightened Kuttner's tie after your speech the other night. When he rescued the maid, Rosa, from Henlein's clumsy drunken pass. I shall miss the opportunity of making him feel like he had something to hide."

"You're a natural contrarian, Gunther," observed Heydrich. "I think your problem is not with the Nazis, it's with all authority. You just don't like being told what to do."

"Maybe."

I glanced around.

"Major Thümmel's here?" I said.

"Yes."

"Is Böhme questioning him?"

"Abendschön is leading the interrogation. He's much more agile than Böhme. If anyone can trip Thümmel up without breaking skin, it's Willy Abendschön."

A minute or two passed before we heard footsteps coming up the broad stairs.

Böhme arrived at the top of the stairs and marched smartly across the hall and into the reception area. He saluted in the usual Nazi way, and under the circumstances I didn't bother returning the compliment; but Heydrich did.

"Let's go and see the prisoner, shall we?" said Heydrich.

Böhme led the way back across the hall and downstairs. At the bottom of the stairs we walked on through a warren of unpleasant-smelling, dimly lit corridors and cells.

"I hear it's down to you, Captain Gunther, that we found Thümmel was the traitor," Böhme told me. "Congratulations."

"Thank you."

Böhme paused outside a cell door. "Here we are."

"Not only that but he has also solved the murder of Captain Kuttner," said Heydrich.

"Then you've really covered yourself in glory, haven't you?" said Böhme. "So who did it?"

I glanced at Heydrich.

"What's the game, General?" I said. "If you've got a card to play here, then you'd better play it, only don't treat me like an idiot."

"In spite of all that, an idiot is what you are," said Heydrich. "A very clever idiot. Only a clever man could have deduced who murdered Captain Kuttner, how and why. But only an idiot could have behaved as you did."

Heydrich pushed open the door to a large interrogation room, complete with a stenographer, several wooden chairs, some chains hanging from the ceiling, and an en suite bath. Besides the stenographer, there were two largish men in the room and a naked woman.

"Only an idiot could have been so easily duped by the Czechs," said Heydrich. "By her."

He pointed at the girl.

It was almost as well he identified her because she was nearly unrecognizable.

The naked girl was Arianne Tauber.

As soon as I saw Arianne, I moved to help her, and found myself solidly restrained by Böhme and another largish man who'd been standing, unseen by me, behind the heavy wooden door of the interrogation room. On Heydrich's order, I was searched for a nonexistent weapon and quickly manacled on a length of chain to a cast-iron radiator as big as a mattress, safely out of harm's way.

I hauled at the chain attached to my wrists and swore loudly, but no one was paying much attention to me. I was like a dog that had been safely kenneled, or worse.

Heydrich laughed, and that was the cue for the others to do the same. Even the stenographer, a young hatchet-faced woman in SS uniform, shook her head and smiled as if genuinely amused by my threats and bad language. Then she straightened the little forage cap she was wearing and adjusted the grip that kept it on her head. She must have sensed me wishing I could have smacked it onto the floor.

I glanced around the windowless room. It was as big as a chapel in a disused church. The walls were tiled in pea green. Dusty, bare lightbulbs were hanging from the heavily cobwebbed ceiling. The floor was covered with pools of water. A slight smell of excrement hung in the cold air. I pulled some more upon my chain, to no effect. It seemed my situation was as helpless as Arianne's seemed hopeless.

She did not move. Her battered purple eyes remained closed, resembling sleeping sea anemones. Her wet hair was coiled around her face, like dark yellow snakes on the head of a dead Medusa. There was blood in her nostrils and she appeared to have lost some fingernails, but she was not dead. The edges of her bare breasts shifted a little as breath entered and left her body; she could not move because she was strapped to a wooden bascule. She was not, however, about to be guillotined, although that was the point of the bascule: to restrain the body and transport the head of a condemned person smoothly through a lunette so that he or she might be quickly decapitated by the falling ax.

Arianne was strapped onto the bascule for an altogether different reason—one almost as unpleasant.

The bascule was positioned precipitously over the end of a bath full of pinkish-brown water so that it worked very like a lever. One of Arianne's torturers kept his foot on the end of the bascule, just under her bare feet, and all he had to do to allow the wooden board carrying her body to tip forward on the fulcrum that was the lip of the bath was to move his black boot a few centimeters; then she would fall headfirst into the water and remain there until either she drowned or her torturers decided to lift the bascule up again. It was ingeniously simple, and although the bath was smeared with blood, from when the bascule at times fell awkwardly—which perhaps explained the several contusions on her eyes, cheeks, and forehead—it was obviously effective.

At the end of my chain, I was at least a meter away from everyone, and this seemed to suggest that others before me had stood where I was, chained to the same radiator and obliged to watch friends being tortured. I couldn't even kick the edge of the stenographer's neat little corner table, with its typewriter, pencil, notebook, magazine, coffee cup and nail file; but I promised myself that if the bitch started filing her nails while Arianne was being tortured, I would take off my shoe and throw it at her.

Looking at Arianne, I found it impossible to believe she was the same woman I had left behind at the Imperial Hotel that morning. Somehow Heydrich or the SD or the Gestapo had discovered something about Arianne that had persuaded them to arrest her. But what? Only she and I knew about Gustav and the envelope he had asked her to give to Franz Koci. Nobody else knew anything. Nobody but Gustav. And even if Paul Thümmel was indeed Gustav, it seemed impossible that her arrest could be connected with his. Not yet. They had to have picked her up at the station *before* I had identified Paul Thümmel as traitor X.

"Has she talked?" Heydrich asked Böhme.

The other man pulled a face. "Well, of course, sir. What a question."

"You think so? What about Mašín and Balabán? You couldn't get them to talk, could you? You had those two Czechos for five months before you managed to get anything out of them."

"They were exceptionally strong and determined men, sir."

"Well, I'm not surprised, now that I've been in here. To me this hardly looks like torture. Somehow I imagined something much worse. Back at my gymnasium in Halle we used to do this sort of thing to other boys just for sport."

"With all due respect, sir, there's not much that's worse than the water bascule. Short of death itself, which would hardly be to the purpose, no other torture quite persuades as much that you are surely about to die."

"I see. So, what has she told us?"

Böhme approached the stenographer, who handed him a few sheets of typed paper; these he passed to Heydrich, and while the Reichsprotector glanced over what was written there, one of Arianne's tormentors slapped her bruised cheeks to bring her out of a faint.

With the sleeves of their striped civilian shirts rolled up above their substantial biceps and their collars removed, Arianne's tormentors looked ready for work. The man with his foot on the bascule was examining his knuckles, probably inspecting them for damage. His blond hair was almost white and he seemed indifferent to Arianne's suffering. The other man was smoking a cigarette, which stayed in his mouth while he was slapping her.

"Come on," he said, almost kindly, like a father speaking to a child who was lagging behind on a Sunday-afternoon walk in the park. "That's it, Arianne. Wakey-wake. Say hello to our important visitors."

Arianne retched bathwater and some vomit that was part blood, and then coughed for almost a minute.

"Come on. Open your eyes."

She started to shiver, probably from shock as much as the cold, but still she didn't open her eyes; at least not until her fatherly interrogator sucked at his cigarette for a second, peeled it off his lower lip, and then touched her breast with it.

Arianne opened her eyes and screamed.

"That's the girl," said the man who had burned her.

It was odd how sorry he looked, I thought; almost as if he regretted hurting her; as if he wouldn't have hurt anyone by choice; right up until the moment he smiled a smile as thin as a razor and then burned her breast a second time, for the pleasure of it. I could see that now. He enjoyed giving pain.

Arianne screamed again and started to weep invisible tears.

"Please, stop this," I pleaded.

Heydrich ignored me. He finished reading the transcript of the interrogation and handed the pages back to Böhme.

"Is this really all that she knows, do you think?" he asked.

Böhme shrugged. "That's a little hard to say, sir. We've only had her for a few hours. At this stage there's no telling how much she knows about anything."

So it was true; her arrest had preceded Paul Thümmel's; in which case they couldn't be connected.

"Sergeant Soppa, isn't it?" Heydrich was looking at the very blond man whose foot was on the water board.

"Sir."

"I believe you are something of an expert in matters like this. It was you who got Balabán to talk, wasn't it?"

"Finally. Yes, sir."

"What is your opinion?"

Sergeant Soppa shifted his feet a little but still managed to keep Arianne's head aloft. She looked like a human torpedo that, at any moment, he might launch into the water.

"In my experience they always keep something back to the end, sir," he said ruefully. "There's always one important thing that they'll hold on to until the last. For their own self-respect, you might say. And they figure you'll miss it because they've already told you absolutely everything else. It's only when they're begging to tell you something they think you don't know—anything—that you can be sure you've got everything there is to be had out of them. Which means that it's always best to keep the interrogation going for longer than seems decent."

Heydrich nodded.

"Yes," he said. "I see what you mean. So, then, I think we shall have to know if she knows something that we don't yet know."

Heydrich nodded at Sergeant Soppa, who immediately took a step back so that the bascule carrying Arianne's naked body tipped forward headfirst and hit the water with a splash.

There was a horrible gurgling sound, like a drain trying to clear itself. Arianne was swallowing water. Her hands and feet flailed helplessly under their restraints like the fins of a landed fish. Then Soppa picked up a length of thick rubber cable lying on the wet floor and started to beat Arianne hard, the way no living creature, not even a stubborn mule, should ever be beaten. Each blow of the cable snapped loudly on her flesh and sounded like a dangerous electrical short circuit.

I watched her beautiful body endure this for several seconds. I remembered the exquisite pleasure we had given each other just a few hours before in the hotel room back at the Imperial. That seemed a very long time ago now. More than that, it seemed like another life, in another place where cruelty and pain did not exist. Worse than this, the body I had known and kissed so tenderly already seemed like a different one from the one I was looking at now.

Why did I agree to bring her to Prague? I could easily have refused her request to accompany me. Surely this was all my fault. I had perhaps foreseen something like this happening, only not quickly enough.

Her hair floated and twisted like yellow seaweed in the water. There was only so much of this kind of treatment she could take. That anyone could take. I told myself I had to do something and I hauled on the chain with all my strength, but was helpless. At this realization, an unpleasant sensation and taste arrived in my mouth from my gut, and I spat it out onto the wet floor. If I'd been thinking, I might have spit it at Heydrich.

"For Christ's sake, you're killing her," I yelled.

"No," said Soppa's smiling colleague. "Not at all." His tone was scoffing. "You might say that we're the ones keeping her alive. Believe me, you have to know what you're doing to take someone right to the edge like this. To almost kill them, and then not kill them. That's the skill, sir. Besides, this little bitch is a lot tougher than she looks. She might panic a bit if ever she was to go swimming again. But, no, we won't kill her." He glanced at Heydrich. "Not unless he tells us to do it."

Arianne's head stayed under the water but Sergeant Soppa stopped beating her for a moment, wiped his brow, and nodded. "That's right. We've been helping people to take the waters in Prague like this for a while now. Just like Marienbad, it is, this place. Or Bad Kissingen."

He grinned at his own attempt at humor. Then he started beating her again.

After a few seconds I turned my face to the wall and, closing my eyes against the edge of my vision, pressed my forehead against the cold, hard tiles. These felt like Heydrich's conscience. I might have closed my eyes but I could hardly close my ears, and the awful combination of sound that was Arianne drowning while she took a dreadful beating continued for another fifteen long seconds before I heard the ghastly dripping creak of the bascule being lifted out of the bath and the banshee rasp of her trying, painfully, to drag air into lungs already bloated with water.

By now I was absolutely certain that Colonel Böhme was right: not much was worse than the water board. Just listening to it seemed bad enough. And when I looked again I saw Arianne was just a few centimeters above the surface of the water, dripping wet, trembling uncontrollably, her body covered with fresh, livid welts; galvanized with the spasms that were her agonized attempts to breathe. Sergeant Soppa had thrown aside his cable and had the heel of his hand on the edge of the water board, ready to do the very same thing again the second that Heydrich or Böhme gave him the order.

Soppa's colleague tossed away his cigarette and turned on a tap to pour some more water into the bath. Had she swallowed that much? Or had it just spilled onto the floor? It was hard to tell. Then he lifted Arianne's head by the hair, shook it like a hand bell, and spoke into her ear.

"Is there anything you want to tell us, darling?" he asked. "Something close to your heart? Next time we'll fucking drown you if we have to. Won't we, Sarge?"

"Sure," said Soppa. "And I'll fuck her while she's drowning." He stroked Arianne's bare behind with lascivious intent and then patted it fondly.

"Ask her—ask her if she knows where Václav Morávek is hiding," said Heydrich.

Soppa's colleague repeated the question into Arianne's ear.

She gulped loudly and whispered, "No. I've told you everything I know. I've never heard of Václav Morávek. Please. You have to believe me."

She swallowed another painful breath, belched, and tried to

say something else, but her previous answer drew a sneer and then a nod from Heydrich, the cue for another ducking. This time her head banged against the side of the bath as she fell into the water. Her body struggled against the leather straps and the buckles, which cut cruelly into her skin, so that a thin trickle of blood ran down her shoulders and dripped into the turbulent bathwater.

I held my own breath at the same time as she went under the water so that I could at least experience some small part of her ordeal. But this time they kept her under for much longer than a minute, and when, with my lungs bursting, I realized I could hold my own breath for no longer, I let it out with a yell, even as Arianne's struggles appeared to have ended for good. Her hands and feet stopped moving. The water calmed. All was still. Including my heart.

"PULL HER UP, you bastards."

"Is she dead?" asked Heydrich.

"No," said Soppa. "Not by a long chalk. Not to worry, sir. We've brought people around who were under the water for much longer than that."

He and the other man lifted Arianne out of the bath and proceeded to use a combination of smelling salts, slaps, brandy, and massage to try to put some life back into her.

"Leave her alone," I pleaded. "For God's sake. She hasn't done anything."

"You think so?" said Heydrich. "I'm afraid that you're wrong about that, Gunther. At least, that was the impression I gained from Colonel Böhme, on the telephone, just before lunchtime."

He turned and faced the stenographer.

"Read the captain what she's already told us, please."

"Yes, sir."

"Just the salient points, if you will."

"Yes, sir."

The stenographer picked up her transcript and read entirely without emotion, like someone announcing the arrival or departure of a train.

Question: What is your name and address?

Answer: My name is Arianne Tauber and I live in a room at flat 6, 3 Uhland Strasse, Berlin, which is owned by Frau Marguerite Lippert. I have lived there for ten months. I work at the Jockey Bar on Martin-Luther-Strasse, where I am employed to be the cloakroom attendant.

Question: You are a Berliner?

Answer: No, originally I am from Dresden. My mother still lives there. She lives in Johann-Georgen-Allee.

Question: So why are you here in Prague?

Answer: I am on holiday. I came here with a friend. I was staying at the Imperial Hotel.

Question: What is the name of that friend?

Answer. Kripo Commissar Bernhard Gunther. From the Police Praesidium at Berlin Alexanderplatz. I am his mistress. He will vouch for me. He works for General Heydrich. Clearly there has been some mistake here. I spent the weekend with him and I was going home to Berlin when I was arrested.

Question: Do you know why you were arrested at the Hibernerbahnhof this morning?

Answer: No. Clearly there's been some sort of mistake here. I've never been in any trouble before. I am a good German. A law-abiding citizen. Commissar Gunther will vouch for me. So will my employers.

Question: But aren't you also working for UVOD?

Answer: I don't know what you mean by that. What is UVOD? I do not understand.

Question: UVOD is the Home Resistance Network here in Prague. We know you are working for UVOD. Why?

Prisoner refused to answer the question.

Prisoner refused to answer the question.

Prisoner refused to answer the question.

Answer: Yes, I am working for UVOD. Following the deaths of my husband and my father in February and May 1940, for which I held Adolf Hitler ultimately responsible, I decided to work for a foreign government against the National Socialist government of Germany. Since I am from Dresden and my mother is Czech, it seemed logical that this foreign government should be Czech.

Question: How did you go about establishing contact with UVOD?

Prisoner refused to answer the question.

Heydrich interrupted the stenographer. "Perhaps I did not make myself entirely clear, my dear young woman," he said patiently. "I asked you to read out only the salient points. What I meant was that it will save a great deal of time if you omit all mention of when the prisoner refused to answer a question."

The stenographer colored a little. "I'm sorry, sir."

"Now continue."

"Yes, sir."

Question: How did you go about establishing contact with UVOD?

Answer: I made contact with an old friend from university called Friedrich Rose in Dresden, a Sudeten German communist, who put me in contact with a Czech terrorist organization that is part of the Central Leadership of Home Resistance—UVOD. I am part Czech myself and I speak a little Czech, and I was pleased when, having investigated my background, they accepted me into their organization. They said a native German could be very useful to their cause. Which is all that I wanted. After my husband died on a U-boat, all I wanted was for the war to be over. For Germany to be defeated.

Question: What did they ask you to do?

Answer: They asked me to leave Dresden and to undertake a special mission on their behalf. In Berlin.

Question: What was this mission?

Prisoner refused to—

"Sorry, sir . . ."

After a short pause, while she tracked down the transcript with a well-manicured fingernail, the stenographer started reading again.

Answer: At the request of UVOD I joined the Berlin Transport Company in the autumn of 1940 and worked for the BVG director, Herr Julius Vahlen, as his personal secretary and sometime mistress. It was my job to monitor Wehrmacht troop movements through Berlin's Anhalter Station and to report on these movements to my Czech contact in Berlin. This I did for several months.

Question: Who was your contact?

Answer: My contact was a former Czech German Army officer I knew only as Detmar. I didn't know his surname. I would give him a list of the troop movements on a weekly basis. The troop movements were passed on to London, I think. Detmar would give me some more instructions and some money. I was always short of money. Living in Berlin is so much more expensive than Dresden.

Question: What else did Detmar tell you to do?

Answer: At first I had to do very little. Just give him the troop movement reports. But then in December 1940 Detmar asked me to help the Three Kings organization in Berlin to plant a bomb in the station. This was much more important work and much more dangerous, too. First of all I had to obtain a plan of the station building; and then, when the bomb was ready, I had to prime it and put it in a place where it had been decided it would cause the most damage.

Question: Who taught you how to prime a bomb?

Answer: I am a qualified chemist. I studied chemistry at university. I know all about handling difficult materials. It's not difficult to prime a bomb. I'm better at that than I was as a stenographer.

Question: What was the purpose of that bomb?

Answer: The purpose of the bomb at Anhalter Station was to cause panic, to demoralize the population of Berlin; and to disrupt troop movements in and out of the city.

Question: Wasn't the real reason for planting that bomb altogether different? Wasn't the real reason that you had inside information about the train belonging to the Reichsführer-SS Heinrich Himmler, that was due to be leaving the station? And that the bomb was meant to kill him?

Answer: Yes. I admit that this bomb was really designed to assassinate the Reichsführer-SS Heinrich Himmler. I planted the bomb in the left-luggage office in February 1941. This is right by the platform where Himmler's train was to leave from; and, even more important, the office is also beside the place on the platform where Himmler's personal carriage was usually located. The assassination was unsuccessful because the bomb was not powerful enough. It was meant to bring down a joist on top of the train and it didn't.

Question: Then what happened? After the failed assassination?

Answer: With the war in Europe more or less won, it was decided by my controller that troop movements in Germany were of less importance to UVOD; a few months afterward I left the BVG's employment. I was not unhappy about this, as my boss, Herr Vahlen, was besotted with me and something of a nuisance. Thereafter I worked in a series of nightclubs. Especially the Jockey Club, where I was supposed to befriend Germans from the Foreign Ministry in order to sleep with them and get information useful to the Czech cause. I did this. Again I was short of money and sometimes I was obliged to sleep with some of these men in the Foreign Ministry for money so that I could keep myself. I also worked for UVOD as a courier. Then in the summer of 1941 my contact Detmar was replaced by another Czech called Victor Keil. I do not know what happened to Detmar and I don't know Victor's real name. But we were very uncomfortable comrades. Victor was a very demanding man to work for, and I did not like him at all. He was not brave like Detmar. He was fearful and he did not inspire much confidence. He didn't understand my situation at all, how difficult it was for me in Berlin. And we often quarreled. Usually about money.

Question: Tell me what Victor asked you to do for him.

Answer: He gave me a gun and asked me to shoot someone for UVOD. I don't know the man's name. All I had to do was meet the man and shoot him. I didn't want to do this. I was worried the gun would attract too much attention and I'd get caught. So Victor gave me a knife and ordered me to use that instead. Again I refused. I am not a murderer. So Victor murdered the man himself at a railway station in Berlin where I had arranged to meet him. He was a foreign worker—Dutch, I think—and all I had to do was ask him for a light and distract him and Victor would commit the murder. Which he did. But it was horrible. And I said I couldn't ever do something like that again.

Question: What station was this?

Answer: The S-Bahn station at Jannowitz Bridge.

Question: What else did he ask you to do?

Answer: Victor had come into possession of an important list of Czechs who were working for the Germans in Prague. I don't know where he got this list. He was intending to return to Prague with it. Leaving me on my own. Which greatly alarmed me, as I suspected he wasn't planning to come back. He was scared he was being followed and so, temporarily, he gave me the list to look after until he was sure he wasn't being shadowed by the Gestapo. Then Victor and I quarreled, again about money. I was broke and I said that if I was going to stay on in Berlin and do important jobs for UVOD, like help to kill people, I wanted more money to cover my expenses. We'd arranged to meet at the station in Nollendorfplatz, in the blackout, but as he went away there was an accident and Victor was knocked down and killed by a taxi. Which was a disaster.

Question: So what did you do then?

Answer: I was in real shit here. Without a contact in Berlin I had no way of getting the list of traitors to our people in Prague. And no way of getting more money. So I resolved to try to go there myself and make contact with someone from UVOD. But it was dangerous and, of course, I was still very short of money. Not to mention a suitable cover story to get myself down to Prague.

Question: So how did you do this?

Answer: After Victor's fatal accident I had become intimate with a police officer called Bernhard Gunther, who was investigating Victor's death. When I met him I didn't know he was a policeman; but when he turned up at the bar one night I got a bit suspicious and searched his coat pockets in the cloakroom and found his Kripo identification disc. At first I thought he was suspicious of me, so I decided that the best thing to do would be to seem to take him into my confidence. And to throw *myself on his mercy and persuade him that I was simply a joy girl who had made a bad mistake. When I told him this he didn't know that I knew he was a cop.*

Anyway, I told him that a man I'd met in the Jockey Bar whom I knew only as Gustav had hired me to give an envelope to a stranger on a railway station in return for a hundred marks. I told Gunther that I got greedy, which is why the transaction went wrong. And I also told him I had no idea what the envelope contained, as I'd since lost it.

Question: Which station was this?

Answer: The S-Bahn station at Nollendorfplatz.

Question: Tell us about Gustav.

Answer: There never was a Gustav. In fact it was Victor who had given me the envelope. And I didn't mention anything about a list of Czech agents who were working for the Gestapo. I just told him about the envelope and that I'd been looking to make an easy hundred marks. Subsequently Gunther revealed he was a policeman and told me that he believed Victor had been working for the Czechs and that I was in danger. I think it flattered him that he could help me; and I allowed a relationship to develop. An intimate relationship.

Question: Tell me more about your relationship with Bernhard Gunther.

Answer: After Victor was killed, I had no one to help me in Berlin. I thought of returning to Dresden, but then the idea of developing Gunther as an unwitting source of intelligence presented itself to me. I knew he was a senior detective in Kripo. So I began a relationship with him. I told him I loved him and he believed me, I think. It was dangerous, but I felt the possible benefits were worth taking that kind of risk. And when he told me he had been posted to Prague, I saw a way of traveling there in comparative safety and comfort: as Gunther's mistress. This seemed a fantastic opportunity that was too good to ignore.

After all, what better cover could I have for traveling to Prague than as a Kripo commissar's bit on the side? He even paid for my ticket and arranged my visa at the Alex. In all respects he was very kind to me.

Question: Did Commissar Gunther know of your involvement with UVOD?

Answer: No, of course not. He suspected nothing, except perhaps that I had been a whore. Or very stupid. Or both. Either that or he didn't care to ask very much. Perhaps it was a bit of both. He was in love with me and he liked sleeping with me. And, of course, also he was too busy with his own work.

Question: Did he talk about his work?

Answer: No. It was very hard to get any information out of him. He said it was safer for me that way. It took me a while to find out that he was working for General Heydrich and that he was coming to Prague to work at Heydrich's country house. But he didn't say what he was doing there.

Question: What happened when you arrived in Prague?

Answer: We arrived in Prague and stayed at the Imperial Hotel. We spent the first day together. For most of the next day Gunther was away on official business. He turned up at night to sleep with me. Which suited me very well, as I had the rest of the time to myself. I had heard Detmar talk about what to do if he and I ever lost contact. The places to go for help. There was a man in Prague, a UVOD agent called Radek. I should go to these places myself and try to make contact with this man. And I decided to go to these places and ask around for Radek. It was taking a risk, but what choice did I have?

Question: What were these places you went to?

Answer: Elektra. It's a café on Richard Wagner Street, next to the National Museum. And Ca d'Oro, a beer restaurant on Národní třída, in the same building as the Riunione Adriatica di Sicurtà. Detmar had given me some instructions in how to go *about this: I should take a red rose wrapped in an old copy of Přítomnost and leave it on the table while I ordered something. Přítomnost is Presence, the weekly review that Masaryk helped to found. I could buy a copy on the black market quite easily. That's what happened. And, having made contact with Radek in the Elektra—I do not know his last name—I handed over the list of traitors.*

Question: Was it Radek who came up with the plan to kill General Heydrich this morning?

Answer: No, it was someone else Radek introduced me to. I'd told them about Gunther and how he was working at the Lower Castle in Panenské-Břežany. How a car from Gestapo HQ with just a driver would come and pick him up and drive him there. A plan was quickly conceived—the opportunity appeared too good to miss. Two men from UVOD would hijack Gunther's SS car and sit on the floor behind the seats so that they might get into the grounds of the castle, walk in, and shoot everyone and anyone they could. Hopefully, Heydrich would be one of these casualties.

Question: By which time you would be safely on a train back to Berlin?

Answer: Yes. That was the plan.

Question: And Gunther?

Answer: He was also to be shot by the two UVOD assassins. But the plan went up in smoke when Gunther's car from Peček Palace was canceled and the poor fool had to walk to the castle and requisition a car from there. After that, there seemed little or no choice but to get on the train as arranged. I'd done all I could. What will happen to me, please?

"That's a very good question," said Heydrich.

He turned to me.

"And at the present moment in time, as you can see for

yourself, things are not looking so good for your lady friend. But I think it answers your earlier remark, Gunther: that she hadn't done anything. Now you know. She tried to murder Himmler. She planned to murder me, and as many of my guests as possible. And she planned to murder you. That's quite an achievement. It looks as if she played you for a fool, wouldn't you say?"

I didn't say anything.

"It's fortunate for you I'm still feeling grateful that you helped us catch Paul Thümmel, otherwise you yourself might now be facing what undoubtedly lies ahead of this deeply misguided young woman."

While the stenographer had been reading, Arianne had recovered consciousness and was at least alive. But she had fainted again, and while I could see no way of saving her from execution, or at best a concentration camp, I did think there was a way of preserving her from further suffering on the water bascule. Much of what I'd heard made sense to me, but it was obvious that she was still concealing things from her torturers; it was equally obvious that I was now in a position to tell Heydrich exactly what I knew and thus save Arianne from herself, even if that meant putting my own head in the Gestapo's lunette.

It was clear that it was I who'd been betrayed by her, and yet as I started speaking, it somehow felt as if it were Arianne who had been betrayed by me.

I guess it made it easier that I despised myself so much, not for what was said now but for what hadn't been said before—in Belorussia, and immediately afterward. I hardly counted the short lecture I had given Heydrich on my first day at the Lower Castle. I had tried to believe that in spite of all that I had seen and done in the East I was a person like her, with a sense of moral purpose and values. As a matter of fact I had no such qualities; and I didn't blame her in the least for wanting to kill me. In Arianne's eyes, I deserved to be shot, like everyone wearing an SS or SD uniform, and I couldn't argue with that. Whatever happened now or in the future, I had it coming to me. We all did. But if my plan was going to work—if I was to prevent her from further suffering—I had to make certain Heydrich understood what I said in the only way he could understand it: not out of pity for Arianne but out of loathing and contempt for her, and a desire for revenge. A sense of my true feelings for Arianne would only have caused her more harm. And for her sake I had to kill any love I had for her, and kill it quickly, too. I had to harden my heart until it was made of iron. Like a true Nazi.

I FISHED OUT MY CIGARETTES and lit one to give myself some puff for what I was about to do. It wasn't easy with my hands manacled to a chain. Nothing about what I was doing was easy. I blew some smoke at the ceiling for nonchalant effect and leaned back against the wall. How much Arianne heard of what I said next, I don't know. None of it, I hope.

"It looks like I've been had, all right." I sighed. "Well, it wouldn't be the first time a fellow like me got given the slow trot around the Tiergarten by a pretty girl. Only it's been a while since I was dummied as well as she managed it. Christ, at my age I should know better, of course, but since I stopped believing in Santa Claus, I don't get many presents that are as nicely wrapped as this little half silk." I shrugged. "I'm not making excuses, General. That's just how it is for a man who likes to think he's still in the game. And I don't sleep so well on my own anymore. The same as Captain Kuttner. She was my version of Veronal. A lot easier to swallow. But probably just as lethal."

I allowed myself a wry smile.

"So she tried to send me upstairs, did she? Bitch. And after all I tried to do for her. That really sticks a hole in my sock. Go ahead and wash her hair again, Sergeant, why don't you? I'm all through pulling my chain about it. Hell, now I can see why she was jumpy when she got out of bed this morning. I thought she was sad because she had to go back to Berlin. Because we were to be parted. What a chump I've been. She's quite a liar, I'll say that for her. It strikes me that you fellows have got your work cut out there, with or without the water board. You could send her to the guillotine and the head on that little cunt would still talk its way out of the basket. And, by the way, make sure you send me a ticket. That's one party I wouldn't want to miss. Who knows? Maybe I can help put her there myself. Because you know, it strikes me that the ration is short on that story of hers, and that maybe I can make up the weight. In fact, it would be my pleasure."

Heydrich gave me a narrow-eyed look, as if he were trying to estimate the distance between what I was saying and what he believed. It was like facing a suspicious parent and, moreover, one who was such a practiced liar himself that he knew precisely what to look for in establishing what was true and what was not. An art expert with a picture of uncertain provenance could not have been more thorough in the way he studied the brushwork and checked the signature on the contrary picture I had painted for him.

"Such as?" he said coldly.

"Such as Victor Keil's real name was Franz Koci." I flicked my cigarette into the bathwater as if I hardly cared that Arianne's head might yet be ducked in it. "I know that because I was the cop who investigated his death; and at the special invitation of your friend Colonel Schellenberg. He was found dead in Berlin's Kleist Park. After the collision she mentioned, with the taxi on Nollendorf-platz, he must have staggered down Maasenstrasse. We found him under a big red rhododendron bush with the knife he'd used on the Dutchman, Geert Vranken, still in his possession.

"I've been thinking about the letter I received from Vranken's father, in the Netherlands. And how Paul Thümmel was the char-acter reference Geert gave the police when he was a potential suspect in the S-Bahn murders. Well, because Thümmel had had some sort of relationship with Vranken's sister, he must have found out from her, I suppose, that Vranken was working on Berlin's railways. That must have been the reason the Abwehr asked to see the files on the S-Bahn murders, which they did, and in particular the interviews with all the foreign workers. The official excuse was that they were on the lookout for spies, but in reality Thümmel must have been on the lookout for Geert Vranken. He was the only person in Germany who could connect him with his Czech controller in The Hague. And when he saw Vranken's statement, which mentions knowing a German officer who might vouch for him, Thümmel must have panicked. Most likely Vranken was killed by Franz Koci at Paul Thümmel's specific request."

Heydrich was nodding now. "Yes, that makes sense, I suppose."

"Either he radioed the request to UVOD here in Prague or, as seems more likely, he told Arianne. Probably she was the cutout between Thümmel and Franz Koci, whom she knew better as Victor Keil."

Heydrich continued nodding. This was a good sign. But an even better one was to come.

"Horst." Heydrich waved at Colonel Böhme. "Release him."

A little reluctantly—he still hadn't forgiven me for being a better detective than he was—Böhme produced a key from the pocket of his riding breeches and unlocked my manacles.

I rubbed my wrists and muttered a thank-you. I didn't say anything about Arianne, who remained strapped to the bascule balanced over the bath of water. It was crucial that Heydrich believe that his revelation about her part in the plot to kill me meant I was now indifferent to her immediate fate; and it was equally crucial that my story was both plausible and authoritative, even though a lot of it was based on sheer guesswork, so that it would seem there was little real point in torturing Arianne anymore; at least for the present.

To my enormous relief he now came to this conclusion.

"Take the woman back to her cell," he told Sergeant Soppa.

"Yes, sir."

Soppa and the other man laid the bascule down on the wet floor and started to unstrap Arianne. She groaned slightly as the buckles were released, but it was hard to tell if her heavily bruised eyes were open, so I had no way of knowing if she saw me.

Either way, it was certainly the last time I ever saw her.

"Let's continue this conversation in your office upstairs, Horst," said Heydrich. "Gunther?" Now he was ushering me out of the interrogation cell, ahead of him.

I walked toward the door. My heart was on the floor alongside Arianne's bedraggled, half-drowned body, twisting over and over like a dying trout.

Heydrich held my arm for a moment and then smiled a sarcastic smile. "What? No fond good-byes for your poor lover? No last words?"

I didn't turn around to look back at her. If I had, he'd have seen the truth in my face. Instead I met Heydrich's chilly, wolf blue eyes, turned a deep sigh into a wry laugh, and shook my head silently.

"To hell with her," I said.

It was, I thought, the only place Arianne and I were ever again likely to meet up with each other.

IN A LARGE OFFICE on an upper floor of the Peček Palace, Heydrich told an orderly to bring us schnapps.

"I think we all need one after that ordeal, don't you, gentlemen?"

I couldn't argue with this. I was desperate for a drink to put a little iron in my soul.

A bottle arrived. A proper one containing real liver glue, but none of the deer or elk blood that Germans sometimes said it contained. That was just a story like the one I was getting ready to tell Heydrich and Böhme. I drank a glassful of the stuff. It was ice-cold, the way it's supposed to be. But I was colder. Nothing's been invented that's as cold as how I felt at that moment.

I went and sat on the windowsill and looked out at the old medieval city of Prague. Somewhere, under one of those dark, ancient roofs, was a fatal creature of death and destruction that was exactly like my own twin brother. Indeed, if the Golem had looked in my eye at what was elusively called the soul, he might well have concluded that I was a man to be shunned, just as people in the street below avoided the Peček Palace front door like it was a Jaffa pesthouse. Given the wicked, monstrous, inhuman events that I'd just witnessed in the basement, they weren't so far off the mark.

Unbidden, I fetched the bottle and poured another glass of the embalming fluid that helps make Germans like me more German than before, and I lit a cigarette, half hoping that it might set fire to my insides and turn me to ashes like everything else that in due course was almost certain to be turned into ashes.

"I expect you're wondering how we got onto her," said Heydrich.

"No, but I would have got around to it before long."

"The list of Czechs working for the Gestapo here in Prague was hardly complete. One of the people Arianne Tauber approached in that other café she mentioned—I can't remember what it was called—he was ours."

"The Ca d'Oro," said Böhme. "It was the Ca d'Oro, sir. The headwaiter is a French fascist who's been working for the Gestapo since the Spanish Civil War. As soon as he saw her sitting there with the flower inside the magazine, he contacted us."

"After that," added Heydrich, "it was only a question of having her followed around the clock. She led us to Radek, about whom Böhme already had his suspicions. Didn't you, Horst?"

"That's right, sir."

Böhme grinned and, taking the bottle from my windowsill, he refilled my glass again and helped the general and then himself.

"That's why your car didn't turn up this morning, Gunther. We arrested the two assassins around the corner from your hotel. And the girl when she arrived at the railway station a little later on. We had hoped there would be someone there from UVOD to see her off, but there wasn't, so we picked her up and put her in the bag with the two killers." He shrugged. "Not that I think there was ever much danger of either one of you being killed. It was a pretty desperate, spur-of-the-moment sort of plan. And chances are, they'd have been shot by the sentries at the Lower Castle before they got very far."

"All in all," said Heydrich, smugly, "it's been an excellent day's work. We have the traitor. We have some more terrorists. It can be only a matter of time before we catch up with Václav Morávek."

"Yes, congratulations, sir," said Böhme, toasting him. "Tell me, what are your orders regarding Arianne Tauber? Do you want her questioned again?"

Heydrich was still thinking this over when I said, "I expect I can fill in the rest of the gaps in her story for you."

"Yes, why don't you tell us again how you met," said Heydrich. "In detail."

I gave him the whole story, more or less; from the circumstances in which I had first met her at Nollendorfplatz Station to my own middle-aged infatuation; there seemed little point in hiding anything other than my true motive for telling him.

"Paul Thümmel was obviously this fellow Gustav she told me about back in Berlin. She might have denied downstairs he exists, but there can be no doubt about that now. I expect that's the one thing she was keeping back from Sergeant Soppa. He was right about that. I also expect that when Thümmel sees her again, he'll fold like a picnic table. Especially when he sees the state you've left her in."

I lit a cigarette and swung my leg carelessly.

"As far as I can gather, it was Paul Thümmel who gave her the list of agents to pass on to Franz Koci. As a major in the Abwehr, he was well placed to know exactly who they were. But when she met up to hand them over to Franz Koci, they quarreled about money, just as she said, and he must have thought she was holding out on him. Maybe she was, too. I expect he demanded that she give him the list and when she wouldn't—at least not until her complaints had been addressed—he got rough with her and decided to search her underwear.

"That was when I saw her for the first time. I assumed, wrongly, that he was attempting to rape her. Or worse. As you know, there's been a lot of that in the blackout this summer. Women attacked and murdered in and around railway stations. I guess it was still on my mind a lot. So naturally I went to her assistance."

"Very gallant of you, I'm sure," said Heydrich.

"Koci and I fought but he got away and ran into the blackout. The next day I was looking at his dead body under a bush in Kleist Park."

"At the request of Walter Schellenberg," said Heydrich.

"That's right. The Berlin Gestapo guessed he was a Czech agent, but they had no idea how he'd met his death. Who killed him, or why. I agreed to help. And soon enough I was able to connect Franz Koci with Geert Vranken."

"But you decided to leave the girl out of it."

I nodded.

"So you could take advantage of her, I suppose."

It hadn't been like that; but it was no good saying that I had honestly believed her to be more innocent than she turned out to be. I needed to give Heydrich the kind of cold and clinical reason he could understand. The kind of reason he would have acted upon himself, no doubt.

"Yes. That's true. I wanted to fuck her. I had the idea she was just a dupe, but that was always me. Of course as soon as I started sleeping with her, I stopped seeing what was right under my nose. That she was in it all the way up to her pretty neck. But it was such a pretty neck."

"The rest of her is not bad, either," said Böhme.

"About that neck, Gunther," said Heydrich. "I won't be able to save it. You know that, don't you? The fact that she was involved in a plan to kill me, well, that's of no real consequence. But an attempt to kill Himmler is a different story. The Reichsführer takes any assault on his personal safety rather more personally than I do."

I shrugged as if I cared nothing now for what happened to her. And I shrugged because I knew Heydrich was right. Nothing could save Arianne now. Not even Heydrich.

"The real question here is what happens to you, Gunther. In many ways you're a useful fellow to have around. Like a bent coat hanger in a toolbox, you're not something that was ever designed for a specific job, but you do manage to come in useful sometimes. Yes, you're an excellent detective. Tenacious. Single-minded. And in some ways you'd have done a good job as a bodyguard. But you're also independent, and that's what makes you dangerous. You have standards you try to live up to, but they're your standards, which means that ultimately you're unreliable. Now that I'm where I am in the scheme of things, I can't tolerate that. I had hoped I might be able to bend you to my will and use you when I could. Like that coat hanger. But I can see now I was wrong. Yes, it's difficult to turn a woman over to the Gestapo, especially a good-looking woman like Arianne Tauber. Some can do it and some can't, and you're just the type who can't. So I have no further use for you. You've become an unfortunate liability, Gunther."

This sounded like the best thing he'd ever said to me, but I was through opening my mouth like that for a long while. Perhaps permanently. He hadn't yet finished telling me my own fate.

"You will return to your desk in Kripo and leave Germany's destiny in the hands of men like me, who truly understand what that means."

He smiled his paper-knife smile and toasted me silently.

I toasted him back but only because, perhaps for the last time, I was hoping to point out a long hair in his chicken soup.

"And the attempt on your life, sir? The poisoning, at Rastenburg? I accept that you no longer wish to have me act as your bodyguard. But am I to take it that you no longer wish me to investigate the recent attempt to kill you?"

He stared at me for a moment, and with a quiet surge of pleasure, I realized he had forgotten all about this incident.

"There never was such an attempt," he said defiantly. "I made it up so that I might have a plausible reason to invite you to Prague with the rest of them."

I nodded meekly, a little surprised that he'd admitted such a thing, and wondered where the actual truth was to be found: if there really had been an attempt to poison Heydrich at Rastenburg, after all.

"Besides, as the most powerful man in Bohemia and Moravia, I think I'm quite safe here, wouldn't you agree, Horst?"

So that clinched it for me; he *was* lying.

Böhme smiled an obsequious smile. "Absolutely, sir. You have Prague's SS and SD at your immediate disposal, not to mention the Gestapo and the German Army."

"You see?" crowed Heydrich. "I have nothing to worry about.

Especially not in Prague. The day the Czechs try to kill me—really try to kill me, not that half-baked attempt we had today, although you mark my words, that will have its own repercussions—the day they try to kill me will be the very worst day in the history of this country and will make the defenestrations of Prague look like a childish prank. Isn't that right, Horst?"

"Yes, sir. In a long line of crazy Czech ideas, that would be the craziest idea of all."

I had my doubts about that. I hadn't been in Bohemia for very long, but from what little I knew about the country, it seemed only appropriate that the idea of the Bohemian—a type of fellow not easily classified and who never acted in a conventional or predictable way—had got started in Prague. In Prague, throwing someone out of a window *was* just a childish prank. A bit of harmless fun. But I didn't expect a Roman Catholic German from Halle an der Saale to understand this. And if I really had been as single-minded and independent as Heydrich said I was, I would probably have told him he was wrong: murder—even political assassination—is rarely ever committed by people who are anything else but crazy, and over the centuries, one way or another, a lot of crazy things had happened in Prague.

So I nodded and told Heydrich he was right when I knew he wasn't.

And that is what makes anyone dangerous.

I MOVED BACK TO the Imperial Hotel and waited for my Berlin rail warrant to arrive. Heydrich liked to keep most people waiting, and I waited for several days. So I saw the sights and tried not to think about what might be happening to Arianne. But of course that was impossible. I preferred to believe that she hadn't actually condoned my murder but that she had felt obliged to go along with it as part of the general plan to kill Heydrich; after all, when you're shooting Germans, it's hard to know who is a Nazi and who isn't. It's a dilemma I understood very well.

Finally my travel papers came through, and on my last night in Prague I remembered my ticket for the Circus Krone, and decided to go along.

It was a cold autumn evening with a clear sky and a full moon, and people were already wearing their warmest winter coats. I sat well away from the rest of my SS colleagues but had a good view of all of them in the front-row seats, and I confess I paid more attention to Mr. and Mrs. Heydrich and to Mr. and Mrs. Frank than I did to the clowns and the animals.

I hadn't seen Lina Heydrich before. She was handsome rather than beautiful. She wore black, with a thick fur stole and a little black pillbox hat. Mrs. Frank wore a wool overcoat with wide lapels and a brown fedora. The two wives sat beside each other and next to them sat their husbands, who were wearing civilian clothes, like everyone else in the SD and Gestapo who was at the circus that night. Frank wore a plain gabardine coat with a white shirt and a patterned silk tie. Heydrich wore a thick double-breasted overcoat and held a black trilby on his lap. He also wore a pair of horn-rimmed glasses that I'd never seen on him before.

Like anyone else, these four marveled at the trapeze and laughed at the clowns and they appeared to enjoy themselves. Like anyone else. That was what struck me most of all. Out of uniform, Heydrich and Frank looked just like anyone else, although even as they sat in their front-row seats, a security crackdown was already under way in the city. Later on, I learned that the mayor of Prague, Otakar Klapka, had been executed, and on the very same day that Arianne was arrested. Hundreds of UVOD collaborators were being rounded up and buildings just across the city were covered with posters listing the names of many others who had been sentenced to death. You wouldn't have known any of that if you'd watched Heydrich at the circus, shaking with laughter as three clowns, behaving like the sort of simpletons the Nazis would probably have murdered for reasons of racial purity fell off chairs and soaked each other with buckets full of water.

Two days later, Heydrich announced that the deportation of all the Jews in the protectorate—some ninety thousand of them—was to begin at the end of the year. To where, he didn't say. Nobody did. Me, I had a pretty good idea, but by then I was back in Berlin.

15

It felt good to be in Berlin again. At least it felt good for an hour or two. Soon after arriving back at my apartment in Fasanenstrasse I discovered to my disappointment that the two Fridmann sisters from downstairs had been deported to some shithole in Poland. Behnke, the block warden, who knew these things, insisted that it was a nice town called Litzmannstadt—formerly known as Lodz—and that they'd be happier there "living with their own," instead of with "decent Germans." I told him I had my doubts about this but Behnke didn't want to hear them. He was more interested in learning Russian so that he would be able to speak to his peasants when eventually he met them. He really thought he was going to get some of that living space in Russia and Belorussia that Goebbels was forever ranting about. I had my doubts about that, too.

It grew bitter. Wind tore the leaves off the trees and hurried them east in their thousands. The water on the Spree looked like corrugated iron. The cold felt like barbed wire. There was one thing to be done before the snows arrived, a sentimental gesture that meant nothing to anyone I had ever met; but I suppose I wanted to feel better about myself. I organized the release of Geert Vranken's remains from Berlin's Charité Hospital and paid for them to be buried in a zinc-lined wooden crate—just in case, after the war, his family wanted to dig it up and take his remains home to the Netherlands.

There was one other person at the funeral: Werner Sachse from the Gestapo. With his black leather coat, black hat, and black tie, he looked like a proper mourner. The short service was conducted by the pastor of St. John's Church in Plotzensee, and when it was over Sachse told me he admired the thought if not the practice.

"Where would we be if policemen paid for every foreign worker who gets killed in an accident?" he asked.

"It wasn't an accident," I reminded him.

Sachse shrugged as if the correction I'd offered hardly mattered. The fact remained that the dead man wasn't German and therefore his death was of little or no account.

For a moment I wondered if telling him why I was doing it was a mistake; then I told him anyway.

"I'm doing it so that somewhere, someone who isn't German will have a better opinion of us than we deserve."

Sachse pretended to be surprised about that, but before we parted we shook hands, so I knew he wasn't.

16

Commissioner Friedrich-Wilhelm Lüdtke was known as Stop-gap Lüdtke on account of his name and because no one had expected him to survive in the job because he wasn't a Party member. But he did what he was told, and when someone told him to put me on night duty, that's what he did. Not that I minded very much. Being on the night shift kept me out of sight and out of mind. At least it did until early on the morning of Monday, November 17. I mention the murder I investigated that night only because it was Heydrich himself who had me taken off the case. I expect he was worried that I might actually solve it.

It was at about five o'clock in the morning when I got the telephone call from Criminal Inspector Heimenz at the police station in Grunewald. There had been a murder at one of those fancy modern villas in Heerstrasse. He wouldn't say who it was on the telephone; all I knew was that it was someone famous.

One of the good things about being on the night shift was that I had access to a car, so I was at the address in less than half an hour. And it was easy to find. Several police cars were parked outside, not to mention a huge silver Rolls-Royce. As soon as I stepped through the elegantly modern front door I guessed whose house it was. But I hardly expected that he was also the victim.

General Ernst Udet was one of the most famous men in

Germany. At the age of just twenty-two he had survived the Great War as Germany's highest-scoring air ace. Only Manfred von Richthofen had more victories than he did. After the war he'd made several movies with Leni Riefenstahl and was a stunt flier in Hollywood. The house was full of film posters, flying cups, and photographs of airplanes. A polished wooden aircraft propeller hung on one wall, and it was several minutes before I could tear myself from all of Udet's memorabilia to look at his dead body. He wasn't very tall, but then you don't need to be tall to fly airplanes, especially when these are experimental: Udet was the director-general of the Luftwaffe's developmental wing. He was also a close friend of Hermann Göring. Or at least, he had been a close friend until someone shot him.

The body was naked. It lay in the middle of an enormous double bed, and surrounded by empty brandy bottles, most of them good-quality French brands. There was a neat hole in his forehead and a hammerless Sauer .38 in his right hand. For a small man—he couldn't have been more than one-sixty in height—he had an enormous penis. But it wasn't any of these details that drew the eyes. Not even the telephone line that was coiled around one of his muscular arms like a Jew's tefillin. It was what was written on the headboard in red lipstick that tugged at my eyeballs and made me think I had walked in on a major scandal.

REICHSMARSHAL, WHY HAVE YOU FORSAKEN ME?

I suppose the choice of words was meant to make one think of Jesus Christ, nailed to the cross, and abandoned by God the Father. But that wasn't what I thought of; it wasn't what Inspector Heimenz thought of, either.

"This is one homicide I'm happy to leave to you boys at the Alex," he said.

"Thanks. Let me tell you, he looks how I feel."

"Cut and dried, isn't it?"

"So *you* take the case."

"Not me. I want to sleep at night."

"You're in the wrong job for that."

"The Grunewald is not like the rest of Berlin. This is a quiet district."

"So I see. Who found the body?"

"The girlfriend. Name of Inge Bleyle. She claims they were on the telephone when she heard the shot. So she drove straight over here in that modest little car you saw parked outside and found him dead."

"That Rolls is hers?"

"So it would seem. Apparently Herr Udet had been drinking heavily all week."

"From the look of things, Martell and Rémy Martin are going to be inconsolable."

"It seems that he and the Air Ministry had had their differences concerning the success of the air war against the British."

"You mean the lack of it, don't you?"

"I know what I meant to say. Perhaps you'd better speak to Fräulein Bleyle yourself, sir."

"Perhaps I had. Where is she now?"

"In the drawing room."

I followed him downstairs.

"Hell of a place, isn't it, sir?"

"Yes."

"Hard to imagine anyone who owned a place like this shooting himself."

"Is that what you think happened?"

"Well, yes. The gun was in his hand."

I stopped on the stairs and pointed to one of the many photographs covering the wall: Ernst Udet and the actor Bela Lugosi, posing on a California tennis court.

"Looks to me as if Ernst Udet was a lefty," I said.

"So?"

"The gun was in his right hand. I don't know about you, but if I were going to shoot myself—and, believe me, I've considered it, seriously, these past few months—I'd probably hold the gun in my stronger hand."

"But the words written on the headboard, sir. Surely that was meant to be some sort of suicide message."

"I'm only sure that's what it's meant to look like. Whether it is or not, we'll only know when a doctor gets him on the slab. You'd expect a powder burn on the skin if he really did press the gun to his forehead, and I didn't see one, that's all."

The inspector nodded. He was a small man with small hands and a small way about him.

"Like I said, this is one homicide I'm glad to leave to the Alex."

Inge Bleyle had stopped crying. She was about thirty-five years old, dark, tall—much taller than Ernst Udet—and good-looking in an understated way. She was wearing her fur coat and there was a drink in one hand and a cigarette in the other, neither of which seemed to have received much of her attention since coming her way.

I found an ashtray, held it under her cigarette, and tapped the back of her hand. She looked up, smiled ruefully, and then put out the cigarette in the ashtray while I continued holding it.

"I'm Commissar Gunther. From the Alex. Feel like talking?"

She shrugged. "I guess so. I guess I have to, right? I mean, I found him, and I made the call, so someone has to start the ball rolling."

"I believe you told the other detective that you were on the telephone with Herr Udet when the shot was fired. Is that correct?"

She nodded.

"What had you been talking about?"

"When I first got to know him, well before the war, Ernst Udet was the life and soul of the party. Everyone liked him. He was a real gentleman. Kind, generous, impeccably well mannered. But you couldn't imagine he was even related to the Ernst Udet of recent memory. He drank, he was short-tempered, he was rude. He'd always drunk a lot. Half of those Great War pilots drank just to go up in those planes. But he always seemed like he could handle the drink. But lately he started drinking even more than usual. Mostly he drank because he was unhappy. Very unhappy. I'd left him because of his drinking, you see. And he wanted me back. And I didn't want to come back because it was obvious that he was still drinking. As you have no doubt seen for yourself. It looks like a one-man house party in there."

"Why was he drinking? Any particular reason? I mean, before you left him."

"Yes, I understand. He was drinking because of what was happening at the Air Ministry. That Jew Erhard Milch was trying to undermine Ernst. All of the people in his department had been fired, and Ernst took that very personally."

"Why were they fired?"

"Because that bastard Göring didn't have the guts to fire Ernst. He figured that if he fired all of Ernst's people, then Ernst's sense of honor would compel him to resign. He blamed Ernst for the failure of our air attacks on Britain. That's what he said to Hitler, to save his own skin. Of course it wasn't true, not a damned word of it, but Hitler believed him anyway. But that was just one reason he was depressed."

I groaned inside. After Prague I needed this case like I needed a pair of silk stockings of the kind Inge Bleyle was wearing on her lovely legs.

"And another reason?"

She shrugged. Suddenly she was looking evasive, as if it had dawned on her that she was talking to a cop.

"What with the war in Russia, well, that was getting him

down, too. Yes, he was depressed and drinking too much. Only . . . well, he wasn't long back from a clinic in Bühlerhöhe. They'd dried him out. He did that for me, you know. Because he wanted me back and I'd made that a condition of our getting back together. But I wanted to wait a little, see? Just to see if it took—the cure." She sipped her whiskey and grimaced. "I don't like whiskey."

"In this house? That's not unusual." I took the glass and put it on the table between us.

"Then, a couple of days ago, something happened to him. I don't know what, exactly. Ploch, his chief of staff at the ministry until Milch had him fired, had just returned from Kiev. He went to see Ernst and told him something. Something awful. Ernst wouldn't say what it was, just that it was something happening in the East, in Russia, and that no one would ever believe it."

I nodded. You didn't have to be a detective to know what Ploch had probably told him. And it wasn't anything to do with airplanes.

"Because of that, Ernst had telephoned Göring to ask him about it, and they'd argued. Badly. And Ernst threatened to tell someone at the American embassy what Ploch had told him."

"He said that?"

"Yes. He had a lot of American friends, you see? Ernst was very popular. Especially with the ladies. The late ambassador's daughter—I mean the American ambassador's daughter, Martha Dodds, she was a very close friend. Perhaps more than just a friend. I don't know."

She paused.

"And he told you all of this on the telephone?"

"Yes. We were talking. Ernst was crying some of the time. Begging me to come and see him. One thing I do remember him saying. It was that he could no longer believe in Germany; that Germany was a wicked country and deserved to lose the war."

The more I heard about Ernst Udet, the more I started to like him. But Inge Bleyle felt obliged to disagree; anyone would have felt the same.

"I didn't like it that he was saying such things. I mean, that kind of talk is not good, Commissar, even if you are a decorated hero like Ernst. I mean, you hear stories about the Gestapo. People being arrested for unpatriotic talk. I told Ernst to be quiet and to keep his mouth shut in case he got us both into trouble. Him for saying such things and me for listening to them without hanging up. That's what you're supposed to do when you hear those things. You understand, the only reason I stayed on the line was that I was concerned for his state of mind."

I nodded. "I understand."

"Then I heard the shot."

"Had he talked about killing himself?"

"Well, no. Not in so many words."

"Did you hear anything else? Voices, perhaps? Footsteps? A door closing?"

"No. I put the telephone down and drove straight over here. I live only a short distance away, in the West End. When I got here all the lights were on. And I still had my key, so I let myself in. I shouted his name a couple of times, and then went upstairs and found him dead, as you saw. I came back downstairs and used the telephone in the study—it's a different line—to call the police. I didn't want to touch the one in his hand. That was an hour ago. I've been here ever since."

"Do you think he killed himself?"

She opened her mouth to say something; checked herself and said: "It certainly looks that way, doesn't it?"

Sensible girl. No wonder she was driving a Rolls-Royce. They don't hand those cars out to just anyone.

After that, two fellows from the Air Ministry showed up:

Colonel Max Pendele, who was Udet's adjutant, and another offi-cer. That was at eight a.m. Then someone from the Ministry of the Interior turned up as well. That was at nine.

At about eleven o'clock I drove back to the Alex to type out my report.

After I'd done this, Lüdtke asked me to come up to his office, and when I got there, he told me I was off the case.

I didn't ask why. By then I hardly needed to. It was plain that someone important didn't want me asking any awkward questions, and there were plenty that could have been asked about the death of Ernst Udet; only after Heydrich's death did I learn that it had been he who told Lüdtke to take me off the case.

Five days later they buried Udet. It was a state funeral. They carried him out of the Air Ministry in a casket covered with a Nazi flag, placed him on a gun carriage, and then proceeded up to Invali-den Cemetery, where they buried him close to his old pal the Baron von Richthofen. Of course, state funerals were for heroes, not sui-cides or enemies of the state, but that was okay, because the story released by the authorities—and this was the reason behind my removal, since of course I knew different—was that Udet had been killed testing an experimental fighter plane.

Hermann Göring delivered a eulogy; the nine-centimeter flak gun in the Tiergarten fired a salute that had many Berliners run-ning for an air-raid shelter, thinking that the RAF was back in our skies. A few days later they were back, although not to drop any bombs.

It was as well I was off the case. Being a detective has made me unreasonably suspicious. I see connections and conspiracies where other people see only the need to look the other way and keep their suspicions to themselves. Another air ace, Werner Mölders, was killed flying back to Germany for Udet's funeral, from the Crimea; and around the Alex there were whispers that there was a lot more to his death—the Heinkel on which he was a passenger crashed as it tried to land in Breslau—than had been allowed to meet the eye.

Certainly the British thought so, for the RAF dropped leaflets over Germany alleging that, like Ernst Udet, Werner Mölders had been opposed to the Nazi regime. And that he had been murdered.

Six days later, Mölders was also given a state funeral, and he was buried alongside his great friend and confidant Ernst Udet in the Invaliden Cemetery.

In retrospect, both of those two state funerals felt like dress rehearsals for what followed six months later in June 1942.

IT WAS SIX A.M. I was on my way home after a night at the Alex when I received a telephone call to go and see Arthur Nebe in his office at RSHA headquarters in Prinz-Albrecht-Strasse. It was a summons I had been dreading. I knew of the attempt on Heydrich's life: on May 27, a group of Czech terrorists had thrown a grenade into his open car as it drove through the streets of Prague. Heydrich had been seriously injured, but as far as anyone knew, he was making a strong recovery. It was only what you might have expected of such a brave hero; at least that's what the newspapers said.

Nebe had already dispatched two senior detectives from the Alex—Horst Kopkow and Dr. Bernhard Wehner—to Prague, to help with the investigation. The assailants were still at large and throughout Bohemia and Moravia a huge security operation was under way to catch them; everyone in Kripo—myself included—believed they would soon be arrested.

Nebe, now back in Berlin after murdering tens of thousands of Jews in Belorussia, looked wearier than usual. But it looked as if these efforts had been appreciated: there were even more decorations on his tunic than I remembered, and in this respect at least he was beginning to resemble a South American generalissimo. His long nose had turned a little purple, no doubt a result of the heavy drinking that was required to complete our historic German tasks, and there were bags under his eyes; he was smoking almost continuously and there were patches of severe eczema on the backs of his hands. The hair on his head was almost silver now, but his eyebrows remained dark and overgrown, like the forest of briars in *The Sleeping Beauty*, shielding the enchanted castle that was his soul from the discovery of the outside world.

He came straight to the point.

"Heydrich died at four thirty this morning."

"He picked a nice day for it."

Nebe permitted himself a wry smile.

"Is that all you've got to say?"

"Yes. I warned him to be more careful. But he wasn't the careful type, I guess."

"I'm flying to Prague in an hour's time. I'll be part of an SS honor guard that will bring his body home to Berlin."

"I think you'll find he was born in Halle, Arthur."

"While I am there, I shall also be reviewing progress in the investigation. As a matter of fact, there isn't any progress. It's fucking chaos down there. Chaos of catastrophic proportions. The local Gestapo is arresting everyone."

"That's one way of catching the murderers, I suppose."

"I need my own man. Someone whose abilities I respect. That's why you're coming with me, Bernie. To find some truth."

"Truth? You're not asking for much, are you?"

"We can argue about it in the car on the way to the airport. Anything you need while you're there, you can buy."

We drove straight to Tempelhof Airport, where a Heinkel was already fueled and waiting for us. We climbed aboard and took off immediately. Viewed from the air, Berlin still looked good. Flying over it was probably the best way to see the city, which looked green and natural, a decent place to live, like the old Berlin of my youth. From up there, you couldn't see the corruption and the savagery.

"You'll observe what's going on. Nothing more than that. Observe and report directly to me."

"Bernhard Wehner won't like that. As a commissioner he outranks me, Arthur. From the way he behaves, I think he outranks Hermann Göring."

"Wehner's not a detective, he's a bureaucrat. Not to mention a cunt."

"Is he in charge?"

"No. Frank thinks he's in overall charge. And so does Daluege. The criminal inquiry is being handled by Heinz Pannwitz."

"I'm beginning to understand the problem. What's Dummi doing there?"

Kurt "Dummi" Daluege was the chief of Germany's uniformed regular police.

"Apparently he was in Prague for medical treatment." Nebe grinned. "Not a well man, it seems."

"What's wrong with him?"

"Nothing trivial, I hope."

"Heinz Pannwitz. I don't know him."

"He's a Berliner, like you and me. And capable up to a point. But a bit of a thug, really. He's been with the SD in Prague since 1940, so he has a fair bit of local knowledge."

"I wonder why I never met him."

"Yes, I heard you were down there last October."

"I had hoped never to go back."

"Rough, eh?"

"Not for me. Not particularly. But there was a girl. Arianne Tauber. It was very rough for her."

"She's the one who tried to blow up Himmler, right?"

"Yes. The assassination attempt that no one talks about. Do you happen to know what happened to her?"

"No, but I could probably find out. In return for your help in Prague."

I nodded. "Fair enough. There was another fellow. The spy. Paul Thümmel. What happened to him? Do you know?"

"Difficult case," said Nebe. "You have two sides to that story. The Abwehr says that Thümmel only ever pretended to spy for the Czechs so that he could obtain information about UVOD's London contacts. The SD, however, insists he was the genuine Esau. And nobody wants to put him on trial so they can prove the case one way or the other. That would be embarrassing for someone important, either way. So Thümmel stays in an isolation cell at the fortress in Terezín, under a false name, the poor bastard."

WHEN WE ARRIVED in Prague we found things even more chaotic than Nebe had described. The streets were empty of everyone except lots of SS troops, who were reportedly trigger-happy, while the cells at Peček Palace and the prison at Pankrác were full after the arrests of almost five hundred Czechs, nearly all of them innocent, of course. But the situation at Hradschin Castle was nothing short of laughable. Daluege was working on the assumption that the assassination was the beginning of an organized Czech uprising; he had called in police reinforcements from Dresden and declared a nine p.m. curfew. Most of the Czechs arrested had simply fallen foul of Daluege's curfew.

Pannwitz and Frank were jointly of the opinion that the ambush was the work of a team of British parachutists and had set in train a painstaking search of every single house in Prague in the hope of uncovering the assassins' hiding place.

As soon as they saw Arthur Nebe, Kopkow and Wehner complained that there was little hope of catching anyone so long as revenge appeared to be the only order of the day, for in addition to the five hundred Czechs who had been arrested, it seemed that the

Gestapo had already shot more than one hundred fifty men and women who were suspected of working for UVOD, including two witnesses to the actual assassination. Which hardly helped their investigation.

Nebe and I viewed the damaged car, the scene of the crime, and other evidence, including a bicycle used by one of the assassins, and the coat he had been wearing; these were on display to the public in the window of a popular shoe store in the center of Prague. Then we went to Bulovka Hospital to view Heydrich's dead body, and found the autopsy was still in progress. This was conducted by Professor Hamperl—who had also handled Captain Kuttner's autopsy eight months earlier—and by Professor Weygrich, also from the German Charles University in Prague.

Nebe, who had no taste for hospitals, left me there to speak to the two professors while he went to the Peček Palace for a meeting with Frank and Pannwitz.

I did not enter the operating theater. Although the whole floor was guarded by several SS men—to me this looked like covering the well after the child had already fallen in—I could easily have entered the theater itself; Nebe made that clear to the NCO in charge of the guard detail. But I didn't go into the autopsy theater. Perhaps I just didn't trust myself not to tell Heydrich that if he had listened to me, then he would have been alive. Perhaps. But I think it's more likely that I wanted to avoid finding the least bit of sympathy in myself for that truly wicked man. So I sat on a wooden bench outside the doors and waited for good news, like an expectant father.

When the autopsy finished, Hamperl was first out of the operating theater, and he greeted me like an old friend.

"So he's really dead, is he?" I asked.

"Oh yes."

I lit a cigarette. I never much cared for big cigars.

We walked along the landing.

"Tell me," asked Hamperl, "did you ever catch that poor captain's murderer?"

The official record showed that Kuttner's murder remained unsolved. Hamperl probably knew that. It was just his way of teasing me. I was hardly about to tell him that he'd just finished dissecting Kuttner's murderer. Somehow that didn't seem appropriate. Besides, in addition to the SS guards, there were several Gestapo men hanging around the floor.

"No," I said. "We never did."

"We? You were in charge of that case, weren't you, Commissar Gunther?"

"I thought that, too. But it turned out I wasn't really."

"Who was?"

I nodded back at the autopsy theater. "He was. Heydrich."

"I expect he's why you're here now. Yes?"

"It's not because I like this place."

"No, indeed. Well, it was good to see you again, anyway."

"No, don't go away. I've come all the way from Berlin to talk to you, Professor."

"I've got nothing to say."

"Come on, Professor. Help me out here."

"It'll be a day or two before Professor Weygrich and I have finished our report," said Hamperl. "You can read it then. Now, if you don't mind, Commissar, I have a lot of work to do in the lab."

I followed him downstairs.

"All I want from you is your probable assessment. And then I'll leave you alone."

"No. I can't help you there. My report is for the eyes of General Frank only. Until he authorizes its release, I can't discuss the case with anyone. That's what he told me. And I wouldn't care to disappoint that man. He's in a mood to do harm to this city. To the whole country, perhaps."

I ran ahead a few steps and then stopped in front of Hamperl.

"I can appreciate that. But I really must insist."

"Don't be ridiculous, Commissar. You're in no position to insist on anything. The report must remain private for now. Now, get out of my way."

I stayed where I was. "Would it make a difference if I said the word 'Rothenburg,' sir?"

Hamperl did not reply.

"I'm sure you know what I'm talking about, Professor Hamperl. The Pension Matzky."

"I was visiting a patient," he said. "In my capacity as a doctor, you understand. That is why I was there."

"Of course. I understand perfectly. What you don't know perhaps is that nothing that happens there is private. Nothing at all."

Hamperl's fixed jaw slackened a little.

"What do you mean?"

"There were hidden microphones."

"I see."

"All I'm asking is that you give me a few minutes of your time, Professor. In private. Do you have a car here, sir?"

"Yes. Why?"

"Perhaps you could give me a lift back into the center of Prague, sir. We might talk a little during the journey."

"Yes. I don't see why not. We could certainly do that. A good idea. Follow me."

THAT EVENING I met Arthur Nebe at the Esplanade Hotel, where both of us were staying, and over an excellent dinner I told him what I had learned that afternoon from Professor Hamperl.

"It seems that Heydrich was making a strong recovery until yesterday lunchtime. He'd just finished a meal cooked specially for him by his wife, Lina, when he collapsed and lost consciousness."

"I hope you're not going to tell me she poisoned him."

Nebe grinned and poured himself a glass of wine. He was doing his best to enjoy himself in spite of everything that had happened, and some of the wariness that was almost always in his narrow eyes was gone. Probably it was just the wine. Nebe was especially fond of good wine and good restaurants. He put his long nose into his wineglass and breathed in deeply.

"Do drink up, Bernie. This is a superb claret."

"It wasn't she who poisoned him, Arthur. But—"

He put down his glass and watched my face for some sign of humor.

"You're not serious."

"Professor Hamperl is scared, Arthur. He'd like the autopsy to report that Heydrich died from anemic shock."

"The man lost his spleen, didn't he? Anemic shock would be a fair conclusion to that sort of injury."

"However, Professor Weygrich wishes to mention the presence of organ damage resulting from an infection. A bacteria or poison." I shrugged. "Well, again, you might expect infection to result from bomb splinters."

"Certainly."

"However."

"Ugh. That word again."

"Hamperl would prefer not to mention this inflammation of the tissues at all. Mediastinitis, he called it."

"I fail to see the need for two ominous howevers. Infection is common in such situations."

"After the patient was making a strong recovery?" I shook my head. "Listen, Arthur. On Tuesday Heydrich had a temperature of one hundred two degrees Fahrenheit. But yesterday his temperature was down and his wound was draining freely. That is until midday, when the infection suddenly returned. A complete reversal of his condition."

"So what are you saying, Bernie?"

"I'm not saying anything. Hamperl is saying it. And frankly he's not likely ever to say it again, to anyone. I had a hard enough job getting him to say it the first time. And here's another thing, Arthur. I'm never going to say any of this again, either. If you ever ask me about this, I'll just say I don't know what you're talking about."

"All right." Nebe nodded. "So let's hear it."

"Hamperl believes the infection was introduced long after the wound was sustained. That Heydrich was infected by a bacterium introduced by an outside agency. In other words, he *was* poisoned."

"Good God. You are serious." Nebe grabbed his glass and drained the contents. "Who did it?"

"He won't say. But I checked through the medical records myself, and they show that Heydrich was initially under the care of Himmler's personal physician, Dr. Karl Gebhardt."

"That's right," said Nebe. "As soon as he heard Heydrich had been injured, Himmler ordered Gebhardt to come to Prague and take charge of Heydrich's treatment."

"But later on, Hitler's own doctor, Dr. Karl Brandt, arrived on the scene and, having examined Heydrich himself, *he* recommended that Heydrich be treated with an antibacterial, sulfonamide. Gebhardt refused, however, on the basis that the drug isn't particularly soluble and, crystallizing in the kidneys, sulfonamide can cause a certain amount of pain. You wouldn't want to prescribe it to someone who wasn't eating or drinking."

"But you said that Heydrich was eating and drinking normally."

"Exactly," I said. "And if he was taking liquids, any pain from sulfonamides would have been considerably lessened."

"So what you are saying? That Gebhardt poisoned Heydrich?"

"I'm saying it's a possibility. When I was last in Prague, Heydrich told me that SS doctors were experimenting with sulfonamide compounds, as a way of treating wound infections. Doesn't it seem odd that Heydrich of all people should have been prevented from taking advantage of a drug newly synthesized in SS laboratories?"

"Yes, it does," admitted Nebe.

"At least until you remember that Heydrich already suspected Himmler of trying to kill him." I shrugged. "Who better than a doctor to finish the job started by the British parachutists? And here's another thing that I found out at the Bulovka Hospital. After her husband died, Lina Heydrich had some sort of altercation with Dr. Gebhardt and actually accused him of killing her husband. It seems that she had to be restrained from hitting him."

"Jesus Christ. I never knew this."

"Apparently she told Major Ploetz, Heydrich's adjutant, that she won't be accompanying your SS guard of honor back to Berlin."

"What?"

"You heard me. It seems she herself believes that her husband's death is not exactly as advertised."

"Himmler will be furious. Hitler, too."

"There is that possibility."

Nebe rubbed his jaw anxiously.

"You're right, Bernie. We never had this conversation." He toasted me with his glass. "I might have known you'd discover a very different culprit from the ones I was hoping to find. I think we'd best leave it there, don't you?"

"I already did. When I get back to Berlin, I'm going to deny I was ever here. As I discovered last October, being in Prague can be damaging to your health. Even fatal."

Nebe uttered a grim sounding sigh.

"About your girlfriend, Arianne Tauber. It's not good news, I'm afraid. I wish I could give you some good news, but I can't. I'm sorry."

"Good news I wasn't expecting, Arthur. I just want to know for sure what happened to her."

"They sent her to a concentration camp near Kraków."

I nodded.

"Well, that's not so bad. People have survived concentration camps before."

"Not this one. This is a new kind of concentration camp. Only part of it is a true concentration camp of the kind that you and I know about. You know, like Dachau or Buchenwald. Mostly this is a special new sort of concentration camp. Much bigger than those others. It's called Auschwitz."

THAT WAS THE FIRST TIME I had ever heard the name Auschwitz. While I was eating a good dinner and enjoying a fine bottle of wine in an expensive restaurant. It seems astonishing now that the name did not stay with me longer, but within a few days I had more or less forgotten it. Years later, I heard the name again, and that time it stayed with me. It stays with me always now, and whenever I think of it I know I can put at least one face and name to the several millions of people who died there.

AUTHOR'S NOTE

The Three Kings were Josef Mašín, Josef Balabán, and Vacláv Morávek. Balabán died in Prague's Ruzyně Prison on October 3, 1941; Václav Morávek was killed in a shoot-out with the Prague Gestapo on March 21, 1942; Josef Mašín was executed in May 1942, as part of the Nazi retaliation for the attack on Reinhard Heydrich.

On June 9, 1942, a special train carrying one thousand Jews left Prague for Auschwitz. The train bore a sign that read ATTENTAT AUF HEYDRICH (Assassination of Heydrich). On the same day, General Karl Hermann Frank ordered Horst Böhme to destroy the Czech village of Lidice, northwest of Prague, because it was vaguely suspected of having harbored some of Heydrich's assassins. One hundred ninety men over the age of sixteen were summarily executed. One hundred eighty-four women were sent to Ravensbrück; eighty-eight children were sent to Lodz. On July 1, 1942, Eichmann ordered the women and children to be sent to Chelmno, where they were all gassed in specially converted gas vans. The village itself was razed to the ground.

On June 16, 1942, Karel Čurda walked into Peček Palace and gave away the names and addresses of many prominent UVOD resistance workers, among them the Morávek family (no relation). Marie Morávek poisoned herself rather than be taken alive by the Gestapo. Her son, Ata, was captured and tortured. His interrogators showed him his mother's severed head before dropping it into a fish tank. Ata Morávek broke down and revealed the hiding place of the Heydrich assassins; this was the church of St. Cyril and St. Methodius in Resolva Street. The Germans called this church Karl Borromäus.

Hiding in the crypt of St. Cyril's (a Russian Orthodox church—not a Roman Catholic one, as might have been supposed) were Jan Kubiš, Adolf Opálka, Jaroslav Švarc, Josef Gabčik, Josef Bublík, Josef Valčik, and Jan Hrubý—all members of an assassination team trained by the British Special Operations Executive for a mission called Operation Anthropoid. A pitched battle ensued, during which all six men were killed or committed suicide. The bodies were identified by "the traitor" Čurda. The entire families of all these brave heroes were sent to Mauthausen concentration camp, where they were executed on October 24, 1942.

On September 3, 1942, the officials of the Resolva Street church of St. Cyril's were tried in the conference hall of the Peček Palace in Prague. The trial lasted three and a half hours. On September 4, Bishop Gorazd, Jan Sonnevend, Vladimir Petrek, and Václav Cikl were hanged.

Adolf Hitler gave Lina Heydrich the Lower Castle at Jungfern-Breschan (the Czech name for this place is Panenské-Břežany) in gratitude for her husband's "heroic work." Heydrich's eldest son, Klaus, was killed in a traffic accident outside the gates of the house in October 1943. The boy is buried in an unmarked grave in the grounds of the house. In January 1945 the Heydrichs left the house for good.

Paul Thümmel was released and rearrested on several occasions. In February 1942 he broke down under questioning and admitted he was a spy. He was imprisoned in the fortress at Terezín (Theresienstadt) under the false name of Dr. Paul Tooman. There he remained for three years. In August 1944 he was divorced by his wife, Elsa, which was the last time he saw her. In April 1945 he "committed suicide" in Terezín.

Karl Hermann Frank was captured in 1945, tried by the Czechs, found guilty, and executed outside Pankrác Prison on May 22, 1946. The whole execution may be found on the Internet for those who are inclined that way at http://www.executedtoday .com/2009/05/22/1946-karl-hermann-frank/

It's only my opinion, but he died rather bravely, for what it's worth.

SS-Standartenführer Dr. Walter Jacobi was arrested by the Americans in September 1945. He was executed in Prague on May 3, 1947.

SS-Obergruppenführer Richard Hildebrandt was hanged for war crimes in Poland on March 10, 1952.

SS-Obergruppenführer Karl von Eberstein testified for the prosecution at the Nuremberg trials. He denied knowledge of and responsibility for Dachau concentration camp, which fell under his authority as the higher SS and police leader for Munich. He died in Bavaria on February 10, 1979.

SS-Gruppenführer Konrad Henlein was captured by the Americans and committed suicide in May 1945. However, he may actually have been a spy for the British.

SS-Gruppenführer Dr. Hugo Jury committed suicide in May 1945.

SS-Brigadeführer Bernard Voss was hanged in Prague on February 4, 1947.

SS-Standartenführer Dr. Hans Ulrich Geschke was most probably killed during the Battle of Budapest in February 1945. He was declared dead in 1959.

SS-Standartenführer Horst Böhme was killed at the Battle of Königsberg in April 1945. He was declared dead in 1954.

SS-Sturmbannführer Dr. Hans-Achim Ploetz. Fate unknown to the author.

Konstantin von Neurath was tried at Nuremberg and sentenced to fifteen years in prison. Released in 1954, he died aged eighty-three in August 1956.

General Kurt Daluege was hanged by the Czechs in Prague in October 1946.

Lina Heydrich died on August 14, 1985. She always defended her husband's name.

The portrait of Adele Bloch-Bauer by Gustav Klimt remained in the possession of the Austrian State Gallery in Vienna until 2006, when an Austrian court determined that it and three other pictures were the rightful property of Ferdinand Bloch-Bauer's niece, Maria Altmann, to whom he had left them in his will, following his impoverished death in Zurich in November 1945. Klimt's portrait of Adele Bloch-Bauer was one of four paintings sold at Christie's, New York, in November 2006. It fetched $88 million and may be viewed today at the Neue Galerie in New York City.

The author visited the house at Panenské-Březany in February 2011. It is closed to the public, however, and mostly derelict. Under the old communist government of Czechoslovakia, the house was a secret weapons research facility.

According to a Prague newspaper in March 2011, Heider Heydrich, aged seventy-six, Heydrich's surviving son, offered to "find finances" for the restoration of the house at Panenské-Březany. The story caused a furor in the Czech Republic. It is, however, the author's opinion that the son is not the father and that this once-beautiful house is worthy of restoration. I imagine he would like to find the grave of his elder brother.

**Philip Kerr's next novel is now available
from Marian Wood Books in hardcover.**

Read on for the first chapter of

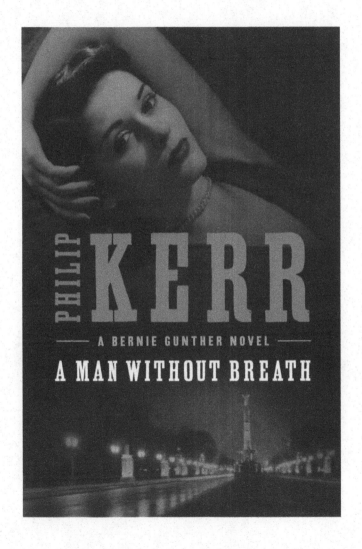

PHILIP **KERR**

— A BERNIE GUNTHER NOVEL —

A MAN WITHOUT BREATH

ISBN 978-0-399-16079-0

1

Franz Meyer stood up at the head of the table, glanced down, touched the cloth, and awaited our silence. With his fair hair, blue eyes, and neoclassical features that looked as if they'd been carved by Arno Breker, Hitler's official state sculptor, he was no one's idea of a Jew. Half of the SS and SD were more obviously Semitic. Meyer took a deep, almost euphoric breath, gave a broad grin that was part relief and part joie de vivre, and raised his glass to each of the four women seated around the table. None were Jewish and yet, by the racial stereotypes beloved of the Propaganda Ministry, they might have been; all were Germans with strong noses, dark eyes, and even darker hair. For a moment Meyer seemed choked with emotion, and when at last he was able to speak, there were tears in his eyes.

"I'd like to thank my wife and her sisters for your efforts on my behalf," he said. "To do what you did took great courage, and I can't tell you what it meant to those of us who were imprisoned in the Jewish Welfare Office to know that there were so many people on the outside who cared enough to come and demonstrate on our behalf."

"I still can't believe they haven't arrested us," said Meyer's wife, Siv.

"They're so used to people just doing what they're told," said his sister-in-law, Klara, "that they don't know what to do."

"We'll go back to Rosenstrasse tomorrow," insisted Siv. "We won't stop until everyone in there is released. All two thousand of them. We've shown what we can do when public opinion is mobilized. We have to keep the pressure up."

"Yes," said Meyer. "And we will. We will. But right now I'd like to propose a toast. To our new friend Bernie Gunther. But for him and his colleagues at the War Crimes Bureau, I'd probably still be imprisoned in the Jewish Welfare Office. And who knows where after that?" He smiled. "To Bernie."

There were six of us in the cozy little dining room in the Meyers' apartment in Lützowerstrasse. As four of them stood up and toasted me silently, I shook my head. I wasn't sure I deserved Franz Meyer's thanks, and besides, the wine we were drinking was a decent German red—a Spätburgunder from long before the war that he and his wife would have done better to have traded for some food instead of wasting it on me. Any wine—let alone a good German red—was almost impossible to come by in Berlin.

Politely I waited for them to drink to my health before standing up to contradict my host. "I'm not sure I can claim to have had much influence on the SS," I explained. "I spoke to a couple of cops I know who were policing your demonstration and they told me there's a strong rumor doing the rounds that most of the prisoners arrested on Saturday as part of the factory action will probably be released in a few days."

"That's incredible," said Klara. "But what does it mean, Bernie? Do you think the authorities are actually going soft on deportations?"

Before I could offer my opinion the air raid warning siren sounded. We all looked at each other in surprise; it had been almost two years since the last air raid by the Royal Air Force.

"We should go to the shelter," I said. "Or the basement, perhaps."

Meyer nodded. "Yes, you're right," he said firmly. "You should all go. Just in case it's for real."

I fetched my coat and hat off the stand and turned back to Meyer.

"But you're coming, too, aren't you?" I said.

"Jews aren't permitted in the shelters. Perhaps you didn't notice it before. Well, there's no reason why you should have. I don't think there's been an air raid since we started to wear the yellow star."

I shook my head. "No, I didn't." I shrugged. "So, where are Jews supposed to go?"

"To hell, of course. At least, that's what they hope." This time Meyer's grin was sardonic. "Besides, people know this is a Jewish apartment, and since the law requires that homes be left with their doors and windows open, to minimize the effect of a pressure wave from a bomb blast, that's also an invitation to some local thief to come and steal from us." He shook his head. "So I shall stay here."

I glanced out the window; in the street below, hundreds of people were already being herded toward the local shelter by uniformed police. There wasn't much time to lose.

"Franz," said Siv. "We're not going there without you. Just leave your coat. If they can't see your star, they'll have to assume you're German. You can carry me in and say I fainted, and if I show my pass and say I'm your wife then no one will be any the wiser."

"She's right," I said.

"And if I'm arrested, what then? I've only just been released." Meyer shook his head and laughed. "Besides, it's probably a false alarm. Hasn't Fat Hermann promised us that this is the best-defended city in Europe?"

The siren continued to wail outside like some dreadful mechanical clarion announcing the end of a night shift in the smoking factories of hell.

Siv Meyer sat down at the table and clasped her hands tight. "If you're not going, then I'm not going."

"Neither am I," Klara said, sitting down beside her.

"There's no time to argue about this," said Meyer. "You should go. All of you."

"He's right," I said, more urgently now as already we could hear the drone of the bombers in the distance; it was obvious this was no false alarm. I opened the door and waved the four women toward me. "Come on," I said.

"No," said Siv. "We're staying."

The two other sisters glanced at each other and then sat down alongside their Jewish brother-in-law. This left me on my feet with a coat in my hand and a nervous look on my face. After all, I'd seen what our own bombers had done to Minsk and parts of France. I put on the coat and shoved my hands in the pockets so as to conceal the fact that they were shaking.

"I don't think they're coming to drop propaganda leaflets," I said. "Not this time."

"Yes, but it's not civilians like us they're after, surely," said Siv. "It's the government district. They'll know there's a hospital near here. The RAF won't want to risk hitting the Catholic Hospital, will they? The English aren't like that. It's the Wilhelmstrasse they'll be after."

"How will they know from two thousand feet up in the air?" I heard myself utter weakly.

"She's right," said Meyer. "It's not the west of Berlin they're targeting. It's the east. Which means it's probably just as well we're none of us in Rosenstrasse tonight." He smiled at me. "You should go, Bernie. We'll be all right. You'll see."

"I expect you're right," I said and, deciding to ignore the air raid siren like the others, I started to take off my coat. "All the same, I can hardly leave you all here."

"Why not?" asked Klara.

I shrugged, but what it really came down to was this: I could hardly leave and still manage to look good in Klara's lovely brown

4

eyes, and I was quite keen that she should have a good impression of me; but I didn't feel I could say this to her, not yet.

For a moment I felt my chest tighten as my nerves continued to get the better of me. Then I heard some bombs explode in the distance and breathed a sigh of relief. Back in the trenches, during the Great War, when you could hear the shells exploding somewhere else, it usually meant you were safe because it was commonly held that you never heard the one that killed you.

"Sounds like it's north Berlin that's getting it," I said, leaning in the doorway. "The petroleum refinery on Thalerstrasse, probably. It's the only real target around here. But I think we should at least get under the table. Just in case a stray bomb—"

I think that was the last thing I said and probably it was the fact that I was standing in the doorway that saved my life because just then the glass in the nearest window frame seemed to melt into a thousand drops of light. Some of these old Berlin apartment buildings were made to last, and I later learned that the bomb that blew up the one we were in—not to mention the hospital on Lützowstrasse—and flattened it in a split second would certainly have killed me had not the lintel above my head and the stout oak door that was hanging inside it resisted the weight of the roof's metal joist, for this is what killed Siv Meyer and her three sisters.

After that there was darkness and silence, except for the sound of a kettle on a gas plate whistling as it came slowly to the boil, although this was probably just the sensation in my battered eardrums. It was as if someone had switched off an electric light and then pulled away the floorboards on which I had been standing, and the effect of the world disappearing from underneath my feet might have been similar to the sensation of being hooded and hanged on a gallows. I don't know. All I really remember of what happened is that I was upside down lying on a pile of rubble when I recovered consciousness and there was a door on top of my face which, for several minutes until I recovered enough breath in my bomb-blasted lungs to moan for help, I was convinced was the lid of my own damned coffin.

I HAD LEFT KRIPO IN the summer of 1942 and joined the Wehrmacht War Crimes Bureau with the connivance of my old colleague Arthur Nebe. As the commander of Special Action Group B, which was headquartered in Smolensk, where tens of thousands of Russian Jews had been murdered, Nebe knew a thing or two about war crimes himself; I'm certain it appealed to his Berliner's black humor that I should find myself attached to an organization of old Prussian judges, most of whom were staunchly anti-Nazi. Dedicated to the military ideals as laid down in the Geneva Convention of 1929, they believed there was a proper and honorable way for the army—any army—to fight a war. Nebe must have thought it very funny that there existed a judicial body within the German High Command that not only resisted having Party members in its distinguished ranks but was also quite prepared to devote its considerable resources to the investigation and prosecution of crimes committed by and against German soldiers: theft, looting, rape, and murder could all be the subject of lengthy and serious inquiries—sometimes earning their perpetrators a death sentence. I thought it was kind of funny myself but then, like Nebe, I'm also from Berlin and it's known that we have a strange sense of humor. By the winter of 1943, you found your laughs where you could, and I don't know how else to describe a situation in which you can have an army corporal hanged for the rape and murder of a Russian peasant girl in one village that's only a few miles from another village where an SS special action group has just murdered twenty-five thousand men, women, and children. I expect the Greeks have a word for that kind of comedy, and if I'd paid a little more attention to my classics master at school I might have known what that word was.

The judges—they were nearly all judges—who worked for the bureau were not hypocrites any more than they were Nazis, and they saw no reason why their moral standards should decline just because the government of Germany had no moral standards at all. The Greeks certainly had a word for that, all right, and I even knew what it was, although it's fair to say I'd had to learn how to spell it again; they called that kind of behavior ethics, and my being concerned with rightness and wrongness felt good since it helped to restore in me a sense of pride in who and what I was. At least for a while, anyway.

Most of the time I assisted the bureau's judges—several of whom I'd known during the Weimar Republic—in taking depositions from witnesses or finding new cases for the bureau to investigate. That was how I first met Siv Meyer. She was a friend of a girl called Renata Matter, who was a good friend of mine and who worked at the Adlon Hotel; Siv played the piano in the orchestra at the Adlon.

I met her at the hotel on Sunday, February 28, which was the day after Berlin's last Jews—some ten thousand people—had been arrested for deportation to ghettos in the east. Franz Meyer was a worker at the Osram electric lightbulb factory in Wilmersdorf, which was where he was arrested, but before this he had been a doctor, and this was how he came to find himself working as a medical orderly on a German hospital ship that had been attacked and sunk by a British submarine off the coast of Norway in August 1941. My boss and the bureau chief, Johannes Goldsche, had tried to investigate the case but, at the time, it was thought that there had been no survivors. So when Renata Matter told me about Franz Meyer's story, I went to see his wife at their apartment in Lützowerstrasse.

It was a short walk from my own apartment on Fasanenstrasse, with a view of the canal and the local town hall, and only a short walk from the Schulstrasse synagogue, where many of Berlin's

Jews had been held in transit on their way to an unknown fate in the east. Meyer had only escaped arrest himself because he was a *Mischling*—a Jew who was married to a German.

From the wedding photograph on the Biedermeier sideboard it was easy to see what they saw in each other. Franz Meyer was absurdly handsome and very like Franchot Tone, the movie actor who was once married to Joan Crawford; Siv was just beautiful and there's nothing absurd about that; more important, so were her three sisters, Klara, Frieda, and Hedwig, all of whom were present when I met their sister for the first time.

"Why didn't your husband come forward before?" I asked Siv Meyer over a cup of ersatz coffee, which was the only kind of coffee anyone had now. "This incident took place on August thirtieth, 1941. Why is he only willing to speak about it now?"

"Clearly you don't know very much about what it's like to be a Jew in Berlin," she said.

"You're right. I don't."

"No Jew wants to draw attention to himself by being a part of any inquiry in Germany. Even if it is a good cause."

I shrugged. "I can understand that," I said. "A witness for the bureau one day and a prisoner of the Gestapo the next. On the other hand, I do know what it's like to be a Jew in the east, and if you want to prevent your husband from ending up there, I hope you're telling the truth about all this. At the War Crimes Bureau we get lots of people who try to waste our time."

"You were in the east?"

"Minsk," I said simply. "They sent me back here to Berlin and the War Crimes Bureau for questioning my orders."

"What's happening out there? In the ghettos? In the concentration camps? One hears so many different stories about what resettlement amounts to."

I shrugged. "I don't think the stories even get close to the horror of what's happening in the eastern ghettos. And by the way, there is no resettlement. There's just starvation and death."

Siv Meyer let out a sigh and then exchanged a glance with her sisters. I was fond of looking at her three sisters myself. It made a very pleasant change to take a deposition from an attractive and well-spoken woman instead of an injured soldier.

"Thank you for being honest, Herr Gunther," she said. "As well as the stories, one hears so many lies." She nodded. "Since you've been so honest, let me be honest, too. The main reason my husband hasn't talked before about the sinking of the SS *Hrotsvitha von Gandersheim* is because he hardly wanted to make a gift of some useful anti-British propaganda to Dr. Goebbels. Of course, now that he's been arrested it seems that this might be his only chance of staying out of a concentration camp."

"We don't have much to do with the Propaganda Ministry, Frau Meyer. Not if we can help it. Perhaps it's them you should be speaking to."

"I don't doubt you mean what you say, Herr Gunther," said Siv Meyer. "Nevertheless, British war crimes against defenseless German hospital ships make good propaganda."

"That's just the kind of story which is especially useful now," added Klara. "After Stalingrad."

I had to admit she was probably right. The surrender of the German Sixth Army in Stalingrad on February 2 had been the greatest disaster suffered by the Nazis since their coming to power, and Goebbels's speech on the eighteenth urging total war on the German people certainly needed incidents like the sinking of a hospital ship to prove that there was no way back for us now; that it was victory or nothing.

"Look," I said, "I can't promise anything but if you tell me where they're holding your husband, I'll go there right now and see him, Frau Meyer. If I think there's something in his story, I'll contact my superiors and see if we can get him released as a key witness for an inquiry."

"He's being detained at the Jewish Welfare Office, on Rosenstrasse," said Siv. "We'll come with you, if you like."

I shook my head. "That's quite all right. I know where it is."

"You don't understand," said Klara. "We're all going there anyway. To protest against Franz's detention."

"I don't think that's a very good idea," I said. "You'll be arrested."

"There are lots of wives who are going," said Siv. "They can't arrest us all."

"Why not?" I asked. "In case you haven't noticed, they've arrested all of the Jews."

HEARING FOOTSTEPS NEAR MY HEAD, I tried to push the heavy wooden door off my face but my left hand was trapped and the right too painful to use. Someone shouted something and a minute or two later I felt myself slide a little as the rubble on which I lay shifted like the scree on a steep mountainside, and then the door was lifted away to reveal my rescuers. The apartment building was almost completely gone and all that remained in the cold moonlight was one high chimney containing an ascending series of fireplaces. Several hands placed me onto a stretcher and I was carried off the tangled, smoking heap of bricks, concrete, leaking water pipes, and wooden planks and laid in the middle of the road, where I enjoyed a perfect view of a building burning in the distance and then the beams from Berlin's defense searchlights as they continued to search the sky for enemy planes; but the siren was sounding the all-clear and I could hear the footsteps of people already coming up from the shelters to look for what was left of their homes. I wondered if my own home in Fasanenstrasse was all right. Not that there was very much in it. Nearly everything of value had been sold or traded on the black market.

Gradually, I began to move my head, one way and the other, until I felt able to push myself up on one elbow to look around. But I could hardly breathe; my chest was still full of dust and smoke and the exertion provoked a fit of coughing that was only alleviated when a man I half recognized helped me to a drink of water and laid a blanket on top of me.

About a minute later there was a loud shout and the chimney came down on top of the spot where I'd been lying. The dust from its collapse covered me so I was moved farther down the street and set down next to some others who were awaiting medical attention. Klara was lying beside me now at less than an arm's length; her dress was hardly torn, her eyes were open, and her body was quite unmarked; I called her name several times before it finally dawned on me that she was dead. It was as if her life had just stopped like a clock, and it hardly seemed possible that so much of her future—she couldn't have been older than thirty—had disappeared in the space of a few seconds.

Other corpses were laid out in the street next to her. I couldn't see how many. I sat up to look for Franz Meyer and the others but the effort was too much and I fell back and closed my eyes. And fainted, I suppose.

"GIVE US BACK OUR MEN."

You could hear them three streets away—a large and angry crowd of women—and as we turned the corner of Rosenstrasse I felt my jaw slacken. I hadn't seen anything like this on the streets of Berlin since before Hitler came to power. And whoever would have thought that wearing a nice hat and carrying a handbag was the best way to dress when you were opposing the Nazis?

"Release our husbands," shouted the mob of women as we pushed our way along the street. "Release our husbands now.There were many more of them than I had been expecting—perhaps several hundred. Even Klara Meyer looked surprised, but not as surprised as the cops and SS who were guarding the Jewish Welfare Office. They gripped their machine pistols and rifles and muttered curses and abuse at the women standing nearest to the door and looked horrified to find themselves ignored or even roundly cursed back. This wasn't how it was supposed to be: if you had a gun, then people were supposed to do what they were told. That's page one of how to be a Nazi.

The welfare office on Rosenstrasse near Berlin's Alexanderplatz was a gray granite Wilhelmine building with a saddle roof next to a synagogue—formerly the oldest in Berlin—partly destroyed by the Nazis in November 1938, and within spitting distance of the Police Praesidium, where I had spent most of my adult working life. I might no longer have been working for Kripo but I'd managed to keep my beer token—the brass identity disk that commanded such craven respect in most German citizens.

"We're decent German women," shouted one woman. "Loyal to the Leader and to the Fatherland. You can't speak to us like that, you cheeky young bastard."

"I can speak to anyone like that who's misguided enough to be married to a Jew," I heard one of the uniformed cops—a corporal—say to her. "Go home, lady, or you'll be shot."

"You need a good spanking, you little pip," said another woman. "Does your mother know you're such an arrogant whelp?"

"You see?" said Klara, triumphantly. "They can't shoot us all."

"Can't we?" sneered the corporal. "When we have the orders to shoot, I can promise you'll get it first, Granny."

"Take it easy, Corporal," I said, and flashed my beer token in front of his face. "There's really no need to be rude to these ladies. Especially on a Sunday afternoon."

"Yes, sir," he said smartly. "Sorry, sir." He nodded back over his shoulder. "Are you going in there, sir?"

"Yes," I said. I turned to Klara and Siv. "I'll try to be as quick as I can."

"Then if you would be so kind," said the corporal, "we need orders, sir. No one's told us what to do. Just to stay here and stop people from going in. Perhaps you might mention that, sir."

I shrugged. "Sure, Corporal. But from what I can see, you're already doing a grand job."

"We are?"

"You're keeping the peace, aren't you?"

"Yes, sir."

"You can't keep the peace if you start shooting at all these ladies, now can you?" I smiled at him and then patted his shoulder. "In my experience, Corporal, the best police work looks like nothing at all and is always soon forgotten."

I was unprepared for the scene that met me inside, where the smell was already intolerable: a welfare office is not designed to be a transit camp for two thousand prisoners. Men and women with identity tags on strings around their necks like traveling children were lined up to use a lavatory that had no door, while others were crammed fifty or sixty to an office where it was standing-room only. Welfare parcels—many of them brought by the women outside—filled another room where they had been tossed but no one was complaining; things were quiet; after almost a decade of Nazi rule, Jews knew better than to complain. It was only the police sergeant in charge of these people who seemed inclined to bemoan his lot, and as he searched a clipboard for Franz Meyer's name and then led me to the second-floor office where the man was being held, he began to unroll the barbed S-wire of his sharp complaint:

"I don't know what I'm supposed to do with all these people. No one's told me a damned thing. How long they're going to be here. How to make them comfortable. How to answer all of these bloody women who are demanding answers. It's not so easy, I can tell you. All I've got is what was in this office building when we turned up yesterday. Toilet paper ran out within an hour of us being here. And Christ only knows how I'm going to feed them. There's nothing open on a Sunday."

"Why don't you open those food parcels and give them that?" I asked.

The sergeant looked incredulous. "I couldn't do that," he said. "Those are private parcels."

"I shouldn't think that the people they belong to will mind," I said. "Just as long as they get something to eat."

We found Franz Meyer seated in one of the larger offices where almost a hundred men were waiting patiently for something to happen. The sergeant called Meyer out and, still grumbling, went off to think about what I'd suggested about the parcels, while I spoke to my potential war crimes witness in the comparative privacy of the corridor.

I told him that I worked for the War Crimes Bureau and why I was there. Meanwhile, outside the building, the women's protest seemed to be getting louder.

"Your wife and sisters-in-law are outside," I told him. "It's them who put me up to this."

"Please tell them to go home," said Meyer. "It's safer in here than out there, I think."

"I agree. But they're not about to listen to me."

Meyer grinned. "Yes, I can imagine."

"The sooner you tell me about what happened on the SS *Hrots-vitha von Gandersheim*, the sooner I can speak to my boss and see about getting you out of here, and the sooner we can get them all out of harm's way." I paused. "That is, if you're prepared to give me a deposition."

"It's my only chance of avoiding a concentration camp, I think."

"Or worse," I added, by way of extra incentive.

"Well, that's honest, I suppose." He shrugged.

"I'll take that as a yes, shall I?"

He nodded and we spent the next thirty minutes writing out his statement about what had happened off the coast of Norway in August 1941. When he'd signed it, I wagged my finger at him.

"Coming here like this I'm sticking my neck out for you," I told him. "So you'd better not let me down. If I so much as get a whiff of you changing your story, I'll wash my hands of you. Got that?"

He nodded. "So why are you sticking your neck out?"

It was a good question and probably it deserved an answer but I hardly wanted to go into how a friend of a friend had asked me to help, which is how these things usually got fixed in Germany; and I certainly didn't want to mention how attractive I found his sister-in-law Klara, or that I was making up for some lost time when it came to helping Jews; and maybe a bit more than only lost time.

"Let's just say I don't like the Tommies very much and leave it at that, shall we?" I shook my head. "Besides, I'm not promising anything. It's up to my boss, Judge Goldsche. If he thinks your deposition can start an inquiry into a British war crime, he's the one who'll have to persuade the Foreign Office that this is worth a white book, not me."

"What's a white book?"

"An official publication that's intended to present the German side of an incident that might amount to a violation of the laws of war. It's the bureau that does all the legwork, but it's the Foreign Office that publishes the report."

"That sounds as if it might take a while."

I shook my head. "Fortunately for you, the bureau and the judge have a great deal of power. Even in Nazi Germany. If the judge buys your story, we'll have you home tomorrow."